A
DAUGHTER
OF
WAPPING

*A Novel of Early England
and the Maryland Colony*

ANN JENSEN

With love and thanks to daughters
Alexis Bond and Erica Jensen-Holmes and siblings
Margie and Fred Dowsett who made this book a
reality.

PART I

I

One Last Look at Home

Step by step, Martha Pratt stared at the chains dragging at the dirt-encrusted ankles of the woman ahead of her. She had no need to see the taunting faces pressing in on them from both sides. Once, she'd been part of such a crowd, pushing and shoving to gawp at the men and women trudging along Water Street to the wharf. Now she was walking as they did, pelted by stones and garbage, iron manacles rubbing her ankles raw. At least she wouldn't end with a noose around her neck.

But there was no such certainty in the colonies where she was bound. Dreadful places, she'd heard. There they'd starve you, beat you, work you til you dropped. That was if you actually reached them. The prospect of the voyage on the ship awaiting them at Blackfriars Stairs was no less bleak.

She brushed at a rotten fig clinging to one shoulder. Bits of egg and shell slithering down the front of her apron were just the latest filth that had rained on them since they left Newgate Prison. People who lived and worked along the route were used to regular convict parades. Some, watching from windows in the begrimed brick and stone buildings, didn't bother to descend to the street. They launched their garbage and verbal abuse from second- and third-story perches.

A sharp cry caused Martha to turn. The girl next in line sank to her knees. A rock had found its mark.

"Bett. Get up!"

Martha raised the bundle she carried to ward off the renewed bombardment of refuse. She grabbed the girl's arm and yanked her to her feet.

"Don't stop. Keep going or they'll be upon you for a certainty. We have only a short way more to go. Let them have their fun with the others."

She jerked her head toward the four women at the head of the slow-moving line. Unlike Martha or Bett and the others who trudged in sullen silence, the four had a ready store of curses to fling back at their tormentors. They'd been the same in Newgate, reveling in any raucous scene they could create. Mag in particular was ever in the lead. Now she was tossing her mass of hennaed hair and swinging close to the grasping hands of men along the way.

"Ahhh. Wouldn't you like a bit of this?"

The men whooped and howled as she pumped her hips, shoving her breasts almost free of her bodice before pulling back with a mirthless laugh.

"You've missed your chance, you scummy bastards!" she screamed at them and swaggered on. "I've had far better 'n you."

Martha ducked her head to avoid clots of offal flung in Mag's wake and pulled Bett after her.

"She has no shame and makes it all the worse for us," said Bett.

"It would be no better without her. No matter what we do, we're all the same to crowds like this. But take heart, we're almost to Blackfriars. Walk on and keep your head down."

Martha looked down at her begrimed bodice and spattered apron. They certainly had nothing to hold their heads high about. She'd once joined such a crowd, thinking the condemned souls were getting what they deserved. She could only pray none in that day's crowd knew her. And if there were any, would they think the same as she had? Several who regularly took their pint of ale and a meat pie at the Black Horse would go out of their way for such a spectacle. Their jeers and laughter were her last memories of the alehouse in Wapping. But they'd had nearly a year to forget her.

God help her if Charley came to the dock. She longed to see his beloved face one last time. But not there, not like that. She blinked rapidly and passed her free hand across her eyes to stem threatening tears. She must not weep.

"Look there, Bett."

She reached back, pulling the girl closer.

"It's not far, now. You can see the masts of the ships. Ach! And smell the Thames."

She had thought she'd never be free of Newgate's stink, but the river's noxious fumes masked even that. And yet, it offered a perverse sort of comfort. In her seventeen years, she'd scarcely drawn a breath on the streets of Wapping that wasn't tinged with the Thames' rancid perfume. She'd be missing even that ere long.

Every day it got harder to fight off her despair. She could see nothing good in whatever prospect lay ahead. Hope was a battered thing, attacked repeatedly over the past months. And pride? That was hard to hold on to in Newgate. It was stripped away at every turn. You did what you must to survive. If you were one of the timid ones, like Bett, you were set upon by hellcats like Mag. You starved. You froze. You sickened. You died.

Over and over again, she had tried to call up some vision of the day, seven years hence, when she'd walk free. Into what, she dared not imagine. It was a blessing her crime earned no more than seven years. Some of those walking toward the Thames would serve double that. But even seven was near half the life she'd already lived.

To think she once felt that life was hard. And Newgate? Those first days and nights?

She'd been sure she'd die there. But she didn't. That was a comfort, however small. It was the talk of what lay ahead that troubled her. They'd use you no better than a slave, if some pestilence didn't carry you off, said those who professed to know.

The fifty or sixty men walking ahead of them would likely be sold for the lowest sort of work in some grimy provincial city or at hard labor on land or water. No great value was placed on transports, men or women. The dregs of London's prisons they were called. The women would be put to the dirtiest labor on a farm or in houses, taverns, or some such place of business. Or worse. In some parts, Martha had heard, Americans were barely civilized, scratching out a living among savages in the wilderness. Transports would be a bargain bought fresh off the deck of a ship like horses or cattle.

She brushed angrily at a clod of dung that still clung to her skirt and caught a glimpse of her broken nails and dirty knuckles. Rubbing her hand on her apron left dirty streaks but didn't clean it. Would a prospective buyer see beyond such things? Likely she'd have no more chance at getting a decent place than some dumb animal. But it did no good to think that far ahead. She had first to reach the end of the voyage.

She let her hand rest over the pocket beneath her apron. Concealed there were ten shillings tightly wrapped in a piece of cloth and

Charley Rawley's penknife.

"You're strong Martha," he'd said when he slipped them into her pocket. "If ever there was one could turn this to advantage, it's you."

He'd also said that he loved her. The memory of his words, his face, and the slim folded blade beneath her hand helped her to raise her head, stiffen her back, to face full on whatever lay ahead.

Which suddenly became reality as Martha and Bett came up on the heels of the women ahead of them. The line of convicts had slowed as they neared the wharf at the end of Water Street. Their way was choked by carts laden with barrels, crates, assorted trunks and boxes, and a crowd determined to reach the waiting ships. They didn't take kindly to being ordered aside to allow the convicts to pass. Their curses mingled with those of the burley stevedores who could count on a tongue lashing at the very least if they were late delivering cargoes.

Shouting and prodding, Newgate's guards forced their charges ahead, clearing a path to the river's edge. They ignored the chained men's angry shouts when bystanders' fists and hard-toed boots connected. Even Mag paid for her brazenness. She arrived at the wharf, flushed and stuffing her breasts back into her bodice. Behind her, a man staggered into the laughing crowd, blood streaming from his nose.

Heartened by the arrival of a club-wielding guard, Martha hugged her bundle to her chest. With her free arm around Bett, she pushed forward, keeping the woman ahead of them moving at a steady pace. Even so, there was no escaping the pokes and pinches. Martha endured them in silence but cringed at Bett's repeated squeals. They only roused her tormentors to greater efforts.

"Pay them no mind, Bett!"

Martha gave the girl's bony shoulder a squeeze, as much out of anger as encouragement. She struggled to make headway, stumbling as a man snatched at her skirt.

Just a few more steps. Just a few more steps.

The litany kept her going until directly ahead she could see the three masts of the black-hulled merchantman stark against a grey sky.

The men were almost all aboard. Mag and the first of the women were right behind. At the wharf's edge, Bett caught Martha's arm as they staggered up the heaving gangplank, becoming as much a hindrance as the ankle chains. At the end, Martha pried her hand loose and stepped down onto the ship's deck. There, she came to a stop with the huddle of women gone suddenly quiet. As one they were struck by the realization that they'd just walked their last on England's soil.

As she stood, unaware of the women huddled around her, Martha looked back. A sooty mist hung over wharves and aged buildings so like the ones she'd known in Wapping, a world she had no hope of ever seeing again. But the ship would pass by the stairs at Wapping as it dropped down the Thames. If just once more she could see the familiar warehouses and shipping offices. But that frail hope died quickly. Ahead of her, the men were fighting their chains as they climbed down into the ship's hold. Soon, she and the other women would follow to be shut away somewhere below.

The rattle of a chain beside her reminded Martha of Bett. She shifted her bundle to put a reassuring arm around the girl's boney shoulders. Martha and several other women carried rough sacks slung over arm or shoulder. Their bundles were stuffed with clothing, a few personal objects, shawls or small blankets, strips of sheeting for their bleeding time, even pots, wooden bowls, spoons, and mugs. All they owned in the world amounted to very little, but they were the fortunate ones. Bett and a few others had only the clothes on their backs. Their calloused feet were either bare or wrapped in rags.

"It's about time!"

Mag's voice roused the other women to move closer to the ship's blacksmith who was at work opening the manacle around her ankle.

"Damn you. Take care!"

As the iron bracelet fell away, the ship's blacksmith shrugged, waiting for Mag to present her other ankle. That done, he moved quickly from one woman to the next. Martha winced at the sight of Bett's bruised and bloody ankles. During their walk through the streets, she'd lost the rags she'd wrapped around her feet before they left the prison cell. Martha's own ankles were sore and spots of blood stained her stockings. When both were free of the chains, she guided Bett to where she could keep an eye on Mag.

The woman had moved up to take first place as the guards herded them toward the dark maw of an after hatch. Mag winked at the sailor waiting at the opening and made a wet kissing sound when he shoved a ragged blanket into her arms. Fumbling to find her footing on the ladder, she left a trail of curses as she disappeared below. Five women quickly followed her.

The rest of the women were hanging back, but Martha guessed that Mag had a good reason for being the first below. She shifted her bundle, pushed Bett toward the hatch, and watched til her head disappeared below. Ignoring the sailor's leer when he handed her a blanket, Martha stepped cautiously over the lip of the companionway and climbed down the ladder into the cabin's low-ceilinged gloom.

II

Where It All Began

"What have you done, Mother?"

Rebecca Rawley stood fists on her hips, glaring at the slender, auburn-haired girl balanced on a stool to hang herbs on the kitchen's soot-blackened beams.

"You said not a word of this to me. What use do we have for some ill-trained country girl?"

Rebecca fought to keep her voice low but couldn't contain her wounded feelings.

"Why must I hear of it from Annie that a wagon had just dropped the wench off? As if I knew. Even Joseph knew of it. And wanted to know where you'd found such a comely wench."

"I saw no need to bother you with the matter."

Hannah Chinn looked up with a sigh.

Now what has set her off?

Impending motherhood did nothing but aggravate her daughter's irascible nature. But then, there was reason enough for her ill temper. Twice Rebecca had been through the tortures of childbirth. She'd been blessed first with a daughter, now bright and full of life. Then, she bore a tiny, ill-formed boy who lived but an hour. That birth left her weak and sickly for weeks. Since then, the thought of going through another birth brought on a wicked, dark mood.

Her daughter's pain stirred troubling memories in Hannah. She'd seen three of her own little ones laid to rest in St. John's churchyard. She still carried the grief, but never felt the anger that harried her daughter. She nodded toward Rebecca's swollen belly that caused her skirt to billow out in front of her like a wind-filled sail.

"You've more pressing matters to concern you. This isn't the time to be worrying about a kitchen wench."

"How can I not worry? What if I don't come through this trial? Will you give so little thought to who will help you with my dear little Mary. And if this infant should live and I don't, you must see to the care of it, Mama. I'm sure Joseph would take another wife... I can't bear the thought of anyone else raising my child."

"Then, don't think of it." Hannah was out of patience.

"Hush your foolishness, Rebecca. You're strong and well and have no need to worry. This isn't like the last time. That poor little mite came too soon after Mary. You weren't ready for it. But don't think of that now. God willing, you'll have a strong and lusty child.

"You do us a disservice if you think Joseph or I would care so little about Mary. You can be sure this girl or any like her would have nothing to do with the care of your children. She's to work for me here in the kitchen. She's not your concern."

"We know nothing about her and you've given her a place to sleep in the garret. She'll have free run of our apartments. There's little enough room up there for the three servants we have now."

"I've spoken to Annie. She doesn't object. Nor do the chambermaids. They expect no more and will get on well enough. Why does it bother you?"

Hannah measured her speech. It was the best way to deal with Rebecca, especially when she'd got her spleen up.

"You didn't tell me, Mother. But you told the servants. What must they think of that?"

"I told them because it concerns them. Beyond that, they'll think nothing of it. It wasn't a matter to concern you. Any more than the wenches you hire for the public rooms are a concern of mine."

Hannah held up her hand to silence her daughter.

"It's done. Let us say no more about it. I'm sure you are needed now ..."

She waved toward the front of the public room where they could hear the growing din of male voices calling to Joseph Rawley for ale and a fresh bowl of punch. Rebecca took one more angry look at the offending country girl and left without another word.

Suddenly very tired, Hannah felt only relief when her daughter left. She knew all too well that their angry exchange had nothing to do with servants. They'd hardly ever been of the same mind and when Rebecca's father died, their differences became irreparable. Despite the unresolved issues, they'd been able to make a success of the Black Horse. But it was a delicate balance, gone a' kilter with the arrival of Sarah Pratt.

That event was a result of Hannah Chinn's mutton, beef, and pork pies and her lasting friendship with Emma Handy, the butcher's wife. The Handy's shop was directly across Nightingale Lane from the Black Horse. But it was Emma's skills as a midwife that deepened their friendship. She'd delivered Rebecca, her sons William and James, and, then, Rebecca's daughter Mary. They were used to asking favors of each other, but weren't prepared for the storm that followed when Hannah agreed to take in Sarah Pratt.

The girl, Emma said, was from a country family with a surfeit of children and no means to support them. She was eighteen and had been put out to service in the kitchen of a nearby manor house. There Emma's knowledge grew hazy, third hand as it was, from a cousin who was a friend of the manor's cook. As she was told, the young man of the house frightened the girl with his untoward advances. She fled and could not be persuaded to return.

"It's not surprising," said Emma, hoisting the carcass of a plump goose onto the table in her shop for Hannah to inspect.

"Word is that she's a pretty thing and has pleasing ways. From what my cousin says, the cook wanted the girl to stay. She knows of the young man and does not doubt there is truth in what the girl claims. Gossips say he has been the ruin of other girls thereabouts. The cook says, if she must lose her, she can vouchsafe that Sarah worked hard, was worthy of trust, and did well with anything she set her hand to in the kitchen."

"And your cousin speaks well of this cook?"

Emma nodded.

"She has known the girl for some time and her family is well thought of."

Hannah poked the goose's breast and studied its feet, testing the softness of the webbing. At that moment, the bird was of greater interest than the girl. She planned to put it on the spit that morning. She nodded her approval.

"This is a fine one. I'll send the boy for it shortly. And, should the girl come to town, send her to me. If she can cook and is willing to work, that will be more than I can say for the wenches I have now."

Hannah didn't think about the girl again

until later that day. As she often did when she had a moment to rest or think, she settled into her rocking chair in the corner by the kitchen's bake ovens. Idly inspecting the stockings she'd left to be darned, she studied the women busy clearing away the remains of the midday dinner. She left Agnes Quinn to oversee the half-dozen women who made up the kitchen staff.

Agnes had been running the inn's kitchen since before Hannah Oxley came to the Black Horse as Arthur Chinn's bride. The older woman had taught Hannah how to plan and cook for a public room that filled daily with twenty or more hungry men from nearby shipyards, wharves, and businesses. Hannah was just eighteen and Agnes's steadiness calmed her panic the first few times she saw the crowd jostling for seats or a drink and impatient to be fed.

Now, twenty years later, Agnes had paid the price for her years of work. She didn't complain, but Hannah could see how it pained her to lift the heavy iron cookware; how she rubbed her back when she bent over to tend a kettle or griddle on the fire. Her work-scarred hands were still sure, but slower as she pounded dough or chopped meat and vegetables for the pot.

Hannah was usually the one to step in to help her. Except for Annie, who Agnes had taken under her wing, most of the kitchen wenches required orders before they'd lift a hand to anything, then needed close supervision and constant reminding. Now, mindful of Hannah's presence, they made a great show of diligence. Hannah wasn't fooled. If Emma's Sarah Pratt could cook and was willing to work, she wouldn't be any worse than the wenches she had.

****

A fortnight later, Sarah arrived. There'd be more than one young man sniffing after her, Hannah thought as she studied the pretty girl following Emma Handy through the taproom. She had the attention of almost every man in the room and the three tavern wenches as well.

Sarah was nearly a head taller than Emma and well-built. Her straw bonnet was tied with a broad green ribbon but barely contained the auburn curls that surrounded her face and fell to her shoulders. Though unfashionably tan, she was smooth-cheeked, unmarred by scars of the pox. Her brown eyes were large and bright.

The girl moved easily into the garret and seemed to get on well with Annie and the other servants. She appeared the next morning ready to work. That first day, Hannah could find no fault with her. Once Sarah found her way around the kitchen, she didn't have to be reminded what was required. She actually seemed to enjoy whatever tasks she was given.

As for Rebecca, Hannah decided she'd

just have to accept the new girl in the kitchen. It was her kitchen, after all. She intended to please herself. Within a week, Sarah proved herself a good cook, skilled in using herbs and spices. She had a knack for roasting small birds and pigeons and frying sweetbreads and other organ meats. Come evening, Agnes didn't have to tell her to fill a kettle to make a hearty soup from each day's leftovers.

Sarah quickly learned to make puddings and sauces and to prepare fish, which weren't common fare in the kitchens where she'd learned to cook. Agnes took a special interest in her, as she had Hannah, and taught her how to produce palatable meals in quantity.

Within days after Sarah's arrival, Rebecca had completely forgotten about her. Her mother's attention was also elsewhere when Rebecca went into labor. As it had many times before, the small second-floor storeroom was put into service for birthing.

With Sarah to help Agnes keep the other wenches at their tasks, the kitchen continued to run smoothly. All they needed from Hannah was the plan for the next day's meal.

When one of the maids arrived with steaming bowls of richly seasoned oxtail soup for Hannah and Rebecca, Hannah knew it was Sarah's doing. But Rebecca didn't. Hannah left it that way and Rebecca emptied her bowl. That was the last time Rebecca thought of food.

Before the next day had dawned, she had presented an ecstatic Joseph Rawley with a strong and lusty son. They named him Charles, or Charley as Joseph preferred. The only one who wasn't happy was Mary. The four-year old would have nothing to do with the baby.

"It's a boy, Mama."

Her small voice was heavy with reproach.

"Send him away. You said I might have a sister."

Rebecca turned hurt, exhausted eyes toward her daughter.

"Look at him in the cradle there, how fine he is."

Close to tears, Mary stamped her foot.

"I don't want a brother."

"There, there."

Hannah tried to console her granddaughter. She took Mary's hand.

"We can't always have what we want. Let's go look at him."

"I will not."

Mary snatched her hand out of Hannah's.

"Then, you will not."

Hannah scooped the little girl up in her arms.

"We'll let your Mama rest now. You'll feel differently on the morrow."

"I won't," were the last words that Rebecca heard as her mother carried the squirming child from the room.

"Is there anything I can get you, Mistress?"

Annie left the cradle she'd been rocking and approached the bed.

"No. Leave me be. Tend to the child."

Rebecca turned away to hide her brimming eyes.

Outside the room, Hannah put Mary down and led her below and through the public room to the kitchen where Agnes and Sarah were preparing the next day's meals.

"I heard young Master Charley was doing well."

Agness' smile chased the fatigue from her face.

"Mistress Mary, what do you think of your new brother?'

"I don't like him. Mama must send him away."

Agnes's eyes widened.

"Oh, my dear. You must not say that. He is God's gift. You must cherish him."

"Why couldn't God send a sister?"

Hannah shook her head to stop Agnes from the reproach she was sure was coming and guided Mary away.

"Let's find something that you would like to do."

"I have just the thing."

Sarah stepped around the table where she was sorting through a pot of dried peas. She took Mary by the hand and helped her up onto a stool at the table. Collecting a small mortar and pestle and a sack of peppercorns, she put them in front of the child and showed her how to crush the seeds. Mary took to her task with vigor, careless of the tiny husks and elusive seeds that popped out of the bowl. Beside her, Sarah resumed her sorting, humming softly as she worked.

Soon, the peppercorns as well as Mary's unhappy disappointment were forgotten. The little girl began to nod, then, dropped her head on her arms folded on the table top. She didn't wake when Hannah lifted her and carried her through the noisy public room and up to bed. As she went, Hannah blessed Sarah Pratt for the girl's good sense and patience.

III

Arthur & Hannah

Young Arthur Chinn had lived in London with his uncle Frederick, a childless widower who viewed the young man more as a son than nephew. He'd found Arthur had a good head for business and hoped his nephew would join him in the West Indies sugar trade.

Not long after Arthur's arrival, Frederick invested in several warehouses and other properties near the Thames in Wapping. One, on Nightingale Lane, was a disreputable alehouse that he took as payment on a loan rather than send the owner to debtor's prison. He'd planned to put the house up for sale, but decided, instead, to give Arthur a year to see if the place could at least pay for itself.

Arthur had quickly found Thomas Quinn, a stout innkeeper, and his equally stout wife, Agnes. They proved their worth as they vigorously discouraged the baser sort of men and women who kept a more respectable clientele away. By the end of his year, Arthur had expanded the pub into the larger house next door to create a proper victualing house with sleeping accommodations above stairs.

Upon the Quinn's advice, he hired a kitchen and a tavern wench, scullery and chamber maids, and an errand boy to serve the growing number of travelers and tradesmen from nearby businesses and shipyards along the Thames. By the second year, he'd hung a sign emblazoned with a rearing black horse above the door. To Frederick Chinn's amazement, the inn was doing well and Arthur returned to take his place in the shipping business.

Until Arthur turned twenty-seven, shipping and inn-keeping had kept him from thinking about taking a wife. Time enough for that, he told himself. In the meantime, he had the money to enjoy the special pleasures women could provide and was content with a straightforward business transaction to satisfy his needs. A whore had no illusions or expectations, unlike the young women he made an effort to meet when he finally began to search for a wife.

As for proper young women, Arthur thought their expectations all too obvious. Some were simply too vain or flirtatious for him to fathom their true feelings. Or worse, they saw the world as a source of goods with which to clothe themselves or furnish a comfortable house provided by a bountiful husband. They seemed to only care for affairs of government or business if they were scandalous or tragic.

When he made the effort, Arthur chafed at playing the role of suitor and the hours spent in drawing rooms. They kept him too long away from Wapping where his uncle's Thames-side offices, ships, and the inn held a greater allure. The beauty or attentions of a young lady never gave him the rush of pride and pleasure that the sign of the Black Horse swinging over Nightingale Lane roused in him. At times, though, he had to admit that he longed to have someone to share that pleasure with.

The last thing on Arthur's mind was finding a wife when he decided on a visit home. The impetus was a letter from his brother Will cataloguing the day-to-day business of the Chinn's public house and ending with a worrisome note and an enticement.

"Ma and Papa long to see you. As do I. They are growing more frail with each passing day. Also, if Papa will allow it, I'm eager to improve upon the old inn and would value your advice."

Arthur was on the road within a week. He thought he might have news of his own. He had, at last, met a young woman he could imagine taking as a wife. A visit with the family and some time among the rough country girls he remembered would surely confirm the correctness of his decision.

****

Shortly after he'd settled in London, Arthur began sending copies of the *London Gazette* and other papers to his father. The elder Chinn laid them out in his public room for customers to read. Eventually, the papers went into the tinder basket by the fire where Hannah Oxley found them. Thrilled by the discovery, she eagerly spread them out on a table to read. Polly Chinn watched in puzzlement.

"I don't know what you find of interest in those papers."

"That's the wonder of it. I don't know. But I can almost always glean something."

At that moment, however, Hannah was struggling through an unfathomable account of an issue before Parliament.

"Well maybe not today."

Disappointed, she tossed the paper back in the basket.

"You'll never get a husband that way"

Polly liked to tease, but was always ready to listen when Hannah found an interesting story to share.

"Don't despair, Polly."

Hannah laughed with a toss of her head.

"Sooner or later, someone will come through the door who also likes to keep up with the news."

Hannah celebrated with the Chinns when Polly married. She even joined in a country dance or two during the festivities, but saw nothing to interest her in any of the men she met. She missed Polly when she left with her husband but soon realized that she missed the busyness of the inn's kitchen and public room even more.

Mrs. Chinn had always considered Hannah to be much like a daughter and gratefully accepted her offer to help in the kitchen. In truth, she got on better with Hannah than with Polly who had no liking for the work of the public house.

As for Hannah, aside from her work there, she looked forward to being able to read the newspapers when the news was relatively fresh. One autumn afternoon, she paused at a table in the public room to spread out a recent copy of the *London Gazette* that she hadn't been able to read.

"You'll find little to interest you there, Lass."

Hannah spun around. She hadn't seen the man seated at the far end of the room looking at her over the top of the latest *Gazette*.

"And why wouldn't I, Sir? It's often worth a look."

"Aye, but I wouldn't think there was much would appeal to..."

"A country girl? Are you mocking me? Do you think because I haven't left the country as you have that I wouldn't care for what goes on in the rest of the world? Or perhaps you're surprised that I can read at all."

Dropping his paper on the table at his side, Arthur Chinn rose hastily.

"You have me at a disadvantage. Should I know you?"

"Aye. I'm James Oxley's daughter. He's a friend of your brother, I think. Robert is it?

"Yes, Robert. Forgive me. It's been a long time. You must be Hannah. Truly, I didn't know you. You've grown so."

Arthur had no trouble calling her father to mind but struggled to see the daughter in the handsome young woman confronting him. But she would have been a child when he last noticed her.

"I must ask for your forgiveness once more. I was a thoughtless youth then and appear to be no better now."

That was a certainty, she thought. Hannah had to turn away to hide the flush that rose in her cheeks. Ninny! She'd been nothing to him then and easily forgotten ten years since. She would have been better off if she'd forgotten him too.

"You mistook my meaning."

Arthur rushed to fill the silence between them.

"Indeed, it's heartening to come upon someone who finds value in a newspaper beyond using it to start a fire."

"You might remember, reading matter is scarce in these parts."

Hannah nodded toward the papers in her hand.

"We thank you for what you've provided."

"Oh, I do remember. But I don't remember Polly or other young ladies of my acquaintance being greatly concerned with the news they contain."

"Perhaps they are put off by the rantings of Parliament."

At last, she had something she could say that would turn their talk to the impersonal.

"It's a bad business, this trade in slaves that has filled the papers of late. It's evil, I think, trafficking in humans, even if they are heathens. Is it true their skin is black?"

"Aye, black as ebony if all are like the one I've seen. A gentleman's servant and a fine looking man. His suit of clothes was finer than any I own. I understand, if he was back in Africa, he'd wear little or none at all."

"That may be, but I suppose he was still a slave, however finely dressed. And from what I've read, the great number of Africans who are taken to the colonies don't fare so well."

"They don't. I don't like the traffic in humans, but there's another side to that coin. The success of my uncle's trade in sugar and that of many other merchants and mariners depends on the work of slaves. The people of the West Indies must have a plentiful supply of Negroes to survive. If there were no slaves, there would be no sugar to sweeten your coffee or cakes."

"There are men enough here in London

begging for work. Can't they be sent to the colonies?"

Damn, thought Arthur, wishing he'd said nothing about the blasted papers. He certainly didn't want to be defending his livelihood to this fiery-eyed girl. He tried to keep his exasperation out of his voice.

"However desperate, none of our countrymen would willingly leave home for the Sugar Islands. Working the cane is as bad as the meanest labor any man must put his hand to here in England. They'd die of the heat and miasmas. The Negroes are better fitted to survive them. There's good and evil in the trade, but it *is* necessary. Ah, come now, you must have other things that interest you."

This country girl with the unruly mass of honey-colored curls and serious blue eyes was beyond the ordinary, he thought. And so was her free expression of opinions, however irritating. He tried to reconcile the young woman before him with a vague memory of Polly's childhood friend.

"As I recall, you and Polly were great companions, weren't you?"

"Yes. It's been a while since I've seen her and have missed her very much. She's to be brought to bed soon, your mother says. I hope to be with her. If Mama can spare me, I will go to her with your mother."

"You're still at home then? I'm surprised you're not in a home of your own."

"No. My mother has need of me."

And do you have someone who needs you at home?

Hannah's mind was racing. She was sure Polly had said nothing of Arthur marrying. But, then, she'd said nothing of him at all.

Please, please let that mean there was nothing of that sort to tell.

"Ah," was all Arthur could think to say, suddenly struck speechless by the thought that this was a woman he would have for a wife. *If* she'd have him.

Hannah never told Arthur that she knew by their second meeting—one that was not by chance—that she would say yes if he proposed. That night, James Oxley stood drinks for every man who happened to be in William Chinn's tavern. Hannah's mother wept with joy. No time was lost in posting the bans and Hannah became Mrs. Arthur Chinn two months later. The next time Helen Oxley wept was when Hannah left for London with her new husband.

IV

The Black Horse

Though Arthur had told Hannah of the city, she wasn't prepared for the reality of it. She'd never imagined such a place. The bustle and clatter of the shop-filled streets crowded with people, buying candles, soap, fresh-baked bread, or butchered meats. It was a wonder.

Arthur had told her that she'd be joining him in inn keeping. It wouldn't be easy, he said. But she couldn't believe that the life could be harder than her mother's had been as a farmer's wife.

Hannah was born to hard work and suffered no misgivings on that count. She did have a moment of misgiving though, when they stepped from the wagon at the door of the Black Horse. With its two public rooms and lodgings above, it was much larger than the Chinn's public house. But the moment she walked into the inn's kitchen, Hannah knew she'd feel at home. There'd be time to learn more of the business. As it turned out, she was busy and happy from dawn til well after dark.

Her life was complete when William was born, followed shortly by Rebecca and James. They and the busy victualing house helped her bear the loss of two others who didn't survive infancy. She had no time to mourn, for by then, Arthur had handed her the keys to the storeroom and office and put the inn's ledgers in her hands.

He was pleased to be freed from the day-to-day worries and operation of the inn and eagerly turned his attention to preparing Chinn & Chinn's brigs *Speedwell* and *Providence* for their outward voyages with goods to be sold in the West Indies. By the time they returned, Arthur would have the Wapping warehouse filled with the brigs' next cargoes and buyers for the sugar, coffee, teak, ebony, and other lucrative cargoes they carried.

The Black Horse served him well for entertaining prospective customers and tradesmen as well as local government officials. As a result, the Black Horse defied easy description.

Customers sorted themselves out before passing through one of its two doors. Few government officials or men of business chose the old alehouse with its door set back from the street in a shadowy entryway. Instead, they went on another twenty feet to a larger, heavier door of oak below a sign displaying a rearing horse pawing the air, its ebony mane and tail flying, teeth bared, wild eyes rimmed with white.

At first, Hannah wished Arthur was more involved in the business of the tavern. Then, one day, as she looked over the crowded public rooms, she realized that she liked being the mistress of the Black Horse and widely acknowledged as a woman of substance. But, in truth, the kitchen of the inn was the chief source of her pride and satisfaction.

There, she and Agnes Quinn had achieved a singular success with the right mix of meats and seasonings in their pies that drew customers from near and far. They hired a second girl and then another to help them keep up with the demand. In time, she was serving food and drink well into the night.

It suited Arthur that she didn't really need or want him to be more involved in the business. He was generous with his praise, especially at the end of each week, when he looked over the inn's account books. On those nights, when they finally made their way to bed, there was no hurry to sleep as they shared the pleasures of their bodies.

Years later, Hannah's thoughts went back most often to such moments. She remembered how nervous she was the first time he sat down with her ledger. She could still see his pursed lips and the deep furrow between his dark brows as he ran one ink-stained finger down each column in her account book.

There was always a short, unruly strand of hair falling across his forehead that he tried uselessly to shove back up under his wig. She teased him about the wig, but he refused to give it up. It was a necessity of doing business, he said. She much preferred his own soft, brown hair to the fussy thing with its rolled curls and queue stiff as the tail of a hog in rut. On those nights, she'd stood silently, hands clinched, looking over his shoulder until he closed the book.

"Humpf."

He turned slowly to her with a frown and pursedlips. His silence lengthened until Hannah was overcome with impatience.

"Well, Mr. Chinn, what have you to say?"

"What must I say? You make it hard, fidgeting and breathing down my neck."

"Mr. Chinn!"

"You have no need to worry, lass. You've done a fine job."

He rose with a broad smile and clasped her around the waist.

"You'd put my clerks to shame."

They dallied no longer below stairs. Many times thereafter, when he wasn't tired or driven by his need, he spent time with her in bed. In the beginning of their marriage, Hannah simply endured their coupling, but as they grew more easy with each other, that began to change. Hannah was bothered only briefly by wondering how he had learned so much about a woman's body. But she was happy that he had. His hands explored her body, responding to her little moans and sighs. He found pleasure spots she didn't know she had. Only then would he satisfy his own need.

Both enjoyed Hannah's discovery that some of the same sorts of caresses that felt good to her, did to him also. From what little her mother and older sisters had told her, Hannah had never expected to know such feelings. Indeed, her would-be advisors had implied that sort of pleasure was a great sin. She was, at first, plagued by the worry that her enjoyment of such physical pleasure was a sin, but could never convince herself of the harm in what she and Arthur shared. She'd come too close to experiencing heaven on a few occasions to believe that God would condemn it.

****

William Chinn began work in his father's warehouse when he turned fourteen. The boy went from checking manifests to preparing them and joined other clerks in the offices of Chinn & Chinn. When William came of age, his father changed the sign to read Chinn & Sons. He included his son James even though he seldom appeared in their offices. At seventeen, James, or Jamie as he'd come to be called, had no patience with office duties and preferred his life at sea working up to first mate of the

Chinns' brig *Speedwell.*

When Jamie announced one day that he meant to take the *Speedwell*'s helm, Arthur had to hide his pleasure despite the brashness of his son's claim. That was as he'd hoped. With Jamie in command of the *Speedwell*, or whatever ship they owned at that time, he'd become a true partner in the business. Arthur had a particular fondness for his younger son, who had his mother's blue eyes and brown hair, though months at sea had lightened it considerably.

Rebecca, a bright and eager child, was a year younger than William. Her cleverness and independence pleased her parents greatly. Arthur seldom returned to the inn without a gift of sweetmeats, a bonnet, or some trinket for her. Though Hannah also doted on her, she found the little girl's volatility a trial as she grew older. She let Rebecca have her way too often and her daughter grew up thinking too much was her due.

When Rebecca was old enough to be useful, she eagerly went about whatever chores were required of her in the kitchen or bedchambers. As she grew older, she much preferred chores that took her into the public room, imagining that she was mistress of the inn. In her heart, she aspired to nothing less and took on more and more responsibility.

Hannah welcomed her assistance with marketing and later, recording each day's accounts. With Hannah's support, the older wenches made sure she didn't get away with a slip-shod job clearing the tables, sweeping floors, tending fires, or whatever other task was required. At first the women were pleased and proud of her, then irritated as Rebecca initiated ways to improve service and increase the overall cleanliness and appearance of the public room.

Hannah was regularly called upon to serve as mediator, but eventually realized that there was another who could do as well. At nineteen, Rebecca had become a handsome young woman and, for some time, she'd suspected something brewing between her and their innkeeper Joseph Rawley.

Joseph had come to the Black Horse as an assistant to Thomas Quinn, the Chinns long-time innkeeper. He was an energetic young man of twenty-four and quickly became indispensable. When Thomas Quinn died suddenly, Arthur had no hesitation in turning over management of the inn to Joseph. His change in status soon confirmed Hannah's suspicion.

Within days, Arthur reported that Joseph had asked permission to marry Rebecca. She'd already guessed that was coming. Joseph and Rebecca were the subject of gossip among women she met at the market and elsewhere. They'd warned her that men of Joseph's age and ambition often used marriage to advance their own interests.

But Hannah had studied Joseph. From

what she knew of him, she couldn't believe he was that sort. Rebecca was actually the more ambitious of the two. But the main reason that Hannah urged Arthur to give his permission was because Joseph was able to manage their fractious daughter when no one else could. He did so, for the most part, because he was content to let Rebecca make the major decisions, stepping in only to explain what she needed to know about running the inn. In that, they worked together with like-minded purpose and shared their accomplishments with equal satisfaction. When they disagreed, Joseph was almost always able to guide them to a compromise.

Arthur was proud and pleased and Hannah was relieved when their wedding day arrived. The Chinns hosted a feast that was shared with any and all present in the Black Horse at the time. Following the festivities, Rebecca and Joseph moved into the empty room next to her parents' apartment. Hannah and Arthur were surprised by their willingness to live in such cramped quarters, but soon discovered why.

For some time, they'd had their eyes on a large, long-vacant, two-story house next to the Black Horse that the owner was eager to be rid of. Armed with facts and figures, the young couple presented her parents with their idea to expand the Black Horse into the second house. Joseph had a small inheritance and had been putting money by. With that and Arthur's financial backing and his eye on their accounts, they were ready to begin work.

Though Hannah worried about allowing her daughter such freedom, she liked their idea. Especially appealing was the opportunity that expanding the business offered her to make some small improvements in the taproom and expand the kitchen and store rooms into the rear of the second house.

She tried to keep that in mind over the ensuing months when she had to feed a small army of carpenters, plasterers, and other craftsmen.

As it turned out, the activity offered her taproom customers a good show and improved the business. Once she'd allayed their fear that the taproom would be closed, the men from Wapping's wharves and shipyards kept every table full. They watched in awe during installation of a handsome lead-topped mahogany bar like those becoming popular in finer West End inns. They could only speculate what was going on above stairs. They knew only that there were two bed chambers large enough to accommodate three or four travelers each and one for the occasional gentleman or a family that liked their privacy.

Their curiosity about the finer beds, tables, chairs, and bureaus was satisfied only when one of the chambermaids told them of the new three-room apartment that the master and mistress were furnishing for themselves. Room by room, Rebecca not only refurnished their apartment, but added bed hangings, curtains, and floor cloths and hired extra maids to clean all the rooms above stairs. Their travelers seldom complained of fleas or bedbugs.

Hannah had to admit that the added accommodations and new public room were a wise addition. The bar set a tone that justified adding a few quality wines to be enjoyed in comfort at the new tables and chairs instead of benches. Also, in the newly furnished public room, gentlemen could sample the wines and sip coffee around tables designed especially for backgammon and whist. Arthur also added a handsome new door to the street so that customers would not have to enter through the taproom. When they were ready for business, a workman arrived to remove the old sign and hang a new, larger sign with a brightly painted but less artful depiction of a rearing black horse.

"What is this? What are you doing?"

Arthur confronted the workman and snatched the faded signboard from his hands.

"Mistress Rawley, Sir. She told me to. I got this new one here to replace it."

"Don't you do anything of the kind."

"But the Mistress, Sir. She said…"

The workman swallowed his words as he watched the angry man tuck the sign under his arm and storm through the new door into the upper public room.

"Rebecca! Daughter! Where are you?"

"Here father!"

"I never agreed to this,"

He held up the old sign.

"We never spoke of removing this."

"Oh Papa, I thought you wouldn't mind. We've got a fine new one that's much more handsome. That one's a disgrace."

"You never thought that before. It's served us well enough until now."

"But now what's to let people know that there's anything different inside? This isn't..."

"Might I suggest something else, Sir."

Joseph hastened from behind the bar.

"We really need both signs."

He took the old sign from Arthur's hands.

"This sign has brought men from Wapping through that door for more than thirty years. It can continue to do so. I'll have the man nail it to the right of the taproom door and hang the new one over the other door."

Arthur's face showed his relief. He never liked going against his daughter's wishes, which seemed increasingly to be at odds with his own and her mother's.

"Well said! That's exactly what we'll do."

Rebecca shrugged and stalked back through the grand new door.

"Come along, Joseph. We've things to do."

Her words trailed back through the door and Joseph followed with a sheepish look.

Arthur remained long enough to see

that the sign he'd so proudly hung many years before was well placed beside the taproom door. When that was done, he went inside to pour a glass of ale to celebrate the sign's rehanging and the certainty that men who worked the shipyards and along the waterfront were still assured of a drink and a simple meal in comfortably familiar surroundings.

****

In growing numbers, shopkeepers, mariners, doctors, lawyers, and minor government officials joined associates for business or pleasure with a more elaborate meal or a game of cards in the upper public room. Because the inn was convenient to the wharves, it catered to a steady stream of travelers, planters from the colonies and those doing business throughout England's empire. They entered under the new sign to dine in the upper public room or in a private chamber above.

In the kitchen, Hannah and Agnes kept half a dozen women busy and had two sturdy boys to run errands and tend the fires. Most days, Hannah welcomed the challenge of offering the finest cuts of beef, pork, lamb, and a variety of fowl from capon to partridge and swan as well as a selection of cheeses, pies, cakes, custards, and fruits in season.

Amidst the turmoil of running a busy inn, Rebecca discovered that she was pregnant.

She refused to let each morning's sickness slow her down and was overcome with guilt when she lost the baby in less than two months. Her life was much calmer and she was more careful three months later when she was pregnant again. The baby girl was delivered safely and they named her Mary. She had Joseph's thick blond hair and blue eyes.

At a year, she was pulling herself up to stand, which delighted Arthur when Rebecca took her to visit her grandfather in his offices. He called her his little yellow bird and proudly carried her down to the wharf to show her the *Providence*, then loading for the West Indies. He was planning his third voyage on her.

Hannah braced herself for their parting, which grew harder each time. On the night before he left, Arthur scoffed at her fears, but he held her until she slept. She was still in his arms when she awoke. He was off at dawn, leaving her on the quay with a kiss before he boarded the *Providence*. Her captain had been waiting for him before giving the order to get underway and, too soon, the brig was standing out in the Thames. Arthur waved from the quarterdeck one last time before the ship disappeared around a bend. And then, the waiting began.

Five months later, Jamie brought the *Speedwell* home from Virginia. One, two, three months passed during which he and William asked for news of the *Providence* from every incoming ship. Finally, the captain of a ship just arrived from Barbados appeared in the offices of Chinn & Sons with papers for William. He'd watched the *Providence* sail from Bridgetown a month ahead of him, he said. She was bound straightaway for London and should have been tied up at her wharf in Wapping.

Jamie was all for going straight away to tell their mother. He knew enough of the sea and was sure that the *Providence* and his father had been lost. But he wasn't sure how long he could contain his grief. He wouldn't let himself cry until he could escape to be alone, to storm and yell and, then, drink himself into a stupor. But first they had to tell their mother.

He couldn't understand when William stopped him.

"We must tell her before she hears from someone else."

"There are things to be done first. Papers. The ship's papers in the office."

"Papers! How can you think of things like that?"

Jamie looked at his brother as if he didn't know him.

"Someone has to."

"But not now!"

As William turned away, Jamie grabbed his arm, but his brother flung off his hand.

"Yes, now. I must do it now. I can't go to her. I won't know what to say."

William wouldn't look at him, but his ashen face spoke of his struggle to hold his feelings in check. There was no point in trying to get William to go with him. Without another word, Jamie broke into a run, racing against the rush of his own pain. At the Black Horse, he found Joseph Rawley at the bar.

"Where's Mother?"

Startled, Joseph Rawley pointed toward the ceiling.

"Above stairs."

Jamie's grim look was enough for him to know there was trouble.

"What's happened?"

Jamie only shook his head, unable to speak, and headed for the steps taking two at a time. He knocked on his mother's door, but didn't wait for a reply. The look on his face brought Hannah out of her chair where she sat by the fire. As her book fell to the floor, she stretched out her hand as if to ward off the news she'd been fearing.

"Your father?"

The tears he could no longer contain were his answer. She opened her arms and, as he stepped into them, her own tears blinded her. She couldn't have said how long they clung to each other, but thanked God that it was Jamie who'd brought the terrible news. He was the only one of her offspring who could share the comfort of such an embrace. Only a frantic pounding on the door caused her to release him. Hastily mother and son wiped away their tears.

"Mother! Are you there?"

They met each other's reddened eyes

and turned toward the door.

"Come in."

William was breathless, a bundle of papers held against his chest.

"I see you've heard. We've suffered a great loss."

For a fleeting moment Hannah wondered if he meant the ship or his father, but that was unfair. William never could express strong feelings.

"Yes. Does Rebecca know?"

William nodded.

"Joseph has gone to find her.

Hannah went numbly through that day and two more. At times, she wished she could do as Rebecca had and close herself away, shutting out family and responsibilities. But they were what kept her going. Especially attending to Mary. The child spent two days and nights with Hannah in her rooms and the kitchen. Solemnly she followed Hannah with trays of food to leave untouched outside Rebecca's door.

On the third morning, Rebecca appeared, ate an early breakfast in the kitchen with Mary, and returned to her office and public room duties as if nothing had happened. Until Mary went back to her family's rooms, Hannah had held her own sorrow close, but when she was again alone at night in the bed she and Arthur had shared, it burst in a torrent.

As he usually did when he was in port, Jamie took his supper with his mother and spent his evenings with other seagoing men in the taproom of the Black Horse or other Wapping pubs. He tried to fill a part of most days with preparations for the *Speedwell*'s next voyage, but could not escape the endless meetings with William and their lawyer in the Chinns' shipping office.

Most dealt with the myriad insurance claims and legal matters beyond their own that involved the losses suffered by customers to whom the brig's cargo had been consigned. When such pressing matters had been dealt with, they came to the matter of Arthur's will. He wrote it before Rebecca and Jamie came of age and, as a result, left the Black Horse and his personal estate to Hannah with the proviso that upon her death, the inn was bequeathed to Rebecca. William would be the principal owner of Chinn & Sons. When they came of age, Rebecca and Jamie would each receive a quarter share of the business.

Because Jamie was already showing a keen interest in going to sea, the Chinns' ships would be his. At the time he wrote the will, he could not have known how much the Black Horse would come to mean to his daughter. Hannah was relieved that he wasn't there to witness the storm caused by his failure to draw up a new will.

"How could he? He knew what this place means to me. It's not fair. When we wed, Joseph had every expectation from Father that we would have the Black Horse. You heard him say as much, Mother. Now this …. It can't be what he intended."

"That may be so, but you were little more than a child. He was so caught up in the business…"

Struggling with the unrelenting pain of her own sorrow threatening to grow into anger, Hannah flung up her hand to quiet her daughter.

"Stop! I don't want to hear any more. He couldn't know he'd leave us so soon. Nothing will change for you and Joseph. It will go on just as it has been. The Black Horse is as good as yours. I'll manage the kitchen as always and will take pleasure in caring for my granddaughter. Nothing will change. Let this be the end of it."

"But…"

"Enough!"

With an abrupt shake of her head, Hannah left Rebecca in open-mouthed silence and retreated to her bed chamber. Behind the door, in the silence of the room she and Arthur had shared, she couldn't escape the pain of his absence. Rebecca's anger and resentment had sharpened her feeling of loss. She'd never felt more alone, but resolved not to retreat into it.

She had no reason to expect understanding from Rebecca, but, then, she'd never understood Rebecca either. More than once she'd wished her daughter had been born with Jamie's easy-going ways. She could better picture Rebecca barking orders from the quarterdeck of a ship. She still couldn't imagine her son in such a role.

In a better frame of mind, Hannah was reminded of Jamie's return from his first voyage to the Chesapeake colonies. He brought back the shell of a large turtle, a terrapin he said the Indians called it, and hung it proudly in the taproom. On another voyage, he returned with a necklace of shells the natives used for money and, from then on, carried small tools and bolts of English cloth that the Indians prized.

He always managed to spend time sitting by her fireside and telling her of the ports he visited and the people he met, from enterprising colonists to the tall, dark-skinned natives who came into colonial settlements to trade. Though she was content with her life, Hannah couldn't help wishing to see some of the places Jamie spoke of. As it was, she could do no more than stand on a wharf watching others leave. She'd pleaded with him more than once to keep the *Speedwell* in England's waters at least.

"You don't have to trade so far away," she'd said. "And if you could put into port here more often, perhaps you could take a wife and start a family."

He'd laughed and hugged her.

"I'm not ready to do that yet. And if you were ever to visit the Chesapeake, you'd know why I return. I wish you could see it. Some call the bay an inland sea, but you're never far from its shores. They're lined with forests and meadows, ashen cliffs, and rivers that offer some fine harbors. But it'll test the most seasoned mariner with its fickle winds and tides that run you aground on its shoals. They've even devised their own breed of sailing craft, fast as a bird in flight. They'll outrun any pirate, but they're not burdensome enough to carry cargo or I'd have one by now."

Hannah had to shake her head.

"Say no more. Just don't forsake us for your new mistress."

She had to laugh at her son's look of shock which wasn't entirely feigned. Mothers were not supposed to speak of such things, especially not in jest. Her light tone didn't express the feelings that she kept from him, the fear that she'd lose him as she had his father.

She'd never thought of herself as the adventurous sort, but on the day she stood on the wharf and watched the *Speedwell* slip its tethers to the land and drop down the Thames, she wished she were sailing with him.

Hannah's life at the Black Horse had been busy enough most of the time to keep her worry and grief at bay. But Rebecca's lingering disappointment and anger caused by her father's final wishes was a painful reminder. She could never relinquish her resentments easily. More than ever, she was ready to take offense.

Hannah credited Joseph Rawley that matters weren't worse. He had good, plain, country sense of the most practical sort. Hardly anything flustered him. Most important, he could curb Rebecca's excess of opinion, which was forever setting her at odds with others. Where her daughter was concerned, Hannah wasn't much better. She had no patience with Rebecca's righteous conceits and worried at the effect she would have on her own daughter. At three Mary was a handful, as willful as her mother, but a sunny child who charmed everyone around her. She didn't understand when her mother became short-tempered and was only mollified when Rebecca told her that, in a few months, she'd have a baby sister to play with.

V

Sarah's Arrival

Rebecca's lying in was brief. She was impatient to work and took no pleasure in nursing and tending to her newborn son Charles, or Charley as he came to be called. Hannah brought her the inn's account books to keep her above stairs. Joseph and the maid Annie, who'd borne the brunt of Rebecca's irritability and impatience, were greatly relieved when Hannah finally allowed her to go below.

Though she couldn't take full charge of running the public rooms, Rebecca still managed to keep the serving girls in a nervous frenzy. They could relax only when she went above to nurse Charley. Within a week of her son's birth, however, Rebecca found a wet nurse, bound her breasts, moved Charley's cradle to the kitchen, and left her mother to take charge of him. Hannah readily agreed but was bothered by Rebecca's lack of interest in her son.

Despite Mary's disappointment at being presented with a brother, she couldn't resist the appeal of an infant. She never seemed to tire of rocking his cradle, which sat close to Hannah's rocking chair in the kitchen corner. When the baby slept, Hannah and Agnes kept Mary busy with small chores. The arrangement suited all concerned. Or so it seemed until the morning that Rebecca appeared unexpectedly.

Without a word, she scooped Charley from the cradle and left the kitchen with a puzzled and noisily unhappy Mary tugging at her skirts. Surprised, Hannah stood for just a few seconds in silence, then gathered her skirts and ran after her daughter. She caught her at the stairs to their apartments above.

"Rebecca, wait. What's happened. What are you doing?"

"You have to ask me? Are you blind?"

At her mother's stunned look, she nodded toward the busy public room.

"We can't talk here. Come upstairs."

As Rebecca busily went about settling Charley in his cradle in her bed chamber, Hannah finally lost her patience.

"What's happened? Why are you doing this?"

"You really don't know? Come, Mother you can't be so blind. Have you looked closely at that girl you've taken in? She's pregnant."

"Pregnant? I..."

Hannah had to stop.

Have I been blind? Or did I just not want to see?

She *had* wondered when Sarah Pratt began wearing a loose-fitting short dress, but assumed it was more comfortable for working in the kitchen. She'd congratulated herself on putting some meat on the girls bones with better food and easier work than she'd had in the country. Now that she had to face the truth, she was saddened, but only because Sarah hadn't felt able to confide in her.

"What difference does that make to the children? It's a pity if she's indeed pregnant, but that's no cause to take the children away. Sarah is good with them. She'll make a good mother with one of her own. And Mary and Charley are happy in the kitchen. I like having them close by me."

"They'll be happy wherever they are. You can be with them elsewhere. Besides, it's time I got Mary to work on her horn book and some simple stitchery."

"You don't need Charley by you to do that."

"Of course not. But I hardly know the child. He'll be out of the cradle in a short while and I want to take him in hand. With a boy that's important. They'll stay with me, Mother."

A long silence stretched between them. Neither was happy with the outcome and neither wanted to be the one to give in.

"So be it. Keep them with you."

Hannah shook her head and, with a

60

rueful look, turned away.

If she expects me to send that girl away, she's sorely mistaken.

"I'll see that Sarah has nothing to do with your children," she said to Rebecca's back.

Returning to the kitchen, she had one of the kitchen boys carry the cradle to Rebecca's office off the public room. From then on, Mary and the baby were with their mother. If she was busy or they required more of her attention than she was willing to give, she sent them with Annie or one of the more reliable chambermaids to the Rawley's apartment above stairs.

****

Hannah couldn't help wondering how she'd been so blind? There'd been signs if she'd been willing to see them. And why hadn't Sarah told her? She'd chosen to think that a longing for home caused Sarah to visit her parents for two days. The girl hadn't begged off a single day of work since she arrived. Hannah easily agreed.

Even when Sarah returned, Hannah accepted her claim that it was smoke or a cinder that caused her to appear so often with red-rimmed eyes. But now there was no denying the truth. She took Sarah aside that afternoon in the relative quiet between midday dinner and supper's demands.

"How long were you going to wait

before telling me?"

Sarah didn't even feign surprise.

"I didn't know how. You've been so good to me. For the longest time, I couldn't think what to do. There was a woman I'd heard of… but, Oh, Mistress, I couldn't go through with it."

The girl stood before Hannah, her hands knotted together in front of her, her large brown eyes bright with unshed tears.

"I had every intention, but when I came to her place, I couldn't do it. It's a wicked practice and I said as much. The woman taunted me for such foolish sensibilities. Then, she said she'd take me in and, when it was time, would relieve me of the baby. She knows of people who would pay for my keep and, then, for the child. But I couldn't stay in such a place, and I wouldn't give her a child for any amount of money."

Hannah had to agree. But that wasn't the only solution.

"What of the father? Do you know…"

"Oh, I do. I'm no whore. I've been with none but him. He spoke of marrying, and I believed him…"

The words released a freshet of tears. Sarah sobbed and wiped her eyes with a corner of her apron, then went on in a rush.

"We even went to look at rooms. But he's a tradesman's apprentice and is forbidden to marry until his indenture is served. I didn't know of his obligation. I'd thought certain we would wed. He claims he didn't think his master would hold him to that part of his contract. But his master would have none of it."

"When he told me we couldn't wed, I was already with child. He can't keep me, even outside of marriage. He has but a few shillings for food and what small things he needs. His master pays for his lodging and would know if I went to stay with him there. It's a mean little room."

The last caused color to rise in Sarah's cheeks and she lowered her head.

"I have not seen him for a month. He's found another room, but his landlord won't tell me where he's gone. It would only anger him if I went to the... to the place where he works."

"I take it, I'd know his master."

The look of distress on Sarah's face kept Hannah from questioning her anymore on that score.

"What about your parents. Did you tell them? Won't they take you in?"

"That was why I went to see them. But my father won't let me come back, and my mother dares not cross him. Nor will my sister and her husband. They won't even speak to me. There are no friends can help. They said I must apply to the parish here. A workhouse might take me in. Put me to making pins or some such. But they'll take my baby from me if I go there. It would be no better than selling a child to that horrible woman. I... I thought maybe I could go on working here and could earn enough to pay for a room and, God willing, keep my baby."

Sarah stopped and gulped back a sob.

"I can't expect you to forgive me, but I would be ever so grateful and would not take advantage if you would let me stay and work until the child comes. I'll put money aside so that I can take a place for us. If I'm working, I can pay for someone to keep the baby."

"It would have been better if you'd thought so carefully before you laid with your young man."

Though Hannah knew that was a foolish thing to say, she needed time to think and wished the girl weren't standing there wringing her hands. She took so long to answer that Sarah turned to leave.

"I'll go then," she said.

"No, wait."

The thought of the kitchen without Sarah pushed Hannah toward her decision.

"You can stay, but I want no trouble over this," she said. "I'll show you no favor. You must do what is required of you, as before. I take it your things are still in the garret."

For an uncomfortable moment, as a look of relief and joy spread over Sarah's face, Hannah thought the girl was going to embrace her.

"Go!" she said more sharply than she intended.

"Yes 'um," said Sarah and ran from the kitchen.

Hannah paused just a moment then

grabbed the shawl she kept in the alcove outside the kitchen door and hurried through the taproom to the street. With a glance at the damp cobblestoned street, she looked skyward from beneath the small shingled roof over the inn's door. The sun still hadn't appeared above that stretch of Nightingale Lane to chase away early fall's chill. She hugged the shawl more tightly around her shoulders.

Curls of smoke from coal fires in Wapping businesses and homes contributed to a sooty haze overhead. At street level, their fumes mingled with the stench rising from the garbage-filled drain that ran down the middle of the street. Mindful of the steady flow of people and assorted hand and horse carts, Hannah gathered her skirts and hurried across to the Handy's butcher shop. She was relieved to find Emma Handy alone.

"I saw a cart leave Sarah at your door. I thought she'd have spent more time at home."

After twenty years, the two friends needed no preliminaries.

"So did I, but I'm afraid she had unwelcome news for her parents. And for me. She's five months pregnant. I never guessed. Or didn't want to see the truth. Her family's disowned her."

Emma Handy shook her head in sad disbelief.

"So there *is* more to the story than she told us."

Hannah's blue eyes grew hard, angry.

"Aye, there is. It's a sorry mother would send her daughter away like that. Or anyone for that matter. I certainly won't turn her out."

Emma Handy had been listening, leaning with both hands on the wood butcher block.

"I wouldn't expect you to. But what about the man's part in it?"

"He doesn't deny it, but is bound by a 'prentice agreement. Now he's run off and she can't find him. I don't need to tell you what choices remain."

"It pains me, Hannah, that I brought this trouble on you."

"You couldn't have known any more than I. And I was more than willing. She's worth more than any two wenches now in my employ. I don't want to lose her."

"You've no need to tell me of her worth. I've sampled enough of her cooking."

"And for that alone she's worth keeping on. I haven't thought what to do when her time comes, but I'll surely need your help."

"You need only call. Perhaps when the girl is delivered we can find somewhere for her to live and someone to care for the babe if she's assured of a place in your kitchen. It's not uncommon."

Hannah was greatly relieved when she finally returned to the Black Horse, wishing only that the issue could be resolved that easily with Rebecca.

VI

Martha's Birth

"Mistress Rawley, come quick!"

The cries of the frightened scullery maid brought all eyes of the breakfasters in the public room up from their plates. The men watched with mild curiosity. The daily business of women was usually not of great interest. With unconcerned shrugs, they turned back to their food as Annie and Rebecca disappeared up the two flights to the garret.

Sarah Pratt lay sprawled on her pallet, but at the sight of Rebecca, she struggled to rise, fighting uselessly against the great weight of her belly.

"The devil take it!"

Rebecca motioned for Annie to help her lift Sarah to her feet.

"We must get her below."

Without a backward glance, Rebecca lead the way below. Struggling against her discomfort, Sarah took care to rest her hand gingerly on her mistress's shoulder. Annie's grasp on the waist of Sarah's skirt was more reassuring as they made slow, precarious progress down the narrow stair. At the bottom, Annie supported Sarah down the broad hall to the small corner room where she eased her onto the low bed.

Rebecca stood in the middle of the room taking a mental inventory of its contents. All was in order, just as it had been five months earlier. She looked with distaste at the bed where she labored to bring Charley into the world. And Mary, four years before that. Except for the bed, the cluttered space was filled with chests of fresh blankets, linens, and extra bed ticks but nothing to show that it was ever a birthing room. Only a sizeable hearth and a table and chair tucked in among bureaus and chests made it habitable. Its only window looked out over the rear courtyard of the inn.

"Stay with her," Rebecca snapped at Annie.

She'd yet to look directly at Sarah or offer any words of comfort and wasn't about to. Annie stepped quickly out of Rebecca's way as she swept past and out the door. Rebecca found her mother in the kitchen where she and Agnes were wrestling a trussed goose onto the spit jack.

"The girl's time has come. I've put her in the corner room. Annie waits with her, but I can't spare her for long."

Rebecca then turned on her heel and left without waiting for Hannah's reply,

Hannah sighed. She didn't regret bringing Sarah Pratt into the Black Horse, but had continued to hope that her daughter would soften toward her. Even though Rebecca and her head told her that was foolish, she'd let her heart tell her otherwise. In the kitchen, she found Agnes.

"You heard."

"Aye. You'd best get up to her."

Quickly they finished the goose, set it in place over the hearth's ruddy coals. Once Hannah'd washed the goose grease from her hands, she looked around the room.

The servant girls stood, just as they had when Rebecca burst into the room, spoons, knives, and floured hands halted mid-task, until Hannah turned from the sink. She knew a long day and night stretched ahead of her, but the girls knew what to do and Agnes would see that they got meals out to the tables on time.

"Where's that boy?"

Hannah asked no one in particular and got no answer. She turned to Agnes.

"Send him for water when he returns and have him bring it up. And send word to Mrs. Handy. We'll be needing her soon."

The older woman simply nodded and waved her hand.

"I'll send word. Now, see to the girl. We'll tend to everything here."

Hannah could have hugged the aged cook, but left her instead with a grateful smile and nod.

In the upper room, Hannah found Sarah sitting as Rebecca had left her. Above cheeks wet with tears, the girl's eyes were brimming. Annie seemed near tears herself as she twisted her apron into clumps of rumpled cloth.

"Let's get you settled," Hannah said with what she hoped was a reassuring smile. "No more tears."

She took Sarah's arm and led her to a nearby chair. Then, with Annie, she pulled the bed away from the wall so they could easily move around the end and both sides. As Annie shook out the bed's plain wool blankets and plumped the bolster, Hannah helped Sarah struggle to her feet. They had to stop until the latest labor pain released its hold on her, then went on to the bed.

"You must rest now," Hannah said. "There'll be little time for that later."

Sarah sank back on the pillows and closed her eyes. Hannah covered her with a blanket and turned to find Annie immobile, still worrying her apron. She tried to hide her exasperation.

"See to the fire. We must get a kettle going."

The girl was clearly relieved to have something familiar to do and disappeared to fetch coals from a fireplace below. Hannah paused to collect her thoughts, then set about making preparations. She had piles of soft cotton diaper and linen cloth and several blankets on the table by the time Annie returned. Soon the girl had the beginnings of a fire in the hearth. In the overcast morning's dim light, Hannah couldn't tell if Sarah was asleep.

That'll be the last rest she gets for a while, she thought.

Moving as silently as she could, she lit the candles in their wall sconces. That was better. And Annie had got a cheery blaze going to lend its warm glow.

"That will do."

She nodded toward the girl.

"Go now and see where that boy is with the water. And bring a bottle of wine and glasses."

Annie wasn't long in returning with the wine. The boy followed close behind with a bucket of water and a kettle. Hannah filled the latter and hooked it over the fire. Hannah nodded her thanks and directed the girl to a stool by the bed.

"I must go below. You sit here by Sarah."

Hannah handed her a shallow bowl of water and a square of diaper.

"Hold her hand when the pains come and wipe her face with this."

She caught a look of distress as she turned away from the girl.

"Don't worry. I won't be long. The babe will come in its own time, and that will be a long while yet."

With one last look at Sarah, she followed the boy down the stairs to find Rebecca waiting at the bottom.

"Annie hasn't finished the rooms, and

she'll soon be needed to serve dinner."

"There are other girls can do as well. I have greater need of her today."

Mother and daughter stood, eyes locked, jaws clenched.

"It won't hurt you to show a little charity," Hannah said softly and continued toward the kitchen.

It pained her that Rebecca could be so unfeeling. Sarah'd never done anything to her. But Rebecca had always been like that. She had no tolerance for any disruption in the order of her life. Or for the frailties of other people. Hannah suspected, her daughter was jealous of anyone who might, in the least, vie for her attention. And could not forgive her mother for allowing it.

In the kitchen, Hannah was soothed by the creaking of the jack turning the spitted goose and the smell of boiled beef, baking bread and pigeon pies, and the slab of gingerbread that Agnes had just removed from one of the bake ovens. When she left, she carried a basket with a small crock of beef broth, a hot pie, a slice of toasted bread, and a wedge of gingerbread.

It was some comfort to see that Sarah, who'd been sleeping, seemed calmer. Hannah suspected Annie had been napping too. She got Sarah up to sit on the side of the bed, offering her and Annie each half of the pie. Annie welcomed it, but Sarah would have none.

"You must keep up your strength."

Hannah poured the warm broth into a bowl.

"Take this now."

They had to wait until a contraction relinquished its hold but, then, Sarah emptied the bowl of broth and took a small piece of the gingerbread.

"So, it's time, is it?"

Emma Handy greeted Hannah with a perturbed look and strode quickly to the bedside. She patted Sarah's hand.

"Don't you worry. We'll just have a look and see how you're coming along."

Her manner was brisk, but not unkind as she ran her hands knowingly over Sarah's distended belly and took a small brass horn from her pocket to listen.

"Heart's beating strong. That's good. Now, let's see how far along you are. "

Sarah clamped her legs together when the midwife moved to examine her.

"There, there, now," she soothed.

"It's the only way to know how things are going. I've brought my share of youngsters into the world and it's ever the same. Mistress Chinn can tell you that."

"Aye, that you have," said Hannah. "There's none better."

Once Sarah had relaxed, Emma made a quick examination.

"You're doing nicely, but it will be a time yet."

She pulled Sarah's skirts down.

"Good. Good."

She nodded approvingly when a contraction gripped the girl.

"A bit of spirits might help," she said to Hannah.

"Have her walk about. It's her first. You well remember. The babe's likely to take its time coming. I must go, but send someone to me if there's a need."

On her way to the door, she stopped, lowering her voice as she spoke.

"I passed Rebecca just now. Her feelings haven't changed, I see. There'll be hell to pay for this. I wish I hadn't brought this trial on you."

"Don't blame yourself for this."

Hannah took her friend's arm as they walked to the door.

"I told you, I've been glad to have Sarah here. I wish more were like her."

At Emma's raised eyebrow, she added. "Well, in most things. I'll send 'round to you when it's time."

Their longstanding friendship required no more talk before Emma was on her way back to her shop. Hannah and Annie spent the rest of the morning walking Sarah back and forth across the room with time on the bed to doze as long as her contractions would allow.

Hannah chose those times to visit the kitchen where she mistook the atmosphere of grim solemnity for concern over Sarah. On one trip below, she snagged the boy again and had him carry her rocking chair up to the room. Of all else she might claim as hers, that chair was the one she treasured. It had served her well during many such vigils.

As the time between contractions diminished, Sarah grew more agitated. Finally, Hannah poured a swallow or two of red wine into a bowl and put it to Sarah's lips. She drank eagerly, but almost immediately began to retch and, then, to cry out as the labor pains seized her again. Sarah sank back breathing heavily when the pain ceased. Hannah gently wiped the sweat and tears from her face and hummed a soothing lullaby. As the day stretched toward night, Hannah spent more and more time trying to calm Sarah's mounting fears.

"Oh, Ma'am, it hurts so."

Sarah's hands were claws gripping Hannah's arm.

"This pain. I know it's God judging me. I didn't know it would end in this. How could I believe that such a man would want a girl like me for a wife? God forgive me, I don't want this child. And now I must pay ..."

Her words were carried on a scream.

"Oh, oh, oh, it ... is ... more than I can bear."

"I know, I know. Hush child."

Hannah brushed damp tendrils of hair from her forehead.

"It will seem like too much, but this pain is a trial we all must bear."

She tried again and again to reassure

75

Sarah, but nothing she said could stop her cries and pleas for God's forgiveness.

"It would be better if I died and didn't bring this child into the world," she sobbed.

"Don't say such things."

Hannah grasped Sarah by the shoulders as if to shake her.

"We can't any of us say if we will live or die. So, there's no sense dwelling on it."

She released Sarah and turned away. The look of despair in the girl's eyes frightened her. Every woman knew that death hung close upon the birth of a child, but Hannah couldn't shake the feeling that she had seen its shadow in Sarah's eyes.

She and Annie kept watch through the night, dozing by turns in the rocking chair by the fire. Emma Handy stopped by in the morning, but could only say that it was not yet time. When the midwife left, Hannah went down with her to fetch breakfast for herself and Annie. In the kitchen, she came upon Rebecca berating Agnes and the girls for roast mutton that was overdone and a custard just the opposite.

"Good day, Mother."

Rebecca was not happy to see her parent.

"I hope your business with the girl will be concluded soon."

"Come with me."

Hannah's grip on her daughter's arm wasn't gentle.

"Let's talk somewhere else."

She guided Rebecca into the alcove between the kitchen and public room where none were likely to hear them.

"Agnes knows better than you or me how to roast mutton and bake a custard."

Her voice was low but shook with anger.

"I have left them instructions and have every certainty that they will be carried out. They don't need your direction."

"You have been away from the kitchen a day and a night."

Rebecca shook Hannah's hand from her arm and waved toward the public room.

"Who will they blame if the dinner is not fit to eat? Mr. Rawley is a reasonable man, but if anything goes awry, he'll look to me."

"I do not have to justify myself to you or Joseph. My kitchen will take care of itself. And I would not expect that from Joseph."

"And what about the rest of the house? You're needed in the kitchen. Let Annie mind the girl."

"I'm where I am needed the most. It's not going well. Annie doesn't know what to do. You have no need of her and no excuse to go on so about Sarah. It was my decision to hire her and mine to keep her on."

"And now we have you and Annie and the kitchen help catering to her needs. Her family wouldn't do as much. Isn't that why she's here? She's taken advantage of Mistress Handy's good heart and yours. But it's too much to ask. She's repaid your kindness with deceit."

"She didn't intend this. It was a girl's heart and a girl's foolishness led her to it, however it came about. I fear she'll pay dearly."

"Humph! She brought it upon herself. Believe what you will. I'll have none of it."

Rebecca turned to leave.

"It saddens me that you feel so, but you must have it your way."

Sometimes, Hannah didn't know this child of hers with the hard eyes and jutting chin.

"But leave the kitchen to Agnes. You are not needed there."

When Rebecca left her, Hannah stood thinking about what her daughter had said. However Sarah came to be with child, there was nothing to do about it now. She could only pray that she was wrong about the hopelessness she'd seen in Sarah's eyes.

Sarah would take no more food by the second evening and wouldn't, or couldn't, get up to walk. Hannah sent Annie for the midwife. Emma arrived prepared to stay. She carried her bag full of vials and packets of camomile, camphor, feverfew, pennyroyal, hyssop, and mustard seed, a mortar and pestle, and two basins. She had her own supply of cloths, but nodded with approval at the supply Hannah had set out and the two eggs nestled in a bowl ready for the poultice she'd apply after the birth. Hannah followed her to the bed with a lantern that she hung on a nearby peg.

"It won't be long," said Emma after she'd examined Sarah.

"The bearing pains are upon her now."

She drew Hannah aside.

"All's not right," she said softly.

"There's some obstruction. I'll likely have to clear it."

The two women gently forced Sarah to stand. Emma held her as Hannah pulled back the blankets and spread a heavy quilt across the end of the bed. After removing Sarah's bodice and petticoat, leaving her in nothing but her long shift, they lowered her to sit on the end of the bed.

The fire in the hearth did little to chase away the evening's chill and Hannah wrapped a blanket around the girl's shoulders. She then hitched up her skirts and climbed onto the bed behind Sarah, settling the girl's back firmly against her chest. Emma put a blanket over Sarah and another around Hannah's shoulders.

"Soon, my dear, soon," Hannah crooned into her ear.

But it wasn't soon. Annie had to take Hannah's place so that she could relieve the numbness and trembling of her legs and arms. In between times on the bed, Hannah paced the room, humming tunelessly, trying to calm herself and shut out the animal screams and a stream of curses the likes of which she'd never thought to hear from a young girl's mouth.

She tried to smile reassuringly at Annie,

whose young face was pale and drawn, her eyes circled by dark shadows. She was no longer fearful, just exhausted. By the time they heard the clock in the public room below strike twelve, she and Annie had exchanged places twice more. Sarah's cries were little more than a whimper when Emma checked her one more time.

"It's in an unnatural position."

She frowned up at Hannah who was standing by her side.

"I must turn the babe to bring it right."

At Emma's bidding, Hannah fetched a pot of goose grease from the kitchen. As Emma slathered the grease over her hands, Hannah again took her place supporting Sarah who reared back in a spasm of pain and, then, sank against Hannah's chest. Emma quickly slipped her hand into the birth canal. Slowly she began manipulating the tiny legs and body, moving the head and shoulders around into a position that would ease their way. Sarah's cries rose to a high-pitched keening that ended only when Emma sat back and wiped her hands on a nearby piece of sheeting.

"It's done now," she said.

She looked up at Hannah who sat biting her lower lip, her head resting against Sarah's.

"Pray that will be all that's required."

The midwife rose and took Sarah's head in her hands.

"You must push, now, Sarah," she said. "With the next pain, push."

Sarah nodded weakly. When the next pain came, Hannah felt the shudder of Sarah's body thrust against her own. She then relaxed no more than the time it took to draw breath before she reared back again. From where she sat cradling Sarah against her chest, Hannah was soon aware with growing certainty and alarm that, with each contraction, Sarah grew weaker in her arms. Her cries were no more than thin gasps.

"Ah! I see it. The crown. We'll have it soon. Just a bit more. Now push, dearie."

Emma coaxed, but Sarah had little strength left to push.

"There! There. It's free!"

The tiny form slid into Emma's bloody hands and her triumphant cry brought Annie from the fireside where she had gone for hot water. Emma slapped the infant's back bringing forth a healthy squeal.

Annie had several pieces of diaper ready and scissors she'd taken from Emma's bag. The midwife's hands were sure as she worked over the infant, tying off the cord and rubbing the tiny body briskly with a piece of diaper. She looked at Sarah, who had slumped in Hannah's arms, her dark hair a tangled mess nearly covering her face.

"You have a girl," she said, but Sarah showed no sign of hearing.

"Sarah?"

Hannah felt nothing but her limp heaviness against her.

"Do you hear? Sarah?"

Hannah untangled herself and stood. She gently lowered Sarah to the bed and knelt to put her ear close to listen. Sarah's breath, escaping through cracked lips, was no more than a faint sighing.

"Don't leave us now," she whispered.

Hannah wiped Sarah's forehead with the damp cloth but she didn't respond.

"In a faint," said Emma.

She hastily swaddled the infant in a fresh piece of diaper and handed her to Annie, who carried her to the rocking chair. The midwife rummaged in her bag and pulled forth a bottle and uncorked it.

"See if this will rouse her."

She handed it to Hannah who put it close enough for Sarah to breathe in the camphor's biting fumes. A sharp intake of breath and a flutter of the girl's eyelids was her only response.

"It's no good. Let her be," said Emma.

"There's one more thing I must attend to."

She collected the two eggs from the table and broke them into a small iron skillet over the fire. She was back in a minute with the barely cooked eggs, preparing a poultice to slow the bleeding and help heal flesh torn by the birth.

"Let me see the babe."

Hannah beckoned to Annie. Perhaps its lusty yowl would bring Sarah around.

"Sarah, you have a fine daughter."

Hannah laid the infant on her mother's breast.

If only the babe could give some of that life back to her mother.,

Hannah quickly shook herself.

Don't give up on her yet.

She picked up the baby and cradled it in her arms just for a minute, before handing her back to Annie. Her squalls were the only sound in the room.

In the meantime, Emma made a pad of sheeting to keep the poultice in place and wrapped more of it around Sarah's hips and thighs to secure it. That done, she and Hannah removed the blood-soaked quilt beneath Sarah and replaced it with a fresh one. Her shift would have to wait. Once they had her back on the bed under a clean blanket, they went to work cleaning the area around the end of the bed, gathering the dirty linens to be carried below.

Hannah realized Annie wouldn't be doing it. The girl and the baby were both asleep in the rocking chair. She gathered up the noxious bundle for a quick trip to the kitchen. Dawn had yet to make an appearance, but Agnes was already at work, building up the fire and preparing for the day. Agnes relieved her of the bundle.

"The babe does well, but Sarah grows weaker by the minute. I fear for her, Agnes."

"Might I see her, Mistress?"

"Aye, come with me now. Perhaps she's come 'round. She's been in a faint. She hasn't even seen her child."

Agnes dropped the kindling she'd been putting on the glowing coals and followed Hannah. The scene was worse than when she left. Emma was grimly intent on stanching the crimson flow that soaked the quilt and a growing pile of bloody rags on the floor. The poultice had proved useless. The sharp scent of camphor cut through air weighted with the cloying scent of blood as Emma poured the liquid on fresh cloths to pack between Sarah's legs.

As Hannah helped Emma, Agnes knelt beside Sarah and took one limp hand. She gently touched the girl's cheek and bowed her head to say a silent prayer. Agnes rose and went over to look at the baby. She was awake again and crying.

Hannah and Emma didn't notice when Agnes left to return to the kitchen. Only when she became aware of the silence in the room did Hannah realize that Annie and the infant were also gone. By then, she and Emma had ceased their ministrations. There was nothing more they could do.

They sat, exhausted, keeping a silent vigil, Emma on the stool, Hannah in her rocking chair. Hannah knew without having to look back at the bed that Sarah would never see her child. The foolish girl had paid far too dearly for her sin, such as it was. And who was she after all? That mite, that last bit of her life, would be all they could know of Sarah Pratt. She closed her eyes and prayed silently that the child would not soon follow her mother. Their watch ended as dawn's thin light filled the window and, with a last, faint sigh, Sarah stopped breathing.

They didn't have to say anything. Each had attended death as often as birth. They got to work. Daylight did nothing to brighten the room. Untended candles burned low and the fire, which was slowly dying in the hearth, invited shadows to fill the room and mask the drawn faces of the two women. Their work-hardened hands moved with efficient caresses to clean and prepare the girl's body.

At the last, Hannah crossed Sarah's hands on her breast. They swathed the body in sheeting and stitched it closed. Only then did Emma Handy gather up her things and take her leave. Hannah stood shoving defiant wisps of greying brown hair back under her cap as she looked from the shrouded form to the new pile of filthy bed linens and rags.

It was a bad business. The last word from the Pratts was that they wanted nothing more to do with their daughter or her child. Sarah would go to a pauper's grave, her baby, poor thing, to a foundling home.

The thought of the infant brought her back to the immediate problem. She left the room, almost bumping into one of the chambermaids.

"Mistress, I've come to help. Annie said the room would be needing cleaning up ..."

"Ah, good lass. Bless you."

Much relieved, Hannah gave the girl a pat on the shoulder and continued downstairs. The kitchen was bustling with breakfast preparations, but above the din she could hear the high-pitched wail of Sarah's baby, momentarily forgotten where she lay in a basket in a far corner.

"I have sent the boy to the watch station and a wagon will be coming soon to take the body," said Agnes. "Should I send the child, too?"

"No!" Hannah said sharply.

She had not thought until that moment that the decision would fall upon her.

"No," she said, this time more calmly.

"Let's see if there is not something else can be done."

She was certain she saw a look akin to joy cross Agnes's face.

"Take care of breakfast. Then, we'll enquire about a wet nurse."

Just then, the boy returned and Hannah sent him up to the birthing room for her chair. Unable to listen to the wailing any longer, she scooped up the infant and sank with her into the chair when it arrived. The rocking soon brought quiet and both Hannah and the baby fell asleep. Which was how Rebecca found them.

"Ah. There it is," she said and leaned

down to take the baby.

"What are you doing?"

Waking with a start, Hannah clutched the infant to her.

"It must go. The constable is here."

"No, she will not. This child will not go off among strangers."

The infant awakened with a squall and Hannah slipped the tip of her little finger between the tiny lips, and the baby sucked hungrily.

"And what will happen to her, then?"

Her daughter stood, frowning down at her mother.

"Go. Send the constable away. I'll tend to this matter in my own time. If I recall, you wanted nothing to do with it."

"Mother. There's nothing to be gained by waiting. And none here to care for her."

Hannah held the infant, closer to her breast.

"Would that be God's mercy?"

"She'll be nothing but trouble. Just like her mother."

"And what trouble was that poor child but at the end? We could do nothing to save her, but *this* we can do. If it was your daughter lying up there and this your granddaughter, would you not want someone to care about what would become of her? We will wait."

Hannah's gaze didn't waver when Rebecca snorted in disgust. She gave her mother a last exasperated look and marched out of the kitchen.

The infant squirmed in her arms, no longer content with a finger to suckle.

We must find a wet nurse.

Hannah thought. The solution was right there in the house, but she quickly dismissed it.

Rebecca was still nursing six-month-old Charley, but she couldn't imagine this babe at her daughter's breast.

Agnes was of the same mind.

"Mistress Handy has sent word that she hopes to have a wet nurse before day's end. And I've prepared a bit of milk and bread to keep her until then."

She handed Hannah a china sucking pot, stored away since Rebecca's Mary had been weaned off the tit. The baby sputtered and turned her head away at first, but on its third offering tried to suck. She did so with little success, soaking the blanket tucked close to her chin. Hannah gave the pot back to Agnes and pressed the knuckle of her little finger to the infant's lips. This time, she sucked and within minutes was asleep.

Steaming platters and bowls were already on their way to satisfy their customers' morning hunger and Agnes was marshaling the staff for dinner preparations. Shortly, Hannah told herself, she'd get up and help, but for a while more she could linger with the tiny person she'd already named Martha.

VII

Life Lessons

Hannah was saddened but not surprised by Rebecca's reaction when she'd decided to keep Sarah Pratt's child. But she wasn't prepared for her daughter's anger when she learned she'd chosen to call the baby Martha.

"How could you, Mother? If I should have a second daughter, I intend to call her that. It will be Mary and Martha, just like in the Bible."

Hannah had to admit that she'd chosen the name for the same reason but had never imagined her daughter thought along such lines. Of course, Rebecca had been almost as disappointed by the birth of a son as Mary had been. Martha would be a perfect name for a sister. The tears in Rebecca's angry eyes affirmed her sincerity and Hannah was ready to find another name. If Rebecca could have stopped there.

"You can't name that whore's bastard Martha."

Hannah felt as if she'd been struck.

"Don't you ever speak those words in

this house again. Not about Sarah, her child, or anyone else. It does you no good to even think such things or to sit in judgement of another."

"How can you say that, Mother? What will people think? Are we to shelter other women like that? Or become a foundling home."

"People know us better than that. They'll have no cause to think one way or another about this child. Unless you make something of it. I warn you. Don't do that. And don't forget your place here. The Black Horse is still mine. I intend to keep this child and raise her here. And her name *will* be Martha."

Hannah was suddenly overcome by a sense of unreality. The young woman standing before her had become a stranger with a look of hatred in her eyes and a hand raised as if to strike. Then just as suddenly, Rebecca lowered her hand, dropped her eyes, and strode from the room.

As the ensuing days stretched into weeks, months, and, then, years, mother and daughter easily avoided each other. Both were consumed with the rapidly growing children and the business of the inn. Though the changing crew of servant girls noticed nothing in the overly distant relationship between their mistresses, Joseph, Agnes, and Annie were cautious in their dealings with matters that might involve both women.

Only Hannah's and Rebecca's love of Mary and Charley and Hannah's compromise of years before concerning the Black Horse kept the peace. Otherwise, they made a habit of avoiding each other.

But not always.

The older Mary got, the less time she spent with her grandmother. Rebecca paid a seamstress a healthy sum to help her daughter learn embroidery and a tutor to teach her how to write a fine hand. Mary seldom appeared in the kitchen where she might soil an apron not really meant for housework. Hannah couldn't remain silent any longer and early one morning sought Rebecca in her office.

"I hardly ever see Mary anymore. She was doing so well, learning to cook with me in the kitchen. She has a knack and was a great help. For all the time she spends in your rooms, the child seems to do nothing useful. Simple stitchery should serve her well enough. And the same with writing. She'd be better off learning how to manage her own kitchen and keep household accounts.

"There'll be time for that, Mother. Or she'll be able to hire people for such things. I mean to see that Mary has better. She doesn't want to live her life out in a tavern or as a shopkeeper's wife. Look at William and Emily's girls. They'll marry well and won't have to work for someone else. If I have anything to do with it, Mary will do the same."

Hannah struggled to contain her anger.

"You do your father and your husband a disservice. This inn and the shipping business are your father's doing. You can't say that you don't take pride in what the Black Horse is today. You and Joseph have done that. I'd wager you'll be able to provide Mary with a dowry that will bring her as fine a husband as William's girls can expect. And I'm certain she'll be a better wife if she follows your lead not Emily's."

Rebecca's look told her nothing would change her daughter's mind.

"But do as you must."

"I *will* Mother."

Hannah shrugged. She had the day's meals to prepare and wasn't about to let Rebecca ruin a perfectly good morning any more than she already had.

****

By the time Martha was seven, Hannah began teaching her to mend simple tears in her clothes. In the process, Martha was easily frustrated as she struggled to control needle, thread, and cloth. To keep her working at her side, Hannah read aloud from her aged leather-bound Bible, turning its well-worn pages with loving care. She realized, however, that the sewing now lay forgotten in Martha's lap.

The child could learn to sew later. Encouraging Martha to stand beside her, Hannah resumed her reading sliding her finger from word to word across the page. Less than a month later, Martha stopped her.

"Let me try it."

She reached for the book.

"You think so? Very well, but this Bible is old and very worn. Be careful with it."

Martha nodded solemnly and pulled up her stool. Once she'd settled, Hannah held out the book open to the page she'd just read.

The words didn't come easily or smoothly but Martha managed to sound out several words, stringing more together as she went.

"You've just held them in your mind. That trick won't benefit you."

"Yes 'um, I did. But I know some of the words. Let me try again."

Martha ran her finger down the page pointing out words she recognized, then proceeded to stumble through a second line that Hannah hadn't read. They finished the page together.

"Well, I'll be..." Hannah sat back slapping her hands on her knees, then laid the book aside.

"If I hadn't seen it with my own eyes, I wouldn't have believed it. But we must put this away for now. There's work to be done below."

"But I'll find you something better to learn from and we'll do some more reading ."

On her regular morning trip to market the next day, Hannah made an additional stop. Martha was with her, as usual, carrying a shopping basket filled with fresh bread, and was surprised when Hannah stopped at an unfamiliar shop. She left Martha at the entrance where she stood staring in wonder at the multitude of books that filled every table top and shelf. Hannah returned quickly and handed Martha a worn, leather-bound book.

"I think you're ready for this. It's a primer and will help you to read. But you must apply yourself. Put that in your basket now. You may look at it later."

"Pens, pens! Ink as black as jet!"

The vendor's song echoed down a nearby street.

"Come, there's something else we must have."

She hurried Martha after the man who strode down the street, his pack on his back and a bunch of goose feathers in one hand. When they caught up with him, Hannah chose a quill pen and two sticks of lampblack ink.

"You don't want that, Madam."

The vendor shook his head vigorously.

"Chinese ink. That's what everyone requires. I've a supply just in on an East Indiaman from the Orient."

"That's not what I require."

Hannah waved away the proffered ink.

"The lampblack will do. Have you pencils?"

She nodded toward the box hanging at his side.

"The finest. Two for a ha' penny." He drew several out.

"Two, then."

After counting the coins into his outstretched palm, Hannah took the items he'd wrapped in a dirty square of paper and put the package with the book in Martha's basket.

"Now," she said with a satisfied air, "we must get on with the marketing."

As they went along, Martha could think of nothing but the things lying at the bottom of her basket. When she was sure Mistress Chinn wasn't looking, she slipped her hand into the basket to reassure herself that the book and writing tools were real and secure beneath the crusty loaves of white bread. She'd never before had anything to call her own other than the clothes she wore, and few enough of those.

She never imagined owning a book. A pen, ink, and pencils? They were a wondrous surprise. She knew their use. She often watched Hannah writing in the evening quiet of her room, pen scratching across the pages of her ledger. As she watched, Martha was beginning to understand what the rows of numbers were, the value of the money they represented, and how they related to the things Hannah bought on market day. But Hannah had never spoken of teaching Martha to write.

Later that day, Martha slipped away to Mistress Chinn's room for a quick peek at the primer and the contents of the little package she'd hidden beneath her pillow.

"What is that you have?"

Martha spun around, startled. The two pencils she was holding fell to the rag rug at her feet.

Mary Rawley was forever coming upon her without warning with a "Stop that!" or a "Don't touch!"

"Look what you've made me do! They're mine."

Martha scrambled to retrieve the pencils and stepped in front of the items still on her cot.

"Mistress Chinn gave them to me."

"Then why are you hiding them? They couldn't be for you. Nana must have meant them for me. I'm in need of fresh pencils. Is that a pen? Let me see it."

"They're not for you."

Martha tried to shove the things back under her pillow, but Mary caught her arm.

"Let me see."

Mary dug her fingers into Martha's arm and pushed her out of the way to inspect the book and pencils that Martha had dropped on the bed.

"Humph. I suppose Nana did mean you to have these. What use would I have for this?"

She held up the primer, then tossed it back.

"And I don't use lampblack or goose quills. Nana knows I prefer a raven's feather. But why do you need to read or write?"

"I have as much need as anybody."

Martha carefully gathered up the pen, pencils, and ink sticks and wrapped them in the paper.

"We'll see about that. But never mind. You'll learn soon enough. Don't you have chores below?"

With a toss of her head that set her honey-colored curls to bouncing, Mary swept out of the room.

When she heard the Rawley's door at the end of the hall slam, Martha shoved the parcel under her pillow and ran to the kitchen. Hannah was waiting.

"Ah, there you are. Fetch that boy for me. Then, I've something for you to do, so don't dawdle."

Off at a run, Martha nearly bumped into Rebecca coming through the kitchen door.

"Watch where you're going!"

"Beg pardon, Ma'am."

With head down, she stepped aside, expecting more, but Rebecca sailed on into the kitchen.

"You must curb that wretched child, Mother. She gets my bile up every time I see her running through the public rooms. She's always running."

Hannah rolled her eyes toward the ceiling in exasperation.

"Aye. I told her to hurry."

"That's no reason. And if she must go about among the customers, can you not see that she knows how to behave? She could be more presentable, too. The state of her clothes is a disgrace. Every apron, skirt, and bodice was Mary's once. I took great care with them.

So did Mary. You could at the very least teach that child to care for the nice things she's given. But you'll do nothing, will you, Mother?"

"She knows full well how she's come by the clothes she wears and she's not ungrateful. Her clothes don't show carelessness. They show hard work. She doesn't shun the meanest chores. You might do something with your daughter on that score. There are things Mary could do to help you in the public rooms ... But that's not what's brought you. I'll talk to Martha."

Mother and daughter were soon sitting head to head, engaged in making a list for the next day's trip to market. Martha heard nothing from Hannah about her clothes.

VIII

Harsh Realities

"Well, what have we here?"

Jamie Chinn sat back in his chair looking in mock surprise at the two children standing by his table in the taproom. Charley spoke up.

"Did they truly hang three pirates at Old Stairs?"

"Why do you want to know that?"

"I...we want to see them. We heard talk. And you told us about looking out for pirates and raising a glass every time you hear one's been caught."

Jamie shook his head. There was truth enough in what he'd told them but it was a worry more than high adventure for him. There were never arms or men enough on the craft he sailed to survive a pirate attack.

Once he'd taken the children to the execution dock, pointing to the gallows and three tall tree-like posts that stood out on the foul mud flats beyond the stone stairway.

"Long before you were born, they hanged Captain William Kidd on this dock.

Time was, they'd have a hanging every week, three, maybe four pirates at a time."

Enjoying the children's rapt attention, Jamie warmed to his story.

"They took them to the dock in a cart. The punishment must have been doubly hard for the last one. He had to wait and watch the others marched out to the gallows. When they stopped twitching and jerking, the hangmen carried their bodies out on the mud flats and hung them on those posts. They stayed there through three tides. Sometimes, when they took them down, they lopped off their heads to put on pikes along the river as a lesson to other's who might be inclined to go pirating."

He'd almost forgotten the incident until Charley reminded him.

"You said they'll stop hanging pirates there soon and be taking them to Tyburn Hill. This might be the last time, Uncle Jamie. I want to see them."

At ten, Charley was impatient to experience everything that he could. And always willing to follow his lead, Martha nodded vigorously.

"That's not a sight you want to see and I'm certain your mother won't like it."

"She won't like it one bit."

Charley paused, looking pensive.

"I suppose it's best we don't go. Probably won't be anything to see now anyway."

He shrugged and pulled Martha after

him toward the kitchen.

Jamie watched them go with a growing suspicion. Charley was a mite too quick to change his mind. Instead of following them to the kitchen, he headed for the street door, arriving just in time to see two small figures running toward the Thames. As he suspected, they'd gone out the kitchen door and around the building to the street.

Following close behind, Jamie had to admire how street wise they'd were, dodging easily in and out among rushing men and women. They were unfazed by people's curses when they tripped someone up. He wasn't concerned by that, but decided, when he caught up with them, he'd have to take a sterner tack on the matter of the vehicles barreling along the streets. Drivers of carts and wagons didn't bother to look out for children who failed to heed the danger. But then, he'd survived on those streets doing just what they were.

As then, Jamie's heart quickened at glimpses of the Thames between buildings. A few steps more and he could see down river to where the shore bristled with the masts of giant ships. Ahead, however, was a modest shipyard with its familiar smell of tar and fresh-sawn lumber. A small boat rested on the stocks, slowly evolving from a bare-ribbed carcass to a fully-planked hull ready for the mast to be set.

The atmosphere changed radically as he neared the execution dock and Wapping Old

Stairs. The horrific smell nearly sickened him. Jamie pulled his kerchief over his nose and chuckled at the sight of the children trying to shield their noses with their hands. By then he'd caught up with them, but they didn't notice. A sight like no other Jamie had ever seen shut out everything else.

On their posts, the three bloated and rotting bodies had already been through two tides. He and the children stared in horrified fascination trying to see men in the barely recognizable forms. Their skin hanging from their bodies was indistinguishable from the remains of their tattered clothing.

"Now you've seen it, let's get away from here."

Jamie startled the children but they didn't object when he hurried them away from the dock. They'd turned pale and looked as if they were about to be sick. Trotting at Jamie's side, they gulped in fresher air.

When they reached Nightingale Lane and the Black Horse, they were breathing normally but still hadn't said a word to each other or the tall man who strode ahead of them. He knew he'd never shake the images he carried with him and was sure the children wouldn't either. They were the stuff of nightmares and he suspected they'd have terrible dreams for many nights to come.

****

Charley usually spent his mornings at school and afternoons running errands for his father. Martha had chores in the kitchen and Mistress Chinn was teaching her to make meat pies. Both children were enlisted to fetch and carry at dinnertime. They grew skilled at moving through the crowded room, dawdling where the talk promised a good tale. Few of the men noticed or gave a thought to the children, except when they bragged of conquests with some wench. Then, they waved Martha away.

"Off with you, girl. This is not for your pretty ears."

It was different for Charley.

"Ah, leave him be," said one with a wink at the boy. "Won't be long before he'll be needing to know."

Later, the children managed to meet to compare notes on what they'd overheard, secreting themselves away behind the old bar in the back corner of the taproom. Most were small events, a cart losing a wheel, the baker's sign coming down nearly killing Mistress Jones. Occasionally an event had everyone talking.

That afternoon, Hannah was sorting through worn napkins at a table in the rear of the taproom when she heard a commotion in the upper public room. It seemed to have proceeded into the street and she was about to follow when Charley raced by with Martha in tow. They didn't see her as they ducked behind the old bar. She quickly rose and moved closer.

"Who was it?" Hannah recognized Martha's voice.

"Mr. Potter, the one who's always coming in for his pie and a pint. The men said he was repairing the bottom of that fishing smack they hauled out in Mr. Hawes' slip a day or two ago. One of the timbers holding her up snapped. Rotten, they're saying. Someone took it from the bottom of a pile. The smack, she tipped over on him. Crushed his chest. By the time they pried him out, he was dead."

Will Potter was a kind man, always came in with a smile. He had several children. One day he'd brought Martha a poppet, like one he'd carved for his daughter who was Martha's age. The little figure was defined by a simple long skirt, a suggestion of arms, and a round-eyed face with a big smile and a mob cap atop. Martha had carried it in her pocket for several days until Hannah suggested she leave it somewhere safe so she wouldn't lose it. Martha had put it under her pillow.

"Truly dead?"

Hannah could hear the tears in Martha's voice and felt a lump rising in her own throat.

"Aye. And that wasn't the end of it." Charley was caught up in telling the tale and didn't notice.

"It started a ruckus. Mr. Potter's brother's claimin' the man who runs the yard knew that wood was rotten. Started a fight he did and pretty soon they'd carried it into the street. I heard some say they was comin' here and I came to tell Pa. Some of the men were already here. They went with Pa down to the end of the street and turned the rest around. I was goin' to see where they were goin' but Pa wouldn't let me."

Good man! thought Hannah, dabbing at her brimming eyes with a corner of her apron. The last thing they needed was a brawl at the Black Horse. But she was glad to know what happened.

Charley paused for breath, which gave him cause to look closely at Martha.

"Are you crying?"

"Aye, his daughter's the same age as me. Others, too. Who'll see after them now?"

"Nobody said anything about that. Let's go see what we can find out."

As the children appeared from behind the bar, Hannah decided it was time to step in.

"Come children!"

Under other circumstances, she would have laughed at the guilty looks on the children's faces. Too bad they knew now that she'd found their hiding place.

"We'll send a basket of food around for his family. I'm sure Mistress Potter will have no time to think of that. You can help me."

In the kitchen, she quickly filled a crock pot with fresh beef and barley soup and wrapped two large, still-warm loaves of rye bread in napkins to tuck into one of her large grocery baskets.

As she was about to cover the lot,

Martha appeared with a half-dozen iced tea cakes.

"Might we send these, too. Mistress Rawley won't mind, will she? For the children?"

Though she knew her daughter most certainly would mind, Hannah nodded.

"That's a good idea. And I'll put in a bit of sugar for them to add to their morning porridge."

She lost no time in sending an errand boy off with the basket and was relieved that supper preparations left her no time to think about Will Potter's family. If his wife had no employment or family to take them in, they'd soon be on the dole or begging on the streets. Not for the first time Hannah would have to harden her heart.

The Potters were just one family among many. She could help with food and maybe a bit of money, but that could only last a little while. It would do them no good to count on that for long. Mrs. Potter would soon have to find the means to survive, and much as it pained her, Hannah knew, she couldn't let herself think about what might happen to the family if she didn't.

The following day, Hannah learned that Will Potter's brother did more than start fights. He took over the care of the family. With the help of a small fund provided by the yard and what little money Mistress Potter made as a seamstress, they found rooms in a smaller, less costly house.

The night after they heard of the accident, Hannah knelt with Martha by her cot to say a prayer for the Potters. She was glad the flickering candlelight wasn't likely to reveal the tears on her cheeks when she saw the child slip a hand under her pillow, as she often did, for the comfort of the poppet Mr. Potter had made for her.

Martha never spoke of it to Mistress Chinn, but the little doll often caused her to wonder about her own father. She chose to imagine him like Mr. Potter. She had nothing else to go on, not even his name or what became of him. His name wasn't Pratt was all Mistress Chinn would say. Or very little more about her mother. Sarah Pratt's story came in bits and pieces.

IX

Mothers & Daughters

"Your mother was a fine, hard-working girl when she came here to help our old cook," Hannah told her. "Sarah was her name, Sarah Pratt. She had a knack for cooking and was as good at it as I've ever seen in one so young. I expected her to be our cook one day."

In time, Martha learned that she was born in the little corner room above stairs at the front of the house. That was where Hannah bore Rebecca, William, and Jamie Chinn. Mary and Charley Rawley, were born there too.

"That was where you took your first breath," Hannah told her. "Your mother wasn't strong though and the Lord took her soon after you were born. She had no family to step forward to take you in, so here you stayed."

Martha tried to imagine what it would have been like, growing up with a mother. From what she'd seen of Mistress Rawley as a mother, the happier she was that it was

Mistress Chinn who was raising her. Unlike Mistress Rawley, she'd never been anything but kind and it puzzled Martha how Rebecca could be so different from her mother. And why they seemed always to be at cross purposes. She learned early to give Rebecca a wide berth. Mary Rawley, too. They were two of a kind and there was no escaping them.

Martha was forever meeting mother or daughter going to or from their rooms above stairs as she pressed herself tight against a wall to let them pass. Rebecca never smiled, often didn't even acknowledge her presence, unless she could find some fault with her. But Mary always managed to have something to say, chiding her on a chore undone, plucking at her clothes to remark on a stain, or pointing to a smudge on her cheek.

"Must you always go about looking like a scullery maid or a char woman's waif," Mary'd say. Or "a gutter snipe" if she was really feeling peevish.

"The wenches take greater care of themselves than you do."

Martha drew some small comfort from knowing that Mary had an equal disregard for her brother Charley who regularly annoyed her and took pleasure in doing so. When he was small, Mary boxed his ears and, as he grew, she found ways to get him in trouble with their mother. She did the same with Martha or found mean things to say that festered long after.

Most of the time, Martha could avoid

Mary and her mother. Rebecca's time was occupied with the Black Horse. Mary had nothing to do with the business of the inn but kept busy in the Rawley's rooms, practicing her stitchery and handwriting or polishing her mother's silver spoons, brass candlesticks, and mahogany tea and breakfast tables.

Such activity took on a feverish urgency when Mary's aunt Emily Chinn and her daughters Alice and Peggy were expected for one of their rare visits. Her uncle, William Chinn, had continued the success of his father's shipping business and provided Emily and his daughters with a comfortable life in a large townhouse east of Wapping. As she approached her teens, Mary spent more time with her cousins than at home. For the first of Alice's and Peggy's rare visits Mary appeared in the inn's kitchen.

"Grandmother, I must learn to make fancy cakes." She waved a sheet of paper at Hannah. "We had such fine ones at Aunt Emily's. I have written out the recipe and I'll have them when Alice and Peggy come for tea day after tomorrow."

Martha looked up from where she was scrubbing a copper kettle at the far end of the kitchen. She held her breath. Such an imperious tone wouldn't sit well with Mistress Chinn.

"Perhaps your cousins would like to learn, too?" Hannah asked.

"They have a cook to do that, Grandmother."

"So, it's *grandmother*, now, is it? You used to call me Nana."

"But I was a child then. I've not heard Alice and Peggy call you that."

Hannah straightened, then leaned with both hands, flat upon the table on either side of her cutting board. The slab of meat she was preparing for the pot at her side lay between them.

"I would have liked it." she said. "Your Aunt Emily does not. How do you know they wouldn't like to learn to make cakes. I have a fine recipe."

Mary looked around the kitchen.

"I think they wouldn't like being here."

With a sweep of her hand, Mary took in Martha on her stool, the kettle in her lap, another yet to be scrubbed on the table, and a red-faced maid at one end of the hearth stirring a pot bubbling on its trivet over the coals. Near her, Grace and a second wench wrestled a pork roast onto the spit. She let her hand drop just short of where her grandmother stood, bare-armed, blood on her hands and the board. All activity around the room ceased.

"It would be good for them to learn. They might not always have a cook. Or a grandmother."

She sighed.

It's not the child's fault she thinks as she does.

"I'm glad you, at least, want to learn. Come back tomorrow when dinner is behind us and we'll make cakes."

"With sugar icing?"

Hannah's nod was greeted with a smile as Mary turned to leave.

"Thank you...Nana." With a quick curtsy and bob of her blond head, Mary was gone.

Nana. At least this granddaughter hadn't forgotten where she came from. But then, William's girls had never been given a chance to find out. Hannah shook her head. Nothing to be gained by dwelling on such thoughts. Suddenly aware of the silence around her, Hannah returned to the present.

"Get back to work," she snapped, attacking the meat with such vengeance that the wenches nearly fell over each other in their haste to get back to what they were doing. By the time the beef was ready for the pot, Hannah felt better.

As had the wenches, Martha hastily returned to her scrubbing before the mistress caught her watching. She decided to find chores far from the kitchen after dinner the next day.

****

In the kitchen, Annie had replaced Sarah Pratt to help Agnes. A quick learner, she worked hard and showed a knack for cookery that earned Hannah Chinn's regard. When Agnes died, Annie took over the kitchen and the old cook's room off the kitchen. She wasn't about to move in until she'd emptied and cleaned it.

"Come with me." Annie grabbed Biddy, who had the misfortune to be the nearest kitchen wench, and prodded her toward Agnes's room.

"Before I can move in there, I'll need your help clearin' out the poor old woman's leavings."

"Poor old woman?" Biddy shook her head. "She were meaner than sin. Creepin' around, watching everthin' I did. Then gettin' after me for this and that and nothin' at all."

"That's got nothing to do with helpin' me." *And don't be thinkin' I'll not be watchin' you.*

Annie shoved a wisk broom and a bunch of dust rags into the girl's arms and pushed her through the door. As Biddy got to work stripping the bed and pulling down the dust-laden curtains, Annie paused at the small table by the bed to pick up Agnes's well-worn Bible. The Mistress might like to have it, she thought as she scanned the small room.

Aside from its single chair, the room's only other furniture was a small trunk of Agnes's clothes. And few enough of those, Annie thought, as she lifted out three much-laundered shifts, two skirts, three mob caps, and a coat. From the looks of the clothes, Annie guessed they once belonged to the Mistress. She was certain that Agnes wouldn't have had a coat if Mistress Chinn hadn't passed on one of hers. Aside from the Bible, all the old woman owned was in that one trunk. Annie shook her head sadly as she lifted out four freshly laundered aprons. There was little else to remember her by. All else was of little matter to her. That kitchen out there. That was her life.

In Agnes's room, Biddy did as little scrubbing and dusting as she could get away with, then returned with similar attention to her kitchen chores. She made sure she was nowhere around when the time came to help Annie move into the room. She let several days pass before asking a question that had been plaguing her.

"If I was you, I'd be afeard o' sleeping in that room. An old woman like that? She lived there a mighty long time. Like as not, her spirit's lingering somewhere's in there."

Annie turned on her with a disgusted shake of her head.

"There's no such thing as spirits. I slept in my Mam's bed after the fever carried her off. It were the very same bed my Pa died in afore her. It was a comfort. And there weren't anything mean about Agnes that would call her spirit back. I've had three good nights' sleep and not a whisper of ghosts. Truth be told, I'm right relieved not to be climbing all those stairs to the garret. That up and down every day was about to wear me down."

Skinny and smart-mouthed, Biddy looked Annie up and down.

"Wouldn't hurt you."

She swaggered off enjoying the other

girls' giggles and their careful looks of sympathy when Annie slapped her. She received her comeuppance the next day when Hannah handed her the pay she was owed and sent her looking for another place of work.

****

Once Martha was able to dress herself, she left Mistress Chinn's room at dawn. Struggling with the last of her skirt buttons, she ran down to the kitchen where Annie was stirring the fires beneath the water kettle that had been warming overnight. That was the only time she missed Biddy who'd always found time to play little games with the child or teach her songs and rhymes.

Though Martha tried not to get in the way, she was forever poking into things or asking questions for which Annie had no answer. Not of a playful mind, Annie found her small chores. The child eagerly did as she was told and Annie was surprised to discover that she could be more help than hindrance.

Martha rose at first light to flee the upper floors so as not to run into Rebecca or Mary Rawley. They seldom appeared until the day was well underway. Hannah knew how her daughter and granddaughter felt about Martha and why the child rushed to the kitchen. So did Annie and she readily agreed to let Martha share her room.

The first few nights, Martha missed the comfort of Mistress Chinn sleeping nearby, but the distance between her and the Rawleys made up for it. And she spent as much time with Mistress Chinn as she ever had. It helped also that her bed fit nicely into the chimney corner, just as it had in Mistress Chinn's room, and that the corner was warmed by the bake ovens on the other side. In the evenings, when they were getting ready for bed, Annie particularly liked to talk, sometimes about events of the day, but sometimes about things that happened before Martha was born.

"You look like your mama," said Annie one night as she braided Martha's hair before bed. Martha's look of surprise made her stop.

"You do! We was friends, Sarah and me. And we shared that little room at the top of the house. I was with her when you were born in that little corner room above stairs. And Mistress Chinn was there helping the midwife the whole time. I was too. Mistress Chinn was right fond of Sarah. That's why she didn't send her off.

But you took a mighty long time coming into this world ... hours and hours. We were right worried about your mama. I don't like remembering that. Or talking about it. I guess Mistress Chinn's the same way. Mistress Handy did everything she could. But your mama wasn't strong. I think she just gave up.

Maybe she wouldn't have, if she'd seen you. You were a beautiful, strong little thing.

They bundled you up and gave you to me, so they could take care of your Mama. When it was all over, Mistress Chinn made sure your Mama was buried proper. And from the start, she took care of you like you were one of her own."

And didn't that send Mistress Rawley into a towering rage.

Annie refrained from sharing that thought. She shook her head, then remembered the child waiting anxiously for her to continue.

"Mistress Chinn named you Martha, Martha Pratt. She took you to sleep in her rooms above stairs. I'd have taken you, but I was sleeping up in the garret then. The rest of the time, she kept you by her in the kitchen. Of course, once you could get around, we were all chasing after you."

"Mistress Rawley didn't like that, did she?"

"She didn't have any say in it... but now, all that's best forgotten."

Her look told Martha there'd be no more talk. With a pat, she gently shoved Martha toward her cot and went quickly to her own bed. That night and many nights after, Martha lay awake a long time imagining what Sarah Pratt might have been like and what it might have been like to have a mother.

X

Possessions

Martha tried to avoid Mary Rawley. Though she was less fearsome than her mother, she was equally unpleasant. Mary made certain Martha knew how miserably she's failed in her manners and comportment. Try as she might, Martha couldn't remember to walk instead of run when she had the chance. She did remember that almost all her clothes came from Mary, but still never knew when or how she tore a skirt or stained a bodice.

Mary was quick to remark that Martha's apron wasn't fresh or her petticoat's hem was tattered. Martha usually ignored such jabs and laughed when Mary doled out unsolicited advice about sweet-smelling soaps and creams for her face and hands. She didn't need more than simple lye soap to get clean. Clean was a smell good enough for her.

Most times, their encounters were by chance. One afternoon, though, Mary appeared in the kitchen, sewing basket over her arm. She lost no time in remarking on a large soot stain on Martha's sleeve.

"You come too easy by nice things."

Mary sounded very like her mother, Martha thought as she prepared for another lecture.

"When you start making your own clothes, you'll take better care of them. But come, I have something for you."

Without looking back or asking permission, Mary headed into the back room. She settled into the rocking chair that once belonged to the old cook and was Annie's favorite place to nap. Nestling the sewing basket in her lap, she drew out Martha's best linen cap and several pieces of bright red ribbon.

"I'm going to show you how to trim your cap."

"I don't need trim on my cap."

Martha was already angry at Mary's invasion of their room.

"You took my cap without asking. What have you done?"

As she looked more closely, she realized that Mary had already sewn red ribbon halfway around the cap.

"You had no leave to do that!"

Martha stood, hands knotted in fists on her hips.

"What else have you taken?"

"Nothing. Sit down. I'll show you what to do."

119

Martha didn't move.

"You're ten years old now. It's time you learned these things. I'm going to help you make a new petticoat for yourself, too. You won't be getting mine much longer."

"I have two petticoats that serve me well enough. Annie will help me if I need another. I won't need yours."

Martha struggled to check her anger. Mary had seen her other petticoat and had to have come into her room and gone into her chest for that cap.

"It's not right, going into my things."

"I mean no harm. Besides, most of those were mine. And grandmother hasn't time to look after a servant. You'll be going into service before long. The sooner you learn to take care of yourself, the better."

"I'll not go into service. Mistress Chinn would tell me."

"Don't worry. Mother will find you a place when the time comes."

"No she won't. Mistress Chinn won't send me away."

Martha snatched her cap out of Mary's hand.

"We can't keep you forever, you know. You're an orphan."

Martha glared at the other girl. She had nothing to say. She knew she was an orphan and had never thought it a bad thing. But could it be reason enough to send her away and Mistress Chinn didn't want to tell her? Mary must have been passing on her mother's words and, if Rebecca Rawley had her way, she'd be gone.

"And you might thank me for the ribbons."

Mary sat straight and prim in the chair and Martha had to fight the urge to tip her out of it.

"I don't want ribbons on my cap. If I do, Annie will help me."

Martha pulled at the ribbons, but Mary's stitches were tight. The cloth began to tear and Martha threw it down.

"Get out! This is Annie's room. And mine. You have no right to come in here."

"I have every right, you ungrateful wretch! You and Annie are nothing but servants. It's you who have no right to be here."

Mary jumped to her feet.

"We have no place here for some trollop's bastard."

Her words trailed after her as as she stormed out.

Stunned, Martha stood looking through a blur of tears at the cap at her feet.

Trollop? Bastard?

She couldn't imagine what the words meant but was certain they were the worst thing that Mary could think to say … something she'd heard her mother say. Whatever their meaning, Martha knew they had to do with her mother. And it was shameful. What could her mother have done to make Rebecca hate her so? Was it the same reason that Mistress Chinn told her so little about her mother?

Martha picked up the cap. Clutching it to her, she fell onto her cot, burying her head in her bolster to muffle her angry sobs. But then, a sudden thought stopped them in her throat.

What if Mistress Rawley has her way? I'll be gone in a trice.

There'd be nothing she could do to stop Rebecca. But Mistress Chinn wouldn't let that happen. Of that she was certain. For the time being, at least. And it did no good to worry about such things.

She'd grown to understand how lucky she was to have been born into Mistress Chinn's house. And fate or good fortune had given her a chance to make something of herself. She certainly wasn't going to laze about like Mary and her cousins. Martha took a wicked pleasure in imagining how they'd fare if they were forced to earn their keep.

She sat up quickly. She had things to do. Shaking out her cap, she went to a chair beneath the room's high, small window and pulled her sewing basket from beneath it. Slowly, carefully, she began to remove Mary's stitches. She was so intent upon her work that Hannah was well into the room before Martha looked up. Hastily, she shoved the cap into her basket and jumped up.

"Sit, child." the mistress said and sank into the rocking chair. Pushing it slowly with one foot, she began to rock, filling the room with a rhythmic creaking. Martha sat, her back straight, hands clasped in her lap.

"I heard some of what Mary said to you. She shouldn't say such things."

Hannah stopped rocking and leaned forward.

"She had no cause to call your mother a trollop. That's just a word she's heard. Your mother was nothing of the kind! Far from it. Your mother's only fault was that she was young. She followed her heart, not her head and had every reason to think she and your father would marry. He didn't do right by her. One day you'll understand, but you mustn't think ill of your mother. Or yourself, whatever people might say."

She ended with finality, clamping her mouth on the last words and sat back. But just for a second. Suddenly she sat forward again.

"And one more thing. This is your home. No one will send you away. Mary knows that now. I've just spoken to her. And to Mistress Rawley."

She frowned and put her head on one side with a questioning look, then rose and beckoned to Martha.

"As for you, what the future might hold and what you choose to do, I can't say. But for now, come, bring your cap."

Martha followed her through the public room and upstairs to her apartment. She stood by as Hannah pulled a basket of rags from the corner where Martha's cot had once been.

"Look at these." She reached in and pulled out a handful of rags.

"You can't always choose your lot in life or even what will happen tomorrow. That's in God's hands. You must make do with what God grants you. Who can say what rags will be in my hand when I draw it from the basket? I certainly didn't choose them."

She tossed back several stained and ragged scraps destined to become tinder or cleaning rags.

"But now that I have them, I can choose the pieces that will go to making something else. A quilt, maybe. What shall I choose?" She dropped one piece, then, another back into the basket.

"A striped piece? Flowered calico? Or, here, this yellow silk. Or maybe linen would wear better. I must choose the ones I want and how I'll stitch them together. Life is no different. You can't always choose what happens but you can choose what you'll do with the lot you're given. Do you see what I'm saying?"

Martha nodded.

"It's of far greater importance than how you choose to make a quilt but the deciding is much the same. You must look at many scraps of cloth, then, choose those that will go together to make a pleasing quilt that will serve you well. In the same way, you must look at how you live your life, what choices you have. If you choose wisely, you'll make your way."

Mistress Chinn pointed to the cap. "I think you might start with that."

"Must I keep the ribbons?"

"No, that's your choice. It wasn't right for Mary to take it without asking. But you must mend it."

"Blue ribbons would be nice."

"Yes." Hannah looked pleased.

Martha put her cap on a nearby table and stepped up to the basket of rags.

"Might I make a quilt, too?"

The mistress nodded, and Martha lifted out several scraps of brightly colored and patterned cloth.

"With these. Will you help?"

"Yes," said Hannah with a catch in her voice and swept the child into her arms. She held her tight for just a moment, then, just as quickly let her go, turning her toward the door as she did.

"It's growing late. We'll do that another day. I have pies to make. Come, child. Let's go below."

Dazed, Martha kept the pieces of cloth she'd chosen and followed Hannah to the kitchen. She liked the idea of piecing her life together like a quilt.

That night, in bed Martha thought over the day's happenings. There was some comfort in knowing that Mistress Chinn wouldn't send her away. But, what if something happened to her? She'd have no place at the Black Horse then. Rebecca would see to that. In the meantime, she vowed, she'd learn to make her way in the world, a world that Rebecca Rawley would have no say in. Her life *would be* the finest quilt she could make of it.

XI

Life Lessons

Hannah and Annie might have noted the passing of Martha's twelfth birthday but there was nothing about that March day for Martha to give it a thought. She knew only by the month that she'd gained another year and two inches. Charley's six month-advantage did him no good on that score. She was as tall as he. And as strong. In a tussle over an apple, she got the better of him. Threw him down. That surprised them both. Long after she'd forgotten, he was still angry.

As he got older, Charley spent more time helping his father.

"Learning the innkeeper's trade," Joseph Rawley said proudly. But he wasn't over vigilant in seeing what his son was learning unless he was within sight. He didn't notice how eagerly Charley jumped at the chance to run errands that took him into the streets to share in the mischief of other boys. Martha sometimes chanced to meet him when she was on an errand for Mistress Chinn.

"Wait, Charley!" Martha waved and hurried to catch up.

"Go on with you, Martha," he said, but didn't bother to look back. "I have things to do."

"I do, too. Where are you off to? We can go together."

She fell into step beside him.

"No. It's no business of yours. I have to go alone."

"Where do you have to go that you have to be alone? And when do you ever have business you can't tell me?"

"There are things you don't need to know. Maybe I just like to go my own way."

Up ahead, they could hear boys shouting, laughing. Charley stopped, held up his hand.

"Go! Now!"

"Why?"

"I don't need you tagging after me."

"You're going off with those ... those wastrels? They're nothing but trouble-makers."

"What do you know about them? You're nothing but a girl."

"If that's what you really think, then you're no better than they are. Go, then. I don't want anything to do with them. Or you."

The instant the words were out of her mouth, she wanted to take them back. But he was already off at a run. She stood, watching him, hoping he'd at least look back. He didn't and soon had joined the boys and disappeared down a winding street.

Martha knew one or two of the boys. Rough. Odd jobbers and errand boys when they weren't up to no good. Most of them were older than Charley and sooner or later they'd lead him into trouble. He'd pay for it when he got home, but that wouldn't be the first time. Without even trying, he could find ways to bedevil his sister or his mother. Martha'd shared in enough of those and they usually went to bed without supper.

Joseph Rawley kept a leather strap by the kitchen door for Charley's more serious offenses. Rebecca saw that he used it. Charley got his first whipping when he was seven. When father and son marched through the kitchen to the courtyard shed, it was hard to tell who was being punished.

Afterwards, Joseph's look was pained as he hung up the strap and stalked back to the public rooms. Martha who was waiting near the door had to jump out of his way. Charley took a while to follow his father.

"He didn't really whip me very hard," he whispered, but his red eyes and flushed cheeks said otherwise.

Whippings didn't stop Charley's adventures in the streets. He accomplished his errands, but often returned with a bloody nose, torn sleeves, or muddied breeches. Joseph Rawley tended to overlook such things with a certain pride.

Rebecca lost all patience with him. Blood on his shirt was of greater concern to her than the wound that put it there. Ruined clothes earned him extra chores — scrubbing floors, cleaning out the hearths, fetching water — the sort of women's and children's work that particularly galled him. Eventually, Joseph called him back to more manly employment, making trips to the storeroom for kegs of rum, pipes of Madeira, or errands outside the house.

One rare sunny spring day of their twelfth year, Martha saw Charley and three other boys sauntering toward Wapping Old Stairs and the Thames. They didn't see her. She forgot her errand to the baker's shop and followed. She had no trouble. Their voices carried above the steady din of the streets. At the Stairs, they found sport in taunting a wild-eyed beggar woman.

Widely known, she regularly scoured the waterfront for anything she could use, sell, or steal. Her layers of rags, rolling eyes, and mass of tangled hair were the stuff of small children's nightmares. Her wild antics and senseless ranting provided amusement for men and boys with nothing better to do.

"Give us a kiss," said one of the boys. He sauntered close to the woman.

"I have a shilling here," he said, holding

out a coin. "What favors will you give?"

Then, it began. Laughing and jeering, they circled the woman, plucking at her rags and leaping away. She clutched her bag to her chest with one hand and leaned heavily on her long walking stick as she hobbled along the wharf.

"Charley Rawley!" Martha couldn't contain her disgust. "Shame on you! And the rest of you. Leave her be."

"Aw, Martha. Go home. We're just having a bit of sport."

He wasn't about to be called to account in front of the other boys. He made a bold feint in the hag's direction. With much more steadiness than she'd led them to suspect, the woman stepped away from him and closer to where the incoming tide lapped at the wharf.

A few yards out in the river, wherryman Duff Malloy sat back to watch the show. He knew what the boys didn't. For all her madness, the hag had no lack of cunning.

"Charley, look out!"

Martha's shout was too late. He danced dangerously close to the wharf's edge. The woman's stick caught him behind his knees and sent him pitching into the Thames. The next swing of her stick scattered the other boys. Running to where Charley thrashed about in the water, Martha barely escaped a blow as the woman strode by. But Martha didn't notice as she dropped to her knees, one hand on the edge of the moss- and slime-covered seawall, the other reached for his flailing hands. Deaf to the wherryman's shout as he pulled mightily on his oars in their direction, Martha tumbled sideways off the wall.

Foul water clouded her eyes, shut her mouth. She fought her shawl that washed up over her face, pushed it away and reached upward. But was it up? She couldn't see, couldn't breathe, couldn't tell up from down. Pain filled her throat, her chest felt as if it might explode. Her hand struck something hard. She struggled for a hold, fighting her sodden skirts. They clung to her legs, dragging her down.

Is this how I'll end? Am I dying? This can't be happening.

She reached again, clawing uselessly at stone. Her arms were so heavy. She fought the water, forced her arms to move. But they were useless. She was too tired to care. So tired. So easy just to let herself go, sliding smoothly through the water, down... down.

On his way toward Martha, the wherryman hauled Charley roughly to the side of his boat where the boy could hold on. He didn't take his eyes from the few bubbles and a stirring of the murky water that suggested where the girl was. Two strokes of his oars and he reached the spot, dragging Charley along with him. Duff raked his boat hook slowly back and forth in the water until it struck something, slipped, then caught.

Martha didn't feel Duff Malloy's boat

hook strike her side, catch on her skirt, pull her up till he could grab a handful of her hair. He pulled her head above the surface. Roughly he caught an arm, lifted her enough to haul her over the side of the boat and let her fall into the bottom. He turned her on her side and thumped her back.

"Come on girlie!"

He thumped her again. Martha convulsed, retching, spewing filthy water all over the boatman's boots.

"There you go! That's the way."

Once she was coughing and spitting and clearly alive, he turned to haul Charley aboard to join her in a sodden heap. Without a word, Duff took up his oars and guided the wherry toward the wharf and tied it to an iron ring.

Charley's friends had fled, but there were plenty of hands along the seawall to lift the children out onto the wharf. Once, he'd climbed ashore, Duff set out, carrying Martha. Charley had to trot to keep up. Anxious not to miss the end of the show, many of the onlookers followed. At the Black Horse, the party left a watery trail across the public room floor.

"Out for a bit of sport, 'e was," said Duff, shoving Charley toward Rebecca.

"And this 'un's yours, too, I believe. Near drowned, she did."

He turned to a nearby table, shoved two men out of the way. As they hastily grabbed tankards and plates, he sat her on one of the benches. Charley sat beside her looking at the floor as the wherryman gave a colorful account of what landed them in the Thames. Clustered behind him, the men who'd followed from the waterfront offered a huzzah or two and fell to arguing over what each thought had happened.

"Thank you, Sir." Rebecca spoke between clenched teeth. The sight of her husband approaching from the bar helped her to overcome her initial fright. Snatching Charley by the ear, she turned to Joseph.

"Mr. Rawley, give Mr. Malloy a glass of punch or whatever pleases him with our thanks. And there are pork pies, fresh from the oven. See he has one."

"Can you walk?" She poked Martha's shoulder with one finger.

"Yes 'um, I think so." She wasn't at all sure. Her head hurt and when she looked up, the room wobbled and pitched in front of her eyes.

"I'm going to puke."

Rebecca had just enough warning to move away and pull Charley with her.

"Sit, then. I'll be back for you."

Still holding fast to her son's ear, Rebecca marched him toward the kitchen. Hannah met them in the doorway.

"You'd best see to her." Rebecca tossed her head, indicating the scene behind her.

"Nearly drowned, they say."

With angry pokes, she shoved Charley past his grandmother and through the kitchen to the courtyard. There she released him to wipe her hands on her apron.

"Ugh!"

She looked down, then, hastily untied the apron to scrub at her hands.

"That's foul!"

Nearly drowned?

Hannah wasn't quite sure what had happened, but one look at Martha after seeing Charley, set her heart to pounding.

Dear God. What if they had drowned?

More than once she'd seen barely recognizable bodies hauled from the Thames. To think of those two... A feeling akin to fear was quickly replaced by relief, then anger that propelled her into the public room.

"Get rags, mop, buckets, whatever you need," she said to two wenches who'd joined the customers who'd gathered.

"And clean up this mess."

Their looks of near horror turned to disgust as they hurried away.

When she saw Mistress Chinn, Martha rose slowly, but had to grip the edge of the table to keep herself from falling. She tried to smile, but her mouth didn't seem to work. She felt more like crying.

Hannah wasn't sure what she felt as she stood looking at Martha, muddy river water puddling around her feet.

Looks like a near-drowned mouse, she thought as she put out a hand to help steady her.

"Come, child." Hannah put a hand on Martha's back and kept it there as she guided her to the kitchen where she met Rebecca in the door to the courtyard. Rebecca waved behind her.

"I don't want those clothes back in the house. The smell sets my gorge to rising."

"Go! If you can do nothing but puke. Leave them to me. Annie's here. We'll take care of the children."

Rebecca wagged her finger in her son's direction. "I'll deal with you later. Call me when he's free of the stink, Mother. And you!"

She looked hard at Martha.

"You're better now?"

She didn't wait to see Martha's nod.

"It's bad enough Charley gets into things like this, but she shouldn't be running the streets. She has far too much freedom, Mother."

With one last angry look at Charley, she flung her apron down on the stones and was gone.

Hannah kicked the apron aside and tucked her skirts up into her waist to keep them out of the filthy water at her feet. She sent Annie back into the kitchen for buckets. They took turns filling them from the pipe in the yard and pouring them over the children.

"Get out of those clothes."

She nodded at Charley and wrinkled her nose at the smell that the water hadn't begun to wash away. As he tugged off the one shoe he hadn't lost and started on his pants, she turned to Martha.

"You too. You'll feel better once the stink is gone."

Gingerly she helped the girl undo her sodden apron, jacket, petticoat, and stockings, letting them fall to her feet.

That done, she and Annie filled the buckets again and doused the children. They stood shivering. Mindful of their naked bodies clearly defined by the wet shirts clinging to them, they cast about for other places to look each time they opened their eyes after a dousing. When all visible river filth was gone, Hannah bade them kneel on the hard stones. Screwing their eyes tight shut, each bent over a bucket. Starting with Martha, she rinsed their hair with vinegar and water, then gave their heads a good scrub with lye soap.

In the meantime, Annie had gathered two worn blankets and an armload of rags that she dropped in the buckets refilled with fresh water and vinegar.

"Now. Off with the shirts."

"No, Nana."

Charley shook his head and sent water flying.

"You've got nothing I haven't seen, young man."

After seeing Martha's equally dismayed look, Hannah paused.

"Ah, that's how it is? We'll do it this way, then."

She stepped between the two children,

shook out one of the blankets, and held it up.

"Now off with the shirt."

She handed the other blanket to Annie who did the same.

Struggling with shaking hands and clinging shirts, the children tugged their shirts over their heads and stood naked hugging themselves.

"You're not finished."

Hannah handed each of them a piece of lye soap.

"You'll never get warm if you don't get on with it. Now scrub yourselves where we did not. Give yourselves a good scrubbing. It will warm you."

By the time they'd finished, their skin was glowing red and they'd almost stopped their trembling. Quickly the women wrapped them in blankets and led them into the kitchen, trailing the smell of vinegar and soap past giggling kitchen wenches.

For several minutes, Martha and Charley sat in silence on stools in front of the fire.

"You had no call to do such a thing to that poor old woman," Martha hissed from under the edge of the blanket she was using to mop at the water still trickling down her face.

"Poor woman? More a trickster, I'd say."

Charley ducked his head, letting a tawny shock of hair fall over his eyes. He wouldn't look at her.

"Were you drowning? You looked near

dead when Mr. Malloy pulled you out."

"Aye, I thought sure I would be. I guess I would have, if he hadn't come along."

Putting the feeling and thought into words made her feel weak and her fingers tremble as she pulled the blanket tight under her chin.

"Why'd you have to follow me?"

She looked at him in disgust, wondering why he had to ask.

"You should be thanking me. I tried to save your life. No one else was around to care."

Flustered, he quickly looked away and started scrubbing himself with the blanket. He was saved from having to say anything more when Joseph Rawley stormed into the kitchen.

Joseph wasn't easily riled, but word of his son and heir's mishap and Martha's near drowning had spread along the wharf. It brought men to the pub to hear the story. He was torn between the sudden business that had come his way and anger at Charley for nearly killing himself and Martha. He'd pretended to laugh along with his customers' jests, but was impatient to get away.

"You shame us, going on like that."

Joseph's growl made Charley cringe and pull the blanket more tightly around him. He'd never seen his father so angry.

"You've got no bloody business running with those boys. Or getting up to such foolishness. Get yourself up from there and get dressed. I'll be back."

But he wasn't back till well after the children had gotten warm and dressed in the clothes that Annie and Hannah found for them. By then Joseph's anger had cooled. The beating Rebecca had urged on him was far less punishing than it might have been. More punishing, for Charley, was the wait. He couldn't eat the hot pork pie his grandmother gave him.

As she helped Martha to dress, Hannah scolded her.

"You knew better than to go chasing after Charley. Now one of the wenches will have to go out and fetch the bread you went to buy. And I'm sure the shilling in your pocket's in the river bottom's muck."

Martha could only hang her head and nod. She had no excuses. When Hannah left her, she returned to scrubbing her clothes and Mistress Rawley's apron. Back in the kitchen, Hannah found her granddaughter waiting.

"I've brought this for Martha."

She held out a red quilted petticoat.

"It's too badly faded for me to go out in, but I think it will serve her well."

"She's in the yard."

Hannah nodded toward the door, wondering as she watched Mary leave what had provoked the gift, if gift it was. She lingered close to the door, hoping for an answer.

"I've brought this for you. If you must run about ruining perfectly good clothes, you'll have use for another petticoat."

140

Hannah shook her head in disgust.

Must she tarnish the gift? But no good will come of it if I interfere now.

"I'm sure I will."

Sarcasm in one so young?

Hannah couldn't help smiling when Martha angrily hoisted the soggy quilted petticoat sloshing water across the stones in Mary's direction.

"You had no call to do that."

Mary snatched up her skirt to look at her shoes.

"You could have ruined my shoes. And look at you, barefoot. No stockings? And where are your shoes?"

"Gone."

"You lost them? The ones I gave you?"

They *were* a fine pair, thought Hannah. Martha had laughed delightedly when, at last, her feet had grown enough to fit them.

"You must be more sensible of what you do. Don't you care what people will think? It's bad enough that Charley doesn't, but he's a boy. You'll pay for it someday. You pretend not to care about such things but you're not a child anymore. Don't act like one. One day you'll have to make your own way and pay for shoes yourself. But never mind. I've brought you this, and I hope you'll be more careful of it. I'll leave it with Grandmother."

Having delivered her gift and message, Mary marched back into the kitchen. Hannah had stepped away from the door just in time.

"Will you please see she gets this when she's done? I almost feel like not giving it to her now. She's lost her shoes, Nana. The ones I gave her. What will she do for shoes?"

"That's no concern of yours. I'm sure she's saddened by the loss. But you have more pressing matters to attend to. She has other shoes."

In the courtyard, Martha dropped the petticoat back into the bucket and crouched, making much of shoving it down in the water. She hoped no one would appear to see the tears that she hastily brushed from her cheek. Those shoes were a greater loss than any damage done to her petticoat. She dearly loved those shoes. It would be a long while before she had any like them again. If ever.

When she'd wrung the last of the river water's stench out of her petticoat, shirt, gown, and the aprons, she put them into a nearby basket and headed with it back into the kitchen. Martha didn't see Hannah at a nearby cupboard as she pulled a wooden rack close to the fire and began hanging the clothes to dry.

"I *will* make my way. And I'll buy my own shoes."

"I'm most certain you will."

Martha gave a start.

"You have good sense, child. You'll do well if you don't let others lead you astray. Don't you have another pair of shoes?"

"Aye, but they aren't so fine."

"They'll serve you for now. Finish

hanging those clothes, then go fetch them."

Martha couldn't look at Hannah, couldn't let her see the tears blurring her eyes. She quickly shook out the clothes and hung them on the rack.

Blast that Charley. What if he'd drowned?

She looked down at the dark pool of frothy water glistening on the stones behind her.

What if I...?

Suddenly she shook with a chill that wasn't from the cold, but from the memory of water all around her, robbing her of air as it pulled her down. Shaking herself as a wet dog might, she fought the image. Carelessly flinging the last of the clothes over the rack, she ran to the back room and scrambled under her cot to find her old shoes. Once she'd pulled them out into the light, she held them gingerly by their soles and shook them hard to be sure no spiders had taken up residence.

Grimacing when she pulled them on, she buckled them as loosely as she could. They pinched her toes but the leather had worn soft. It would stretch. And she didn't drown. Neither did Charley. That was all that mattered. She hurried back into the kitchen to help with supper preparations.

XII

Fictions & Fact

Martha tried to be happy for Charley when he joined his father at the bar. She couldn't blame him for being proud. He'd just turned fifteen and was doing a man's work. Better still, he was no longer at his mother's beck and call. And well past time, she thought.

Should be for me, too. I'm just five months younger and spending most of the day helping in the kitchen. Or, worse, darning stockings, mending tears I can't explain, or toiling over some such womanly skill the Mistress says I'm sure to need one day. I'll never know how to make my way in this world if I keep to that. I'm old enough and I've got a lot more sense than Charley.

"Might I have a word, Mistress?"

Hannah looked up from the recipe book she was thumbing through, surprised at such formality. She nodded.

"I want to go to work in the taproom."

At Hannah's look of surprise, she went on in a rush.

"I'm not really needed in the kitchen. I know I can do it. They're always in a great rush getting the midday dinner out. What with the men calling for more ale or more bread to sop up the gravy or what have you. I can get a pot or bowl out to the tables as well as any other wench. And I can learn how to figure what's due for a meal or a drink. I won't let anyone take me for a ninny. And sooner or later, I'll need to know how to make my way."

" I'm sure you can do it, but you needn't worry about that yet. Let me see what Ellen and Nancy have to say."

Hannah spoke the truth about Martha's ability, but worried that the two women who had charge of the taproom would say about having her there.

At fifteen, Martha had grown tall with a woman's body that caused men to notice and the taproom wenches to glare. She paid the men no mind, but the wenches were a different matter. Ellen Peck and Nancy Shaw especially. An unlikely pair of friends, they weren't much older than Martha when they began working in the taproom. With dark eyes and an abundance of dark curls, Ellen was a sharp-tongued temptress skilled at keeping men in their place when it suited her. Blue-eyed Nancy was blond with a ready smile and a lively but less willing nature than Ellen.

Though they could have earned more

serving the gentlemen in the upper public rooms, that wasn't for them. Better to work for Hannah Chinn than under Rebecca Rawley's heavy hand. And over the years, Hannah had left service in the taproom to them. The other wenches either deferred to them or didn't last long.

The two women knew how Martha came to be at the Black Horse and had watched Martha grow up. They knew also the trouble Sarah Pratt had caused between Hannah and her daughter and admired their mistress all the more for taking in the orphaned child. But Martha was a young woman now. She caused men to look twice and could easily compete for those most likely to slip her a coin or two.

As it turned out, she proved to be more help than hindrance and showed no sign of trying to take customers away from them. They willingly shared what they knew and took pride in her success. She proved a match for any customer who tried to take advantage of her youth and inexperience to get away without paying what he owed.

Martha would stand before him with a pleading look and an outstretched palm.

"That's three pence more please, Sir. The Mistress will take it outa my hide if I come up short."

That amused the regulars. They knew Hannah Chinn would do nothing of the sort and had great sport with the offender. Martha also managed to shame would-be cheats, who claimed not to be able to pay for a drink or a meal.

"Don't you worry, Sir."

She leaned close but could be heard by those at nearby tables.

"I won't let on you haven't got the coin for a meat pie. I guess it's hard times you're having."

Over the weeks, Martha also learned to fend off customers' playful pinches and attempts at a hug or kiss without giving offense. Most customers took her rebuffs in good spirits.

For the first time in her life, Martha had money to call her own. She kept it in a small purse she tucked under her pillow with the little wooden doll. At night, it pleased her to feel the purse and its contents or in her pocket beneath her apron when she went out during the day. Except for an occasional sweet or piece of fresh fruit, she spent very little of her earnings.

Just once, she stopped by the neighborhood bookshop of Josiah Hood where Mary Rawley was a good customer. Martha had borrowed some of the fantastical romances that she brought home, but usually returned them unfinished.

"Why should I care for such far-fetched tales? I hear better on the streets and more to care about."

"I don't understand you, Martha Pratt."

Mary took the little volume from her.

"My friends were much taken with the story. I'll take the stories of gentlemen and ladies over your fish wives and butchers."

"And how many gentlemen and ladies do you see in a day?"

"Scant few to see here," she said with a toss of her head, "but I have no need when I can call upon the Chinns. Alice and Peggy know the ways of being a lady. But I suppose you care nothing for that and would just as soon remain a tavern wench."

"From what I've read, the skills of your ladies and gentlemen are beyond any I would want to practice. I haven't time to waste on such things, but thank you for the book."

Mary marched off with her book and an offended air.

Not long after that, Martha stopped into Josiah Hood's shop to see if he had some other sort. The bookseller immediately pressed a book upon her. After reading a page or two, she set it aside. It was another of the romances that Mary was so fond of. He looked down his long nose with disapproval when she picked up another that had caught her eye.

"The History of Miss Betsy Thoughtless", she read on its cover. Opening it, she arrived at Chapter I, which declared, "Gives the reader room to guess at what is to ensue tho ten to one but he finds himself deceived."

Now, there was a promising start, she thought, and likely to be a better tale, addressed as it was to a man. She wasn't disappointed. The first sentence fulfilled the opening's promise.

"It was always my opinion that fewer women were undone by love than vanity and, that those that the sex sometimes are guilty of proceed for the most part rather from inadvertency than a vicious inclination."

"How much will this one be?" she asked.

"Ah, that would not do for a young lady like yourself," he said, snatching the volume from her hands.

"Mistress Rawley would never forgive me if I were to allow you to bring such into her house."

"Mistress Rawley has nothing to do with what I bring into the Black Horse. Nor does she care. I do as I please."

Martha reached for the book. "I will take it."

"I don't think that's so," said Mr. Hood and put the book on a table behind him.

"I'll not have Mistress Rawley angry. Let her tell me herself that you may purchase what you will and you may have this book. I'll set it aside for you."

"There's no need. I'll find it elsewhere. You won't get my money."

Martha didn't wait to hear his response and nursed her anger all the way home. Some days later, on an errand for Mistress Chinn, she found the shop of M. Tolbert, Esq., Bookseller, as the battered sign over his door announced. M. Tolbert was a very different sort from Mr.

Hood. He nodded pleasantly when she entered and returned to dusting books on the shelves as she browsed through several on a table at the front of the store.

When nothing captured her interest, she cleared her throat. Immediately he turned.

"Yes, Miss?"

"I'm looking for a book called *The History of Miss Betsy Thoughtless.*

"Ah, yes. I know the book, but I don't think I have it. If you really want it, I'll find you a copy at no more expense."

"Thank you, Sir."

Martha was surprised and greatly pleased to find a bookseller who wouldn't judge her choices.

"Perhaps you have another that I've read about. It's the story of a child born in Newgate."

With a broad smile that piled his plump cheeks up under his eyes, the bookseller clapped his hands and quickly disappeared among the shelves at the back of his shop. He returned almost immediately with a small volume.

"This one is much in demand these days. As you see, this copy is well used, but none the worse for it. I don't know what you've read, but I must warn you, it's not of the sort that gentle folk approve. Indeed, I'll wager that you'll find much in it distasteful."

He handed her "The History and Misfortunes of the Famous Moll Flanders".

She took it from him and eagerly turned to the first page. She read that and several more that told of an infant born in Newgate, of a mother soon to be transported, and of the grim futures the orphaned child could face. But like herself, it seemed, Moll was offered a better start in life.

Martha stood transfixed as she read of the little girl's fear of being placed out to service to "run errands and be a drudge to some cook-maid."

That was a fear too close to those that beset her as she went about her work in the public room. She could read no more with the bookseller looking on. That was a story she must read alone, for the thoughts stirred by those few words caused her breath to catch in her throat.

"I'll take this one," she said, fumbling for the purse beneath her apron.

"You're sure?"

His cheery smile was replaced by a look of concern.

"I don't want to do you a disservice."

"Oh no."

She was moved by the fact he noticed how the book affected her.

"It touches on things I often think of and the ways of people I know. It's not the plight of those poor souls in Newgate but of orphans that is my interest."

"Ah yes, that is sad enough. But you'll find much more than that, and if it does not suit you, you may return it for the three pence you pay today. Or for the *The History of Miss Betsy Thoughtless*."

"Thank you, Sir."

Martha had to restrain herself from throwing her arms around the gentleman.

"One way or the other, you can be sure I'll return."

Her step was brisk when she left M. Tolbert's shop. The pleasing exchange with the bookseller had driven off the distress she felt reading the first pages of *Moll Flanders*. It was just a story, after all, no worse than the real stories that fueled talk in Wapping's public houses. They came fresh daily, often with the news of thieves and cutpurses, brutal beatings, wanton women, or another body dragged from the foul black waters of the Thames.

Back home, she put her book on the table by her bed, then, worked through that evening's supper with an impatience that brought comments from some of the regular customers.

"You have a gentleman waiting for you that you can't tarry for a word with an old man?"

Duff Malloy seldom missed his supper of pigeon pie. Martha had a special fondness for the wherryman. And he for her. Neither ever spoke of the day he'd hauled her from the Thames. For her part, she'd as soon it were forgotten.

"It's a book, I have waiting."

Martha felt easy enough with the grizzled waterman to speak the truth.

"You should be doin' better than that on a cold night like this, lass."

"For now, the company of a good tale suits me."

She sat on the empty bench across from him.

"I see none who come in here that are better company than you."

"You flatter me, but I think you're right. Few come in here would be good for passing the time. And you have time enough to be lookin' for a husband. Fifteen years have you?"

Martha shook her head.

"Sixteen this past March. And what makes you think I'm looking for a husband?"

Martha made a face at him to show her disgust at the thought, but couldn't deny that she studied the men who took their meals at the tavern.

"It's time you did. You're a fine lookin' lass and have the look and way of one older. You may not be lookin' now, but you got plenty eying you. If I were a mite younger and had aught to offer, I'd be thinkin' that way myself."

Martha's look of mock surprise caused him to pause.

"Naught to worry there, lass," he said with a snort.

"But there's others…"

A call for Martha's attention from across

the room ended their conversation.

"It wouldn't be such a bad thing, what you were thinking."

She left him with a wink and a quick hug, which wasn't lost on others in the room. She spent the rest of the evening fending off their efforts to earn a similar embrace.

None of those were the sort she'd want for a husband. Ever since she began to work later at night, she knew of too many who drank away their day's earnings without a thought for wives who spent those same days and nights in drudgery. Or their children who ran wild in the streets and went to bed hungry.

There were a few who came for their midday meal that she liked the looks of … an apprentice shipwright from the shipyard caught her eye, as did a hard-working young ship carpenter with wood chips in his hair. They were clean and sober. At least at midday. She had yet to see them at night. Perhaps they already had wives, ones young enough to keep them home at the end of the day. Martha didn't deceive herself. Not many men came to a tavern looking for a wife.

The two men from the shipyard often cast sideways looks at her but never offered more than a nod or a word of thanks to acknowledge the dish or cup she placed before them. She envied the girls whose talk flowed as freely as the ale from Joseph Rawley's tap. She'd seen Charley eying the younger wenches when she went to the bar for a customer's drink. They made much of him.

And why not? He was the innkeeper's son. And fair enough to look at. But he gave her no more than a nod and a smile in an all too brotherly way as he handed her a glass or mug.

She'd read enough of the books Mary loved so well not to expect more from him. Or from herself. She couldn't imagine trying to amuse Charley or any other man with flattery and lively conversation the way the women in Mary's novels did.

There's no more substance in that than watery gruel. Is that all a man wants? Why would I want to spend my life with any of the foppish men the women in Mary's books seem to adore. She's welcome to them, if such men even exist.

As for gentlemen, Martha had little to do with those who came to the upper room of the Black Horse. Unless they were shorthanded, Mistress Rawley seldom called on her to work there. When she did, Martha saw little beyond their fine clothes and studiously polished airs to commend them. Perhaps, she thought, it was easier to love a story than the real man. That would most surely be true of the great majority of men she served regularly. Many a night, she'd watch them leave, reeling from drink. Come morning, she'd help the scullery maids clean up their puke from the floor or where it was spewed across the inn's doorstep.

XIII

Taproom Wench

Martha had worked only a night or two before she learned that many of the men came to the taproom of the Black Horse craving more than ale or rum. She couldn't always escape their hands when her own were laden with brimming jugs or pitchers and tankards. Most meant nothing by the liberties they took. But as they left after an evening of drink, some were dogged in their attempts to slip a hand beneath her skirts or hug her to them. Often she'd feel a man's swollen member as he pressed against her. They roused more disgust than fear and certainly no desire.

Mistress Rawley was enough of a cooling presence to keep most of them from forcing the issue. Martha studied the bar maids who successfully managed to hold off unwanted familiarity. Soon she too grew skilled at keeping glasses filled and the customers happy with winks and kisses that came nowhere near another's skin. She learned to dodge and dance among them, laughing and making jests delivered with not altogether playful jabs and slaps. Most customers turned their attentions to more willing wenches.

Occasionally, gentlemen brought lewd women into the tavern with them. Tarts and sluts, Mistress Rawley called them and chased the women out. Joseph was usually close by to remove the woman and, if needed, their companions.

"This is not a brothel," Rebecca'd lecture the man. "I'll not have such women here."

Martha thought it puzzling that she didn't insist upon the men leaving. Often, they didn't. Many of the tavern's wenches were good company. Some of the upper room's regulars knew, if they went down the two broad steps into the taproom, they'd find a wench or two who could satisfy them if they could escape Mistress Rawley's notice.

Martha suspected that Rebecca knew what Ellen, Nancy, and some of the other wenches were doing. Whatever that was. She wasn't exactly sure as she watched them slip out of the taproom with a customer. Finally, her curiosity prompted her to follow Ellen. She went just far enough to see the couple duck into the dark alley between the Black Horse and the baker's house next door, then went back inside.

Ellen caught Martha when she returned.

She stood close, her nails digging into Martha's arm.

"You keep your mouth shut. What you saw is none of your affair and nothing to be tellin' Mistress Rawley about."

"I wouldn't do that! I just wondered…" Martha pulled away.

"There's other ways to find out than creepin' after and spyin'. I'd be happy to tell you what you want to know. It's past time you learned a thing or two."

Martha was relieved when a shout for more ale took Ellen away. The woman had a knack for insinuating her way into other people's affairs. She'd be asking more than telling, Martha was sure.

When Martha first began working nights, she was watched with suspicion by the other women in the taproom. They were wary of her kinship to Mistress Chinn and of the way she willingly worked harder than they chose to. At first, they didn't trust her with their gossip, especially the more wanton ones who whispered behind their hands if she was near. Little by little, they realized that she carried no tales and were less cautious, accepting that she was not a spy for Mistress Chinn or Mistress Rawley.

In truth, they were disappointed that she had no secrets to share about their mistresses or customers, but lost no time in educating Martha about what happened in the shadows of the alley and why a girl disappeared for a day or so, then returned pale and claiming she was ailing.

Most of the time, the girl had gone off to visit to an old woman on Red Maid Lane; or perhaps to an apothecary who had powders that could help eliminate an unwanted pregnancy. Not until Ellen arrived and pulled Nancy aside with the news that Nelly, one of the other wenches wouldn't be returning to work did Martha realize what a dangerous solution that could be.

"She went round to that butcher on Red Maid Lane," said Ellen. "Then, she came home and went straight to her bed ..."

Ellen had to stop to swipe angrily at brimming eyes.

"She didn't get up. Dead, she was."

"But how ... what happened?"

Martha remembered Nelly, not much older than she was.

"It's easy enough. Could happen to any of us. But you can't go around thinking about dying. There's worse things than that. No good'll come of trying to keep some bastard's spawn. Most likely, you'd end in the workhouse and the child would be sweepin' chimneys or doin' somebody's drudge work. If it lived. Like as not it wouldn't. You don't know how lucky you were... Your mother comin' here and causing all manner of trouble..."

At Nancy's disapproving look, Ellen clapped her hand over her mouth, but Martha guessed that she knew exactly what she was saying.

"Pay her no mind." Nancy glared at Ellen.

For a second or two, Martha stood, looking from one woman to the other, trying to ignore giggles from two other wenches who'd come close to hear the news, then, turned and ran through the taproom to the kitchen and her room beyond. Startled, Annie looked up from her darning.

"What's happened?"

She put her work aside.

For a moment, Martha didn't know what to say.

Bastard. Trollop.

The hateful things that Mary had said to her long ago came back in a rush.

"Did you ever hear tell how I came to be here?"

"Why in heaven's name do you want to know that?"

"Ellen's says that Nelly's dead because she tried to rid herself of a baby. She said that dying could be better than having a...a baby got like that, and I don't know how lucky I am. She said my mother caused trouble."

"A pox on the woman! What good is there in bringing all that up, now?"

"Does everyone know but me? Mistress Chinn never said anything of my mother causing trouble. What don't I know about my mother?"

With a heavy sigh, Annie waved Martha

160

to sit on her cot.

"Let me think where to begin."

"Where did my mother come from?"

"She'd never say for sure, but she was from the country. Had some trouble with a man there. She was a good, honest girl, your Ma. She wasn't loose like those wenches you been talking to. Oh, and did she ever have a way with cookin'. That was why Mistress Chinn kept her on when she learned she was with child. And she worked hard.

"Anyway, she'd found this young man after she got here. Thought he was a fine, upstanding sort. She loved him dearly, she did. I was quite taken with him, but he worried me at the same time. She'd hear nothing said against him. She was so happy and I hoped she was right. A strong handsome boy, and tall. You take after him that way. He had dark eyes, like your Ma"

Annie paused and busied herself with putting her darning in the basket by her side.

"He was an apprentice and talked of marrying her... Makes me angry, just thinking about it. He kept after her to lie with him...You know what I mean?"

Martha nodded.

"Well afterwards, he tells her they can't wed. Not so long as he's an apprentice. He wasn't about to be givin' that up. He was no good after all. Wouldn't do anything to help her and moved to where she couldn't find him.

"There was those told her to go looking

for help up off Red Maid Lane, but you Ma couldn't do it. Wasn't right, she told me. She was scared to go home, afraid what her family'd do, but she couldn't think what else to do. And sure enough, when she went back, her family turned her out. Said she brought shame on them. It was Mistress Chinn saved her from the work house and you from going to the foundling home like Mistress Rawley wanted. That was a sad time."

Annie dabbed at her eyes.

"It's been a long time since I've thought on that. Your Ma and me, we'd been livin' in the garret for near two years. Sarah was as good a friend as I've ever had. I was there when her time came, helpin' Mistress Chinn and the midwife. But there was no savin' that poor girl."

"You was strong, though. When you came back from the wet nurse, Mistress Agnes, the old cook, she took great care of you and loved you dearly. And I guess that's all I can say. 'Cept don't let those wenches put worrisome ideas in your head. You might not have a mama and papa, but Mistress Chinn and me, we set great store by you. And there's no shame in how you come into the world, whatever people say."

Long after Annie fell silent, Martha sat staring at her hands clenched in her lap. When at last she was sure she could speak with a steady voice, she looked up.

"Thank you. I was afraid to ask Mistress

Chinn, because I was sure it was tangled up with Mistress Rawley, that I was the cause of the trouble between them."

"I don't think Mistress Chinn would tell you more than I have. And, you've no need to worry about her and Mistress Rawley. There'd be trouble between them, one way or another, even if it wasn't to do with you. As long as I've been here, and that was before your ma came, they were at cross purposes."

She reached for her sewing.

"Aren't they going to be lookin' for you?"

"I'm surprised they haven't already come looking."

Martha rose slowly. She dreaded going back out to face Nancy and the rest. They'd surely been having a fine gossip while she was gone. At least it was a relief not to see Mistress Chinn in the kitchen. The pair of wenches scrubbing pots by the sink didn't look up. Did they know too? She paused in the shadows of the alcove to sort out her thoughts before stepping into the light of the public room.

What was the shame in being born? How can they blame me for the way my mother got me? And if the world thinks I'm to blame, so be it. Let them think what they will. They aren't going to shame me. Maybe she was foolish, but it wasn't just her fault.

The more Martha thought about it, the harder it was to be angry at her mother. Sarah Pratt was beginning to feel more real than she ever had before. Her father was another matter. Whatever Annie thought about him, Martha felt justified in hating him for what he did to her mother.

Most painful was realizing that between them, they'd killed her, he by getting her with child, her by being born. What was more, she vowed that she wouldn't let her heart rule her head, or risk everything for whatever pleasures were luring Ellen and the other wenches out into the alley.

Was it the natural way of men not to care about what might happen to a woman? If that was so, then it was pure foolishness for women to risk their lives that way. And for what? She'd heard Nancy describing the special attributes of this or that customer, though she could only guess at the means by which Nancy measured a man's rod.

She hadn't seen a male organ since she spied Charley pissing in the stable yard when they were small children. She wasn't blind to how a wee thing like that had grown to what now stretched the crotch of his tightest britches. Why a girl would care about such a measurement was beyond her ken.

Nancy and the others spoke from knowledge they chose not to share with Martha. Free as their talk was, it explained nothing of what they did that involved a man's sex. She couldn't imagine any of the men she saw in the public room enticing her to find out. But Charley?

She felt heat rising in her cheeks.

164

Whatever men and women did together, she suspected it had to do with the yearning that came upon her at the very thought of Charley. He was ever present in the muddle of her imaginings. She saw him every day, and when she didn't, he was still in her thoughts, as clearly as if he were standing before her, his blue eyes alight with laughter.

For a long time she'd been aware of the stirring in her body at the thought of Charley's lips on hers, their bodies pressed together, their hands.... What would their hands be doing? She'd seen Charley watching her when he thought she didn't know it. Most times, it was when she was fending off the attentions of a customer. Sometimes, when he was teasing one of the tavern wenches with a pinch or a playful kiss, she wished he'd feel as free to do the same with her. Did he want to?

His mother would certainly put an end to it if he did. As it was, if Charley and not his father happened to take Martha's orders for more beer or punch and they had time to say a few words, Rebecca swooped down like an angry crow to end any further conversation between them. Even so, if he caught her eye, Charley'd give her a wink and a rueful smile as he turned away.

Martha knew she was the only one Rebecca objected to. Let another wench loiter at the bar, angling for a kiss, and his mother barely cast an eye their way. She'd never let anything of a serious nature develop between her and Charley and had probably already lectured him on the subject.

But that had nothing to do with what she had to face that evening. Taking a deep breath, she stepped into the taproom and was soon pushing her way through the crowd at the bar to set three tankards down with a loud thump that caused Joseph Rawley to look up with raised eyebrows. She was relieved to see that Charley was nowhere about.

XIV

Charley

One busy night, Ellen chose to disappear. Martha and the others were hard put to keep the customers' tankards and glasses full. At the bar, Joseph Rawley had all but lost his usual patience and good humor. When he heard a call for Ellen and she couldn't be found, he caught Martha and sent her off to find the girl. It was a good thing the Mistress retired early, she thought as she checked the kitchen and necessary.

When she saw that Joseph wasn't looking, Martha slipped out the door to the street. As she approached the end of the building, she heard a grunt, then Ellen's throaty laugh coming from the side alley. The full moon cast just enough light for her to see Ellen pressed up against the wall, her skirts hiked up, legs wrapped around Billy Nunn, his hips thrusting savagely.

"You've got no business here," Ellen snapped at her over Billy's shoulder.

"Mr. Rawley sent me to find you."

"And now you have."

"Maybe she wants to have a go at it..."

Billy laughed and cocked his head to see Martha. Still looking, he resumed his thrusting, and laughed again as Ellen yanked his head back toward her. His next breath was a long drawn-out groan as he collapsed against her.

"Go on with you," Ellen hissed. "I'll be in soon enough now."

Martha tossed her head with a nonchalance she didn't feel and didn't wait to see them get untangled. She wasn't sure what they were doing, or how, but knew it was what Ellen and the other girls whispered about. She envied them and their talk that flowed as freely as the ale from Joseph Rawley's tap.

That night, after she left Ellen and Billy Nunn in the alley, thoughts of Charley came unbidden. She'd seen the younger wenches making much of him, especially if his father was otherwise engaged. He was the innkeeper's son, after all, and a fair lad to look at. And she was sure it wasn't by chance when they leaned over the bar to take a glass or mug from him that loose bodices ill-concealed the swell of their breasts. But what was the meaning of Charley's occasional wink when they blew him a kiss as they left with the drinks he'd poured? At night's end, when the girls left for their lodgings, did Charley go with his father up to the Rawleys' chambers or follow one of them for a favor promised earlier in the evening?

And what if he did? What right do I have to approve or disapprove what he does? Does he ever think of me that way? We were once the best of friends. Now we hardly ever talk. He doesn't even tease me the way he used to.

"Learned a bit of somethin' tonight, did you?"

Ellen's pinch on her arm brought her back to the present.

"Don't you be speaking of that to Mistress Rawley," Ellen hissed in her ear, "or you'll have me to reckon with."

"You needn't worry. I won't."

Martha shook her head, rubbing her arm.

"See that you don't."

Without a backward glance, Ellen went back to work, swinging her skirt and stopping by tables to collect orders and empty tankards. Martha was relieved that Ellen did no more than pinch her. They managed to work through the night without incident. Trouble, however, came from another quarter.

The following night, as she passed close to Billy Nunn's table, he grabbed her by the waist and pulled her onto his lap. He was drunk and she easily escaped to take a firm grip on his ear, leaned close, and jerked his head toward her.

"I'd not try that again," she whispered and gave his ear a vicious twist.

His howl turned heads, but Martha was

on her way out of the room. The few nearby were a long time letting Billy forget it. As Martha passed near her, Ellen caught her arm.

"Be careful," she said. "He's a mean one. He'll be biding his time, but one way or another, he'll make you pay."

****

Sometimes, if one of Rebecca's regular wenches failed to appear, Martha worked the upper public room. The men who chose to eat and drink there generally ranked themselves above those who gathered in the old taproom. Rebecca certainly thought they were. It puzzled Martha that Rebecca never called on Mary to help when they were short-handed. Some of the younger men were clearly from good families, just the sort Rebecca would want as a husband for her daughter and the sort she'd be likely to meet when visiting her cousins, Alice and Peggy Chinn.

If such men were to see Mary working in a pub, that would very likely banish any thought of marriage. But from what Martha saw of them, Rebecca's admirable gentlemen had nothing to commend them beyond their fine clothes, well-groomed wigs, and affected manners. Most were just as raucous, drunk, and disgusting as the men who filled the old taproom.

Martha had long since gotten over being offended by Mary and Alice and Peggy Chinn looking down on her. Over time, that became an advantage. They thought nothing of speaking freely in front of her, as they did any servant, especially one such as she. Other than their talk of clothes and young men, she'd overheard various fictions Mary and her cousins concocted about how her parents made their living. Martha was most bothered by how Mary felt about the Black Horse and especially about her mother running it. She and the Chinns struggled to call it anything but a pub.

At various times it was an inn or a coffee house or they avoided the issue entirely. In extreme situations, the Chinn sisters weren't above leading young men to think that Mary was their parents' orphaned niece. Martha was often tempted to confront Mary about how she belittled her mother. Didn't she see how, as Mistress of the Black Horse, she was no less successful than her brother, Alice's and Peggy's father? But, in the end, Martha said nothing. She had more immediate problems with Mary.

Martha cared nothing about the genteel life Mary and her mother valued so highly. To her way of thinking, the fine needlework that occupied Mary and her Chinn cousins was too tiresome and generally useless. To stitch a straight seam and keep her clothes mended was all Martha required of a needle and thread. And what use had she for learning to write a fine hand? She could write well enough for any to read. What's more, she could keep accounts, which she guessed was more than Mary could

171

do.

Though she didn't like the books Mary admired, Martha did value reading and spent much of her free time exploring the shelves of Mr. Tolbert's shop. She would willingly have spent every cent she earned there, if the bookseller didn't let her borrow books for next to nothing. To repay him, she brought rags on her visits and dusted the shelves, straightening books as she went and looking for ones of interest.

Strange, thought Martha that night, as she absentmindedly scrubbed the bar.

If I could choose the sort of life I'd want, I'd like to be a bookseller. Or the wife of one.

When they had a moment free of customers' demands, Charley joined her at the bar.

"You're quiet tonight. Nothing troubling, I hope."

"No. I was just thinking that I'd like to be a bookseller."

"A bookseller?" Charley snorted. "I can't see you working in a dusty old shop with nothing but books for company."

"Sometimes I'd rather have books for company than some who come in here."

"How long have you been thinking that?" he snapped.

The sudden anger in his tone made her frown.

"Why does that make you angry? It was just something I was thinking about. And I

172

might not always have a place here."

"You needn't worry about that. I have some news that might change your mind about that. Mama and Papa say it's time I learn the business. I'm going to be helping Papa here at the bar."

He looked around and when he was sure there was no one nearby, he went on.

"I think I'll like that. At least I won't be at Mama's beck and call all the time."

"I thought you wanted to go to sea with your Uncle Jamie."

"There's no telling when he'll be back. And I still have to persuade him to take me on and help me persuade Mama. Til then, I'll try to make the most of bartending."

Martha was busy in the kitchen and taproom and did little more than listen to his plans. It bothered her that the more he talked the more he left unsaid. She wasn't a part of the life he described. Though she saw Charley every day as she carried drinks from the bar to taproom, they rarely had time to talk as they once had.

There could have been an ocean between them, or in reality, something more formidable. Ever vigilant, Rebecca Rawley made very sure they had no time to talk and especially that her son had no time to notice what customers were beginning to notice. Martha was becoming a handsome and self-assured young woman, particularly appealing to the men she served occasionally in the upper room.

Over time, Martha had come to realize that often a customer wanted to talk, to have someone to listen to their trials or triumphs. Gradually, she'd learned how to get them talking, how to make them laugh and forget what bothered them for a short while. But that was all they wanted to talk about. When it came to talk of serious, worldly matters, they didn't want a wench around.

She regularly read the discarded copies of the *London Gazette* and other newspapers and could have asked a reasonable question or offered an opinion, but the opportunity never came. Not even Charley wanted to discuss such things. Or anything of a serious nature, it seemed. As a result, they discussed little more than taproom business and their customers' likes and dislikes.

****

"There's a bolt of linen in the little corner room." Annie caught Martha early one morning.

"It's in the bureau on the right, bottom drawer, if memory serves. Fetch it down for me."

"And what if Mistress Rawley catches me going into one of their rooms?"

Martha had suffered too many unpleasant encounters over the years to relish the idea of meeting Rebecca outside her own

174

apartment at dawn's first light.

"It's a storeroom. She can say nothing about that. And it's early yet, she won't be up now. She'll be after me if I don't get started on making some fresh napkins. So, go now."

Martha said no more, but took her time climbing the stairs. She tiptoed to the door of the little room. Cautiously she turned the knob and slowly pushed it open, praying that the hinges didn't squeal. She paused after shutting the door, scanning the dusky interior. Pale daylight from the small window did no more than create a room full of shadows.

From what she could see, Annie hadn't visited the room in a while. A trunk stood in the middle of the room and on the bed in the corner, bedding was piled in disarray. Well, that wasn't her business. Quickly she went to the tall bureau and pulled out the bottom drawer. In the poor light, she had to feel the several bolts of cloth to determine which was the linen they used for napkins. She'd stitched enough of them to know. Finding it at last, she pulled it out. Standing, she shoved the drawer closed with her foot.

"What are you doing!"

The man's voice was thick from interrupted sleep. Martha froze, clutching the bolt of linen to her chest. Was it Mr. Rawley? Some lodger? A thief in hiding? How could he have come in without her hearing him? There was movement behind her. She spun around.

"Charley! What are you doing here?"

"Who did you think it might be?"

"There shouldn't be anyone here. You gave me a fright. You're lucky I didn't black your eye."

"You think you could? And what about you? Creeping in like a thief and waking me from a fine dream?"

"So I see."

Martha could feel the color rising in her cheeks along with relieved laughter. She struggled not to look down toward the protrusion beneath his long shirt. It was his turn to blush.

"Go about your business," he mumbled.

"Let me take care of mine."

With a great show of nonchalance, he turned and pulled the chamber pot from beneath the bed. For what seemed an exceedingly long time, the only sound in the room was his steady stream hitting the bowl. She turned away and pretended to be looking for something in the top drawer of the bureau as he hastily pulled on his breeches. Finally he returned to where she stood.

"Why are you in here?"

"Because of that rascal Joseph. Mother's decided he's old enough and doesn't need to sleep in their chamber anymore. So, she sent him into my bed. He may be small, but he's all arms and legs flailing about. I couldn't get a decent night's sleep. So now he has the bed to himself. This room suits me well. I've no need of more. But I suppose I should ask Mother for the key."

He grinned. Martha cocked her head to look into his face. Not only had he gotten to be a head taller than she, the new timbre of his voice left no doubt of his manhood, of which she was suddenly uncomfortably aware. Her heart wasn't pounding out of fright but the few inches that separated them, despite the bolt of linen she hugged tightly to her chest. She was keenly aware of the closeness and heat of their bodies in the cool room, the intermingling of their breath, coming quickly now. She sensed he felt it too and was frightened. Dragging her eyes away from his to the linen, she tried to step past him.

"Annie is waiting for this below."

"No, wait."

He caught her arm.

"There's something I've been wanting to ask you. The men in the taproom talk about you and every night, I must hold myself in check when I see how some put their hands on you. They treat you just like they do the other wenches."

"And am I not? You would be forever black and blue if you didn't check yourself. I can take care of myself. Don't worry."

"But I do and I don't like it. You could stay in the kitchen. I'm sure Grandmother has need of you."

"And who are you to say what I should or shouldn't do?"

"I didn't mean it that way. I..."

"Oh, I know, but I don't like kitchen work, Charley. It's much more lively in the public rooms. If I must make my way one day, I'd do better as a serving wench. Your grandmother won't always be here to see that I have a place. You know as well as I that your mother won't keep me."

"She'll have to if I have any say in it."

"You can't be sure of that, but I'm glad you'd stand by me. And I'll manage."

"But you shouldn't have to. If Mother puts you out, I'll go with you."

"You know that's foolishness. I love you for it, but that would just make two of us with no place to live and no sure way to make a living. Besides, a lot can happen between now and then."

"What did you just say?"

"I said, a lot can happen…"

"No, not that. Do you truly love me?"

"Of course, I do. We've been like brother and sister."

"Oh."

He looked so crestfallen that Martha took a step back the better to look in his face.

"What is it?"

"I have sister enough in Mary. What I feel for you isn't like that. I'm very glad we're not kin because what I feel isn't brotherly."

He blushed and looked away.

"Hang it all, Martha, I've been thinking about what I'd say if I ever got the chance. I even stole a look in one of those books Mary's always studying. They're nothing but a lot of foolish nonsense as near as I can tell. If I talked to you like that, you'd have every right to laugh me out of this room."

He stepped back to stand ramrod straight, one hand over his heart.

"Ahh, Mistress Martha, I have longed for this moment to tell you of my devotion, my adoration..."

Martha clapped her hand over her mouth to contain her laughter.

"Stop Charley. You'll bring your mother in on us for sure!"

How familiar that felt, the two of them, up to mischief and hiding from Rebecca. But this wasn't mischief. Her laughter was bringing her close to tears.

"Blast, Martha! Don't laugh. I've no fine words, but I had to say something before you... before someone else does. There've been a couple of fellows thinking about it... ."

"How do you know that?"

"They asked me if you were spoken for. I said I didn't know. They haven't said any more, so I figure they haven't asked you yet or got an answer they couldn't brag about."

"Well , no one's been asking."

She was heartened by his broad smile and look of relief. She had no idea who those men might be, but, then, none of them really interested her. And Charley had never caused her to think that he might care what she did or that he'd notice if she showed an interest in other men.

"I don't care about any of them. You're the only one that has meant anything to me for as long as I can remember. But how could I know your mind on such things? We never really talk anymore. And I see you with the wenches. They tell me about the things they do with you. If I can believe what they say, you've sampled more than their lips."

"Aw Martha, they don't mean anything to me and whatever I might do when I'm with them is just sport. They're not worth a cinder compared to you. And I'm not the only one thinks so. It plagues me that you'll find someone…"

"I haven't. And it's your mother we have to worry about. She'd do anything she could to keep us apart. Let's not give her a reason. There'll come a time when it's right to let her know about us."

Fine words, but she didn't believe them. Martha had to look away to hide the threatening tears.

"Are you crying? Why are you sad? We'll find a way."

He hugged her to him.

"We don't have to say anything now. They'll surely say we're too young, and that's true."

Releasing her, he pulled back just enough to slip one knuckle beneath her chin and lift it so that he could see her face.

"We must make Mother see the

rightness of it. Papa will be easy enough. And I'm certain Nana will stand by us. We'll just have to think out what we do. And be careful."

That wasn't new, Martha thought. She was forever mindful of what she was doing if Rebecca was anywhere around. But till then, she hadn't thought about how she acted around Charley. They'd never seemed to need words to understand what each was thinking or cared about. Now, everything seemed different. At least, if they were careful and luck was with them, they could take pleasure in this new-found secret they shared. With a laugh, she brushed away the tears.

"I'm not sad. I'm happy. For so long I've feared you would...Oh never mind. I must go."

She stood on tiptoe and kissed him lightly on the lips, but before she could turn to leave, Charley's arms were around her again, his lips on hers. Forgetting all else, their lips explored the familiar, yet new terrain of much loved faces. Despite the bolt of linen she still clutched between them, Martha could feel him growing hard against her, her own body responding with a frightening need.

"No, Charley. We can't do this." She turned her head away. "Not now."

He let go of her and stepped back, a flash of anger in his blue eyes that she remembered from times past.

"Don't be angry. This isn't the right time. I've already been away too long. If we're not careful, Annie will be up here looking for me."

"Why must you always be right?"

"Because I usually am."

With a grin, she slipped past him, but stopped, just out of reach.

"Let's think on it and find a way to meet. At least we can talk and none the wiser."

She cocked her head.

"Can't we?"

"Aye." He sighed.

"That we can do. Go, now."

For a moment they stood looking at each other, feeling strange and searching for the person they once knew in the one they'd just discovered. Without another word, Martha left, taking care to close the door quietly.

XV

A Fateful Encounter

John Randolph was often the subject of public room gossip. He'd once prospered in the East India trade, it was said, but had been brought low by his scandalous dealings. The look of him, Martha thought, said as much. His wig was ill-kept, his waistcoat well-worn, and his shirts far from fresh. Several of the wenches had warned her about him.

"He's a mean one." Several of the serving wenches warned her.

"If he's far gone with drink, don't get near him."

She gave their warning little thought. He wasn't the only customer who took liberties. The first time he attempted to lift her skirts, she made light of it and easily stepped out of his reach. The next time, he pulled her onto his lap and grabbed her breast. His pinch wasn't playful. Nor was her slap that reddened his cheek. His surprise gave her just enough time to twist out of his grasp.

"Looks like you've met your match, John."

His drinking companion clapped him on the back and laughed as others at the table joined in.

"We'll see about that."

Feigning indifference, Randolph turned back to his tankard of ale.

****

"Martha!"

Rebecca's summons called Martha to her from across the taproom and shoved a bottle of wine and a glass into her hands..

"We've a new lodger just come in and he's ordered this sent up. There's no one else. He's in the corner room.."

"Come!"

The man's command was an imperious bark. Martha cautiously pushed the door open. The gentleman was standing, his back to the door, fanning himself by the open window. Hanging loosely from his shoulders to his slippered feet was a long, cream-colored silk gown adorned with a faded cascade of vines and flowers. A similarly-patterned cap covered his wigless head of short, unkempt hair.

"Well, don't just stand there, girl."

John Randolph turned away from the window.

"Come here."

184

His face had the red, mottled look of one overly fond of drink. As the door clicked shut behind her, Martha realized who he was. He recognized her too. His thin lips curved in a sneer.

"We've met before."

"Yes Sir."

She took a step back toward the door.

"I'm glad to see they've replaced that other one. Too much meat on her bones. What do they call you?"

"Martha, Sir."

"How old are you, Martha?"

"Seventeen, Sir."

She didn't like his smile or the way he looked at her.

"Put that here."

He snapped the fan shut, pointing it toward the table by his side and the tray with the remains of his dinner. She avoided his eyes, but was uncomfortably aware that he was watching her intently as she carried the bottle to the table and put it down. She was close enough to take in the rank smell of his body.

"Will you share some of this fine wine with me, Martha?"

"No, thank you, Mr. Randolph. I can't. I'm needed below."

"Come now, I'm sure they can spare you for a while. I can make it worth your while."

"Truly, Sir, I have work below."

She took a step back, but he moved with surprising swiftness and grabbed her right arm.

"See here, what I have for you."

He opened his loosely tied gown, revealing a pale body and full evidence of his manhood rising from its dark mat of hair. His lip curled at her look of revulsion. Pulling her toward him, he took her left wrist and thrust her hand toward his crotch.

"What? You think you don't like this? How can you know unless you try it? I assure you, many a fine lady has been well pleased."

Before she could snatch her hand away, it brushed against hot flesh. She shoved back, but his hold on her right arm was firm as he twisted it behind her and drew her close.

"Be still, you little slut! I'm sure your Mistress Rawley didn't send up one like you just to deliver a bottle of wine."

"You've no reason to say such a thing. This isn't that sort of place. I've just come with your wine."

He swayed against her and Martha realized how drunk he was. She renewed her struggle. Twisting and turning, she threw him off balance. Breaking his hold, she fled to the door. Behind her, she heard him laugh.

"You value yourself too highly for a common trollop."

From the direction of his voice, she knew he wasn't following and looked back. John Randolph's eyes were hard.

"There'll come a day when you'll regret not taking my offer."

In the empty hall, Martha sought the wall's support until she could get her trembling legs to carry her to the storeroom at the end of the hall. Inside, she leaned against the closed door scrubbing her hands on her skirt. But there was no getting the sour, sweaty smell of him off her. Or the shame of it.

In all the times she'd turned aside mens' roaming hands, none of them, not even the most insistent, had left her feeling so dirty and humiliated. When she could finally bring herself to leave the storeroom, she ran downstairs.

Though she badly wanted to tell someone, she didn't. Who could she tell? The wenches would be all ears and sympathy. Rebecca would surely say it was her fault. Worse yet, Charley would go after Randolph and possibly get himself killed. And Mistress Chinn needed no more worries where she was concerned. She was relieved when no one seemed to notice anything amiss. That night, she lay awake, plagued by thoughts of John Randolph.

At dawn, the next morning, Annie had to call her, hovering about as Martha dragged herself out of bed.

"You worried me, not getting up as usual. Are you ailing?"

"No, nothing's ailing me. I just couldn't sleep. I'll be right along."

"You look like you need a good physick."

"What I need is to get to work."

Martha snapped at her and was immediately sorry.

"Pay me no mind."

She gave Annie a quick hug and headed into the kitchen. Breakfast preparations kept thoughts of John Randolph at bay until she was called out to the taproom. Praying she wouldn't have to face him, she couldn't breathe easy until she heard that he'd left London. Bound for Virginia reported the harried boy who'd helped get his baggage loaded into a carriage.

"Had nothin' to give me, not even thanks," said the boy.

"Good riddance, I say."

Amen to that thought Martha. She took a moment's mean pleasure imagining him staggering drunkenly up to the ship's deck where he was washed overboard.

XVI

Randolph's Revenge

Annie caught Martha outside the laundry room door and shoved a bundle of bed linens into her arms.

"It won't take a minute, but I ain't got a minute."

Her face was flushed, sleeves pushed above her elbows exposing arms reddened by lye.

"Mistress Rawley will have my hide if these don't get upstairs now. She told me a while back, then gave me a heap more to finish. She thinks they've already gone up. I don't know where Lilly's got to. It won't take you but a minute."

"I sent the boy round to find Lilly, but he says she's not at home. Which I don't believe. But there's no one else and the Mistress will be back here any minute now. I don't want her to find out Lilly's not here. She's a good girl and needs this work. I've told Lilly, there's plenty others can do what she does. She should be glad to have a place. But does she listen?"

Martha raised a hand to stop the flood of words.

Annie could have had these linens upstairs in the time it's taking her to complain about the girl.

She sighed. It wasn't the first time she or someone else had stood in for Lilly, but this, she vowed, would be the last time *she* did.

"And see if there's any dirty dishes to bring down."

The woman just can't stop.

It didn't take much for Rebecca to get things out of kilter, Martha thought as she climbed the stairs. In the room, she put the linens on top of a bureau but instead of dishes on the table, she saw a stack of books. The words etched in gold on the spine of the topmost one drew her closer.

Paradise Lost.

In the taproom, sailors were forever talking about this or that paradise. She liked the sound of the one they called Virginia. She tried to picture it from their descriptions, but most of those were of favorite pubs and back streets that offered other pleasures. She couldn't resist. Lifting the book, she rubbed her hand over the cool, smooth leather before she opened it. She read one line, then another, growing more and more confused and discouraged. There wasn't a word about

Virginia or any paradise she could picture. Like parts of Mistress Chinn's Bible, the words were strung together in strange combinations she had to struggle to understand.

Disappointed, she closed the book and was about to put it back when the chamber door opened. As John Randolph strode into the room, she froze, the book forgotten in her hand.

"So, we meet again."

Martha's breath caught in her throat at the sight of him and the glint of triumph in his hard eyes.

"And what have we here? Thought you'd steal that, did you?"

A few long strides brought him to her side. Grabbing her arm, He snatched the book from her.

"How fitting."

"No, Sir."

Martha tried to keep her voice steady.

"I wasn't stealing it. I was just looking at it."

"And why would a girl like you be interested in a book except to steal it? You'd reap a pretty penny from this one."

"I would not steal it, Sir."

Martha tried to twist her arm out of his grasp, but this time, he wasn't drunk. His look was cool and calculating.

"So you say. But come, Martha, we had some business before that wasn't concluded to my satisfaction."

Without looking away or letting go of

her, he put the book on the table.

"We can settle that now, and I'll forget what you were about to do."

"I wasn't going to do anything. I just brought up your fresh linens and thought to look at the book."

"Don't play me for a fool, girl. Come, now, we can put a much better end to this."

He pulled her toward the high canopied bed at the far end of the room and shoved her back against it, pinning her there with the weight of his body.

"Be still, damn you!"

Leaning back, he slapped her with a force that left her head spinning and the taste of blood in her mouth. The blow knocked the fight out of her and gave Randolph the seconds it took to reach across the bed to pull off the sash of a dressing gown he'd flung there. In a practiced motion, he quickly wound it around her wrists, shoved her to the floor, and tied her bound hands to the leg of the bed.

Martha fought the pain in her head to clear it and think how to stop him.

"The Rawleys will have the constable after you."

Randolph's look was cold as he turned to the table to snatch a napkin from his dinner tray. Grabbing her chin, he forced her jaw open and stuffed the waded linen into her mouth.

"Maybe next time you'll know to keep your mouth shut."

He straightened to shed his waistcoat

and toss it on the bed. Unbuttoning his breeches, he quickly had them off and sent them after the coat.

"Do you think they'll believe you ... or me when I tell them how you offered yourself to me? Came up here lifting your skirts and tempting me beyond all reason. How could I resist? It's you the constable will be coming for. Now, be still. Unless you want this to hurt more than it ought to."

Helpless and frightened almost beyond reason, Martha pulled uselessly at the sash binding her hands. But one look up at Randolph's hairy legs and what rose above them turned her fear to anger and revulsion.

As bad as what he had in mind was, Randolph wasn't going to kill her. She'd make sure he wouldn't have an easy time of it. When he bent toward her, she brought both legs up and kicked catching him square in the gut. He doubled over with a grunt. His hold on the side of the bed was all that kept him from falling.

"You're going to pay for that."

Randolph's words came in gasps between clenched teeth.

Martha had a fleeting glimpse of his fist as it drove into her jaw. For a moment there was nothing but darkness, then a throbbing pain in her head and his hands roughly shoving her skirts up around her waist. He fell on her with the full weight of his body and his foul breath in her face. Then, there was only a searing pain that went on and on and grew until her screams, trapped in her throat by the wad of linen, nearly strangled her. The pain didn't stop when he stopped and pulled away. Panting, he sat back on his haunches with a look of malicious satisfaction.

"So, I'm the first. It's been a while since I've had the pleasure. That's good. There'll be no disease. You'll not leave me with a reminder of this."

The sight, the stench of him made Martha want to retch. Fighting to prevent it, she wildly twisted her head from side to side.

Randolph grabbed her chin and forced her to look at him.

"Vow not to make a sound and I'll take that from your mouth."

She closed her eyes and nodded. When he yanked the cloth from her mouth, she choked and took her first full breath. One, two, three more deep breaths helped to clear her head. As he stood, Randolph shook out the napkin and shoved it between her legs, then turned to the sash binding her wrists. Cursing when its knots wouldn't give way easily, he turned to his writing case on the bureau for a penknife. After he'd cut her loose, he stood looking sadly down at the butchered sash.

"That was a regrettable loss."

With a shake of his head, he dropped the pieces on the floor and stepped away from Martha.

Rubbing her chafed wrists, Martha pushed herself up, fumbling hastily for the napkin to stop the bloody mess that ran from her and onto the floor. She could do no more than hold the rag in place until a wave of dizziness passed and was barely aware that he'd left her side. When she could look up again, she saw that he was at the wash basin across the room. Her head had begun to clear when he returned.

"There's more water in the pitcher." He pointed to the wash stand. "Go make yourself presentable. And not a word of this when you go below. No one will believe you anyway. Do you understand?"

Martha stared at him, struggling to understand what he was saying, what had just happened. She wanted to shut it out, but the pain in her head and nether parts wouldn't allow it. She nodded.

"Say it!"

Her lip was swollen and tasted of blood. It was all she could do to move her aching jaw to speak.

"I won't say anything."

"Now, get up."

Slowly, on trembling legs, she used the bed post to pull up. Willing herself to stand straight, she stumbled to the wash stand. She took a quick peek in his direction but he was busy getting dressed. Even though he wasn't paying attention, his very presence made her feel dirty. She dropped the bloody napkin on the floor. Trying foolishly to hide herself she bunched her skirts under one arm and used the bath sheet he'd discarded to scrub everywhere she could reach.

She had to get his filth and the stink of him off of her, anything that would let people know what had happened. She could only guess what she looked like. One last length of sheet hung on a rod by the washstand. Quickly, she folded it lengthwise, tucking one end under her waistband in front, the other in back, then let her petticoats drop. Her mouth tasted of blood. She could imagine what she looked like and one look at her skirt told her there'd be no hiding the stains.

Across the room, Randolph had reached the same conclusion. He came back to where she stood and walked slowly around her.

"That won't do. There'll be questions. Stay there."

When he returned from the bureau he had two notes in his hand.

Martha flinched as he reached toward her.

"Be still. I'm just going to get rid of some of that blood."

Slowly, he used the bills to wipe her bleeding lips and then, a bloody section of her kerchief. Satisfied that they were well covered, he stepped back.

"Now let me look at you."

He walked around her, studying her as if she were a piece of furniture.

"Yes, that will do."

He came to a stop in front of her and

196

waved the bloody notes in her face.

"You value yourself too highly and are going to be sorry you did. When I'm done with you, you'll find that you're not worth the least portion of one of these notes you were trying to steal."

"You know I did no such thing!"

"And who's to take the word of a common wench over mine?"

There was no mirth in his satisfied grin as he grabbed her wrist.

"How can you say I took them? No one here will believe you."

He shook the bills in her face.

"They'll believe your blood on these. It'll be gaol for a thief like you."

Jerking her after him through the door, Randolph dragged her roughly toward the stairs to the public room, yelling for someone to fetch a constable.

Dizzy with the horror of what was happening and the pain in her head, Martha struggled to keep from falling. At the bottom, her head cleared at the sight of Rebecca Rawley advancing across the room toward them,

"What is the meaning of this?"

She scowled at Martha.

"Look at you. What have you done?"

"Nothing. He's the one. He..."

"Mistress Rawley, will you send for the constable?"

Randolph managed to sputter, his face red with an anger he'd nurtured on the way down the stairs.

"I want this girl taken to the magistrate straight away."

"To a magistrate? What's she done, Sir?"

"I caught her stuffing these in her bodice."

He shook the crumpled notes at Rebecca.

"Took them right off my table. Lucky for me I looked around when I did. She'd have made off with them for sure. She's a hellion, that one. As you can see, I had to take them from her by force."

He jerked Martha's arm as she tried to pull away.

"Be still, slut."

By that time, several servants had gathered and the few men at the bar turned to watch.

Rebecca turned on Martha.

"How could you do such a thing?"

"I didn't. He's lying. He..."

What am I doing? Why am I defending myself?

Martha stared in disbelief at Rebecca.

How can she even think...?

But she knew. Rebecca could.

That and the sudden memory of what Randolph had done struck her with a force that froze the words in her throat. All she could do was shake her head and fight to stem her tears of frustration, anger, and growing despair. Her relief was overwhelming when she saw

Hannah pushing through the servants and customers who'd gathered behind Rebecca

"What's going on here? Take your hands off that girl."

Hannah's voice shook with anger as she shoved her daughter aside.

Randolph tightened his hold on Martha's arm and gave her a jerk.

"As I was telling Mistress Rawley here, this wench is a thief. I grant you, I should not have left money lying about, but I had no reason to suspect thievery in a place like this."

"I never touched those notes. I never even saw them. I don't need money. He's lying."

Randolph turned to Martha with a nasty grin that only she understood.

"So, you want the whole dirty business to come out do you?"

He gave her arm a vicious twist and turned back to Rebecca, intentionally ignoring Hannah.

"I was prepared to pay her for her...ah, service, shall we say. As I'm sure you expected. I must admit I was surprised that you employed such wenches here."

There was a collective intake of breath among those within hearing.

"How dare you!"

Rebecca's accusatory glare took in Randolph and Martha.

"This is a proper house. I will have nothing of that sort here. How could you do such a thing?"

Martha stared at Rebecca in disbelief. What was she doing?

She should be defending me. Not the Black Horse.

Rebecca seemed as if she'd hadn't heard a word she said.

"What you suggest is despicable."

Hannah stepped in front of her daughter, forcing Randolph to acknowledge her.

"We've never had such a thing here. Not until you came into this house. I don't know what happened, but what you say can't be true. Release her, Sir. She won't go anywhere."

"You may have confidence in her, Madam, but I don't."

Hannah reached for Martha's arm, but Randolph yanked her away.

"Oh, no, you don't. You're not making off with her."

Hannah rounded on him, an imposing figure even if a head shorter and a woman.

"I will hear what she has to say. And what you've done to her. Let her speak."

Randolph renewed his hold on Martha arm, but nodded. She took a deep breath and willed the words to come.

"Oh Ma'am. I never touched those notes, didn't even see them until... Please, Ma'am, don't make me say more. Not here."

She looks just like a cornered animal. Lord, what has he done?

But Hannah knew the answer. It was

there for all to see in the stains and disarray of Martha's clothes. She had to get her away from that man, to find out how badly she'd been hurt.

"Let her go, Sir. Mistress Rawley and I will speak to her in private."

"If she has more to say, let her tell it to the magistrate. She's staying right here."

Wildly Martha tried to think of something to say that would end the horror, but it was too late. Billy Nunn was charging back through the public room with the constable in tow.

"Ah, good, you're here at last."

Randolph tossed Billy Nunn a coin and shoved Martha toward the constable.

"Take this wench. I caught her trying to make off with these."

He held the notes out to the constable."

"What's all that blood?"

Constable Dugan wasn't about to touch them.

"She fought when I tried to get them away from her and I fear I had to strike her rather hard. She'd hidden them in her bodice."

He poked a finger at Martha's chest.

"I did no such thing, Mr. Dugan."

The man knew her. Martha was certain he'd listen at least, but her words were drowned out as Randolph continued his angry tirade.

"I caught her red-handed."

Hannah couldn't remain silent any

longer. She pushed forward.

"You know this girl, George Dugan. And you know she wouldn't do such a thing. What she says is the truth."

"You waste my time, constable. Do your duty."

Though John Randolph wasn't as heavy as George Dugan, he was a taller, more formidable man. The constable shrugged. He wouldn't look at Hannah.

"You must come with me, girl."

Pulling manacles from his belt, he clamped them on her wrists.

"You have no need of that. She'll go with you."

Martha could only nod. She felt numb except for the rough iron bracelets already scraping her wrists.

"Sorry, Ma'am. It's what I must do in all cases. Come along now."

Clearly uncomfortable, he didn't look at Martha as he pulled on the chain, forcing her to follow him out of the Black Horse. Her last glimpse of the inn was of the tables full of staring men. With a mocking wink, Billy Nunn raised his tankard.

XVII

Newgate Prison

"Out of the way! Make way!"

Order in hand, Dugan dragged Martha out of the magistrate's office to his cart waiting in the street. The constable made the most of his authority. He and his charge quickly collected a crowd of street urchins in their wake.

"Snatched a purse, did she?"

"Sellin' watered ale, I'll wager."

"Or somethin' else..."

The boys winked and laughed and elbowed each other knowingly.

"Get on with you, or I'll be takin' you in, too!"

Dugan shoved Martha up on the seat as he hauled himself up beside her. With a sweep of his cudgel, he drove the boys back out of the way and slapped the reins on the pony's rump.

Martha had only a dim sense of cold stone walls and iron bars as they approached

Newgate's looming towers. After hitching the pony to a post, Dugan helped Martha climb down. To keep her at his side, Dugan's grip on her arm was firmer than necessary. It was some small relief when he let go to push open the prison's massive iron door. As it growled shut behind them, he grabbed Martha's arm again to face the raucous scene before them. Gathered in the cavernous, grey-walled room filled with a wild assortment of people fighting, crying, cursing, and kicking at the warder's snarling dog, which was soon sniffing and poking around the hem of Martha's skirt.

"Come on with you!"

Dugan swung his cudgel at the dog and ducked his head. He'd lost his swagger. It wasn't so long since he'd come close to being in Martha's place and was anxious to be done with her and his business at the prison that day. He jerked the chain to hurry her along. As the manacles cut into her wrists, Martha pulled back. Dugan's more vicious yank nearly pulled her off her feet as he stalked on without a backward glance.

Desperately she grabbed the chain to ease the pain of the iron bracelets' cutting into her wrists and hurried to keep up with him. She was glad he didn't look at her. She was near tears. The iron rubbing her wrists raw not only sharpened her fear but was yet another painful reminder of how badly Randolph had used her. But all thought of the pain left her as they were suddenly in the midst of the crowd clamoring for a moment with the keeper.

The dog had left her and was in a tangle of teeth and flying fur with another mangy prison dog at the far end of the dingy entry hall. A few of the men and women waiting there passed the time by making wagers and cheering them on. Many more, like Martha, were wrapped in their own private misery. Few had hope of gaining release.

She struggled to keep up with her captor as she dodged groping hands and tried to ignore hissed propositions coming at her from all directions. Could they tell what had happened to her, she wondered as she pulled away from a grimy hand. When at last they reached the warder, he barely looked up from his ledger, took the magistrate's paper, then nodded with a grunt toward a place off to the side.

"Wait there. The turnkey'll be out to fetch 'er."

Dugan fidgeted as they waited, nervously scratching his chest under his dirt-greyed shirt and running his fingers through hair that sweat had plastered to his forehead.

"You gonna just stand there?"

The turnkey shouldered his way through the people around Martha and the constable. He nodded toward the manacles.

"Get them off her."

Startled, Dugan jumped. Flustered by the guard impatiently jangling a large ring of keys, he fumbled clumsily with the locks. When they fell away, he nudged Martha toward the jailor, gathered up the chains, and hurried off without a backward look. Handing Martha a threadbare blanket, the man shoved her roughly toward a stone-arched opening at the far end of the room.

"Move along."

He was close behind, poking her with his club every step or so as they went deeper into the dungeon's cavernous interior. Her nostrils filled with the stench of rotting humanity. No matter how fast she walked, she couldn't escape the man's prodding.

From cell doors came woeful entreaties for money; from deeper within, screams, howls, and other outpourings of anger and abuse beat in her ears. At last, he stopped her in front of a barred door. Martha strained to see what she could of the cell beyond, but its battered lanterns revealed little of the crowd of women and children contained within its dingy grey stone walls.

"Move yer besotted arses."

The jailor jabbed his club through the bars, prodding women who didn't move away fast enough. Cursing the man and each other, they moved back just enough for Martha to escape the iron door as it clanged shut behind her. She had no time to think before the women were on her, snatching her cap and scrabbling for the few bone pins that fell from her hair. Her apron went next.

Hitting and punching, she fought her

way to a nearby wall and turned with her back to it. Through the screen of her hair, loosened from the restraining cap and pins, she saw a blur of angry faces and open mouths full of rotten teeth. They reminded her of a pack of street dogs. She'd once seen such a pack tear a cat to bloody scraps of fur, skin, and jagged bones. She couldn't save it, but went after the dogs, ignoring their bared teeth and snarling mouths, kicking, grabbing ruffs, flinging them away, and throwing stones as they fled.

This felt too much the same. But this cat could fight back. Quickly, she covered her head with her arms, ducked, then came up fast, driving one fist beneath the chin of the nearest woman and catching another in the chest with her elbow. Barely noticing the pain, she spun again. And again she struck out blindly, fists, elbows, knees, connecting with as much force has she had left in her and an anger that, till then, she'd held at bay. Then, suddenly, she was all alone in a small space, the women standing back just out of her reach. Bless you, Charley, she thought, taking deep breaths to steady herself. He'd taught her a thing or two about fighting.

"Leave her be."

A tall woman with a gruff voice and a tangle of wild grey hair stepped forward. She nodded at Martha.

"They'll leave you alone now."

The woman turned slowly and looked at the others, who shuffled back a bit more.

"Go now," she said to Martha.

"Find yourself a place."

She pointed off to her left and the nearest women began to step back. Martha didn't move at first, then took a tentative step, no more sure she could walk than she was of what she might walk into as the closest woman stepped away. Her body was such a bundle of pain, she couldn't distinguish the afflicted parts.

"I said, go!"

The woman nudged Martha in the direction she'd pointed, and, as she walked forward, the women made way for her. Beyond them, the clutter of bodies presented obstacles at every step, but none moved to stop her. She could think of nothing but to keep going, hoping she'd find some small unpeopled spot.

As near as she could tell, every bit of open space was taken by women sitting or lying on the stone floor. Most had no more than a prison blanket, but some had grimy bed ticks. A few had commandeered space enough for cots, pillows, stools, and assorted belongings. They huddled in small clusters around games of dice and cards.

Martha wasn't sure if it was the fear or the fighting or the stale, foul-smelling air that made it hard for her to catch her breath. But for the moment, there seemed to be no immediate threat. Most of the women didn't even look up as she passed.

When she finally reached a buttress, she

stopped to lean against it and was again conscious of the pain that enveloped her whole body. Trying to ignore it, she let her eyes adjust to the dim light as she scanned the cavernous room. Its dirt-streaked stone walls contained a crush of women, girls, and scrawny children crammed together in a space never meant to hold so many. Somehow she'd have to find a place among them.

Cautiously, she followed a meandering path around the edge of the room and was uncomfortably aware that several women were eying her with calculating looks. A tug at her skirt caused her to look around, then down into the dirty face of a small boy, no more than waist high.

"A penny for a bit of bread, Mistress."

He held out a small, grimy palm. His look was pitiful, pleading.

"I wish I could, but I have no money."

"Bitch!"

A snarl twisted his pinched face as he landed a sharp-toed kick on her ankle and a glob of spit on her skirt, then swaggered off amidst cheers and laughter. Stunned, Martha looked down at the spittle and a muddy smudge left by the boy's hand on her skirt. Suddenly it struck her, why the women were watching her so intently, why the boy came begging. Though not fine, her clothes were well made and too clean compared to the dingy rags that most of the cell's occupants wore.

Only a few, she realized, were

adequately clothed. And they seemed to command the choicest spots where the floor slanted up to a wall out of the filthy slime that coated much of the cell floor. Not only did they rest high and dry, they appeared to have cohorts to help defend their territory, however small and mean. The rest of the cell's occupants, the weaker ones were a shifting population that held only a tentative claim to patches of damp stone floor in the center of the room and on its darkest, coldest fringes.

Martha continued on her way, searching for a relatively safe place to settle. Finally, on the far side of the cell, she was surprised to see an empty patch. It lay between a snoring, gap-toothed hag and a girl, perhaps her own age, sitting with her back to the stone wall, her arms hugging her knees to her chest. As Martha approached, the girl looked up with wide frightened eyes.

"My name's Martha Pratt. Might I take this place?"

"Tis no business of mine."

The girl's voice was barely above a whisper. She looked away, then lowered her head to her knees.

"I guess it comes to that."

She paused just long enough for the girl to give some sign she'd heard, then added.

"I mean you no harm."

Silence.

So be it.

Martha's own emotions were so spent

that she had none to spare on a pitiful stranger. Turning aside, she folded her blanket and claimed the empty patch of stone floor, lowering herself to sit with her back to the wall. She was careful to leave as much space as she could between herself and the wreck of a woman to her right.

She couldn't imagine curling up to sleep and decided it best to sit with her back against the wall as did the girl and several others. She pulled her knees up, tucking her skirt more closely around her legs to keep it away from the damp floor and the woman who gave off an overwhelming stink of piss and worse.

Before long, Martha thought bitterly, her own clothes would look and smell as bad as everyone else's. And likely that wouldn't be the worst of it. Numbed by everything that had happened since she opened her eyes that morning, Martha stared out over the crowd of women ranting at each other or at the children scrabbling freely among them.

A few who were ill or had no fight left simply wandered around to no purpose or stood vacant-eyed in the middle of the room. That was safer, Martha guessed, than trying to sit or lie down out there. Here and there, a heap of rags suggested someone drunk or ill who'd collapsed and been kicked or dragged out of another's way.

Then the horrible reality of where she was swept over her. Even if she dared close her eyes to shut out the wretchedness around her, the cold, the dank floor, the rough stone wall at her back allowed no escape from the despair and disbelief that gripped her. Stone, filth, blood. This couldn't be happening.

But it was. The pain in her head and in every part of her body was a constant reminder of the attacks that drove her to that miserable plot of stone floor. Flexing her fingers, she gingerly touched their blood-encrusted knuckles and hoped there were women somewhere else in the cell nursing their own cuts and bruises.

As light began to fade from the cell's narrow windows, sections of the room disappeared into darkness remedied only by the feeble glow of a few lanterns. She was relieved that one of those was close enough to offer some protection from the shadows' dangers. Beside her, the girl crumpled into a heap on her side, curled as tightly as she could manage on the small patch of floor covered by her scrap of blanket.

Suddenly, Martha was very tired. Slowly, tentatively, she curled as the girl had, her knees bent, facing the room, her feet toward the woman on her other side. She fought to keep her eyes open, slipping between dreams and wakefulness, one condition no better than the other.

Throughout the seemingly endless night, she eased her aching body by alternating one side, then the other, against the wall, until dawn's sickly light struggled to brighten the sooty windows. Coming upon the heels of the previous day's and night's waking nightmares, the fear and uncertainty she faced made the prospect of that morning and the coming days unimaginably grim.

When the hag beside her flung out an arm and struck her, Martha was pulled abruptly into the immediate present. She scrambled to her feet just as the wretched woman pitched forward, then flopped back, her heels drumming the floor.

"Blast!"

Martha turned to look down on the pitiful creature. She'd suddenly gone still, mouth slack, eyes rolled back in her head.

"It's the devil."

The girl spoke so softly, Martha wasn't sure she'd heard.

"What?"

"The devil's taken her. She's sufferin' the torments of hell. That's what *they* say."

She nodded toward the center of the room where silence had fallen among the women closest to them.

"Three days, I guess, she's been here. Havin' more and more of them fits. That's why none has settled by her. They won't come near, but I figure that's a good thing."

"It is that."

Martha had to agree as she bent to look more closely at the woman.

"She won't be keeping them away much longer. She's dead."

The girl turned disbelieving eyes to peer at the woman.

"How can you tell."

"I've seen plenty dragged from the river, or turned up dead on the street. They've got a look…"

Martha reached out with the toe of one shoe and lifted the woman's arm where it lay on the floor and let it drop limply again to the stones.

"Oh, no!"

Martha fumbled for her apron only to remember it was gone. Instead, she cupped her hands to cover her nose and voiced the obvious. She could hear someone calling for the warder.

"Loosed her bowels."

Beside her, the ashen-faced girl had risen to cringe against the wall like a beaten dog.

"They'll have our place in a trice."

"Not easily, they won't."

Martha put an arm around the girl's narrow shoulders.

"Stay close to me."

They waited for what seemed like a long time before the warder appeared accompanied by a male prisoner with a hand cart and a bucket full of water strong with the smell of vinegar. With a stream of curses delivered through kerchiefs they'd tied over their noses and mouths, the two men loaded the body. That done, the warder snatched the remains of an apron from the old woman and handed it and the bucket to Martha.

"Get to work."

He pointed at the bloody brown stain on the floor where the woman had been and left.

Martha was glad it was many hours since she last ate. She couldn't control her retching as she used the vinegar-soaked rag to push the putrid mess toward a spot away from where she and the girl had been sitting.

"Hang it all."

She straightened to look out into the room where several women were watching her. Leaning back against the wall, she reached up under her quilted petticoat and undid the ties that held her embroidered linen petticoat and stepped out of it. She shook it out, making sure others could see.

"I've a fine linen petticoat here. I'd hate to use it on this mess. Any of you want to trade?"

The chorus of "ayes" ended abruptly.

"I'll have it."

Once again the tall woman stood before her. Just one glaring look over her shoulder silenced the few bold enough to object.

"You're a smart one."

The woman spoke through a kerchief she held over her nose.

"I could use a fresh petticoat."

She fingered the material in Martha's hand.

"A fine one. What put you in here?"

"I was wrongly accused…"

"Weren't we all. No matter. What's your name?"

"Martha. Martha Pratt."

"What place you from, Martha Pratt?"

"Wapping. The Black Horse."

"I know of it. There'll be someone coming to see to your welfare, I'd wager."

"Might be."

The day's events had shaken Martha's confidence in any such possibility.

"You see they bring you money, or something of value, I'll see nobody bothers you."

Martha looked at her long and hard, trying to judge the truth of the woman's words. The woman must have guessed her thoughts.

"Ask 'em."

She tossed her tangled mop of hair back toward those behind her.

"My word's good, ain't it?"

"Aye!" Several women hastily spoke up.

"They call me Mag. Margaret in the warder's book to those as need to know."

Martha reached behind her to pull the girl forward.

"You'll see they don't bother my friend either."

"Friend, huh? You expect a lot for one petticoat."

Martha remained silent and held the woman's gaze.

With a quick nod of her head, Mag

beckoned to a nearby woman who produced two ragged prison blankets.

"It suits us, too, if you get that cleaned up. Use those. I come back and smell shit, you'll pay with your other petticoat."

That said, she swung around and followed a path that opened as she crossed the room.

Rolling up her own blanket, Martha gave it to the girl to hold and got to work as fast as her stomach would allow. She used one of the blankets soaked in vinegar water to scrub the place where the woman died and as much space around it as she could before the cloth was too foul to do more. She went back over the floor with the second blanket and the last of the water until all she could smell was vinegar. Finally, she gathered all the rags and put them in the empty bucket.

For a moment, she stood weighing her chances of getting to the cell door and back and would find the girl and her place as she'd left them. But if Mag meant what she said, Martha figured her chances were good. She turned to the girl.

"I'm going to get rid of this and get fresh straw. I'll be back shortly. Don't move from this spot."

There seemed to be no likelihood that the girl would. She hadn't moved since Martha began to clean. As she was turning to leave, Martha stopped.

"I don't know your name."

"Bett. Bett Williams."

Her voice was hardly more than a whisper.

"Will you come back?"

Martha had to lean close to understand what she was saying.

"Aye. Don't worry. I'll be back."

For a moment the girl lost her worried look. Martha smiled her reassurance, but wished she felt more certain. At least saying it bolstered her own courage.

XVIII

Bett's Story

At the cell door, Martha set the bucket out of sight just inside before asking for the straw. She was well away and lost in the crowd of women when she heard the warder's angry curses at the discovery of the bucket and its foul contents. She was as relieved to see no one had moved in to take her place. Bett greeted her with wide-eyed disbelief.

"I told you I'd be back."

Once Martha had spread the straw over as much of the stone floor as she could, she shook out Bett's blanket and wrapped it around the girl's boney shoulders. As she pulled hers around her, Martha realized how very tired she was. Even the rock-hard floor was welcome when she lowered herself to sit. Despite her heavy quilted petticoat and woolen bodice, she was soon acutely aware of the stones' cold bite and the girl shivering beside her. Bett's linen shift, threadbare petticoat, and tattered blanket were no defense against the cold. Martha touched her shoulder.

"If we sit close, we'll be warmer."

The girl lifted her head with a puzzled look.

"Come closer. Here, like this."

Martha opened her blanket and her arm and pulled Bett close. She was surprised at how little substance there was to the girl, all sharp edges with nothing between flesh and bones.

"Bett. That's for Elizabeth, isn't it?"

"Aye, but Bett's all my mam ever called me."

"Does she come see you?"

"No, not once since they brought me here. She's glad to be rid of me."

Martha had to wait for a fit of coughing to subside before Bett continued.

"The older I got, the men weren't as eager to pay. I hated it and couldn't play at wanting to please them, however much she beat me."

Martha was glad that Bett couldn't see her face when she grasped what the other girl was saying. She was sure that Bett was younger that she was.

"How old were you then?"

"Twelve, I guess. But she'd been using me to get her money before that. Soon's I could go out alone and not get lost, she had me on the streets beggin'. She'd not let me come home till I had coins to give her. And if I wanted more than her leavings, I had to beg for food at shop doors. There was some saw I got a meal every so often, but I dared not tell my mam that. Other times, she acted like I was no concern of hers. Specially at night. She'd go after me with a switch if I come out from behind the coal bin to use the pot."

"Behind the coal bin?"

"That's where she put my pallet, so's the men who came at night wouldn't see me. Sometimes, I thought they was killin' her, and I had to cover my ears. And after a while, God forgive me, I almost hoped they was..." Bett's voice trailed off into a long silence as Martha sought something she could offer to fill it..

She'd seen women like Bett's mother in the streets of Wapping. Sometimes, if he didn't know better, a man would bring one into the taproom and maybe buy her a meat pie, but more likely a mug of rum or ale, before he went off to collect his payment.

Most of the time, the men with such women didn't get to stay long enough to eat or drink. Forever on the lookout for them, Rebecca Rawley would send Joseph or the bar man to run them off. The women left, screaming curses at the men who brought them and whoever was throwing them out.

Softly, Bett's voice brought Martha back from her memories.

"I've never told a soul about that."

She stiffened as Martha began to turn toward her.

"No don't. It's easier if I'm not looking at you. I'm thinkin' you don't know nothin' about that kinda thing."

"But I do. I lived my whole life in an alehouse."

"Is that where your mama is?"

"My mama died. Right after I was born. The Black Horse, that's where she was working when I was born."

Martha suddenly felt guilty about ever thinking *she* had a sorry lot in life. Now it didn't seem half bad.

"I don't know who my father was."

"Me neither. My mam didn't know. Whoever he was, she said, he wasn't worth the trouble he'd left her with."

"Mistress Chinn, who owned the Black Horse, was as close to a mother as I ever had. She raised me. She taught me to read and write and mend my clothes. She took care of the kitchen and the old taproom and I've been working there for a while now. ... well, I had been. That was the part of the Black Horse she started out with and she kept it, but she let her daughter, Mistress Rawley, add on to it. They made it a right smart inn offering food and lodging for gentlemen."

The thought of all she'd lost made Martha's words catch in her throat. Beside her Bett shook her head.

"My mam didn't teach me anythin' good like that."

Both girls were silent for a long time

before Bett continued, her voice low, her words coming faster the longer she talked.

"When my bleedin' started, I thought I was dying. It bloodied my skirt and I thought sure she'd beat me. So I couldn't understand why she was so happy when she found out, or why she went out and bought me a new dress and petticoat and laughed and pinched my tits when she saw they was growin'. Bout a week after the bleedin' stopped, I found out why she was so happy.

"One night, she dressed me in those new clothes and sat me up on her bed. Told me to wait and off she went. Wasn't long before she was back. She had a man with her and told me to do whatever he wanted. Then she just left. Didn't even look back..." Bett's last words trailed off in a sob.

"You don't have to go on."

Martha raised her hand to stop Bett from continuing. Hearing what happened to Bett, she knew, would bring back the memories of John Randolph that she fought so hard to shut out. But the tears in Bett's eyes and the intense look on her face begged Martha to listen. Bett had to tell it all now she'd got started. Martha nodded for her to continue.

"I been keepin' this to myself for too long, I guess. I didn't know how good it'd feel to let it out. If you've a mind to listen some more."

"Go on."

It wasn't easy to hear what Bett was saying, but it was better than returning to silence and her own thoughts.

"That time was the worst. My mam's beatin's were nowhere near as bad as that, but even worse was the shame of it. And, later, the things other men wanted to do. If I tried to stop them, they'd hit me. But if they left a mark, my mam would never let them come back... She saw they all paid, though... I never knew their names. Not a one of them."

"How'd you come to be here?"

"It weren't for that. One night, a year ago, I guess, a ha'penny fell out of a man's pocket and he didn't notice it in the bed. I took it and when he was gone, I went to my place behind the coal bin and hid it in a chink in the brick wall there. My mam was still sendin' me out during the day to beg. I took the coin with me. I walked a long ways to where no one would know me and tell my mam and bought me a bit of stew and some fine white bread with that ha' penny.

"After that, I started lookin' for ways to get at the men's money. I guess, 'cause I was young, they didn't think they had to be careful. I never took more than a few pence, not enough for most to notice. I didn't keep it around long, in case my mam took it in her head to go looking around my little corner. I only spent it on food, or a tot of ale ever so often, nothing I'd have to hide at home.

"I almost looked forward to the men comin' and the chance to get a penny or two that didn't go into my mam's purse. That was worth as much as anything I spent it on. But I was getting greedy, takin' more than pennies. I shoulda known I'd be no better at thievin' than at pleasin' the men.

"I guess it's been a month or more now, she come in with a man too much in his cups. He couldn't even get his britches off an' asked me to help. There was two guineas in a pocket of them britches and a gold watch. I don't know what possessed me to take those coins and the watch too. He didn't know they were gone until the next mornin' and he came back with the constable."

"They were accusing my mam, an' she was crying an' tearing her hair, saying it weren't her. For once, she was saying the truth. Course, they didn't believe her and were goin' to take her away. I shoulda let em.

"But I got scared. What would become of me all alone? Then, she was saying 'Bett, tell em. Tell em it weren't me. They'll hang *me*! But you're young. A child. They'll go easy on you. I'll tell em you didn't know what you was doing... Bett. Please! Do you want to see your ma hangin' from Tyburn Tree?'"

"She took me to see a hangin' once. I hope never to see such a horrible sight again. They had to pull on that poor woman's legs to stop her dancin' in the air. Much as I hated her, I couldn't let them do that to my mam. And I'd heard enough talk. I knew what she said was true about me. I went and got the watch and the two guineas from where I'd hid them under the scuttle, and all of a sudden, they were draggin' me off to gaol. I was crying and beggin' her to come and speak for me. She didn't say a word. Just stood there in the door watchin'."

By then, Bett was crying. Martha tightened her arm around the girl's boney shoulders. It was a wonder, she thought, that she hadn't already been carted out like that wretched woman. Just another nameless corpse to be dropped into a common grave.

Gradually, Bett's sobbing diminished. Martha eased her down to lie on the back half of the blanket where she fell asleep almost immediately. Sore and exhausted, Martha shifted her own position next to her so she could face the room. She wasn't about to turn her back on it.

She lay awake for a long time watching, feeling every inch of the stone floor that no amount of turning could make more comfortable. She didn't expect to sleep, but when, in the morning, women around her began to stir, Martha started awake. Slowly she pushed herself up, groaning with the pain of every move and a churning in her empty belly. Behind her, Bett was still asleep. A blessed escape, Martha thought, but returning from it made reality all the harder to take.

****

At first Martha wasn't sure what was causing the commotion at the cell door, but as the women began to return to their places with bowls and chunks of bread, she realized that the warder was passing out food. And she was hungry, hungrier than she could ever remember. No wonder her stomach was in turmoil.

"So, you've decided to join us?"

Mag stood back watching the women crowding forward.

"Here, I've saved you some of the swill they call food."

Martha hesitated, looking at the clump of hard bread and some disgusting mess in the bowl Mag held out to her.

"Don't be turning up that fine nose of yours. This is all you get if someone doesn't come with provisions. Or money. There's nothin' free in here. I've even got 'em to give you a double portion. I don't think that girl's had more than bread to eat. Doesn't even have a spoon."

"And you did naught to help her?"

"Figured there was no use in doin' that. That one's got no fight left in her. Anything I'd give her would be taken away soon as I turned around. It's enough to keep my own body and soul together. I got my boy to mind too. I think you met him..."

She grinned when she saw Martha's look of recognition and disgust.

"But if you got family or whatever comin' to help you, then, maybe you can take care of that one too. Meantime, you remember,

I'll be comin' round for an accountin' before too long."

She shoved the food into Martha's hands and handed her two bent pewter spoons.

"Don't let those outa your sight."

Martha's thanks and attempt at a smile got only a hard-eyed look in return.

"That ain't no gift. That's business. Let's call it a debt I'll be callin' in soon."

Martha took the food and spoons and turned without a word, praying that someone would indeed be coming from home. She found Bett awake and handed her a piece of the bread and the bowl and spoon.

"We'll have to share that. Mag got us a double portion. You eat first."

Bett shook her head and pushed the bowl back toward Martha who shook her head.

"Eat! I'll not sit by and have you die of starvation."

She tore the bread in half and kept a piece as she turned away.

"I'm going to find something to help get this down."

The warder was still at the door sloshing the allotted pint of ale into pewter mugs that the women held out to him. He gave Martha a full mug but refused to give her a second for Bett.

"She got one when she come in. That's all's allowed. Move on."

Martha finished her piece of bread, taking sips from the cup to get each bite down.

She wanted badly to drain the cup, but with the last of the bread and one more sip, she took the rest back for Bett. The girl was waiting, the half-empty bowl clutched with both hands in her lap.

"I guess they knew you'd be comin' back. Nobody tried to take this."

She lifted the bowl for Martha to take.

In exchange, she gave Bett the cup but after a large gulp, she insisted Martha take it back.

"You'll be wanting it after you eat that."

She gestured with her head toward the bowl. Just one small taste of the bowl's lumpy, grey porridge-like contents nearly made Martha gag. Bad as the food was, though, she was still hungry and had to stop the grinding in her belly. She took a deep breath and forced herself to take another mouthful. The lumps were small enough, at least, to swallow without chewing and releasing more of the bitterness that seasoned the heavy mix of peas and disgusting chunks of unidentifiable meat. Gratefully, she took the last swallow that Bett had left her in the mug.

Before settling down, she gathered the bowl, mug, and spoons, tucked them behind Bett and left to relieve herself. Her nose told her how to find the brimming bucket not far from where they sat. Only when she began gathering her petticoat around her waist did she remember John Randolph and what he'd done. The bath sheet she'd tucked in the waist of her skirt was still there. As well as the pain she hadn't given a thought to until then.

Quickly she looked up to see if anyone was watching, but the women around her were otherwise absorbed in their own business. Carefully she pulled away the sheeting. Relieved to see only small spots of fresh blood, she squatted and winced at the sting of her piss on still raw flesh. After folding in the bloodstained side of the sheet, she tucked it back in her waistband.

She vowed to pay attention to when next the waste bucket was emptied so that she could use it soon after and almost laughed when she was struck by a perverse thought of Mary Rawley trying to hide her bare nether parts and keep her lace trimmed petticoats from the muck. Bitterly she thought of the many times she wished she could get away from Mary Rawley but, at that moment, she would have welcomed doing the older girl's haughty bidding just to be out of that godforsaken hole.

XIX

Hannah's Visit

"Martha, get up. They're calling your name."

Bett nudged her awake.

"They're calling for you. Go quick."

Martha needed no urging. She could see Mistress Chinn standing with the jailor at the cell door. The man's cudgel had driven the women back enough for Hannah to enter. She stood trying to get her bearings, clutching the straw-filled bed tick for which she'd paid far more than it was worth.

She almost didn't recognize Martha. Above her begrimed petticoat and bodice, her kerchief was in disarray and a dark bruise marred one pale cheek. Martha's look of joy was clear though, and beneath the tangled mass of her hair, her eyes were bright with a familiar spark of defiance. Hannah hardly noticed when the jailor nudged her forward and slammed the cell door shut.

"Oh, my dear…"

"Wait. We can't talk here. Come with me. I've a place."

Martha extended a grimy hand to take her arm then quickly pulled it back and beckoned her to follow.

"Stay close behind me."

Hannah nodded. She intended to. Hugging the bed tick, she tried to ignore the tugs at her skirts, the dizzying stench of the place, and the sea of dirty, hollow-eyed women that moved grudgingly out of their way. Their slow progress through the crowded cavern of a room seemed to be getting them nowhere. Hannah was about to reach out to Martha to ask how much farther they'd have to go when the girl suddenly stopped and turned.

"This is where I sleep."

She indicated a ragged blanket on an open patch of stone floor, but couldn't look at Hannah.

"I wish you didn't have to come in here."

"Don't think of that, child. I wouldn't be anywhere else right now. And I hope we'll soon have you out of here."

She couldn't imagine trying to sit, much less sleep in the spot at their feet, and remembered the bed tick she carried.

"They said you'd be needing this."

She was heartened when Martha took it eagerly.

"That will be much better than the blanket they gave me. Now Bett and I will have more to keep us warm."

"See here, Bett, what we have."

She turned aside and dropped the bed tick beside a wretched girl who looked up from where she sat huddled behind her.

No more than a child.

Hannah was shocked at the look the hopelessness in the girl's eyes before she dropped her head back on her bent knees. What she saw of Martha was equally disturbing.

"This is no good. Let me have a look at you."

Hannah gently lifted her chin to confirm the bruise she thought she'd seen on the side of her cheek. She touched it lightly, frowning.

"What is this?"

"It's nothing ..."

"And this?"

Hannah pointed to another on the side of her neck, then took her hand to examine her bruised knuckles.

"It's the way of this place. I can take care of myself."

"Ah Martha, there's no justice in this. An unkind fortune has brought you here. And that vile man. There must be a way to set this right and get you out of here."

"I don't know what it can be. He ..."

Hannah raised a hand to silence her.

"I know. And I know he lied. He wouldn't speak to any of us, just gathered his things, and left before we could do anything.

William's making inquiries, but he tells me we can do nothing until the trial. None have anything good to say about that man. But I won't lie to you, he's got friends in high places. That worries me. But tell me child, are you badly hurt?"

"No more than you see, I think."

She looked away embarrassed.

"You don't have to say any more. And don't ever let anyone shame you. But you must tell me if... Oh bother. I must stop my blathering. You know there are many who want to help you."

Hannah shook her head in irritation.

Martha struggled to keep her feelings in check. She wanted to tell Mistress Chinn what had happened, but didn't know how. And what would it matter that John Randolph had raped her against his claim that she'd taken the twenty pounds?

Rebecca Rawley wouldn't be the only one who'd believe Randolph's lie. But when had Rebecca ever taken her side? Martha could imagine her gloating. If that despicable man had his way, she'd be rid of Martha well and good. Gone. Out of the way forever. Rebecca couldn't have devised a better outcome.

"You must be strong. You're not alone in this. It's all the talk in the public rooms. They know you wouldn't steal, whatever he might say. The taproom's been full of men wanting to know what's become of you. They don't believe a word that man said. And of course Charley raised a great commotion."

Martha had to smile. She could picture Charley stomping about, cursing as much as he dared, and raking his fingers through his hair til it was a wild tangle. He was good at raising a commotion. Hannah was heartened by Martha's smile.

At least they haven't taken all the fight out of her.

"I intended for Charley to come with me, but his mother found work he must do straight away. I couldn't wait. He said he'll be here as soon as he can."

Martha silently cursed Rebecca and looked away. Only then did she remember Bett. The girl had risen and was standing wide-eyed, watching them intently. Martha gently turned Hannah toward the other girl.

"This is Bett Williams. We're learning the ways of this place together."

Bett's awkward struggle to stand caused Hannah to put out a hand to stop her, but she quickly drew it back when the girl flinched.

"No, no, don't get up. I'll only be here a minute more."

So young. And like a frightened animal. God help her. What could that child possibly have done to be here?

Hannah nodded in Bett's direction and turned back to Martha.

"We must get you out of here. The warder spoke of cells where you can be away from all this. Look at you."

She took Martha's hand again.

"There will be worse than this the longer you stay here."

"That's too costly, and I'll be all right here for now."

Her words were spurred more by Bett's look of dismay than by reasoned thought.

"You mustn't worry about money. I'll speak to the warder."

"No, please don't. I hear, those cells can be dangerous. Anyone able to pay the price can gain admittance. No questions asked. Worse things can happen to women alone in private cells than are likely here."

"Well, I know you can use a shilling or two. And victuals."

"I do need a fresh petticoat. I gave my linen one to be sure I would sleep safely through last night."

She raised her hand, showing Hannah her bruised knuckles again.

"Fighting isn't the only way to survive in this place. Safety, here, comes with favors or coin and goods to barter. It seems there are laws here, too, and not so different from what's outside these walls. Please, don't bring anything of great value, just small things to trade."

Cunning, thought Hannah, almost relieved. *At least she's better able to survive this than poor little Bett. But for how long?*

Still wondering about that, she gave Martha a long hug and one last worried look as she said farewell. She left behind a shilling and six pence and the wool shawl she wore.

XX

Mag

Martha clutched the shawl to her face, taking in the scent of it as she watched Hannah disappear, then wrapped it around Bett. She was spreading the bed tick out when Mag swooped down demanding payment.

"That's too fine a shawl for the likes of her."

She reached down to feel the heft of the cloth covering Bett's thin shoulders.

"We had a bargain, did we not?"

"We still have that bargain. Leave the shawl. I've a shilling here. My mistress promises more. And food. I expect someone will be back before sundown. You'll be well satisfied."

Mag eyed her for an uncomfortably long time, then, with a quick nod, she stalked back across the room. Martha let out a great sigh of relief and sank onto the bed tick next to Bett.

"Ah, that's better."

Looking around she was surprised to see Bett's cheeks wet with tears.

"It is better, isn't it?"

"No one has ever done me such a kindness."

Sniffling, the girl lifted the edge of her skirt to wipe her eyes and nose.

"Is that your Mistress Chinn? She's a bit fearsome, but has a kind heart, I think."

"Aye, she does."

Martha had to look away. She couldn't start crying now or she'd never stop. Hannah hadn't held her like that since she was small enough to sit on her lap, and, then, not often. Martha sat back, stunned by a sudden thought.

It was late morning. Mistress Chinn came when the kitchen would be in a turmoil of dinner preparations. Martha couldn't remember her ever leaving it at that time of day. Mistress Chinn wouldn't even allow her own illness to keep her from overseeing dinner.

But she was here at just that time. For me.

Martha drew her knees up and hugged them tight to contain the urge to laugh and cry and scream in anger that she should discover now how much Hannah Chinn cared for her.

****

Near dusk, Martha was again called to the cell door. But that evening, the warder was standing alone outside. Had Mistress Chinn paid for her to move to another cell? She didn't dare let herself think that she was to be set free. As she neared the door a woman stepped in front of her.

"That's a fine one you got waitin' out there. Ain't yer gonna share 'im?"

The woman's grin revealed a mouthful of broken teeth. Puzzled, Martha said nothing, pushing her way around her and through others crowded around the door. The reason for the comment was clear once the jailor opened it.

Charley was standing back as far as he could, red-faced and angry, his knuckles white around the knotted end of the sack he carried.

"Ya got a guinea on ya, I could find ya a place, private like."

The warder's sideways look at Charley was equally obsequious and suggestive. Charley grabbed Martha's arm and pulled her into the hallway.

"I'll speak to her here."

Overwhelmed by a wild mix of feelings that lingered from the morning, Martha almost burst out laughing from the strain of the moment, its unreality, and the gruffness of Charley's voice. It was a voice he hadn't used in a long while, not since he was all swagger and bluster, trying to impress older boys on the street. The thought helped Martha swallow the lump rising in her throat.

"Have it your way."

The man gave an angry shrug and pushed Martha toward Charley who managed to catch her with his one free arm.

"Make it quick."

As the warder shuffled off in the direction of the cell door, Martha had already forgotten his presence. She was aware of nothing but Charley's arm around her shoulders, the beat of his heart beneath her hand where it came to rest against his chest, and the clean, male smell of him that was almost smothered by the stench of her own filthy clothes. She tried to push away, but his arm tightened around her for just a few seconds before letting her go.

"I wish I could carry you away."

His voice was a whisper, close to her ear.

"You shouldn't be here."

His cheeks were still flushed, his blue eyes angry and dark in the dungeon gloom.

"I went looking for that man Randolph. They say he left as soon as the constable took you off. I couldn't find him."

"It's a good thing you didn't. You might be near as tall as he is, but he's got a full four stone's weight on you."

"He sent a man to collect his things. Papa tried to get him to say where he was taking them, even offered him money, but he wouldn't say. That coward's afraid someone will find out he was lying. It was a foul thing he did to put you in here. Papa's been in a rage ever since. He's mad at himself for not knowing what a scoundrel Randolph is. Grandmother is going to the magistrate to see if she can get him to set this right."

"We haven't much time, let's not talk about that, now. Isn't there something better we can speak of? What have you there?"

Charley held out the sack and rolled his eyes toward the jailor.

"He wasn't going to let me see you, just leave this. Says I must come earlier. But a shilling got him to call you out so I could be sure you got it. He's had his filthy hands in it though. Said he had to check. I didn't see him take anything."

He looked toward the barred door and the women beyond.

"Grandmother said to use these provisions wisely but see you keep enough to give you some small comfort. Is it true, like she says, you'll be trading them to keep from being set upon in there?"

"That's the way of it. Let me see what you've brought before I carry it inside."

She quickly untied the neck of the bag, relieved to have something to do but fling herself back into his arms. Charley took the sack again and held it open so she could look through the contents. On top she was pleased to see a fresh linen petticoat. That would satisfy Mag for a while. Two large pieces of cheese, three crusty, round loaves of bread, and six hard-boiled eggs, made her mouth water, but the meat pie wrapped in a napkin at the bottom threatened to bring her to tears. As the savory smell of it reached her nose, she realized that the minute she carried it into the cell, she'd have the women swarming all over her. She lifted out the wrapped pie and handed the sack back to Charley.

"I thought I'd never taste one of these again. I'll have a time getting past that crowd at the door. They'll smell this the minute I step through and will be after me like a pack of dogs."

With shaking hands, she tore off a small piece of the pie and shoved it in her mouth, using a corner of the napkin to wipe away the juice running down her chin. She realized what she must look like and blushed

"Its shameful what you become after just a short time in here. I imagine dogs get better fare than they give us. I never thought for a second about the food we ate."

"Eat all of it. There'll be more coming."

She shook her head, but couldn't resist eating another small piece. Then, reluctantly, she wrapped the rest in the napkin.

"There's another needs it more than I do."

"Do you need money? Grandmother said she gave you some. I have a few pence."

Martha stopped his hand before he could draw the coins from his waistcoat pocket.

"I still have what she gave me. It's better I don't have much. Damn and blast!"

She looked beyond Charley to where the jailor's negotiations with one of the women seemed to have turned sour. He was headed back toward them with a stormy look.

"You've had enough time. Get on with you, now."

He waved his cudgel at Charley to indicate the long hallway out and grabbed Martha's arm, yanking her away.

"I'll be back. And Grandmother, too."

She had to strain to catch his words above the screech of the cell door's hinges as the warder dragged it open. She had just enough time to see him wave before she was shoved through the door.

The sob that rose in Martha's throat as Charley disappeared died as Mag appeared at her side, her fingers digging into Martha's wrist.

"We've got accounts to settle, you and me."

"I've not forgotten."

Martha pulled free of the woman's grasp and eased open her sack. Drawing out the petticoat she handed it over and dropped the sack on the floor behind her.

"That should do it."

"It's not just me you've got to please. Night's comin' on and there's others don't take lightly to someone not sharin'."

"I'll have to take my chances."

Martha picked up the sack and tied it shut. Mag followed her back to where Bett was waiting.

"You stay here, you don't stand a chance. If you come to the other side, I'll find a place for you, a penny a night. That's two pence if you're bringing her along."

Mag pointed at Bett hunched over her knees at their feet.

"And a part of what food you get."

"What if they don't bring more food?"

"You pay more. As long as you pay, you can stay. Is that meat I smell?"

"Aye, I've half a meat pie should buy us a night or two. I've bread, cheese, and boiled eggs. We'll be needing another bowl and a cup."

She reached into the bag, pulled out the pie, and tore off a piece. There was still nearly a half left. She wrapped it up again and handed it to Mag along with two eggs.

"Come round before dusk."

Mag rolled up the petticoat and shoved it with the eggs into the large pocket under her apron. Without even a look back she was off, a path opening for her to the other side of the cell. Martha handed Bett the last piece of pie and licked her fingers.

"You heard?"

Bett simply nodded. Her mouth was already full of crust and meaty filling, a look much like ecstasy on her pale face. Impatient for her to finish, Martha gathered up the bowl, spoons, and cup and put them in the sack. Dusk wasn't far off. Mag didn't have to tell her. Martha knew evil lurked in the dark. Much as

245

she wanted to, she didn't rush Bett, guessing it was a meal like nothing she'd ever had, certainly not in her mother's house.

At last, the girl was finished, licking her lips and fingers, chasing stray crumbs that had fallen to her lap. Rolling up their two blankets, Martha handed them to Bett, then, folded the sack in the bed tick. She hugged the cumbersome bundle to her and beckoned for Bett to follow.

Unlike Mag, they made slow progress, dodging and weaving as they were kicked, shoved, cursed at every step. At their destination, Mag waved a woman out of the way. She scuttled happily to another space, as Mag approached.

"You've been lucky. Don't think it'll last. You stir up trouble, you're gone. Your people don't come through, you're gone. I'm not the only one needs paying."

She rolled her eyes toward the coterie of women busy around a small brick firebox. They'd stopped to watch the exchange.

"Quite your gawping! You got nothing to do, I'll find you something."

Whatever that was, the prospect moved the women back to their meal preparations and a pot bubbling over the coals in the firebox.

"We all have our chores. I'll decide what yours will be tomorrow."

With a now familiar toss of her head, she was gone.

"That woman had good reason to leave

this spot."

Bett was staring with disgust at the waste buckets in an uncomfortably close corner. A woman nearby turned with a laugh.

"That's your job now. First thing every morning."

Several others joined her laughter, including the one who'd just vacated the spot. That was the last time anyone paid them any attention. Quickly the girls got to work, laying out their beds, this time with their feet to the room as the other women seemed to have done. To sit, they pulled the bed tick up behind their backs to lean against the wall. How little brings pleasure, thought Martha bitterly.

When she was sure the women were occupied with their supper and getting drunk, she pulled the sack into her lap. Unnoticed at the bottom were two rolls.

"Don't let them see you," she said slipping one into Bett's lap. "Tear it into small pieces and eat slowly." She followed her own bidding, shielding the roll in the folds of the sack. Only a cup of ale to wash the bits of soft bread down would have completed the pleasure in it.

When she was sure no one was looking their way, she reached into the bottom of the sack. There had been one last thing she felt when she took out the rolls. Slowly, she pulled out copies of the *London Gazette*. Her throat tightened at the sight of them. Mistress Chinn was the only one who knew how she treasured having a book to read or the occasional newspaper. And the time to read them.

But time was all she'd have now. The passing of it would be one of the hardest trials she'd have to bear. Keeping most of the paper in the sack, she folded the few pages into quarters to better conceal them. With a quick look at one page, she shoved it back with the rest wondering if she'd have a chance to actually read them. She figured very few of the women could read, but she'd already seen that they valued newspapers. They were much in demand for lining shoes and shielding a body from the prison's cold stone floor. Reluctantly she pulled a page back out of the sack.

"Bett, give me your shoes."

At the girl's look of alarm, she smiled.

"Don't fret, you'll have them back better than before."

Quickly she tore the paper in two and folded the pieces into the bottoms of the shoes Bett handed her. Martha was glad she'd thought to do it, because the shoes' soles were as thin as the paper and worn through in spots. The more Martha thought of it, the more she realized she'd probably do very little reading. The rest of the papers would surely get them a cup or two of rum to warm their insides, or vinegar to scour the floor around the slop buckets, or one of the many other commodities Mag traded in.

How strange. A simple thing like the newspapers had lifted her spirits. Whether she read them or not, they were a reminder of who she was, or had been, and, with luck, would be again. That night, Martha was less troubled by the horrors around her, than by the flood of memories she'd held at bay until Charley's and Mistress Chinn's visits had brought them on in a rush. Everything happened so fast, she'd had no time to really think of what she'd lost. As night fell, her spirits plummeted and reality overwhelmed her.

How could such a foul concoction of lies bring her to this? She had little hope that Randolph would not press charges against her and the court wouldn't judge in his favor... Damn the man. And Mistress Rawley. How could she have stood right there, too ready to believe what he said? But, then, Mistress Rawley had no love for Martha, and would never believe a gentleman could have such pure meanness in him. The painful memory of it caused a new gripping in her stomach. Again and again, she relived the nightmare of the despicable act and lies of a vengeful man that had swept her life away.

XXI

The Old Bailey

Martha told her story as clearly as she could when it came to her turn in the witness box. She searched for a bare section of wall to avoid looking directly at the judges, jurors, and barristers. They stared at her, stone faced, except for one or two who dozed off during the proceedings. They were attentive, however, when John Randolph entered the box to present his grievances against her. He referred to her only as "that tavern wench" whenever he looked at her with his haughty sneer.

Charley Rawley was the first to come forward on her behalf. Her nod and rueful smile were all she could do by way of thanks before he hastily looked away. His voice was strong and clear and his look earnest when asked about Martha.

"She's been like a sister, forever chiding me for telling falsehoods and taking things that weren't mine. Martha would never do such a thing as she is accused of."

"This young man *may* have a brotherly affection for the wench…"

Randolph's knowing sneer suggested something less innocent.

"But he wasn't in the house at the time to know what transpired."

The judge nodded in agreement and dismissed Charley, allowing Randolph to continue his prosecution. Mistress Chinn was next.

"This tavern wench has been in your employ for some time, has she not?"

"She is not a tavern wench as the gentleman chooses to call her."

Hannah glared at Martha's prosecutor.

"I have raised her from an infant. She's like a daughter to me. And I have put much trust in her. There was never a more honest or hardworking girl. She has been wrongly accused, your lordships."

"And who is it receives the moneys this girl might make from the work she does for you?"

Randolph leaned forward. He was taking great pleasure in his role as prosecutor *and* victim.

"Or from pilfering money and valuables from those hapless souls she lifts her skirts for."

The jurors sat forward at that, relieved to hear something of greater interest than Randolph's tiresome account of the hardship the loss of the money would have caused him.

"Her money is her own. And she does no such thing. The Black Horse is not that sort of place."

"I'm sure you think not, Madam. But I fear you don't know all that goes on in your establishment or what girls like this one do behind closed doors."

He turned away toward the jury before Hannah could say more.

"Nor did I until I found that one in my room. She offered herself, indeed, tempted me beyond all reason. And I'm ashamed to say I gave in. But I'll not say more, in deference to those with finer sensibilities."

As if there are any of that sort in this place, thought Hannah looking at the painted eyes and mouths of several women. They'd clearly come from the stage or the city's back streets.

"When our business was concluded," Randolph continued, "she took two pounds from where I'd left them on my bureau and was careless in hiding them away in her bodice. I first noticed the edge of a note above the cloth and then saw they were missing. When I attempted to take them from her, she fought me and, I'm ashamed to say, I had to strike her to wrest them away."

His look was smug as he turned toward Martha.

She raised her eyes and immediately closed them. The sun, which a cleverly positioned mirror directed into the eyes of an occupant of the prisoner's box, forced her to open them slowly to squint at the man whose malice seemed boundless.

"I did not touch his money. He's lying."

Martha's voice caught in her throat.

"Speak up, girl!"

"Yes, your lordship."

She turned toward the bewigged magistrate and, then, the jurors. It took an effort to steady her voice, to give it a ring of confidence.

"I did not take his money. I did nothing to...to deserve what he... He *attacked* me."

"As I have testified, I had no recourse but to strike this wench when I saw she had my notes. I had no reason to think ill of her. Til then she'd been most accommodating."

He gave the jury a commiserating look and turned back toward Martha.

"How was I to know that my carelessness would leave me prey to a wench with a criminal frame of mind. Ah, but no matter. The fact of this case is that I caught her with the notes on her person and am not of such comfortable means that the loss of such a sum would not cause me great distress."

"I never saw them until he..."

The sight of Randolph's poor attempt at a look of distress caused her to pause and take a deep breath.

"That wasn't why he hit me... He struck me because he was trying to have his way with me. I tried to stop him."

She had to look away from the jurors who now were eagerly leaning forward in their seats, here and there a mouth agape. She continued with a sudden flash of anger.

"He's lying. He struck me again so that he could... he could accomplish what he set out to do. He raped me. I never saw those notes until after he'd done it. He wiped the blood from my mouth with the wretched things."

Martha bit her lip to keep from saying more and was painfully reminded. She could tell that Randolph was taken aback. He hadn't expected her to actually say what he'd done. For a moment, he seemed at a loss to respond. But he recovered quickly.

"Are we to take the word of a person like this tavern wench?"

A slight inclination of several heads suggested the jurists might not.

"As you have just heard, she's quick with her lies and comely enough, in a rough sort of way, to make the gullible believe her. It shames me to admit that I was taken in, a stranger in this place, far from my family and loved ones on the other side of the world. I've not often been in a city such as this and it is most certainly not my custom to consort with the likes of such women. Indeed, I thought I was lodging in a respectable establishment. Which was not the case, as it was my misfortune to discover."

"That is not so! That's a slanderous lie!"

All eyes in the room swung to the

witness box where Hannah stood, red-faced, shaking with indignation.

"Silence, woman!" The judge snapped. "You may step down."

Stunned, Hannah didn't move until a bailiff appeared to take her by the arm and lead her to the row of benches where Rebecca and Joseph Rawley waited. Rebecca pulled Hannah down between them and kept her mother's arm locked in hers. But there was no need.

Hannah's energy was spent. She was stricken by what she'd heard said, not just about Martha but about the Black Horse. The place had been her life and source of pride since she came to London as a bride. And now her own daughter was taking that despicable man's word about what happened.

As silence again settled on the courtroom, the jurors began moving around restlessly on their hard benches. Martha had no doubt she was doomed. They'd already made up their minds. It wasn't so hard to believe that a girl such as she would offer herself to a handsome, well-bred man such as Randolph; that she'd think nothing of taking money left lying about. The judge turned to peer down at her from his bench.

" Have you anything more to say?"

"No, your lordship."

He, then, affirmed that John Randolph also had no more to say and asked Martha how she pleaded. She stood straight and spoke out in a clear voice.

"Not guilty!"

In his summation, the judge's words were weighted on the side of the aggrieved victim when he instructed the jurors. They huddled just a short while, their bewigged heads bobbing, and found Martha guilty of theft. Though she'd expected it, Martha was nearly overcome by a feeling of hopelessness. She had no sense of what was happening as she was led from the courtroom and down the stairs to the underground passage that would take her back to a holding cell to await sentencing. Dead Man's walk they called it.

How long she sat there, she couldn't have said and when the jailor called her name she rose in a daze to return to the prisoner's box. The blinding sun was gone and she could clearly see the public galleries where Mistress Chinn and Charley sat. Had they been there all the while? The worry was stark on their drawn faces. She found Randolph, too, at the other end of the gallery, sitting back, his chest puffed out, obviously pleased with his day's work. The judge cleared his throat and Randolph sat forward eager for the sentence.

"Can you offer any reason that judgement should not be passed upon you?"

"No, your lordship."

Martha shook her head.

"Then, for the crime of theft, your sentence shall be seven years' transportation to the American colonies."

Martha felt a cold weight settle in her

chest. Afraid she'd cry, she couldn't look at Mistress Chinn or Charley. She wasn't going to let herself do that.

At the judge's pronouncement, Hannah felt a cold weight grow in her chest but it had no time to settle there. She quickly had to grab Charley's arm as he lurched from his seat.

"Be still! We need cause her no more pain by having you arrested."

And I could not bear any more pain. America? She's going to some godforsaken colony? She's just a girl. What will become of her? What had Jamie said of transports? Treated as badly or worse than the black Africans the Americans kept as slaves.

Martha dared not look toward Mistress Chinn or Charley and had to clutch the rail in front of her to keep from falling. The sentence could have been death. But what did this one mean? Would it be any better? She bit her lower lip, determined not to cry.

She tried to remember what she'd heard of the American colonies but where she was bound was a small matter weighed against the chance that she'd survive to see it. Or have a life there after she arrived.

XXII

Another Soul in Hell

Hannah and Charley took turns visiting over the passing weeks. Each time, they left Martha with a few shillings to buy a bit of cooked meat, fresh bread, or an extra ration of ale. They also brought provisions that kept Mag happy and put a bit of color in Bett's cheeks. Martha was heartened by the occasional bit of palatable food she felt like eating.

Those first days, no more than a few bites of the prison's fare sent her rushing to the waste bucket. She convinced herself that it was the ever-present stink of rotting food, sweat, and human waste and bargained with the warder for extra vinegar to clean the patch of stone she and Bett occupied. But even its cleansing odor sickened her. She had to accept what she feared. She hadn't bled for two months. Randolph not only had condemned her but another soul to hell.

However much Martha found to do, she couldn't escape the thought of the infant that had been growing inside her. On her worst days, she couldn't even think of it as a living being. Come night, she'd lie awake, pounding and kneading her belly, hoping to dislodge it. Eventually, her sleeplessness drove her to walk the perimeter of the cell, wandering heedlessly through the gambling brawling women.

Most were so drunk they attacked any and all within reach unable to distinguish friend from foe. Martha didn't even see the punch that sent her sprawling to the floor. She looked up just in time to see a kick coming and grabbed the woman's foot. A quick twist was all it took to send the besotted woman reeling and allow her to scrabble out of reach.

Once she was well clear and sure no one was following, Martha staggered to her feet, a hand pressed to her belly. She felt as if she was about to puke, but more from the thought of what might just have happened than by the blow itself. Had that damned woman done what she'd been unable to do? Had she killed the child? Until that moment, she hadn't thought what she had been trying to do. She'd never been able to think of actually killing anything. Well maybe a rat. And John Randolph. He'd certainly qualify as that form of vermin. But not a child. Even it it was his.

She gently rubbed her hand across her middle. This child shouldn't suffer for what it's father did. It was hers too. And hers to protect for now and for whatever lay ahead. If anything happened to her, there'd be no Hannah Chinn. She'd have to be strong for both of them. Whatever lay ahead, she realized, she wanted to face it head on, wanted to keep herself and the child she carried alive. No one must know of it. Not until she was settled in the new world and somehow was prepared to care for it. In the meantime, she'd have to find ways to stay out of trouble and pass each tedious day.

****

"I wish you'd read the news like you used to."

Bett had sat watching Martha play with an indistinguishable lump in the gruel that passed for breakfast for some time, then, cautiously touched her arm. She patted the pile of unread papers between them.

"It helps to pass the time."

Martha stared at her, not really understanding what the other girl had said, then, shaking herself as if she'd just come awake, she rummaged through the pile to pull out the earliest paper.

"You're right. Let's see what's been going on in the world that we've missed."

As Martha read aloud to Bett, one or two other women came close to listen, if for no other reason than that it helped a little to make the time pass. At last, in early autumn, Martha learned that she, Bett, Mag, and some of the others would be sent to the colony of Maryland on a ship loading at Blackfriars Stairs. She now had a greater reason to read the papers, but found little mention of the colony. It was on the Chesapeake Bay and that she knew from Jamie Chinn's tales of his adventures. But that did nothing to reassure her.

The only Virginian she knew was John Randolph. What little passed for news of Maryland was a stew concerning English troops at war with the French and Indians in its hinterlands. She didn't read those accounts to Bett. The girl needed nothing more to frighten her about what lay ahead for them. Nor did she mention more disturbing reports that French privateers were attacking English ships, which added to her own nighttime worries.

For the most part, Martha registered very little of what she read anymore. The news couldn't compete with her overwhelming dread as the day of their departure drew near and she'd have to say farewell to the Chinns, never to see them again. The day before Martha was to leave, Hannah paid the warder handsomely to allow them to meet outside the cell. Despite all the things Martha wanted to say to them, when they stood face to face, she could think of none of them.

"You'll need these things."

Hannah thrust a a large bundle into Martha's arms.

"Don't open it until you're on your way.

It looks like nothing and it's better no one sees what's inside."

Martha only glanced at it and nodded. Mistress Chinn was right. Disguised as it was in a very large, dirty, and well-used kerchief, the bundle suggested no contents of value.

"And don't let any see this either."

Charley hastily slipped something into her pocket. She nodded and tried to smile but when she looked into Charley's stricken face she was nearly undone. Hannah's was no better. Martha couldn't remember her ever looking so old, her forehead creased with worry, dark shadows under her eyes.

Numbly Martha nodded as Hannah gave her Joseph Rawley's farewell wishes. He'd always been kind to her and she'd miss him. Rebecca and Mary sent no messages, but she said William Chinn had a message about his brother Jamie who was then at sea.

"Jamie's due back soon and William has cargo waiting to go back to his Virginia agents. Jamie knows those waters well and Maryland lies near there. William will ask him to find you. I'll send you a letter."

When Martha could only nod, Hannah continued in a rush.

"We can come to see you off on the morrow."

Her eyes hadn't left Martha's face since she arrived. Martha could barely speak for wanting to scream and cry and cling to them as long as she could. To endure another farewell was more than she could stand.

"That parting would be harder than this. Let's do it here."

As she and Hannah wept in each others arms, Charley stood by, helplessly struggling to contain his own tears. With thoughts of what lay ahead for her on the voyage and in Maryland pressing upon them, they had no more words to express their feelings. Though they'd dreaded it, the warder's knock was almost a relief. Unable to delay their parting any longer, Hannah let Martha go and stepped back.

"Remember child that I was proud to say it in the court that you're very like a daughter to me and always will be. I'll pray that God watches over you. I know Jamie will find you. Let him know if you need help. You'll be at a great distance but you won't be lost to us."

Martha gave Hannah one last hug.

"You'll always be in my heart."

Even as she spoke the words, Martha felt as if that heart was being wrenched out of her chest at the thought of never seeing Hannah or Charley again.

Until then, Charley had said hardly a word. He cleared his throat, stepped forward, and clumsily took her in his arms.

"If there was anything I could do to save you from this, I would. But for now, just know my love goes with you. It's the best part of me."

His voice broke, but he forced himself to go on.

"I don't know what more I can say."

"That's all I need, Charley, just knowing that you have loved me. That gives me strength."

"And you're strong Martha. If ever there was one who could turn this to advantage, it's you. I'll be waiting to hear that you've made a fresh start in the colonies. You'll make a life for yourself there. Of that, I'm sure, and I'll wager it will be better than you could get here."

"But it won't have you in it, and that will be hard to bear."

She clung to him for a moment more, then stepped back to have one last look at their dear faces.

"Go now," she said as tears blurred her vision.

"Go!"

She almost shouted the word when Hannah hesitated and couldn't watch as Charley hurried Hannah to the door.

Martha had no more tears as she waited for the warder to take her back to the cell. She couldn't have described the path that took her back to where Bett waited, didn't notice the girl's worried look.

She sank onto the bed tick, curling up with her arms around the bundle, too numb with the pain of the parting to even cry. When night had fallen and she was aware, at last, of the raspy breathing that told her Bett was asleep, she sat up. She set the bundle aside to open later. Mistress Chinn was right, but there was no ignoring the things Charley had slipped into her pocket.

Her fingers quickly identified a small cloth sack of coins, several shillings, she guessed from the feel of them. The metal object beneath the sack wasn't familiar at first. Certainly nothing she'd held. Slowly she ran her fingers around the sides, then the edges and she knew. It was his folding knife. Where had he gotten the coins? Charley never had money to spare. And the knife was his most prized possession. She wrapped her fingers around it and felt the cold metal grow warm. Small comfort, but it was enough for her to cling to as she curled up on her side. Using the bundle to pillow her head, she escaped into a dreamless sleep.

XXIII

Aboard the Sea Nymph

The air in the *Sea Nymph*'s low-ceilinged cabin was thick with a sickening stench that Martha suspected came from rat carcasses rotting in the bilge. Bett was just a step ahead of her at the foot of the ladder, afraid to step into the gloom. Martha paused there too, waiting for her eyes to adjust in the feeble amber glow of three lanterns evenly spaced down the length of the cabin. She could just make out what looked like narrow sleeping shelves along the bulkhead. Clearly made of fresh-hewn lumber, she guessed the cabin had been hastily fitted out for human cargo.

Mag's sack of belongings was already on a shelf near a greasy pine table beneath the center lantern. The first of the women were vying for shelves near her. In the cabin's shadowy depths, the last lantern revealed a pair of crude boxes attached to the bulkhead at the far end. Martha guessed that it wouldn't be long before there was a new stink rising through the holes in their lids.

"You gonna stand there forever?"

So that's how it would be. Martha felt a tightness in her chest. She let her bundle drop to her feet. It would be no different from Newgate. In the cell it was usually possible to stay out of Mag's way, but, there'd be no escaping her or anyone else in the cabin's cramped space.

Mag reached out to grab Bett, but Martha was there before her. She pushed Bett out of the way and slipped her hand into her pocket as the woman advanced on her with a self-satisfied sneer.

"You ain't gonna get your way here."

Mag's hand reaching out to seize her was all it took. The tightness in Martha's chest burst like a chestnut too long in the fire, releasing a rotten, angry thing. In the space of a breath, Martha grabbed Mag's outstretched arm, hooked a foot around her left ankle, and pushed hard. Mag fell backward, the breath knocked out of her, too surprised to make a sound.

Before she could recover, Martha was upon her, a knee on her chest, her right foot pinning one arm, her left hand gripping the other. Her knife was open at the stunned woman's throat. Afraid to speak or move her head, Mag's eyes swung wildly from side to side, seeking help among the women hovering in the cabin's gloom. They'd taken a step back, waiting to see who would be the victor.

"We'll choose where we make our bed."

Martha spit out the words between breaths. She shifted her weight to lean closer and felt soft, yielding flesh under her knee. Months of privation in prison had left nothing to cushion Martha's sharp-boned knee weighing on Mag's breast. Martha was gratified by her grimace.

"Aye!"

Mag gasped. In her eyes was a fleeting look of fear, but the hatred that replaced it, Martha knew, occupied the better part of Mag's soul. However that contest ended, it would not be finished between them. She tightened her grip on Mag's arm and cocked her head.

"I didn't hear you."

She pressed the edge of the blade a little harder against Mag's throat, just to remind her of its presence.

"Aye!"

That time, it was loud enough for all to hear. Martha knew she couldn't hesitate. Leaning back, she sprang to her feet and stepped away. She stood knife ready, eyes on Mag. Without a look in Martha's direction, Mag turned over and dragged herself up, first to her knees, then to her feet. She steadied herself against the table and turned back toward Martha. They stood, eyes locked, breathing hard, each waiting for the other to make the first move. Finally, Mag tossed her head.

"You might have your pig sticker now, but the guards'll have it off you before this day's out. Then, you'll not be so quick to say who chooses what."

"I'll take my chances."

Martha looked beyond Mag to the other women and raised her voice.

"When they take mine, they'll be looking to see what more the lot of you have got."

Mag snorted and made a great show of putting her clothes in order. She glared at the other women, expecting some show of support. As one, they turned away to busy themselves at their plank beds. With a boldness she didn't feel, Martha picked up her bundle, folded the penknife, and slipped it back into the pocket under her apron. She looked quickly around the cabin, then, turned her back on Mag.

With more force than she'd intended, Martha grabbed Bett's arm, pulling her toward a stretch of planking barely within the closest lantern's circle of pallid light. Bett sat heavily on the berth, her arms clutching her blanket to her narrow chest. She looked fearfully at Martha, but Martha couldn't meet her eyes. She wasn't ready to deal kindly with anyone.

She turned instead to put her bundle on the shelf next to Bett's and closest to the ladder and companionway. She paused and gripped the knotted cloth with trembling hands to wait until her heart settled and her breath came easily again. How could she have been so foolish as to show the knife? She had to bite off

269

a bitter laugh. A penknife! How many of them knew that? No matter. If it kept Mag and any others at a distance, it was worth it.

She'd endured worse until she'd learned Newgate's ways. She'd been cursed at, spat upon, pummeled, and kicked. She still had bruises and scars from the sharp-nailed rakings and the pinches that drew blood. She could defend herself, but she'd never attacked another. Martha looked down at her hands. They had actually held the knife to that woman's throat.

She'd seen real fear in Mag's eyes. To have that power, to control what happened to you... For six weeks she'd been denied any say in her life. But not this time. She stood straighter, filled by a sense of power that stilled her shaking hands and held off the fear she'd been living with. She might face worse in the coming months, but, for the moment, she felt equal to whatever the upcoming days and weeks might bring.

Was it like that for the men and boys she'd seen brawling on Wapping's streets? Flailing arms and legs, butting heads, all bloody lips, noses, and bit ears? Charley was always in the midst of it and usually went swaggering off when all was over.

She'd watched the women in prison fly at each other, kicking, scratching, and biting like cocks fighting to the death. Was it the feeling of victory or just a rush of relief to have come out alive? She tried to call up the faces of the women in the cabin behind her. Was there another Mag among them?

She lowered her hand to find the hidden knife, but quickly had to take in a deep breath to fight the bile that rose from the churning in her gut. Mag might threaten to tell the guards about the knife, but Martha doubted she would. Even if they had no weapons, several, she was sure, had coin or some other things of value the guards would take. The women could no more trust them than they could each other. No. Neither Mag nor any who heard their exchange wanted the guards searching them or their belongings. In that, if nothing else, they were allied.

"Would you have cut her?" Bett whispered.

Bett's whisper brought Martha back to matters at hand. She shook her head, not sure of her voice.

"I don't know," she ventured. "Mag would surely have if she'd had a knife."

That Martha knew for sure. She also knew that, from that moment on, she'd have some say in what happened to her. At least, within the cabin's bounds. Martha looked over at Bett still hunched on the edge of her berth. Untying her bundle, she took out two brown wool blankets and shook them out. Coaxing Bett to her feet, she wrapped one of the blankets around her thin shoulders, then eased the ragged ship blanket from Bett's arms to spread it out on the bare wood planks. She forced a smile.

"It's a sight better than we've had."

She motioned for Bett to climb onto the berth, then followed, pulling her second wool blanket around her own shoulders. The two girls tucked their feet up under them and leaned together against the bulkhead.

"I wish I was brave like you. I fear what she'll do next."

Bett looked across the cabin to where Mag was rummaging through the sack she carried aboard.

"You have nothing to worry about from her. It's me she'll be after. And I don't expect she'll be looking for a fight any time soon. She'll think of something else to settle the score. But don't trouble yourself with that. Rest now."

"It's thanks to you I can do that. You're my only friend in this rotten world."

Bett's sad smile of gratitude tugged at Martha's heart. She gave her a gentle pat as Bett drew the blanket more firmly around her and curled up in a tight knot. She was asleep almost as soon as she closed her eyes.

What *will* become of us?

Martha looked down at the girl who'd shared a patch of cold stone floor with her for more than six weeks. That and whatever miserable future they would face in America was all they had in common. The frail girl looked as if she'd break at the slightest touch. She had no meat beneath her skin or color in her sharp-boned cheeks. A piece of string held back her thin brown hair that lay across the narrow stalk of her neck.

Except when they used her weakness to their advantage, Bett had never attracted anyone's notice. And that, Martha suspected, was what had kept her alive in the cells. She certainly had nothing anyone would want to steal. The most memorable thing about her were her brown eyes, overlarge and stark against the pallor of her face. They never lost their look of fear. And not without reason. They woke most mornings to the jailor hauling away some dead or near dead soul.

Martha didn't presume to credit herself with the fact that Bett hadn't come to such an end. From the look of her, she could still end up a nameless corpse dropped into a common grave. But as long as they shared the same fate, Martha vowed to see that didn't happen and that Bett would have a few hours of untroubled sleep that night. Martha envied Bett her ability to sleep. Tired as she was, she didn't dare relax her vigil.

If nothing else, having someone to look after helped her forget about her own plight. But it wasn't just her own fate she had to worry about. With all that had happened over the preceding weeks, she'd given little thought to the tiny being growing inside her. Indeed, it had given no cause. She almost thought, almost wished, she'd been wrong, but the passing of nearly three months without her monthly bleeding told her otherwise. And if it survived, the child would be in even greater need of care and protection than Bett.

Shoving that thought aside, she turned her attention to the cabin's other occupants, sorting themselves out as Mag directed her own small coterie to this or that chore. None seemed over eager to take the berth next to Bett's and Martha's. She caught the eye of an older woman who'd been standing silently near the foot of the ladder studying the scene before her with sharp, angry eyes. As near as Martha could remember, the woman had been behind her when they climbed down.

With an attempt at a smile that was little more than a bitter twist to her mouth when their eyes met, the woman slung her bag on the berth next to Bett's. Using it as a pillow, she stretched out as far as the narrow space allowed and lay staring at the dark beams above her. Martha watched her idly for a bit longer before looking up through the hatch. That glimpse of daylight helped her push away the heaviness that clung to every thought until, with a creak and a thump, someone above slammed the hatch shut and darkness closed in around her.

Once her eyes had adjusted to the dim lantern light, Martha moved to her own berth. She sat with her back against the rough wood. Behind her, she could hear the slurp of the Thames lapping at the side of the ship just inches away. She pulled her knees up and rested her head on them, but was no less vigilant, listening to the voices of the women.

They fell silent, though, when they heard the pounding of feet overhead and shouts of the crew preparing the ship to get underway. Martha had seen enough such activity to imagine the sailors scrambling hand-over-hand to loose the sails, others standing by the lines below, brawny landmen at the capstan awaiting the order to raise the anchor. The captain would be standing close by the helmsman.

Muir was the captain's name she'd heard. There was no sign of him when they were brought aboard. She badly wanted to see the man who traded in humans. Was it a sop to his conscience that his ship carried English men and women in chains and not black Africans? At least some of them would walk free one day. Those that lived.

Most of the blacks, though, would have only death to set them free. Did he feel it was a great service he rendered clearing England's gaols and workhouses. Wasn't transportation a kinder fate than hanging? A fine distinction. Death would sail with them and would stalk those who reached America. But that mattered nothing to the captain. He'd pocket the money she and the others would bring.

The groan and reverberating squeal and clank of the anchor chain brought her attention back to the situation at hand. The noise and sudden motion of the ship woke Bett and forced the women still on their feet to retreat to their berths.

"Are we off, then?"

"So it would seem."

But they weren't. Not long after the ship got underway, the rumbling protest of the anchor told them they'd simply cleared the quay and moved out into the river. By then, Martha had lost all sense of time. They came aboard late in the day. It had to be night. She leaned toward Bett.

"I suspect we'll catch the morning tide. Go back to sleep. I'll keep watch."

Bett curled up again, but Martha didn't see her eyes close in sleep for a long time. It wasn't so easy to do this time. Slowly, Martha pulled her bundle into her lap and untied it. In the prison, she dared no more than a peek at the things Mistress Chinn had packed so cleverly and brought to the prison that last day. None would think there was anything worth taking wrapped in the dirty, ragged cloth.

For the two days before they were marched out of Newgate, the bundle never left her hands. Now, as the stained, tattered kerchief fell away, her throat grew tight. She blinked her eyes rapidly to keep back the tears she'd controlled for so long. She hastily wiped the back of her hand across her eyes and looked up to scan the cabin, but the others were taken up with bickering and settling into whatever poor spaces they'd claimed.

Martha lifted out the dark green folds of her woolen cloak. It still carried the smell of the pine chest in her room at the Black Horse, as did a brown cloth petticoat, two linen shifts, and a red-striped linen apron. Putting them aside, she gathered up the small patchwork quilt, holding it to her face to wipe away her tears and breathe in the scent of wood smoke just as she did when she curled up on her bed in the chimney corner in the room behind the inn's kitchen. Carefully, she refolded each item with a prayer that they might hold fast some of the smells of home and set them aside.

Near the bottom, rolled in linen sheeting were a pewter spoon and mug; a tin box containing a bit of cloth threaded with four needles; two spools of thread, one black, one white; a thimble; a pin cushion; a pencil, pen, and two small blocks of ink. And, at last, wrapped in a fresh muslin kerchief was her little wooden doll, just large enough to fit in the palm of her hand, and a small, well-worn Bible, older than she, its leather binding oil-darkened by years of handling. The doll caused such a catch in her throat that she quickly put it aside to open the Bible.

Martha was quickly overcome with early memories of Mistress Chinn reading from it, then using it to teach her to read. She opened the little book and leaned forward to let the lantern light fall on the page, but fresh tears blurred the words. Martha closed it quickly and tucked it away again in the kerchief. It would do her no good if the other women saw her crying.

She busied herself with repacking the bundle and shutting away the memories that the things had stirred in her. Across the cabin, Mag had a noisy game of cards going. She or someone else had produced a flask that was passing from mouth to mouth. They kept at it well into the night. Martha lay under her wool blanket watching them until, one-by-one, they drifted off to their berths. Eventually Mag fell back in a drunken stupor. Except for a discordant chorus of snores, the cabin was still. Martha raised her eyes to the lantern swaying to the gentle rocking of the ship. From the deck above came the mournful bawling of the cows.

Poor dumb creatures. Angrily she turned her back to the cabin, pulling her blanket more tightly around her. Better to be dumb than wondering what was to become of them. A sob filled her throat, threatened to break free. She buried her head in the blanket, unable to stem the flood of despair that overwhelmed her. Would she be no more able to direct her own course than her mother had?

XXIV

Misery at Sea

The *Sea Nymph* wasn't long at sea before she ran into ocean storms that added to the misery of the cold, damp space the women shared beneath the closed hatch. Most of them were seasick. The cabin reeked of vomit, urine, feces, and the compounded odors of too many bodies in too small a space. Once a day, the women drew lots to see which ones would carry the four buckets, brimful with their waste, to the deck. They were cursed roundly by the sailors if they failed to pitch the foul contents over the leeward rail.

On days when the weather was fair, the ship's captain ordered the guards into the cabin swinging their clubs to chase the women up to the deck to spend time in fresher air. Threats of a beating were all that could get Mag and her band to leave their games of cards and dice.

Once a week, the women dragged their bedding with them to shake and beat it and let the sun and wind work on the dank ticking.

279

Their efforts never succeeded in driving out the lice. On those days, they also scoured the cabin's tables and fought the filth and odors with mops, brushes, and buckets of vinegar and sea water. That done, they continued whatever gaming, fighting, or bartering had begun below. Guards and other members of the crew who had no pressing duties, regularly loitered near where the women gathered. Soon after their arrival, Mag and one or two others disappeared. Their business was quickly done and no one remarked their return.

From the beginning, Bett and a fair number of the women huddled together in fear that they'd be thrown into the sea from the pitching deck. Even when calm, the vast ocean was a fearsome thing, taming some of the most brazen women. Martha didn't share their fears. She was so used to a bilious stomach that she didn't know if the sea or the infant inside her was to blame.

As bad as the food was, she forced herself to eat, not for herself but for the child. She wished she could do as much to ease Bett's discomfort. In rough weather, the girl couldn't keep anything down. During her bouts of dry retching, the best Martha could do was keep a reassuring arm around her shoulders.

"Let me help."

The woman rose from her berth on the other side of Bett. Until then she and Martha had only exchanged nods.

"My name's Joan, Joan Thornton."

She lowered her voice.

"I'd like to help."

Martha could have hugged her.

"I'd welcome that. My name's Martha Pratt. This is Bett."

From then on, they took turns caring for Bett when rough weather brought on the sickness. In the long, tiresome hours when Bett slept and there was nothing else to do, Martha and Joan talked of the lives they'd left behind and what brought them to that ship bound for Maryland.

Joan's days and nights were still haunted by the piteous cries of her four children when the constable hauled her out of the miserable room they occupied. She was reminded of them daily when she looked at Bett who had the same pale skin and brown eyes as her youngest daughter.

"I could get a few pence cleaning and mending for two or three ladies, but there was never enough."

Though the memory was painful, talking about it helped.

"My little ones were near starving. At the last, all I had for them to eat were scraps of food one of the ladies left out for her dogs. I had to get them something better than that. God forgive me, I pawned a linen shirt the lady gave me to mend. I expected to earn enough to get it back before she wanted it. As it was all I could buy was a bit of cheese, some stale bread, and milk for the children to soak it in."

Joan paused to dry the tears that had been falling unnoticed. She was unable to reclaim the shirt and the woman had her arrested. At trial, the woman not only accused her of the theft of the shirt, but also of taking scraps from her family's midday dinner meant for the dogs. Joan never saw her children again. A neighbor visited her in prison with the news that her children were taken to the foundling home. Their future, she knew, was every bit as bleak as hers and very possibly more so. Caring for Bett offered some comfort and a meager hope that her own children might be treated with kindness.

****

As the days stretched interminably, Martha seized every opportunity to get out of the cabin. She earned the gratitude of several women by taking their turns at emptying waste buckets. In the open air, her stomach didn't bother her as much. She grew accustomed to the heaving of the deck beneath her feet and sure-footed enough to let her body relax into the rise and fall of the ship.

If she had a choice, Bett wouldn't go on deck. She never lost her fear of the sea. Even when the sun shown and the winds were calm, she shivered uncontrollably.

"No flesh on her bones," Joan said to Martha.

The three had just returned to the cabin.

Almost immediately, Bett retreated to her bed and curled up beneath her blankets.

"She had no strength to begin with. Now the seasickness has weakened her even more. She eats less than one of those blasted rats.

Joan cast her eyes toward the dark ceiling.

"She said when we were up there that she wished she had the will to fling herself overboard. She doesn't want to live and fears the worst if she does reach America. Ah, Martha, I fear she won't see the end of this voyage."

On stormy days, the women stayed below beneath the closed hatch. A sailor handed down buckets of bread or ship biscuits and hard, moldy cheese with increasingly foul water or, on rare occasions, ale to help get the food down. Better days allowed three or four of the women to prepare their day's meal in the ship's galley. There was little satisfaction in it. No amount of trying could make the leathery meat and bug-infested peas more palatable. Martha took her turn in the galley just for the chance to be above deck. She seized every opportunity to escape the foul-smelling cabin to stand for just a minute, gulping down great breaths of cold, sea air.

In the galley, Martha chafed at waiting as their daily portion of salt pork or beef and peas was bubbling in the kettle on the galley's brick hearth. The other women enjoyed their gossip and squabbling in the warmth of the fire and paid no heed when Martha climbed to the deck. She pitied the male prisoners, who still wore leg irons and were kept under guard when they had their time in the air. The women were supervised only by whatever sailor had the watch on the quarterdeck.

No one ever stopped Martha when she stepped to the ship's rail to gaze seaward, nor missed her as she wandered slowly out of sight behind the pens where, now, only three cows and five hogs watched her with doleful eyes.

If only she could see what lay beyond the horizon stretching ahead of the ship. It was no use thinking about what lay behind. That life was gone forever. And ahead? She could imagine the look of the land from stories overheard in the public room of the Black Horse. But when they got to port? To be sold to a stranger to do his bidding for seven years terrified her. She'd heard that buyers examined them like horses or cattle and haggled over their price as they would a piece of meat in a market. Most would be sold off to the plantations. That she knew.

She knew, also, that she was young and strong and would very likely be sold into the country. That could be better than some of the possibilities she'd heard about. She'd heard talk of the brothels in American ports. Convict and slave women were common fare, the sailors said. *Newgate speculation*, she told herself. Her imaginings were darkest when they included the small life she'd carry with her into bondage. Those always ended as dark as the storm clouds that piled along the western edge of the sea.

****

A month into the voyage, Martha let her thoughts keep her too long looking out over the ocean. She didn't hear the guard's approach, didn't sense his presence until he was standing behind her, so close she could feel his breath on her ear and the pressure of his body forcing her against the ship's bulkhead.

"Be still!"

His voice was a low growl. Before she could turn to see his face, he brought his club up under her chin, both hands on it forcing her head back against his chest. Martha clawed at his hands and the club that trapped her last breath in her throat.

She had to stop him, stop the pain that seared her throat and chest. She was near fainting when she let her body go limp, her hands drop to the rail.

"Ahhh. There's a good lass. You're not supposed to wander up here. It's not safe."

His growl became a gravelly purr. He eased the club's pressure, and Martha sucked in the welcome rush of air.

"Don't move!"

He let the club fall to swing on the leather thong around his wrist and replaced it with his arm.

"Make no cry." He tightened his hold.

"It would be easy to break your neck and pitch you over. None would be the wiser."

Martha had to hold her breath to keep her body still when she felt his hand groping at her kerchief and the neck of the shift above the laces of her bodice. His fingers were course against her throat, sliding down, pushing the cloth aside, stretching the frayed laces, then, digging painfully into her breast.

Oh God. Not again.

Her thoughts raced wildly, terror building as she tried to turn. But she was no match for his strength or the weight of his body ramming her hard into the unyielding wood, his arm tightening around her neck. She stopped struggling.

No! Not this time.

The resolve calmed her.

"You learn quick."

He eased his hold on her throat. With a last squeeze, he removed his hand from her breast.

"You be good and do me this little favor, and I can make your life better on this godforsaken ship. Mag'll tell you. There's extra rations and rum in it for you, favor for favor."

Martha went cold inside.

Mag! The bitch. And this was Hal, the one Mag called Lovey.

"She told you I would take kindly to your offer?"

Martha fought to keep her voice steady.

"Aye. *She* finds our arrangement to her liking."

"How can I know it's to my liking when you treat me so harshly?"

She spoke softly and forced herself to lean back against him.

Never taking his hands off her, he let her turn.

Ahh. She knew that face. A hard one, scarred and weather darkened, lit only by brown, scheming eyes. She tilted her head and raised her eyebrows. Could she make herself appear the bawd? His grotesque leer, broken teeth behind a humorless grin told her yes.

Martha gently shoved him back and slid her hand down toward his waist, fingers searching for the buttons of his pants. With her other, she began to gather her skirt and raise it slowly.

"Ahhh, there you go ..."

His eyes narrowed and he tilted his head back. The hiss of pleasure escaping between his clenched teeth was cut short when Martha brought her knee up hard into his groin and pushed him away with all her strength. But he was too tall. Her knee didn't deliver the stunning blow she'd hoped. And she was no match in strength.

"You filthy whore!"

In a practiced motion, he had his club in hand and swung it, opening a gash just over Martha's right brow. His other hand went for her throat, only to find her teeth clamped tightly on the soft skin between thumb and forefinger. He snatched his hand away and she staggered back, slumping against the rail, her arms shielding her head.

But the next blow didn't come. She lowered one arm enough to look. Hal stood, his club dangling from his wrist, staring at his bleeding hand. Martha tried to think. She had to get away but her head was reeling. Blood cast a red veil over her right eye. If he didn't strike again, he'd surely pitch her over. He reached for her, and she tried to move away but was overcome by dizziness.

"Damn you!"

He dragged her back away from the bulkhead into the shadows cast by the animal pens. When he let her go, she had to fight to stand upright, clutching at the cow pen's rough boards before the swirling behind her eyes sent her careening to the deck. She clung there, eyes closed. Taking in deep breaths to clear her head, she waited for him to hit her again. When he didn't, she slowly turned to face him. He was frowning, tugging at the kerchief around his neck with his good hand.

"Don't you move," he snarled.

The idea of moving almost made Martha laugh.

"I won't."

She winced. Speaking brought a stab of pain. Gingerly, she raised her hand to her forehead.

The whole side of her face throbbed. She

feared she'd puke when she lowered her bloody hand. Blood had been running unnoticed down her face and neck and into the folds of her kerchief. The taste of it filled her mouth. She spit, sickened by the thought that it belonged to Hal. But her tongue quickly found that it wasn't his but her own blood. She must have caught her lip when she bit his hand. Trying to focus, Martha waited and watched him.

She had only one good eye. The other had already begun to swell shut. She had no delusions, little time, and little to bargain with. Her thoughts raced. She was a convict servant, of small value in the world of bound labor. On the block, a slave would fetch a better price than she.

Buyers expected little value for their money when they bought a convict. They wouldn't pay well for damaged property. The captain would be lucky to get what it cost to transport her. If they traced it to Hal he'd get a dozen lashes with the cat-o-nine-tails. Unless ...

"The captain will have you on the rack for this," she said softly.

Hal looked up tugging at a corner of the kerchief he was wrapping around his hand. He gripped another corner in his teeth.

"But that will do me no good. No one on this ship thinks a convict's worth that. It will be worse for me than before."

Hal simply grunted through his teeth and glared at her over his hand, then spit out the corner of cloth.

"It was you led me on, always goin' off alone. What's to keep me from gettin' what I come after, pitch you over, and none the wiser?"

"You don't look like the murderin' type."

She prayed she'd read him right.

"How were you to know I wasn't like Mag said? It's common knowledge some give their favors for extra rations. And reason enough to think all will be generous that way."

Not that you wouldn't have taken the advantage without Mag putting you to it.

"Aye, that's how it were."

The man looked almost relieved.

"Some are easy that way. And how was I to know you was a different sort. That maybe you'd be wantin'..."

He cut his last thought short, frowning as he looked down at her bloody clothes, registering the damage for the first time. He realized he had a more pressing problem.

Martha guessed his concern.

"It's more blood than serious hurt. If any ask, I'll tell them I fell against the rail."

She nodded toward the bulkhead but the move set the world to spinning and a new pounding to start in her head. Steadying herself, she cautiously felt her cheek. The bleeding seemed to have stopped.

"You've seen players, haven't you? On fair days?"

Hal who'd been silent, scowling at the

deck, looked up puzzled.

"Just watch me."

She'd often seen wandering groups performing on the streets of Wapping.

"I'm such a clumsy wench."

She winked her good eye.

"Wandering off to puke like that."

She gritted her teeth against the pain and made a retching sound, clapping her hand to her mouth.

"If it weren't for you, I'd be lyin' there, my life's blood seeping out on the deck."

In truth, she realized, it wouldn't all be acting. She'd need his help to get back to the cabin.

"Aye!"

He grinned, understanding at last. He quickly grabbed her as she swayed and nearly fell.

"You've got it!"

She had to get them moving before he had second thoughts. Leaning heavily against him, she took a step forward, then another and they moved out from behind the animal pens to the open deck. Martha's stumbling progress across the deck was real misery. Though the first mate eyed her quizzically, he didn't interfere. For him, at least, the story she told was convincing enough to save Hal from a flogging, whatever the other sailors or women who'd lifted their skirts for him thought.

With the help of one of the women called from the galley, Martha made her way

291

down into the cabin. When she gained her footing at the bottom of the ladder, she straightened with care so as not to move her head. She turned aside the hands reaching out to help and walked with slow, shuffling steps to her berth. Bett, she saw, had risen to stand shakily, eyes wide, her hand to her mouth.

"Let me be for a bit. My head is fairly spinning."

Martha sank onto the bed and tried to smile reassuringly at Bett but saw from the fear and alarm on the other girl's face that she was making a poor job of it. A quick glance down at her kerchief told her why and also why she had to take care not to look down again. She fumbled for the slop bucket beneath her berth and pulled it out just as the vomiting began. Martha thought at first, the comforting hand on her shoulder was Bett's, but realized the worn shoes beneath a tattered hem belonged to the one other soul she felt she could call friend.

Joan had guessed what happened to Martha, as had most of the other women. The girl wasn't the sort to lose her footing, nor to follow Mag's path. They saw the loose lacings of her bodice and her kerchief in disarray. And Joan saw Mag, whispering and grinning with one of her cronies. She had no doubt that Mag's hand was in whatever happened. But there were more pressing matters to deal with.

She filled a bucket with sea water from the barrel near the bottom of the ladder and wet a rag that she handed to Martha when her retching stopped. Martha wiped gingerly at her mouth and winced at the sting of salt water on her cut lip. She settled for holding the cloth against her lips. With a deep breath to quiet her stomach, she leaned back against the bulkhead. Once she was still and could keep the dizziness at bay, Martha was aware of the blood caked on her cheeks and chin. She began to scrub at it.

"You're making a mess of that."

Joan took the rag to finish cleaning the blood crusting over Martha's face and neck. She had less success getting out the blood that had deepened the reddish brown of the hair falling across her forehead.

"We need to make a bandage for your head. Have you something we can use?"

"Aye."

Martha couldn't say more. Speaking hurt. She fumbled behind her to pull several folded strips of sheeting from the corner where she kept her belongings. They were meant for her monthly courses, but she kept them only so that none would guess she had no need. Unable to care what happened next, she closed her eyes to shut out the cabin that was again spinning around her.

"Rest," Joan said, and Martha hoped her mouth had formed a smile in response. She was afraid to open her eyes.

Joan tore off a bit of sheeting and folded it into a square to press over the wound, then secured it with another strip of the cloth. She put the rest of the sheeting close by. It would be needed soon enough. By the time Martha had eased herself back on the berth, blood was already seeping through the bandage. Relaxing at last, Martha was grateful to be left alone.

"Where is she?"

The voice rumbled down through the hatch. A shadow suddenly blotted out its small patch of daylight and took form as a pair of thick, knotty legs. Mr. John Wigg was a large man whose movements demanded space. Above his grease-stained waistcoat, the ship's barber-surgeon's ruddy face was stormy.

He was in an ill humor after being called away from his dinner to tend some convict wench. Cringing in his wake, the captain's cabin boy clearly didn't want to be there. Shying away from him, the closest women pointed toward Martha.

"You there. Come here."

He waved a hand in Martha's direction. She shoved herself carefully to her feet. With Joan's help, she walked to the stool Mr. Wigg kicked to a spot in the lantern's light.

Martha gripped the side of the table and eased herself down to the stool. She winced as the surgeon roughly untied her bandage and lifted the pad covering the wound.

"Curses."

Muttering angrily, he quickly replaced the pad to stop the blood that had begun to flow again. He looked around to find the cabin boy who shrank back against the ladder. The surgeon apparently thought better of it. He beckoned toward Joan.

"Here. You there. Come hold this."

He waited until Joan had her hand on the bandage and turned again to the boy.

"Go to my cabin. You'll find my bag there. Bring it."

Relief sent the boy up the ladder in double time.

"You've not done anything else to yourself have you?"

For the first time, he looked directly at Martha.

"No."

She was grateful that Joan's hand on her forehead reminded her not to shake her head.

"Humpf"

The surgeon looked hard at the girl. The captain said she was young and still fair to look at. He'd caught the captain's meaning. Clear eyes. At least the one he could see. The color of a ripe hazelnut. And just a few marks of the pox. And teeth?

"Open your mouth, girl."

Ah, yes. Good teeth.

"Took a bite out of your lip, I see. Not serious."

He continued his thought in silence.

Someone will pay well for the likes of this one. Just a little repair is all she'd need.

"Bucket!"

Martha gestured wildly. Joan shoved the bucket in front of her just in time, but her retching only brought up yellow bile.

"Dammit to hell."

Mr. Wigg stepped back looking as if he, too, might be sick.

"It's the spinning. It brings on the puking."

Whatever the cause, Wigg didn't care. When he was sure the girl had finished, he moved close again and lifted the hair on her forehead. His prodding around the wound brought tears to her eyes.

"It's not cracked."

He was speaking mainly to himself. With thumb and forefinger he pinched her chin and lifted it toward the light, the better to see her eye when he pulled back the lid.

"Good. No blood. The wound will mend right enough. Where's that damned boy?"

"Here, Sir."

The boy, who'd been crouching at the top of the ladder, scrabbled down with a battered brown leather satchel and handed it to Mr. Wigg. From the bag, the surgeon pulled a small stone mortar and pestle, scissors, and a corked bottle containing a light brown powder. He shook some of the powder into the bowl, mixing it vigorously to a paste with a bit of sea water from the barrel. He picked up the strip of sheeting he'd untied, dropped it on the table and cut a piece of it that he folded into a small narrow rectangle. Working quickly, because the sticky plaster was drying, he removed the bloody square of cloth and cleaned around the wound pinching it closed. Loading the tip of his finger, he applied the plaster in lines along the edges of the wound, pressed the rectangle of cloth over it, and held it tight.

"This will close the wound. By the time we see land, it will be no more than a bit of a scar."

Martha had been sitting with her eyes closed. When she didn't respond, he poked her shoulder.

"You mind what I say. Keep it dry and don't meddle with it."

After tying another bandage around her head and gathering his tools into his bag, Mr. Wigg seemed well satisfied with himself.

"What's the matter with that one, there?"

He directed his question toward Joan as he pointed where Bett sat hunched beneath a shawl and blankets on her berth. Her eyes, dark and alarmed, looked overly large against the pallor of her face.

"It's the seasickness." Joan answered hurriedly. It would do no good for the doctor to think it was more than that.

Wigg stood, looking hard at Bett, then, with a shrug, turned toward the ladder. As he climbed, he took in a breath of fresh air. He looked forward to giving the captain a good report, but, of greater importance, he hoped the cook had kept his dinner warm.

Normal activity returned with the surgeon's departure. Martha declined the bowl of boiled beef Joan brought her and returned to her berth. She curled up with her back to the cabin, her head on her folded blanket and assessed her aches and pains. Her whole head hurt and her lip was swollen and painful. If she was careful not to move, the spinning stopped. She was sure there was a black and blue mark on her hip where Hal shoved her up against the bulwark. She guessed she'd have no more trouble from him. There was satisfaction in that.

She felt sick at the thought of Hal's groping hands and how close he'd come to taking that final painful liberty. Memories of John Randolph came back in a rush. Would she forever be preyed upon by such men? A convict? What decent man would look beyond that for the truth about her? About who she really was?

But then, could she ever again feel about a man the way she felt about Charley? That seemed like such a long time ago. So much had happened. And now she wasn't the only one who could be hurt. She laid her hand over her belly, but could feel nothing to assure her the child sheltering in her womb was safe.

Martha dared not think what might lie ahead where she was going. As she listened to the squabbling of the women behind her in the cabin, she wondered if enough ill use would make her as hard as Mag. Suddenly too tired to think, she let her eyes close, and fell into an exhausted sleep.

XXV

Journey's End

"Martha. Wake up."

Martha struggled against the heaviness of sleep and lurched upright. She could barely make out the face above her in the near darkness.

"Mistress Chin?"

"No. Wake up, Martha." Joan put a hand on her shoulder and turned away.

"You must come. It's Bett."

Still half asleep, she rose, but the scene in the next berth jolted her full awake. Joan was seated beside Bett trying sooth her, but the girl seemed not even to know her. She flung her head from side to side, great frightened eyes searching wildly for an escape like a cornered animal.

"Don't touch me! You mustn't. No more."

Her voice was weak, pleading, her breath raspy, passing through cracked lips in quick labored gasps. Joan took Bett in her arms, whispering and rocking until she grew still.

"They're gone, dear. They can't touch you. Hush. Hush."

When she grew quiet, Joan lowered her to the bed and looked up sadly to hand Martha the wet cloth she was using.

"Wet this again for me."

"Should I rouse someone to call the doctor?"

"What can he do? He'll want to bleed her or will offer some worthless nostrum. I think there is nothing anyone can do now. She must fight this alone. If she has the will..."

Joan's voice trailed off. She slowly shook her head and turned away so Bett couldn't hear her.

"She said she'd as soon die as go where we're bound."

Martha knelt to take the girl in her arms. She was shocked at how little substance there was left of her, nothing but bones.

"Bett! You mustn't leave us."

"I don't want to leave you, but I'm so tired. I can't do this anymore."

Bett reached up to touch Martha's cheek.

"You've been so good to me. I've never had anyone who cared. You've been the best thing that's ever happened to me. Both of you."

She looked up at Joan with a bitter smile.

"I wish I'd had a mother like you. Wherever I go from here, I won't forget either of you. Now I'll rest a while."

Martha held Bett until she appeared to have fallen asleep, then laid her back on the bed and rose.

"Perhaps all she needs is to rest."

"Perhaps."

Joan's face said otherwise. A sudden hoarse gasp drew them back to the bed. Bett lay still, too still. Her eyes were sunk deep in their dark-rimmed sockets, open wide, but beyond seeing.

The following morning, most of the women gathered around the ship's rail where a narrow bundle wrapped in canvas and tied with rope lay on a rough plank. Captain Muir stood near the end of the board. Two sailors waited on either side, ready to tip its burden into the ocean. Martha and Joan faced each other across the canvas swathed body.

"Does she have a name?"

The captain's words broke the silence. He looked from Joan to Martha.

"Elizabeth Williams."

Martha had to force herself to speak through threatening sobs.

"Ah, good. May you rest in peace, Elizabeth Williams. The sea is an honorable grave."

He nodded toward the sailors.

Martha couldn't stop herself from reaching for the shrouded form as it slid down the plank with a harsh rasping sound. She watched, tears streaming down her cheeks, as the narrow bundle plunged into the water where the ballast stone at its foot took it spiraling swiftly out of sight. It's trail of bubbles joined the froth of the ship's wake.

****

Martha lost all track of time between the creak and thud of the hatch closing at night and opening at the first light. On rainy days, the hatch remained shut, locking them in shadows created by the lanterns' weak light. Until their shouts brought someone to investigate, they had to endure the stench of their waste bucket at the back of the cabin that hadn't been emptied. Only when a sailor lowered the day's paltry ration of bread, cheese, and stale beer, were they allowed to carry the foul buckets above.

Martha could only guess that they'd been at sea two months. It seemed like more. However long, she had to force herself to get through each successive day. She wasn't sure which was preferable, the monotony of calm seas or the terrors of the vicious storms which they thought they'd never survive.

The most she could look forward to was a trip up on deck, if only to empty the buckets of waste. Joan sometimes joined her in that onerous task or to collect buckets of sea water laced with vinegar for scouring the cabin. The only other times the women were allowed on deck was to collect their rations or take their turn in the galley to prepare the midday meal.

Joan and one or two others actually did the cooking. While they were so engaged, Mag and her followers spent their time above deck nurturing mutually beneficial relations with particular guards and members of the crew. Later, they made great show of the rum, extra rations, fresh bedding, and whatever else they'd earned. Those who were unwilling to pay the price did without and cherished the hour or so of fresh air that could make the rest of their existence more bearable.

Martha seldom joined in the cooking. As she had before Hal attacked her, Martha sought a place at the ship's rail, but now in full view of the quarterdeck watch. There she let her thoughts travel back to Wapping, as painful as that memory was, and used it to build a fragile hope that she'd regain some semblance of that life when she reached Maryland. At first she kept an eye out for Hal, but soon was gratified to see that if he happened to be on deck, he made much of avoiding her.

She wasn't as quick to notice Captain Muir on the quarterdeck, which she realized was almost daily. He appeared to be studying the women. Calculating what they'd earn him when they reached Maryland, she guessed. She usually paid no attention to him as she stood at the rail, letting her mind wander with less direction than the waves curling along the side of the ship. Then, one day a barked order announced his descent from the quarterdeck.

She turned slightly not expecting him to do more than pass her by or send her below. Instead, he stopped beside her.

"You're the one was injured, aren't you?

Martha shifted, more fully to face him.

"Aye."

"Let me see."

Puzzled, Martha didn't move.

"Turn your head, girl."

He grabbed her chin between thumb and forefinger twisting her face from side to side. With a frown, he roughly flicked a strand of hair out of the way the better to see the ragged scar above her right eye.

"A fall, the surgeon tells me."

"Aye."

His closeness and his hands on her made Martha flinch and pull away. He took no notice.

"Humph. You seem too sure-footed to fall easily."

"I was sick, Sir, or I wouldn't have."

Had he been watching her? The sun in her eyes made his hard to see under the broad brim of his hat. Suddenly she was chilled by the memory of the box in the Old Bailey, John Randolph grilling her, the sun nearly blinding her. But then, she'd still had hope that she might go free. What hope had she now? The captain's manner suggested none.

"Sick?"

She nodded.

"I was rushing to puke over the side so

as not to foul the decks. I hit my head on the rail."

"I think you're not one to suffer from seasickness any more than you'd lose your footing."

"Most times that's so, but I *was* truly sick, Sir."

What does this man want of me?

"But it wasn't the sea caused it. It was foul water. I knew better than to drink, but I had a real thirst."

That wasn't entirely false. And high time the captain knew of it.

"I've heard nothing about the water. Wasn't it Burton did this?"

So that was it. But to what purpose?

"Burton, Sir?"

"The guard. They tell me he was with you."

"Hal's what I've heard him called, Sir. He helped me to the cabin."

The captain scowled at her.

"It's hard to believe that's all there is to it. He's more the sort to take advantage."

"I wouldn't know, Sir. I'd have been a long while getting back to the cabin if he hadn't come along."

"Was it someone else you were meeting then?"

"I wasn't meeting anyone. That's not my way, Sir. I like to clear my head and watch the sea."

"You're an uncommon whore, then."

"I'm no whore, Sir!"

Martha stepped back, her anger clear in her eyes.

"You have no right…"

The captain grabbed her arm and held fast.

"I have every right. And I don't think I have to remind you how you came to be on my ship. It'll give me great pleasure to put you on the block when we reach Annapolis. I expect to make a good profit on you. And perhaps you'll benefit from some honest labor in America."

He released her arm, but clearly wasn't finished with her.

"You don't know how much better you're treated than on most other ships. Trash like you are no more than livestock to most traders and are treated no better. I'm losing money on this venture and don't plan to repeat it. That girl we delivered to the sea was no loss, but six men have died and another likely to. It would have been more if I thought as little of human life as some who trade regularly in criminals. I've allowed too much freedom. If I see you wandering about alone again, I'll have you back in chains."

He started to turn away, then stopped.

"And mind you, we'll make landfall ere long. If it isn't whoring you've been set upon but escape, I'll be watching you."

"What would it serve me to escape, Sir? I can't swim, nor would I know where to go if I could reach land. And what would I do there alone, knowing not a soul, and not a penny to my name?"

"See you remember that. Now get below."

More shaken than she had thought, Martha didn't join the women in the galley, but went back to the cabin. She lingered at the hatch a long time to feel the wind and sun on her face as she looked out to sea. Would that be lost to her now too? Was it true, what the captain said? She turned and stepped through into the cabin's dark. Might their lot have been worse than this? And when they reached the place he called Annapolis? What then? For the first time, she let herself think of the immediate future.

An auction block? She had no doubt that she and the others would provide a great public spectacle. She'd seen buyers examine, paw, and dicker over livestock bound for London's butchers waiting at Smithfield Market. Would they really be treated the same as those doomed cattle and sheep? Her dark thoughts followed her below where fetid air enveloped her as she stepped off the ladder and into the cabin's gloom.

****

The women had enjoyed a full week of clear days when they heard a cry from the deck above.

"Land! Land!"

From her place near the bottom of the ladder, Martha was the first to reach the deck. Could it be true? She couldn't believe what she'd heard, but the shouts of the ship's crew swept away any doubt. The rest of the women were close behind her, pushing and shoving their way through the hatch. Immediately several guards appeared on the run, their sticks at the ready.

"Hold there! Get yer arses below. There's naught to see yet."

Martha, Joan, and a few others were already at the rail, straining for a first sight of land, but they hadn't the advantage of the sailor high in the rigging. There was nothing but the sea stretching off to where it became a part of the sky.

"Get on with you."

Hal and two others prodded them none too gently with their cudgels.

"Wait!"

Martha had caught a new, sharp, clean scent on the air.

"Do you smell it? That's fir, Joan. Can you smell it?"

"Aye, there are pines aplenty on the Capes," said a nearby sailor. "We'll be seein' them come morning."

Hal waved his cudgel toward the open hatch.

"But if you don't get below, the captain'll have you put in irons."

They started to leave the rail, when a

sailor's shout pulled them back.

"Look there!"

He pointed excitedly off to the north where they could just see a flock of birds, their white wings flashing in the sunlight as they swooped and darted toward the ocean's surface."

Hal, too stopped, but only for an instant.

"That's enough gawkin'. Get below."

The guards pushed and shoved the protesting women back into the cabin and, for good measure, slammed the hatch.

When three women were allowed up to prepare the midday meal, Martha persuaded the guard to let her go above to empty a nearly full waste bucket. She took her time tying the rope to the bucket's handle and checking to be sure it was tight. Lost buckets weren't quickly replaced. She lowered it for the sea to wash the last of its foul contents away.

Letting it trail bumping against the side of the ship, Martha drew in deep breaths of cool, pine-scented air as she stared at the dark band that now marked the horizon beyond the *Sea Nymph*'s bow. Reluctantly she hauled up the bucket and carried it below. Returning to her berth, she looked back up through the hatch and was heartened to see a white bird flying through the small patch of sky.

Martha had heard they must pass through two capes to enter the Chesapeake Bay. Late that day, she guessed the brig had done just that when they heard the protest of the anchor chain being let out for the first time since they left England's channel. The Bay's welcome wasn't hospitable. Almost as soon as the anchor took hold, a pounding rain drummed on the closed hatch and the sudden storm brought frightening claps of thunder that caused the ship to shudder and toss about wildly.

Within minutes the women were sick and fighting over buckets. With a blessed swiftness the storm receded leaving only a distant rumbling to remind them of its passing. In its aftermath, they were left with damp air thick with the smell of vomit and buckets brimming with waste at the back of the cabin.

Struggling to control her stomach, Martha climbed the ladder to beat on the hatch until a guard lifted it away.

"You must let us up! The stink down here is making us sick."

"Stay below!"

The guard shoved her back and threatened her with his stick until she backed down. He leaned through the opening swinging his cudgel and with a gasp quickly backed away.

"I'll tell the captain."

He didn't leave until two other guards came to stand watch at the open hatch.

At last, they allowed the women to hand buckets up to them and with a steady stream of curses emptied and washed them. Beyond that, watery ale and a breeze that followed in the wake of the storm were their only relief.

The brig was underway again at dawn. She seemed to be making only desultory progress with a light wind that did nothing to freshen the air below the open hatch. When the ship's anchor was lowered again, Martha could hear shouting and activity that suggested other ships nearby and the *Sea Nymph*'s boat being lowered. But they still weren't allowed on deck. Several hours later, one of the guards lowered cans of blessedly fresh drinking water and equally fresh ship's bread free of mold and weevils. He told them they were anchored in the roads off a Virginia port called Norfolk.

Martha realized that the captain had been paying attention when she told him the water made her sick and he rose a notch in her estimation. Then another when the guard told them they'd also taken on fresh provisions for the ship's passengers in chains as well as the crew.

"Fattening us up for the kill, the captain is."

Mag was the only one who thought that was a joke.

"I fear she's not far from wrong."

Martha leaned closer to Joan who had taken Bett's berth to be closer to the hatch and whatever fresh air it offered. She and Martha could talk more or less in private. She had told Joan what the captain said about the sale they'd face when they reached their destination.

"It would be a fine thing if you and I

311

were taken up by the same person, don't you think?"

"I have no hope of that, unless we're sold to the plantations. It's the men the colonials will be wanting in great numbers. Ah, Martha, let's not think on that now. I wake in the night wondering...It's almost as bad as thinking what might have happened to my little ones. I can find no good in any of this. Bett is well out of it."

Martha nodded and they returned to the silence of their own thoughts. The news that they'd be leaving on the morning tide to head up the Bay to Annapolis did nothing to lift their spirits.

****

"Git yer arses movin'"

The guard seemed over-zealous that morning, thought Martha, dodging a kick to follow Joan to the ladder. Behind her, the cabin was filled with angry voices. Since they entered the Chesapeake Bay, the women had grown more sullen and mean-spirited with each day that passed. That morning, they were a sorry lot. Slowly, amidst groans and curses, they forced aching bodies to stand, minds to shed their dullness to move toward the ladder and the hatch above.

Martha was impatient to be above deck. At the top, she and Joan, caught up with Mag, and three others stumbling ahead of them into the late morning sunshine, squinting and shielding eyes seared by the light. Silently, Martha cheered Mag as she cursed and slapped at the men who shoved them along toward the open space where the animal pens had been. The distraction was enough to allow her to ease her way toward the port rail where she could search the distance beyond the brig's rising and falling bow.

As she had for three days, now, she scanned the shore, but could see neither harbor nor city. She pounded the rail in disgust. The *Sea Nymph* was still in the middle of the Bay, still on her northerly course. For all Martha could tell, she was looking at the same stretch of forest she'd seen the day before. And the same meadow in the shade of giant red and gold-leafed trees, but this time there were deer, a dozen or more grazing. She knew nothing about farming, but guessed the land she saw had never been scarred by a plow. The air was surprisingly warm for autumn and thick with an unfamiliar earthy scent, so different from the stink of the Thames she once knew.

Unlike the Thames, whose waters offered no sign of what lay below, this bay was clear. The day before, she'd seen a great creature one of the sailors told her was a turtle, swimming just beneath the surface. And that moment, there was a churning with flashes of silver on the water's surface followed by an amazing fish, larger than any she'd ever seen gutted in the kitchen of the Black Horse. Were

she in different circumstances, she thought
bitterly, it would be a pleasant prospect, far
better than the grey existence London offered a
girl of her station in life. She was finding it
harder and harder to be patient now that they
were so close to ending the uncertainty of what
lay ahead.

Will this wilderness never end?

She was suddenly struck by a longing
for Wapping's familiar streets, its shipyards
and docks, the shops and houses where she
knew every soul. And the Black Horse. At least,
there, she knew what to expect from one day to
the next. It had been nearly a year now since
she last awakened in her room behind Mistress
Chinn's kitchen and the pain of the loss nearly
brought her to tears.

She was pulled back into the present as
two other guards and several sailors appeared
with buckets of the clear bay water, then stood
back to watch. Hal handed each woman a cake
of lye soap.

"You ladies are in luck," he said with a
sneer. "After you've cleaned up, you're getting
new clothes. So get rid of the ones you're
wearing."

"Not here. No. Never."

The angry chorus brought Hal up short.

"Captain's orders. If you don't we'll have
to help you."

The water carriers cheered.

He scrubbed his chin, puzzling over
what he should do as he scanned the group of

angry women.

"The captain wants you rid of your stink. If you're gonna make good use of the soap, those clothes have to go."

"No!"

The women spoke as one and made no move to comply.

Anxious to end to the confrontation, Hal shook his head.

"You will do this, and do it now, but you can keep one thing. A shift, a skirt, whatever. The rest must go."

He was answered with a chorus of curses as he waited, arms crossed over his chest. Mag and her cohorts were first to oblige. Huddling together for cover, Martha, Joan, and the others followed slowly, trying to shut out the cheers and lewd remarks from crew on the quarterdeck and in ship's rigging above. There was no hiding from the dozens of eyes hungry for the sight of bare flesh. Most of the women had put off their kerchiefs, bodices, and the few aprons that were still in one piece. They stood hugging themselves, uncomfortable in their shifts, as near naked as they'd ever been outside of closet or bedchamber.

The guards and sailors weren't the only ones enjoying the show. Some of the cheers came from amidships where the male prisoners were enjoying the show as they, too, stripped. Some had small clothes, but many had nothing beneath their shirts and trousers. They thought nothing of their nakedness.

"Damn your besotted arse!"

Mag's curses rose above the gasps and cries of the other woman as the cold water hit them. Martha spit and wiped the briny water from her eyes. Beside her, Joan was doing the same. They braced for another sloshing as the guards and several sailors advanced on the women huddled in small groups scrubbing their bodies under their shifts with the harsh soap. The men made great sport of hauling water. For once, it was no great chore.

"Let me help you."

The sailor leered at Martha, his hand with a scrap of soap stretched toward her chest. She slapped it away and bared her teeth.

"Keep your scurvy hands to yourself."

After Hal, such men roused more disgust than fear in her. For their part, the men were wary. Though Hal kept the truth of it to himself, a few guessed what happened between him and the girl. But she was comely enough to risk pressing against her in tight quarters and making lewd propositions when she came within hearing.

They guessed rightly that she wasn't one such as Mag. That one was worn and too well used. She encouraged the attentions of any and all, whatever their desires, so long as they had money or favors to exchange. This one would be a prize for any could get her to lift her skirts. Too bad the time for a chance at her was growing short.

"Filthy bitch, you'll learn to be more

obliging once we reach port."

The sailor's breath was foul as he leaned close so only she could hear.

He would have ventured more, but Captain Muir appeared on the quarterdeck with Mr. Wigg by his side. He stood, arms crossed on his chest, watching the activity below him. Martha had rarely seen him since they spoke and only from a distance. She was almost certain that he was studying her in a cold calculating way before he turned to say something to the surgeon. But she couldn't think any more about the captain. The sailor she'd rebuffed had returned to fling water in her face with malevolent force.

"I should have seen that coming."
Martha said to Joan.

"They'll tire of this soon."

Joan was wiping her eyes and wringing the water out of her hair from her own dousing. As it turned out, that was the last of it. The captain's presence had put an end to the sport. The sailors filled several buckets and left them for the women to finish their washing. Martha and Joan rinsed quickly, the salt water stinging skin red from the caustic soap. They could do no more than rake their fingers through matted hair, wringing and shaking as much of the water out as they could.

They had little more success with their shifts. The male prisoners were already rooting through the barrel of clothing set out for them. For the women, the captain arrived with two sailors carrying a large basket between them. The sailors began pulling out clothes and handing them to the women.

"Why do you suppose the captain takes such an interest in this?"

Joan looked sideways at Martha.

"I suppose he must see that we're going to show well on the block. One thing is most certain, we'll all look of a piece."

Besides petticoats that were of black and white stripes or blue and white checks, they each received a shift of white linen, a dun-colored short gown, and a blue linen handkerchief to tie up their hair. The clothing seemed to be less uniform in size. There was much haggling and exchanging of items when the women went below to put them on.

Though the clothes were ill made of sturdy common cloth, Martha gloried in the feel of clean fabric against her skin. Her own shift was of finer linen and well cut, but it had grown stiff with sweat and dirt. She could put on the clothes Mistress Chinn packed for her, but was glad she wouldn't have to use them until some better prospect presented itself.

When the women were dressed and on the deck again, the sailors brought out a large basket of shoes. By then, they were welcome as most of the women were poorly shod. The stitching in Martha's had begun to give way. She grabbed two of the over-large and badly cut shoes for herself and two for Joan. They'd put bits of their old clothes to use as wrapping for their feet to keep the shoes on. Martha was on her way back to the cabin to do just that when she looked beyond the *Sea Nymph*'s fo'c'sle.

"Joan, look!"

The ship was moving slowly toward a point of land that rose in a gentle slope to neatly trimmed hedgerows, gardens, and a swath of green lawn in front of a stately brick house. To the right, a river defined the point's north shore disappearing westward between heavily treed banks.

The *Sea Nymph* was bound, however, for a second, smaller waterway following its marshy shoreline to the southwest. Sheltering there were several ships around which swarmed punts, lighters, and other small craft. The marsh gave way to crude houses and the wooden stairs of a wharf leading to a wide street that wanted only paving and buildings of any substance to be called a boulevard. What structures she could see were modest homes, shops, and outbuildings, some brick, but most of plain clapboards gone grey with the streets' dust.

They anchored just off the entrance to a small harbor, guarded by a low brick and timber battlement where the noses of perhaps a dozen small guns were trained toward the open bay. What enemy they might repel, Martha couldn't imagine. She'd seen the king's warships pass on the Thames. These guns wouldn't stand a chance against the fire from

319

just one of their great cannon.

Behind the battery, she could see more small houses and a shipyard, where men worked around a small boat drawn up on a shipway. The yard was open, unlike the walled shipyards of the Thames. She wondered at the sawn planks that lay unguarded beside a sawpit and assorted tools and supplies inside the open doors of several sheds. Did these colonials not worry about thieves?

On the opposite side of the dock were wooden wharves and warehouses peopled by great numbers of dark-skinned men moving boxes, barrels, and crates between boats, warehouses, and wagons. More wagons and carts passed back and forth over the broad rock and shell strewn street that lay between the water and a block of stores and shops.

From where she stood on the deck of the *Sea Nymph*, Martha could see the rest of the town rising in a series of wooded hillocks to a crest topped by a large brick building of official stature. Scattered among the trees in between were several brick houses large enough to be called grand but, to Martha's eyes, the town had an unfinished look. This Annapolis was nothing like London where age-worn buildings were packed cheek to jowl along cobbled or brick streets. Was this really the metropolis of Maryland? Town maybe, but certainly not a city.

A dread, like the weight of a stone, settled in her stomach, crushing her eagerness for the voyage to end. What chance for a life could she find in a place like this? And it wouldn't be just herself she'd have to worry about. She rested her hand on her belly as she and Joan stood silently by the rail, ignoring the cursing guards driving the men back into the ship's hold.

"Poor excuse for a city." Joan shook her head.

"What will become of us, Joan?"

"I don't care. But you are young and strong. You'll make your way."

I must, thought Martha, but couldn't speak. Joan sounded so much like Mistress Chinn, it almost brought her to tears. Soon she'd be losing Joan, too, and could see little promise of a happy future in what she saw of their destination.

"You there! Get below."

The guard pulled at Joan's arm and then Martha's and shoved them toward the companionway. For the first time since she'd set foot on the ship, Martha was glad to climb down into the cabin's gloom. At least there, she knew what to expect. Perhaps this Annapolis would look better on the morrow.

PART II

I

Sold

"You'll see, gentlemen, I have brought you a fine selection of skilled men ... a cooper, carpenters, a tailor, a shoemaker... good workers all. I have also a goodly number of strong men to work your fields and bring in your harvests, and women who'll serve you well as cooks, house servants, seamstresses ..."

Captain Muir turned from the cluster of townsmen on the *Sea Nymph*'s deck to indicate the indentures with a sweep of his hand. A man at the back of the crowd shook his head.

"Straight out of Newgate, I hear tell. Pickpockets, pilferers, whores. We don't need London's foul rubbish here."

"Not rubbish, Sir. They're men and women who've fallen on hard times. They've been sent here in need of honest work to pay for what small crimes they've committed. You can't disagree there's plenty of work goes

323

wanting. And you won't find labor at a better price."

Adam Muir beckoned the men to step forward. He was pleased with the turnout and anxious to get his sale underway before other detractors could speak. The previous afternoon he'd posted his notice on the boards in several taprooms around town. In some, he lingered for a pint and a chance to tell any and all of the next day's sale aboard his brig.

He tipped his hat to a serious young man standing off to one side.

"Good day, Andrew."

On his rare visits to Annapolis, he'd stopped at Andrew Faal's public house just off the dock.

A good prospect for a sale, he thought. But why the tall self-assured man at his side might be interested in that day's business, he couldn't imagine. He simply acknowledged Faal's companion with a nod. He knew Daniel Pyke and his unpredictable temper all too well. They'd competed for cargoes in many of the same coastal ports until Adam Muir's ambition took him into the more lucrative English and European trades.

Martha stood with the other women, trying to hide her fear and loathing as she studied the approaching buyers. Most seemed more interested in the men until Mag shoved her way to the front. Making a great show of swinging her hips, she tugged her bodice down to offer a view of her full breasts. She'd seen the captain acknowledge the two men and caught the eye of the older, more seasoned one. With tilted head, she winked at him and licked her lips.

With a grin, Daniel nudged Andrew but he wasn't amused.

"Let's be done with this business, Daniel.

Daniel looked back at Mag with a shrug and mock bow.

"What about her?"

Andrew nodded toward a stout woman with a weathered, but pleasant face.

"Ah Andrew, Andrew. You must be more careful. Look at her hands. Do they look like the hands of a woman who's worked in a kitchen? Or anywhere indoors?"

Andrew looked more carefully. Broken nails, a little finger permanently bent at an unnatural angle, skin rough and stained by years of working the soil or worse. Daniel was right.

He stood back to look over the group more carefully. What would he look for if they were horses? Right off, he'd lift a lip to check their teeth. Then, he'd run a hand down their legs and along their backs and haunches.

Fool.

He chided himself. They weren't horses and the last thing he wanted to do was touch any of them. Easy enough to tell the old or worn out ones. A single look eliminated others. The task was harder with the remaining few.

"Now there's one."

Daniel nodded toward a dark-haired girl standing in the shadow of the quarterdeck.

Little wonder he noticed, Andrew thought. She seemed to be studying the prospective buyers with a speculative look that equaled their own. Sure to be headstrong. That would disqualify a horse. But she was young and strong and looked healthier than most. Too comely, though. That would surely mean trouble. For all the reasons the men who filled his public room at night would like the girl, he knew his mother wouldn't. And it was on her orders that he'd come looking for a servant.

Reluctantly, Andrew turned toward a woman standing near the girl. Plain-faced with a solemn gaze, she seemed sturdy enough. Well-shaped hands, long fingers accustomed to women's work he guessed. Cooking. Sewing perhaps.

Before he could think further, a man stepped up to the girl. Like most people in town, Andrew knew James Wilson. He owned a small plantation south of Annapolis.

"You there."

Martha turned to face him. Wilson crooked his finger at her.

"Step out. What's your age."

"Eighteen, Sir."

"Turn."

Everything in her screamed against obeying, but Martha knew that would only make things worse. She flinched and stepped back when he reached for her arm.

"Be still!"

He gripped her arm, his nails digging into her as he felt for muscle beneath the cloth. Not by accident he dragged his filthy hand across her breast before he stepped back to peer at her face. His foul breath caused Martha purse her lips and turn aside.

"Look at me, girl. Open your mouth."

He pulled her head around, grabbed her chin, and forced her mouth open.

With a self-satisfied look, he let go.

"Looks healthy enough."

Martha was relieved when Adam Muir appeared behind the man.

"You like the looks of her, Mr. Wilson?"

Martha looked at the captain in alarm. Until that moment, she hadn't really thought how the sale might go, that she actually could end up in the hands of such a horrible man.

"Aye. I've need of a young one, someone strong enough to ease my wife's days. Scouring, washing, drudge work. And, if she can learn it, milking and tending the kitchen garden."

"I'm no drudge, Sir. I've..."

"Quiet girl." Adam Muir stepped close to her.

"But Sir..."

"You'll wait till you're told to speak."

Was that an order or a warning?

"So what'd she do to get herself transported?"

Wilson looked her up and down.

" Working the streets, was she?"

He reached down and lifted her skirt almost knee high.

"That's enough, Sir."

The captain stepped between her and Wilson.

"She was taken up for theft. Bills of exchange, I think. A common enough crime. Her first from what I understand. That shouldn't be a concern.

"I was wrongly accused, Sir."

"Hah, a liar as well as a thief, I'd say."

Wilson looked smug. He turned to another man who'd been watching the exchange.

"Needs a good lesson in mending her ways. But she's young. She can be made to learn. Mistress Wilson won't have lying or thieving servants, but you can beat that out of 'em."

He turned to the captain.

"What's your price?"

"Wait."

Andrew Faal stepped forward, ignoring Daniels's raised eyebrows and nod of approval and James Wilson's angry glare.

"You say you're no drudge. What work can you do?"

Surprise and relief tied Martha's tongue.

"Speak up, girl."

Pleased by the prospect of competing buyers, Adam Muir stepped forward.

"Answer the gentleman."

"I was born and raised at the Black Horse, Sir. A tavern in Wapping."

Martha looked from Andrew to the captain. He nodded for her to continue.

"I can read and write and keep accounts. I served in the public rooms..."

"And in the bed chambers, I'll wager. You can't take a convict's word."

Wilson threw up his hands in impatience.

"What's your price, Captain?"

"Nine pounds."

"That'll buy nothing but trouble. Seven."

Adam Muir shook his head. He hoped he'd correctly judged the depth of Wilson's purse.

"That hardly pays the cost of transporting her. She's worth nine pounds even if she can do half what she claims. I have others for that price. And you, Mr. Faal? Do I hear an offer? I'd think you could use a wench like this."

Andrew was already sorry he'd opened his mouth. All he'd wanted was to get her a hearing. But to think of her or anyone else falling into James Wilson's hands sickened him. The man was said to use his slaves and animals harshly. The thought of a horse going to him was distasteful enough, but a girl? A young one... And now, damn it. What had he got himself into? He could tell from the look on her face, she thought he'd buy her indenture.

"Perhaps. But I'd like to consider one or two others."

He nodded toward the solemn-faced woman beside her, trying to shut out the girl's look of distress.

"What's your skill?"

"I've raised and cooked for a family, Sir. But I've made my way mending and sewing simple clothes and most anything else the lady of a house might be wanting."

"And your crime?"

"My children were hungry, Sir. I pawned a shirt I had to mend and bought some bread and milk for my four young ones. My poor little wretches had eaten nothing but other people's table scraps for two days."

James Wilson stepped forward.

"Come, come. Let's settle on the girl."

By then, he didn't care if he got her. He just didn't like being bested by the younger man.

"I'll be wanting a man, too."

He turned to the captain.

"Let's make it seven pounds ten shillings for her."

"Eight."

Surprised and relieved, Adam Muir turned toward Andrew.

"You'll take her?"

Surprised at himself, Andrew looked around hoping someone else would come forward, but all he saw was Daniel's wide grin.

"Mr. Faal?"

The captain's voice was insistent. Andrew nodded.

"Sold!"

"Well played, Andrew!"

Daniel slapped him on the back.

"That's unlike you. I'm the one always going off half-cocked."

"Aye, and there'll be the devil to pay when I get her home."

"I'd wager you won't be sorry. Your mother will come round. But I must be away now. I'll stop by later for a pint to see how you're faring."

Daniel knew it wouldn't go well if Andrew's mother thought he had anything to do with buying the girl. Mehitabel Faal had no use for him. Or most others in town for that matter. It would go better for Andrew if his mother didn't think he was connected with her son's purchase. Daniel clapped Andrew on the shoulder and, with a wink and a nod, was gone.

Though Andrew was sorry to see Daniel leave, he guessed the reason. His friend had gotten him through plenty of hard times, but dealing with his mother wasn't one of them. He didn't look forward to what lay ahead. But, truth be told, he didn't regret what he'd done. Prodded by that thought, he hastened to settle affairs with Adam Muir's clerk.

II

First Step on American Soil

Heedless of the activity around them, Martha and Joan clung to each other weeping. Finally, Joan pulled away.

"May God help you, child. You must be strong."

"No more than you."

Joan shook her head.

"I don't care where I go. All I ever cared about was taken from me. I'll get on one way or another, but you have a chance to make a good life for yourself here."

Martha had to look away.

If it was only my life.

She wished she'd told Joan of her pregnancy. What did she know about birthing a baby? Or caring for one.

It's too late now. I'll have to get through this on my own. And at the mercy of that solemn man. He'll surely feel deceived. And rightfully so when he finds out. And what will his wife think?

332

What if he doesn't have one?

But things could have been worse. She couldn't shake the memory of the cruel-eyed man, his pock-marked face close to hers, his broken-toothed leer, his rough hands pinching and prodding.

Oh God! What if Joan should fall into his hands or go to some other despicable buyer?

Martha tried to smile and hugged Joan again.

"I pray you'll get someone who'll use you well. God willing, we'll meet again. Once I've got to know this place, I'll try to find you."

"God willing."

Joan gently but firmly shoved Martha away with a light kiss on her cheek.

"Go now. Fare you well."

Without a backward glance, Joan returned quickly to where several men were walking among the other women, poking this one, questioning that. Martha saw no sign of the evil Mr. Wilson, but continued to watch hoping to see what might befall Joan.

"It's done."

Martha turned with a start. The man had come up behind her.

"Come along. We're done here."

"Yes, Sir."

Without a look or a nod, he turned away and she found herself speaking to his back.

Martha hastily scooped up her bundle and followed him toward the gangway. At the bottom, she stumbled with her first steps on solid ground. The feel of it was strange after being so long on heaving decks. When she recovered and looked up, the man had disappeared. Instead a pair of black men blocked her way. Clad only in flapping knee breeches and loose-fitting shoes, their bare upper bodies glistened with sweat from the heat and strain of the large box they carried between them.

Despite their load, they were more nimble than she and quickly stepped aside to let her pass. Though they were fearsome to look at, their faces were impassive, their eyes, glancing ever so briefly at her, told nothing of what they might be thinking or feeling. It was better, she guessed, to hide your feelings if you were a slave. Or a convict servant for that matter.

Once beyond them, she caught sight of the man. He'd stopped to look back.

"This way."

Nodding for her to follow, he set off with long, loose-hipped strides. Martha hurried to keep up, dodging another slave rolling a great barrel creaking and thumping along the wharf.

Does he not worry that I'll run off? But where could I go? I'd soon be in worse hands than his. So this is how it'll be? Doing his bidding and trotting obediently at his heels like a dog? It won't be easy learning a servant's lot. Newgate was almost easier ... once you learned how to stay alive. But here? It won't be that straightforward. And this man?

What must I call him? Master? That won't be easy. He can't be much older than I am. He has such a dark look, almost angry. As if I was the cause of it. And the other one. A rogue from the look of him. The sort to give Mag a chance to earn a coin or two.

Martha was glad that other one had left. She didn't like the way he'd been looking at her, speculating the way men in the taproom of the Black Horse did. In spite of the heat of the sun, she felt a chill. What did that man have to do with the one striding ahead of her with not a word or backward glance?

Once away from the wharf, they turned onto a wide unpaved street. Till that day, Martha had thought there couldn't be streets as foul as those of Wapping. But this roadway's deep ruts collected a stinking mix of horse and cattle dung. A dusty walkway separated from the street by a row of rough-hewn posts was little better. They did nothing, however, to keep her from being driven back out into the street by a large, sharp-snouted pig rooting through some vile mess of garbage strewn there.

She swung her bundle at the ugly creature, but it simply grunted and went back to its meal. She guessed its owner lived in one of the street's small plain-fronted clapboard houses. The pig certainly seemed at home. Little distinguished one house from another except for a crude weathered sign over one door showing the dim outline of a tankard.

A poor excuse for a public house, she

thought, and prayed their destination was a better one. Beyond the pub, houses gave way to the rear of the small shipyard she'd seen when the *Sea Nymph* entered the harbor. Several men paused in their work to watch her pass.

"Got yerself a fine one there, Mr. Faal."

Ahead of her, Martha saw the man's back stiffen, but he gave no other sign that he'd heard them.

"How long you think afore he beds her?"

He'd lowered his voice and Martha was sure that last was meant for her ears only. She swallowed the angry reply she wanted to fling back and wished she'd seen who it was for the pleasure of putting him in his place one day.

"Get back to work!"

Martha looked up and forgot everything else at the sight ahead of her. Behind a high brick wall was a large stone building. At first glance, it had a promising look of substance, which was all the more remarkable for its serviceable plainness. And its small barred windows.

Martha stopped, her breath caught in her throat. The bars, the impassable wall, and now she could hear curses, an angry shout. The solid, lumpish thing was a prison. She clutched her bundle to her chest and stared in alarm. Mr. Faal had stopped in front of it, waiting, watching her. She couldn't move.

"You've nothing to fear from that. The poor sods kept there are well- guarded. Though I grant you, it's a sad thing to have for a neighbor."

Andrew stepped closer to the girl, aware that the prison must be a sorry reminder of the place she'd come from. He put his hand on her back to guide her to the opposite side of the street but dropped it when he felt her stiffen. He went ahead of her, leading the way toward a fair-sized, relatively well-kept clapboard house.

"Follow me."

He disappeared into a walkway along its side. In its shadow, Martha suddenly felt light-headed. She steadied herself with a hand on the side of the house, then stepped from its shade into a sunny yard. A waft of warm air carrying the smell of fresh-cooked meat and bread quickly cleared her head. He stopped as they approached an open door.

"They're about to serve dinner. My mother should be in the kitchen. I hope you spoke the truth. She's in great need of a serving girl willing to do what's required of her in a taproom."

"I don't lie, Sir. And I'm willing to work."

Was that just a dutiful son's regard for his mother? He was a strange one. But, if this was an inn, she was sure she could handle whatever was required. For the first time since the awful day she'd been hauled away to prison, she felt a twinge of hope. But it was short-lived, passing as she stepped through the kitchen door and came face to face with Mehitabel Faal. In that moment, Martha understood the man's concern.

"Who is this, Andrew?"

Martha forced a smile and tried a curtsy.

"My name is Martha Pratt, Ma'am."

"I did not speak to you. Stay there. Andrew, come with me."

She snatched her son's sleeve and turned him away from Martha.

"What have you done, Andrew? I've heard the talk. Captain Muir didn't bring indentured servants. They're convicts. How could you think I'd want you to bring such a creature into our house?"

The woman made no effort to lower her voice.

Martha bit her lip to keep silent. Hugging her bundle to her, she glanced around the room. She wasn't the only one watching the exchange. A black woman standing by the fire was only half attending to the contents of the kettle she was stirring. Her worried look was mirrored in the face of a dark-skinned girl who stood nearby. Their mistress's displeasure had clearly given them reason for concern.

"How could you bring someone like that into this house? I'll not have it."

"She's bought and paid for, Mother. She says she's worked in a tavern."

"How can you know that? Such a person can't be trusted. Look at her. She has the look of a strumpet."

"You judge too quickly. It's done. You wanted someone with experience. Let's see what she can do."

338

"It's your judgement I question, Andrew."

She turned away from her son to level the full force of her outrage at Martha. The slave woman felt it, too. She quickly drew the girl closer to the hearth and handed her an iron to stir the coals beneath the steaming kettle.

Mehitabel Faal came to a stop, ramrod straight in front of Martha.

"What have you to say for yourself?"

Martha faltered, trying to think of something that wouldn't anger the woman any further.

"Speak up. I didn't send my son to purchase Newgate's dregs. Why shouldn't I send you back there?"

"That's your right, Ma'am. But if you'll let me, I'll show you that I spoke truly. I've every reason to serve you well and do what I must to make my way here. I come from Wapping and was born and raised in a public house. I worked some in the kitchen, but mostly in the public rooms. I can read and write. I did the marketing and helped keep the kitchen accounts."

"So you say."

Martha had to look away, fighting to keep silent. The woman glowering at her wasn't about to be convinced. Her son simply stood stiff and uncomfortable behind her. Martha could plainly see the kinship between mother and son. Both were thin and tall. They shared the same blue eyes and tawny hair, though what little showed beneath Mistress Faal's cap was streaked with grey. Her son's was a sun-bleached cinnamon. Scars left by the pox and lines traced by age and care hadn't quite erased the fact that Mistress Faal had once been a beauty.

"I was wrongly accused and taken from my home because of a wicked man's lies."

Martha had to stop. She couldn't let herself think of all she'd lost. Nor could she give way to her anger at the look on Mistress Faal's face. It was clear the woman neither believed nor cared what she had to say.

"I'll give you no trouble, Ma'am. And I'm used to hard work."

Mistress Faal snorted and threw up her hands.

"Take her to the garret, Andrew. I can't spend more time on this. Let her wait there."

She looked again at Martha and handed her son a ring of keys she took from her pocket.

"And lock my chamber door."

She pointed at Martha's bag.

"What are you bringing into this house?

"I... I have fresh clothes, Ma'am, and some few other things."

"Let me see."

Andrew, who had stood silent, a muscle twitching at the side of his jaw, stepped forward.

"We have no right to ask that."

"We certainly do. Who knows what verminous things she might be bringing in?"

Struggling to hold her tongue, Martha lowered her bag to the floor.

"I'll show you, Ma'am."

Slowly, she untied the knot and the kerchief fell open to reveal her belongings. Biting her lip, she shook out her woolen cloak, her blanket, the patchwork quilt, and unfolded the old petticoat, apron, shift, and short wool jacket she'd worn through the cold months of the voyage.

"What is that?"

Mahitabel pointed at the neatly folded cloth bundle. Unfolding it, Martha was careful to keep the kerchief's dull blood stains hidden as she took out her spoon, mug, and tin box.

"And that?"

"Just a few small things of little consequence."

"Open it."

Everything in Martha cried against complying, but she held herself in check. At least she'd have the satisfaction of seeing the woman's disappointment when she discovered what Martha said was true. It was a good thing she'd kept Charlie's knife and the ten shillings wrapped in a scrap of cloth in her pocket. She turned out the sewing items, her pencil, pen, and the small blocks of ink.

"You see. It's nothing."

Martha did a poor job of concealing her pleasure in her triumph, however small.

"Impudent slut. Put them away and go. No. Wait. What is that book?"

The little Bible had lain hidden at the bottom of the pile until Martha began refolding the shift and revealed it. She reached for the comfort of its worn leather cover.

"It's my Bible."

"That's enough!"

Andrew startled Martha. And his mother.

"She's done what you asked. You. Come with me."

Without another look to see if Martha was following, he turned abruptly and walked to the door.

"I'll show you where to put your things. Then, we'll see what you can do."

After quickly gathering her belongings, Martha passed well away from Mistress Faal as she hurried to catch up with him. By the time they'd crossed the shell-covered walkway between kitchen and house, she could hear Mehitabel berating the slave woman for some failure. Martha guessed that she, and not the slave, was the cause of the anger.

In the house, Andrew led her past a rough bar and around two long tables flanked by benches. Empty bowls and dishes with the scant remains of several meals had yet to be cleared away. Pieces of a broken pitcher lay on the hearth. Ahead of her, Andrew's boots left prints in the unswept dirt on the floor as they crossed the room.

Oh yes. I can do much for this place. If I don't lose my temper. That will be the hardest thing. There'll be no escaping Mistress Faal. But at least I know what to expect.

They passed through the far door to a short hall and a door o the street, she guessed. Through an open door across the hall, she caught a glimpse of another public room before hurrying after Mr. Faal. He'd already disappeared around the curve of the wide spiral stair and was waiting at the top.

"You'll stay in the garret. There are pallets and bedding up there."

He pointed to yet another spiral stair, this one of rough wood treads between bare-timbered walls unlike the whitewashed ones below.

"Just leave your things there for now. I'll wait for you in the taproom."

"Yes, Sir."

She ventured a quick look back to see him watching before the turn of the stair took her out of sight. Shortly, she heard the sounds of a key grating in a lock and his footsteps on the stairs.

At the top of the stair, she stood gasping for a cool breath in the room's oppressive heat. The afternoon sun coming through a small front window showed her a room clearly used for storing unwanted furniture. To one side, beneath the slanting roof, she could just see a cot and bed tick covered by a thin sheet. A small table and a battered chair stood nearby. Boxes, trunks, and broken chairs took up the remaining space under the eaves.

She ducked her head to drop her bundle on the bed and stepped back again to stand upright. Light from behind the chimney that rose in the center of the room told her there was another window. She went quickly to open it. If she was to occupy that cockloft, she had to cool it. A thump of the heel of her hand swung it open to let in a weak but welcome breeze. Beyond the roof of the kitchen, she could see what looked like a stable and gardens.

She guessed that the water gleaming not far distant was the river she'd seen when the *Sea Nymph* came into port. Looking beyond it to the east, she could see the bay. Was it just yesterday, she and Joan were out there on the brig's deck? And what of Joan?

A tightness in her throat warned her not to think anymore of her friend, her only friend now lost to her forever in this rough place. She offered a prayer for Joan's well-being and forced herself to think of her own future. She went back around to open the front window but found no relief from the heat. The unsettling sight of the prison's grey stone wall across the street sent her quickly back down the stairs.

III

Confrontation

If only for a few minutes, Andrew was relieved to be rid of the girl to sort out his warring feelings. Whatever possessed him to purchase a convict? And a girl such as that one? However capable she might be, she was sure to displease his mother. But, that wasn't new. Ever since his father died, nothing suited her. The house slaves, Sukey, Belle, and her husband Nate bore the brunt of her ill humor. James and Harry, the two younger ones, were fortunate. They worked outside the house, usually beyond his mother's reach.

Now he'd brought another target for her temper. But this one, he feared, wouldn't be so easily intimidated. He could only imagine what the girl had been through, but she didn't have the whipped or hardened look of someone who'd been treated badly. He had no doubt there'd be a constant testing of wills between his mother and this Martha Pratt.

His mind didn't rest easy about the effect her appearance in the public room would have. He'd seen Daniel's interest. Every other man who came into the Faal's ordinary for a drink or a meal would share it. Though she had none of the bawd about her, the girl had a look and ways that were bound to draw attention. He couldn't deny she'd attracted his and not as a servant. Nor as the women he'd had dealings with since he arrived in Annapolis.

Early on, Daniel had introduced him to the house by the town gate. There the women were obliging and could be had any way you wanted them for a few pence. He had no doubt one or two of their kind were among the convicts, but this girl wasn't one of them. But if her crime was theft, he supposed he'd have to keep an eye on her. Or not. His mother, he could be certain would be doing that. But if she was half what she claimed to be, she'd be what they needed.

He had yet to deal with his mother and her anger broke upon him the instant he walked back into the taproom.

"What were you thinking, Andrew? You defy me at every turn. You wouldn't dare, if your father was still alive."

Mehitabel's voice shook with her anger.

"Straight out of Newgate? Who knows what crimes she's committed? I'm sure you don't. Do you?"

He didn't even try to answer.

"Of course you don't. She's sure to be a thief. Or worse. I expect you to watch her. You didn't have to take such a one as that. Who knows what foul things she's been caught up in. Straight from a bawdy house I'll warrant. You know as well as I what sort of place Wapping is.

Nothing but brothels and overrun with thieves and whores and every other sort of river scum. Bad enough that we've come to a place these people used to call Wapping. And why was that, tell me? I'll not have anyone think we're bringing that back. This is a proper house and I expect you to see that none think otherwise."

"You're wrong about where I come from, Mistress."

Surprised, Mother and son turned to face Martha.

"I don't know what people think of your Wapping, but none could ever speak ill of where I lived. My master and mistress would never allow anything unseemly to go on in the Black Horse.

Forgive me, Lord. It's just a small lie.

"You'd find nothing untoward there. And, in your house, I'll do nothing would cause you trouble or offense."

"That remains to be seen," Mehitabel snapped. "And if you don't want any trouble here, you'll keep your silence."

"Yes 'm."

Martha's attempt at a curtsy brought on another spell of lightheadedness. She barely managed to catch herself and lean against a table.

"Are you sick? Have you brought disease with you?"

"No, ma'am."

Martha forced herself to stand and face the woman.

347

"It's the heat, I think. I've had naught to eat or drink since this time yesterday."

Andrew stepped forward, prepared to catch her if she fell.

"We can do something about that. Our cook will find you something left from dinner."

"No. She will not, Andrew. That's for tonight's supper. You'll not waste good food, on her. There's likely something left from last night. If those Negroes haven't eaten it all."

With two steps, Andrew had his mother's arm, drawing her away from Martha. Stunned into silence, Mehitabel listened to the unfamiliar authority of her son's angry whisper.

"I'll hear no more of that, Mother. Good food isn't wasted on her or the Negroes. I've said this before. And I meant it. They'll eat whatever food we eat. We've more than enough. They can't serve us well if they're half starved."

Leaving her to recover from her shock, he returned to shepherd Martha into the breezeway between the main house and the kitchen. There, he stopped her.

"I'll see that you're judged fairly, but nothing more. You'll obey Mistress Faal. You'll have to earn your keep here and don't contrive to dishonor this house. Or rob us. Or run away. It goes very badly here for thieves. In all else, you must set your own course."

"Yes sir, I understand. I'll do as you wish. I may come to you from Newgate, but I've done nothing to dishonor myself or anyone else. I'll earn my keep. If Mistress Faal will permit it, I'll be of use beyond that. I do know something of running a tavern."

"You come by words easy enough, but mind you, I'll be watching. Now, let's see what Belle has for you to eat."

"Thank you, Sir. You're kind."

"Just minding my investment."

Andrew left Martha seated at a small table in a corner of the kitchen. She had just a few minutes to wait before the girl Sukey put a pewter plate heaped with pieces of roasted chicken, black-eyed peas, chunks of bacon, and fresh corn bread in front of her. Before she'd swallowed her first bite, Andrew returned with a mug of small beer, set it by her plate, and was gone again.

As she took a second large mouthful of food, the Negro woman approached and touched her arm. Startled, Martha pulled back with a frown.

"I means no disrespect. I jes think you needs to know, you be sick if you eat too fast. I'm thinkin' it's been a while. Your innards can't take too much all at once."

"Aye, that's true."

Martha was ashamed of her reaction.

"I'm feeling like I might puke. It's been a long time since I've had a proper meal."

I must get used to these Negroes.

Fast on the heels of that thought was the realization that Belle had already decided about her. The black woman would never have presumed to touch Mistress Faal.

She forced herself to sit back until the churning in her stomach subsided.

Belle nodded her approval and left, taking the door to the kitchen yard. Martha tried to eat slowly, hoping Mistress Faal wouldn't suddenly appear. Once finished, she took her dish and mug to a large basin of water in the corner of the room where the slaves had left a coarse cloth and assorted dishes to be washed. Quickly, she washed her dish and mug, then picked up two china plates. Mr. and Mistress Faal's, she was certain. The rest of the food encrusted plates were of pewter, which she soon had scrubbed clean. She finished several tankards, a pottery bowl, and assorted spoons and knives.

As she scrubbed, Martha was amazed at herself. She'd done everything she could at the Black Horse to avoid washing dishes, but here, in this rustic kitchen, she was exhilarated as the clean utensils accumulating on the table. When all were done, she found a broom and swept the brick floor. She was crouched brushing ashes back into the fireplace when she heard a noise behind her.

Mehitabel was standing, hands on hips, staring at the table full of dishes and kitchenware. She hadn't seen Martha until she stood up.

"What is this? Where is Belle?"

"I think she's out in the garden."

"You did these?"

"Yes'm."

"This is Belle's work. You're not to corrupt my Negroes by doing their work for them."

"She was waiting for me to finish eating, Ma'am. I could see she was busy outdoors and I had nothing else to do. This isn't their doing."

"From now on, you wait upon my orders."

Mehitabel picked up one china plate, then the other and a tankard and several spoons. Dropping the last on the table with a noisy clatter, she glanced toward the door.

"It's about time they got to the garden. But that should have been done before now. They haven't done the public room."

She turned back to Martha.

"It's nearing supper time and that room will be full before it's done. Left to themselves, nothing would get done. The least distraction and everything goes out of their heads."

She glared at Martha who was clearly the cause of it as far as she was concerned. Suddenly in need of something to make her point, she snatched up a pail of water standing by the breezeway door and shoved it toward Martha.

"And this has gone right out of that Sukey's head. Take it. I'm sure you can do no worse."

Vinegary water sloshing out on Martha's hand was redolent of Newgate and the ship's

351

dark hold. She fought the retort that nearly sprang to her lips.

All it required was someone to oversee the job properly.

"Yes, Ma'am, I'll do it right away."

She took the pail and broom and hastened to the house, happy to be free from the woman's carping. Though her mind and body were tired, she welcomed the chore and the chance for a closer look at that part of the house. From what she'd seen, the public rooms were in no way a well-regulated business.

Methodically, she went through the main room, collecting dirty mugs and dishes, sweeping the floor, scrubbing tables and benches. She noted a corner cupboard full of heavy crockery bowls and cups, a few tea cups, a good supply of pewter plates and tankards, and a coffee pot. On a sideboard, she paused to admire several dust-covered, but well-made tin cups, a tin pitcher, and a candle box. From the last, she took two candles to replace the stubs in a pair of pewter sconces. The most promising sign was the room's well-stocked bar in a corner near the rear door, but the stained bar shelf was crudely made. Martha took one last look to be sure she'd left nothing for Mistress Faal to find, then headed for the second public room across the front hall.

She made quick work of cleaning the room's two tables before inspecting what appeared to be a shop. At home, she would have visited three or four shops to purchase the assortment of goods clustered in one corner and scattered along a wall. Someone had tried to create order among the rolls of linen, worsted, and broadcloth; a small stack of piece goods; baskets of laces, ribbons, and threads; and women's hose, gloves, and mittens. Mistress Faal's doing, Martha guessed. Their thin coating of dust suggested that few, if any, ladies visited the shop.

The rest of the goods were scattered about on a few shelves and in barrels and crates. One nearly empty barrel held cream-ware plates and bowls resting haphazardly in straw packing. A wooden box held beeswax candles and sealing wax; another contained candle snuffers, razors, pocket knives, a small bundle of memorandum books, and other serviceable items.

"We'll replenish the supply come autumn when the tobacco fleet arrives."

Martha turned to see Andrew Faal standing in the doorway.

"I was just wondering about that. You must do well then."

"We can do better."

The sharp edge to his voice brought her back to who and where she was.

"Beg your pardon, Sir. Mistress Faal wished me to finish this quickly. I must go."

She gathered up her pail and broom, gave a last swipe with the cloth at a stain on one of the tables and hurried out of the room.

She wondered at the hard look in his

blue eyes, but of one thing she was sure. She must tread carefully in this household. Some deep trouble festered between this man and his mother. For all she knew her life in this place could depend on it. Or, at the very least, the manner in which she lived it.

IV

Andrew's Story

Andrew Faal was five, running after his brother, heedless of the people and wagons that filled Liverpool's cobblestoned streets. He didn't remember the shove that sent him sprawling, didn't understand the scream, the man's shout, and the strong arms snatching him up.

"Don't look, boy! Don't look!"

But Andrew did look.

Will was lying in the street, crushed by a barreling carriage, when he'd pushed his younger brother out of its way. At the edge of the street, Andrew stood staring, willing his brother to jump up laughing and brush himself off.

"Come away, now."

The man took Andrew by the arm. "We mustn't leave him."

Andrew struggled to pull himself free, but the man's grasp was firm.

"Others will see to him. We must get

your father."

Ignoring Andrew's protests, the man tightened the grip on his arm and dragged him away. Word had already reached William Faal's shop. He didn't even notice his younger son as he charged out the door. Just inside, his mother stood white-faced, unseeing, her mouth twisted in an awful grimace.

"Mama."

Andrew tugged at her skirt, but she yanked it away and stumbled blindly through the front hall to the stairs and her room above. He was close behind, but at her chamber door, she shoved him away and disappeared inside. Abandoned in front of the closed door, Andrew couldn't think what to do. He stood staring through his tears at the dark wood, helpless and frightened by the muffled keening he heard behind it.

When he couldn't bear it any longer, he stumbled to the stairs and sank to a step halfway down. There, he tried to staunch his tears that soaked his shirt sleeve. Suddenly two men flung open the outer door just below. His father staggered through carrying Will's limp body. Once he'd passed, the men stood back motioning for Andrew to follow his father toward their large front room. All Andrew could see of Will was a leg swinging shoeless over his father's arm.

William Faal gently laid his son out on a large table cleared by neighbor women who'd gathered to attend him. He didn't look back as he pushed his way back through the crowd. There, he found Andrew pressed against a wall.

"You mustn't go in there."

He scooped Andrew up and carried him to the stairs where he sank to a step clasping the frightened boy to his chest.

"You must be strong, boy."

William gently pried Andrew's arms from around his neck.

"I must go to your mother."

Pulling a handkerchief from his waistcoat pocket, he mopped his eyes.

"We both must be strong and take care of your mother. Go to the kitchen now. Someone will be there to tend to you."

****

"Have you nothing better to do than pester me?"

Mehitabel Faal shook her duster at Andrew.

He ducked and scuttled out of sight. When he was sure she wasn't following, he snuck down to the kitchen larder where he carefully cut a thick slice of bread and another of cheese. Folding one over the other, he hungrily took a bite. As usual, if he didn't get to the kitchen when his father did in the morning, he went without a meal until midday's dinner.

It had been so since Will's death. His mother's attention was cursory at best. If he tried to help her, she shooed him away as if he were a nuisance. He finally decided simply to stay out of her way.

She didn't have to say anything. He knew that he'd taken from her the most beloved of her sons; that he might be grieving as much, if not more, than she. He and Will had been inseparable, exploring, wrestling, playing tag as they'd been doing the day Will was killed.

His father urged Andrew to get to know other boys in the neighborhood, but without Will, he wasn't comfortable with the boys' rough and tumble play. Instead Andrew joined his father in his carpentry shop, building houses and forts with wood scraps.

Because he avoided her, Andrew was a long time noticing his mother's widening middle. His father said nothing and left him to draw his own conclusions when he led Andrew proudly into their bed chamber to see a tightly swaddled, red-faced infant in a cradle at his mother's bedside.

"Don't make a sound."

His mother hissed from the heap of pillows that supported her in the bed.

"And don't touch her."

He didn't dare. Later, Andrew accompanied them to the church of St. John for Emily's christening, but couldn't bring himself to go with them to visit Will's grave following weekly services. At home, he wasn't about to chance doing anything that might harm his infant sister and welcomed the half of every day he spent in school. His mother was no more loving toward him after Emily's birth, but Andrew's time at home was more bearable as the baby claimed more and more of their mother's attention.

Once more, Mehitabel took great pleasure in her sewing, adorning the neckline of Emily's shifts with delicate vines and daisy chains and stitching birds and flowers on bodices in colors to match tiny patterned skirts. By the time Emily was four, Mehitabel was giving her small chores around the house and in the kitchen.

For his part, William Faal doted on his daughter and his wife. Mehitabel responded, if not with open affection, with a genuine concern for the state of her husband's clothes and the meals she set before him. Andrew shared the meals and knew to take his clothes to her to be mended or have seams let out as he grew. He was also quick to run errands and finish the chores she set for him, but she seemed to have no use for him otherwise.

There was no affection in the occasional nod of approval she gave him for a task well done. He expected no such thing from her and took pains to stay out of her way. Once out of her sight, he knew he was out of his mother's thoughts and that suited him.

When he wasn't in school, he was in his father's workshop earning a few pence to spend in the local book seller's shop. William encouraged him to try his hand at carpentry, but Andrew found his interests took him into another trade. With scraps of leather and canvas and William's help, he made a crude knife case and straps for holding tools on the wall over his father's bench. Instead of buying books, as he once had, he spent his earnings on leathers.

By the time he was twelve, Andrew had left school and was working in the local livery mending harnesses and other tack. On his own, he crafted a belt especially for his father's tools, a leather money pouch, and a razor case. With his father's encouragement, he took his leatherwork to a local saddler and harness maker who took Andrew on as an apprentice.

With his earnings, Andrew bought his own clothes and other necessities, but continued to take his meals at home. He often saw his father during the day, but the only time he had to spend with Emily was after supper when he read to her. He scoured the local booksellers' shops especially for books that would bring out her merry laugh. Emily was a small and delicate child and her sunny presence brightened the Faals' days. But her time with them was all too short.

Soon after she turned six, Emily was claimed by the feverish sweating sickness that claimed many in their neighborhood. Once again, Mehitabel closed herself away from her husband and son. They bore their grief alone. Those were probably the darkest days that Andrew could remember. He missed his sister and the evenings he spent reading to her. She'd been a pleasure that kept him at home most nights, preferring her company or a new book to an evening drinking at the Red Lion.

Though he and his father didn't speak of their loss, William acknowledged their kinship in sorrow and asked Andrew to go with him to the Red Lion the evening after Emily's funeral. There, over a pint of ale, they accepted gruff condolences and, for a night or two, took comfort from the pub's camaraderie. If it hadn't been for his father, Andrew would have left home to escape the sadness that prevailed there.

As for his mother, she remained closeted for two days after Emily's death. When she finally left her room, she made sure Andrew and his father were out of the house. Alone and weeping, she carried Emily's pretty clothes to the kitchen and there, fed them to the fire. She saved only the christening dress she'd embroidered before young Will's birth and used for each of her children. She packed that away and without another sign, went back to keeping house.

Mehitabel took little interest in her home though, or in the sort of meals she put on the table for William and their son. She accepted and returned William's tender attentions in bed at night, but allowed nothing that would get her with another child she might lose. They didn't speak of it, but both understood he was fulfilling his needs elsewhere.

Mehitabel found comfort of another sort. Unless there was heavy rain, snow, or bitter cold, she disappeared for hours every day.

"Errands," she answered with a wave of her hand, when Andrew asked.

But his mother hadn't been one for keeping things to herself and his puzzlement increased. She wasn't dressed for visiting and wore her heaviest cloak, even on relatively mild days. He finally had to satisfy his curiosity and followed her one day. She walked purposefully to the nearby churchyard. Weaving through its gravestones, she came to a stop at the simple stones that marked Will's and Emily's graves. Pausing to speak a silent prayer at each, she pulled her cloak more tightly around her and settled on the nearby wall.

On that day and the next, to be sure nothing untoward happened, Andrew lingered nearby. Each day, she read from her Bible for a short while, then took out some mending she'd carried with her. When he told his father, William simply shrugged.

"Let her be. She'll come round in time," he said. "But I will speak to the parson. I'm sure he will look out for her."

Though he assured Andrew that all would be well, William didn't tell him of his visit to the parsonage. To his surprise, the pastor's greeting was barely cordial. Mistress

Faal, he said, had refused in no uncertain terms to go into the church or to accept his offer to pray with her by the graves. Nevertheless, he'd assured William that he'd been doing his Christian duty and keeping an eye on her.

Relieved that she would suffer no more than winter's chill and a hard, cold seat on the stone wall, William hoped she would find the comfort there that she didn't seem to be getting from him. In truth, her visits to the graveyard did little to ease her feelings of loss, but they were the only thing that gave her any feeling of being close to her beloved children.

Indeed, William Faal wished he too could find an escape from his own memories. In the evenings, he began paying close attention to talk in the Red Lion of the American colonies and opportunities to start anew there. His questions took him beyond the pub to Liverpool's waterfront where ship owners and masters encouraged him to consider leaving England for the new world and its opportunities. Not until he was sure what he wanted to do, did he tell Mehitabel and his son of his decision to leave Liverpool and for a colony called Maryland.

His son, as he'd expected, was overjoyed. Andrew had ended his apprenticeship and was hoping to move beyond the saddlery where he'd perfected his trade. From the beginning of his term as an apprentice, Andrew had been setting aside part of his earnings to buy the best leather-working tools he could afford and made a fine leather case to hold them. From all he could learn, Andrew believed he'd be in business for himself within weeks after arriving in Maryland. That would be unlikely for several years, he knew, if he remained in Liverpool.

Mehitabel surprised both her husband and her son. She listened intently to what William could tell her about the Maryland colony and Annapolis, the city in which they'd settle. The idea of a capital city that was the home of wealthy colonials appealed to her. She'd long been chafing at the solitude she'd created around herself and couldn't escape the sadness that clung to every thing and every place she looked. Upon their agreement, William gave up the lease to his shop, then bought the passage to Annapolis that made their decision final.

When the move became a certainty, Mehitabel busied herself with mending and cleaning her family's clothes for packing and spent many days shopping for a variety of linens, cottons, silks, and sewing supplies to set herself up as a seamstress in the colony.

Mehitabel regretted leaving the few acquaintances in Liverpool she'd never see again, but had no family beyond her husband and son to miss. The hardest part was leaving her children's graves. Before they set sail, Andrew made charcoal rubbings from Will's and Emily's gravestones that his father framed for Mehitabel to take to their new home.

V

Annapolis Arrival

"What is this place they've brought us to, William? I thought we were coming to a capital city. Is this voyage not yet at an end?"

Mehitabel Faal clutched the *Good Fortune*'s rail, her knuckles white, unlike her face, reddened by an angry flush.

William couldn't answer his wife. He and Andrew stood mute. They were as shocked as she was. Less than an hour before, their spirits had soared at the sight of a distant harbor crowded with vessels. They'd been certain the *Good Fortune* would soon deposit them on the wharf of a large and prosperous town. Touted as the metropolis of Maryland, it was also the capital of the province. But what lay revealed before them as the brig eased her way through the ship-filled harbor had nothing of a capital city about it.

Laid out in an irregular plan, the place had no paved streets and very few substantial houses to commend it. A wharf hardly deserving the name was surrounded by a wide open shore bustling with horses, carts, and people stirring up small clouds of dust as they went about their business. As if that weren't enough, the majority of men toiling there were half-naked Negroes, the most the Faals had ever seen. The only other Negro they'd ever seen was a well-dressed servant waiting with his master on the Liverpool quay.

"Oh, my."

Mehitabel took hold of William's arm. She had prayed daily for the voyage to end. Now, with the prospect at hand, she viewed the scene before her with distress.

"Must we go amongst them?"

"There is nothing to fear, Mistress Faal."

William placed a reassuring hand over hers.

"They're fearsome beings, William. How can they let them roam freely like that?"

"They're not animals, Mother. They're human beings."

Andrew looked shoreward hoping no one had heard her.

"They're most likely servants, not savages, my dear."

William patted his wife's hand and frowned over her head at his son.

"I trust we'll have no dealings with them."

"We must, Mother. You'll soon become accustomed to them."

Andrew pretended not to notice his

father's dark look. He was intrigued by the town, the Negroes, and the abundance of cargoes they were manhandling onto lighters along the shore.

"They're slaves, Mother. And the only ones doing any labor by the look of it."

The rattle of chains and a thump that shook the deck under their feet ended any further talk of slaves. At last, the gangplank was being made fast to the wharf and the Faals hurried below to gather whatever they'd carry when they were allowed ashore. Returning to the deck, they joined the other eager passengers filing down the gangplank.

William left Andrew to attend to the unloading of their trunks and other baggage and escorted his wife away from the ship. As he led her across the unpaved expanse at the head of the dock, Mehitabel clung to his arm. With her free hand, she gathered up her skirts to keep them out of the dirt and animal dung, then hastily dropped them to pull a handkerchief from her bodice. The bit of cloth was poor defense against the smells and dust assailing her nose and eyes. She tucked it back where it came from and gathered up her skirts again.

"We're almost there, Mrs. Faal."

William guided her past a brick tavern, several rough sheds, and a small stone warehouse to a narrow lane and Mr. Ashbury Sutton's inn. At the door, Mehitabel hung back.

"Is there no place better than this?"

"No my dear, not now. The captain tells

me the province's government is in session. The best places are taken up. He assured me that this will suit us until we can find more permanent lodging."

The innkeeper was expecting them.

"Ah Mistess Faal, welcome to our house."

Ashbury Sutton was a large, imposing man .

"We've been awaiting your arrival. Captain Jameson sent word as soon as he arrived in port."

Just inside the inn's door, Sutton's wife greeted them. She quickly took Mehitabel in hand as the innkeeper led William off to the public room with the promise of a pitcher of beer.

"I've prepared our best rooms for you. Come, my dear, you must rest and get settled in. A glass of cider, perhaps? Mr. Sutton brews a fine apple cider."

"But my husband…"

"He'll be along shortly. Mr. Sutton will show him up."

Hoping soon to be rid of the irritating woman, Mehitabel yielded and followed her upstairs to a large, sunlit room.

"Now just sit yourself down, here…"

She took Mehitabel's cape and bonnet and guided her to a large wing-back chair by the open rear window. It looked out on a neatly laid out summer garden of fruit-bearing trees and beds of herbs, vegetables, and an array of blooming flowers.

"I'll be back in a flash."

And she was gone.

Mehitabel half rose, intending to follow, and then sank back into the chair. It felt too good to sit comfortably in a proper room with a gentle breeze that smelled of earth and carried flowers' sweet scent. Better still was the lack of the ship's motion with its creaks and groans and the watery sounds of the endless expanse of grey sea. She sat back listening to the songs of birds in the trees and even found comfort in the solid rumble of an unseen wagon on a nearby street.

As they recovered from the shock of their first glimpse of the town, William and Andrew walked the streets of Annapolis from end to end and side to side. They soon discovered its dimensions weren't considerable. Come evening, they visited one or another public house to listen as the locals assured them that opportunities abounded in their city.

"Might not look like it, but our city's growing. Should'a been here ten, fifteen years back. Those as don't mind working will prosper. A carpenter like you? Just look around, you'll see there's places a-building all over town. And more needed."

The man nodded toward Andrew.

"There'll be work for saddlers too. The governor and his people have got some fine horses. And plenty others have leather work.

Come to think on it, I got a belt needs mending. So I'll be hoping you get set up soon."

Others joined in.

"Wapping's the place to look. It's close by the dock and just the place you'll be needin'."

To a man, they all said more of less the same thing.

"Course, some don't call it Wapping any more."

The man shook his head disgustedly.

"This place is gettin' above itself, you ask me. They're calling it Prince George's Street now. But if you're looking for a house over that way, see John Ervin. He's got a place across from the shipyard."

William discovered that word traveled fast in the little town. John Ervin found him before he'd had time to search him out. The house was a tavern, Ervin said. It served men who worked the water or in businesses nearby, especially the men from the shipyard. They all but assured the innkeeper a living.

The house was easy to find, being across from the shipyard and the town gaol. But Ervin assured him that never put anybody off. The warder was known to lift a glass there a couple of times a day and some stopped in at night just to hear the tales he had to tell. The tavern was closed, just then, but not for want of business."

He shook his head mournfully.

"I let it to the wrong man, I'm shamed to say. But how was I to know Tom Pool had more of a liking for liquor than for selling and serving it? Stumbled off the wharf at the end of the street just a fortnight ago. That was a sad scene. Men from one of the ships in the harbor found him caught up under the wharf when they came ashore the next morning. Crabs and turtles had already been at him…"

The look on his listener's faces told Ervin that the rest of the tale was best left untold.

"The poor sod's wife and children just moved out and into other lodgings. The bar's still stocked and, except for fresh victuals, the kitchen's ready to use. A little scouring and clearing out and you could open your doors in a week or less. The Widow Pool kept it going till folks started calling in Tom's debts. She hadn't the where-with-all or the heart to continue after that. But come. Let me show you. I think it will suit you well."

William and Andrew inspected the house from ground floor to sweltering garret, and from the front to the kitchen house, stable, and outbuildings behind. The lead-topped bar in the main front room, scattered chairs, tables, and crude beds throughout told the story of a once busy, but sorely neglected, public house. Even so, the Faals were intrigued and saw its promise.

VI

A Suitable House

Rested but in no better mood, Mehitabel set in with her complaints the minute she stepped outside Sutton's house.

"Are there no paved streets in this town?"

She quickly drew out her handkerchief and covered her nose and mouth as the three Faals followed John Ervin through a broad alleyway along the prison's brick wall. Once past it and well out onto Prince George's Street, a sudden burst of angry shouts and screams from the walled prison yard drove Mehitabel into William's arms.

"It's nothing, my dear."

He gave her a hug and tried to lead her on.

"You've nothing to fear."

"Nothing!"

Mehitabel shook herself free from his

protecting arm for a good look at the source of the racket. The solid iron gate and stone building's barred windows quickly provided the answer.

"You call *that* nothing? Where are you taking me?"

"We're almost there. Just look. It's a fine house."

He turned her to look across the street and hoped his sweeping gesture would draw her attention away from the offending building.

"What does it matter how fine it is? How could you even think of living anywhere near that!"

Her voice was thick with reproach as she looked from the prison to the house across the street.

"I will not live there. I'd be afraid to close my eyes at night. How could you think I'd ever consider staying in such a place?"

Andrew stepped forward.

"It's a good house, Mother. Just have a look."

She swatted away the hand he extended to take her arm.

"Andrew's right. It is a good house and we *are* going to look at it, my dear."

Andrew looked at his father in surprise. William Faal seldom spoke to anyone with such sternness and never his mother. Andrew was doubly surprised by his mother's stunned look as she took the arm William offered.

From his vantage point across the

street, John Ervin breathed a sigh of relief. He wished only for the business to be completed. And quickly. At the door of the house, William stepped back and placed a hand firmly on Mehitabel's back to guide her forward.

"Once you've looked around inside, you'll see. It's a fine house and will suit us very well."

"What makes you think that? A fine house? I have yet to see anything fine in this place. That house is mean and plain like everything else."

Mehitable walked with William through the three ground-floor rooms in tight-lipped silence, then followed Ervin as he scuttled past to direct them back to the front hall and a winding stair to the upper floor. He followed them through the first large bed chamber where a battered chair, table, and bed heaped with stained bedding caused Mehitabel to take out her handkerchief again. The second bed chamber was no better. She turned to the landlord.

"It would appear that the innkeeper has been resting cheek to jowl with his lodgers. Are these the only sleeping chambers?"

"A garret above, Miss'us, but you'd only want to use it for stowing goods or slaves."

"Slaves?"

She ignored William's scowl.

"Or a servant, if need be. Wasn't much need for more bed chambers. I imagine the Widow Pool and her brood was sleeping in one of the chambers. And the others took care of what few lodgers she had. There was none at the last."

Andrew's call from the other bed chamber took a relieved Ervin off and freed Mehitabel to speak her mind.

"And this is the place you'd have us live, William?"

"We can't afford more until I've made myself known here. This street, they say, is the best for that. It will just be till we get settled, Mrs. Faal. You'll find this house more to your liking when we've had it cleaned properly and our furniture delivered. We must have a place. The captain will soon order our things removed to the dock."

He led her back to the other room where Andrew stood looking out a rear window.

"There's an orchard just behind the stable, and I suppose those chickens come with the property."

He pointed to the poultry milling about outside the stable door, then turned to his father. He'd heard his mother's complaints.

"Mr. Ervin says there's much improvement in this neighborhood. There'll be no shortage of other places that offer lodging, so I think that it won't profit us to do that."

Grateful for his son's intercession, William led her farther into the room.

"And we'll put these chambers to better use. I'm sure, my dear, you'll make these rooms a comfortable apartment for us."

"An apartment?"

Mehitabel's face brightened for the first time since they'd entered the house. She looked around the room more carefully and returned for a second look at the other bed chamber. With a nod of thanks toward his son, William followed her to add a thought that had come to him soon after John Ervin told him of the house.

"I've been thinking, my dear, from all I hear, there should be profit in keeping a tavern. At least until my work is supporting us. We don't want to use up everything we've put by to get started."

Stunned for a second time, Mehitabel didn't know what to say. For the first time in their years together, she didn't know her husband. Or what to think of his proposal.

Is it not enough that I'm here? What more must I accept in this God forsaken place?

William read her angry look.

"Don't worry, my dear. Andrew and I will see there's no carousing or rowdiness. I've no more liking for that sort of thing than you. We'll make it known that the lower sort aren't welcome here."

"Clearly, you have already decided."

"You might find it to your liking. "

William dared not say how much he liked the thought of keeping a public house. His idea was couched in memories of Sam McCall's Red Lion in Liverpool where he'd passed so many agreeable evenings. Sam made running the tavern look easy, at least from what William saw of it. Losing the comradery he'd enjoyed in the Red Lion was one of the things he regretted most when they left Liverpool.

What harm could there be opening a pub? ... Just in the evenings? ... It would be easy enough.

He'd checked behind the bar and discovered that Mrs. Pool had left a modest supply of wine and rum. They'd have enough to get started. But now wasn't the time to think of that.

"Come, we'll go below. You'll be pleased with the kitchen, I think."

With Andrew leading the way, they found Ervin waiting. Pleased to be nearing the end of his ordeal, he led them through the rear taproom door and a breezeway to the kitchen.

Unlike the clapboard of the house, the kitchen was built of brick with a flagstone floor, a great stone fireplace, and ovens that took up the entire back wall. The room's chief furnishings were a large, well seasoned pine table, and two sturdy chairs, with an array of iron kettles, skillets, and a variety of pots on hooks hanging along the walls and from beams overhead. Elsewhere several shelves held an assortment of crockery. Every surface was in want of a good cleaning, but it was clear that Mistress Pool had managed her kitchen well.

"Oh, my!"

"Now, my dear..."

William fully expected another protest,

but one look at her caused him to bite off what he was about to say.

Mehitabel sorely missed her kitchen in Liverpool, but it couldn't compare to the one before her. One day, on impulse, she'd bought a cooking book, but never had the space or means to prepare its recipes. Beneath the dust, she saw before her was the kitchen she'd always wanted. She was already making plans.

"I'll need people to clean this, William. A good man and woman should be enough."

As William, his son, and John Ervin masked their shock and relief, Mehitabel disappeared into a storeroom at one end of the kitchen. Ervin followed to stand in the doorway.

"I'll see to getting this cleaned to your satisfaction, Ma'am. And you'll be needing proper help. A wench or two in the house and men to work the garden and tend the stable."

The Faals followed him out into the kitchen garden.

"I'll send a man 'round to get this ready and planted when the time comes. Might be, he can get some things in that will be ready by harvest time."

He paused pointing to the clump of apple trees behind the stable.

"And in a month or so you'll be having apples aplenty for making cider."

When the Faals looked nonplused, he hastened to add.

"If you're not of a mind to make cider,

folks hereabouts will buy your apples. But you might want to keep some, Ma'am, for baking tarts and pies and what have you. And the fowl there will keep you in eggs."

Mehitabel walked gingerly around the creatures strutting and pecking around their feet. The only chickens she'd seen this close she'd bought ready to clean and cook. As William left to investigate the stable, she returned to the kitchen to look around again. But it was too much.

Suddenly, she didn't want to begin to think about cooking in that kitchen, much less living in the house. As soon as William reappeared, she urged him to go with her back to the Suttons'. With his mind on pubs, his shop, and settling in, he failed to notice his wife's distress.

"We've much to do, Mrs. Faal. And little time to get about it."

He rubbed his hands together, eager to begin.

"I'll leave you to see that the rooms are furnished to suit us. Mr. Ervin can send that woman to you here..."

"No, William. Not now. I'm tired. I can't think of that now."

Surprised and disappointed, he accompanied her back to the Suttons' house where Mehitabel sank onto the bed, then stretched out, shoes and all. William stood speechless. She'd never done such a thing.

"I'll rest now. Fetch me a glass of rum.

That will help."

"Rum?"

Mehitabel seldom took anything stronger than an occasional glass of canary wine.

"Rum, William. I want to sleep."

"Yes, my dear."

He left her staring at the ceiling.

The wonder of the kitchen was just a momentary distraction, not enough to erase the sad memories or replace the feelings of loss she'd endured since before they left home — their real home where her dear, dead children now slept alone with no one to keep their memory alive. Whatever this place might have to offer, it would never feel like home. Sobbing, she let her tears flow until she heard William's voice speaking to someone below and his footsteps on the stair.

Wielding her handkerchief, she wiped her nose and eyes as she sat up. She was fluffing the limp curls at her temples when William came through the door. He could see she'd been crying, but had no idea how to comfort her. Silently, he handed her the glass of rum, and gently squeezed her free hand. He waited just long enough to see her take a sip, then left. As the door closed behind him, Mehitabel took a deep breath, downed the rum in three slow swallows, and fell back on the pillow.

No more tears, Mitty. You must make the most of it.

Her mother's admonition was as clear as if she were standing there in the room. With a snort, Mehitabel shook her head.

You never had to face what I must, Mother. But you were right. For now, I'll just take a little nap. Then I'll be ready to face anything.

William looked in on her when he returned from signing the lease for the house on Prince George's Street. She was sound asleep and he slipped out quietly so as not to wake her.

VII

A New Life

As John Ervin had predicted, the tavern did well with men who worked the waterfront. William Faal took easily to innkeeping. He was a jovial host and within six months was making more from the taproom than from his carpentry. Though William was a master carpenter, he was new to the colonies and had to compete with younger men or those already well established in Annapolis. To find work, he'd have to go on the road.

He didn't relish the thought of traveling for weeks at a time through what he viewed as a vast wilderness. Mehitabel wouldn't hear of it. Thus, William settled comfortably into his shop with occasional small commissions to occupy him when he wasn't needed in the taproom.   William was more pleased than he dared admit as men gathered nightly to drink, talk, and play at dice, whist, or backgammon.

Though he'd at first stocked Malaga,

Canary, and Madeira wines, he found most of his customers chose New England rum, strong beer, or flip when the weather cooled. Once he'd mastered the art of it, he enjoyed the drama of making flip, measuring out beer, molasses, and rum, then, with a flourish, stirring it with a red-hot iron till it frothed and bubbled to the rim of a mug.

As customers gathered to drink, William welcomed travelers' tales and talk of trade and ships that had recently come into the harbor bringing news along with their cargoes. He was generally a tolerant host but had no liking for talk of politics which too often led to fights. An overheated debate got customers tossed out onto the street.

Sport, however, was another matter. During fairs and sessions of the court, wrestling matches and races afoot or on horseback roused more amiable, though no less passionate, rivalries than did politics. William didn't dare tell Mehitabel how much he liked his business and life as an innkeeper. Nor did he tell her that he no longer intended to move away from the waterfront.

****

Not long after the Faals settled in Annapolis, Andrew put a notice in the *Maryland Gazette*. He soon had work in town and was sharing his father's little-used shop off the taproom. Before long, however, he realized that a great number of the colonials who came from beyond the town needed saddlery and harness-work for their horses, oxen, sledges, carts, and carriages.

Often those who came to the tavern from farms and plantations spoke of the need for a saddler's skills. He had offers from several but declined. He'd have to depend on them for transportation to and from plantations that were often a day's ride away. Though he welcomed the chance to see more to the countryside, he didn't want to be trapped on some rustic's farm.

As a result, he put out the word that he needed a horse, assuming that riding was a skill easily acquired. Much to the amusement of local liverymen, he was either thrown or simply fell off the first horses he tried. At last they took pity on him and brought forth a sturdy bay gelding with an easy and forgiving temperament. With *Robin* he was soon able to take his trade into the surrounding country where he found more than enough leatherwork to justify his purchase of the horse.

On the road, he took his time, stopping often to ease his legs and backside until his body adjusted to the new demands on it. At plantations, large and small, he got to know the people and their ways. In the process, he mended bridles, stirrup leathers, harnesses, and other tack a farmer had and accepted payment in goods or coin along with a place to sleep, meals, and fodder for *Robin*. Though his accommodations were rustic more often than not, at twenty-two, Andrew gloried in a freedom he'd never known in Liverpool.

By the end of the first year, he had orders enough and business from his ad in the *Maryland Gazette* to make it worth his while to stay at home. Not only was he repairing saddles and other tack, he was working with leather trappings unique to the needs of local businesses, especially the shipyard across the street.

The shipwrights and other workmen there required a great variety of leather goods for which he'd never had requests. He welcomed the challenge and required no more than a drawing or a worn leather strap or belt to be replaced to fill an order. He quickly became one of the steadiest customers of the tanner at the western edge of town.

Andrew never regretted his time on the road, though he often wished he hadn't been limited by the heavy packs of tools and supplies that kept him from giving *Robin* a good run. When *Robin* was unhampered and Andrew could give him his head, he discovered the gelding was a fast, sure-footed sprinter. He also found that there was no dearth of young men eager to test their country-bred horses. On a quarter-mile stretch of open road, *Robin* easily outran most challengers.

Back in Annapolis, his bay was barred from the fall races on the long course on the outskirts of town. Only blooded horses

385

imported by the governor and other Maryland gentlemen could run there for the entertainment of their fellow gentry as well as cheering crowds of townsmen.

On race day, the names of horses, riders, and race results were the subject of much debate in the Faal's taproom. Many of William's customers knew of Andrew's successes with *Robin* and fueled enthusiasm for a fall scrub race at Annapolis. The call quickly went out and two horses were found to challenge *Robin* on a rough three-mile course south of town.

It seemed as if half the town turned out to stand along the country course to watch *Robin* win two out of the three races. Andrew's pride in his horse lingered long after that race. So did the memory of his father waving his hat and cheering him on as *Robin*'s dust filled the mouths and eyes of the riders behind them. That was among the few good times with his father that Andrew remembered.

****

The Faals weren't long in Annapolis before Andrew and his father were at odds over the hired help. William easily found white tavern wenches to serve in the public rooms but that wasn't the case with men to work the gardens, stable, and orchard. White labor was scarce and an unnecessary expense when slaves for hire were readily available. Over Andrew's objections, William hired the labor of two slaves.

"I know what you've come to say, Andrew and I'll hear none of it."

"I don't understand how you can justify this, Father. You know you exploit those Negroes twice when you hire them. Not only are they enslaved, they get nothing from their labor. This town must have men in need of work. We're sure to find someone who'll suit us."

"I've tried, Andrew. The work needs to be done. I don't find you eager to get out there with a hoe. We need them now. And it's done. I've signed an agreement with Mr. Jones and will hear no more on the matter from you."

Stunned, Andrew could only watch as his father strode away. They had differences enough, but never so angry. He looked beyond the kitchen yard to where the two black men were already turning a sizable section of long-abandoned earth into soil that could produce a garden crop.

His father was right on one count. He didn't want to work the garden. He'd already broken a perfectly good wooden rake and had no idea how to split wood to build a rail fence for the garden he'd have to plant.

Just once he took up the wedge and iron-banded maul and tried his hand at splitting cordwood for their fires. His shoulders ached for days afterward. When he returned to his workbench, he sat, head in hands, until his breathing returned to normal and his anger cooled. But only briefly. When he picked up an awl, he realized that his blistered hands weren't going to let him use his tools that day. Tossing the awl aside, he rummaged at the back of the bench to pull out a cloth and oil and went to work on a waiting leather harness strap.

VIII

Daniel Pyke

"Damn you! Move on!"

The shout brought Andrew into the street where a heavy-set man was mercilessly beating his cart horse. A few passers-by looked away in disgust, but none took an interest in the animal's fate. Already no more than a sharp-boned rack for its hide, the sorry animal's owner seemed determined to finish it off.

The carter had no idea what hit him until he was sprawled in the dust. Standing over him, Daniel Pyke flicked the tip of the man's whip perilously close to his head.

"I've a good mind to put you in harness and give you a taste of this."

Daniel looked for all the world as if he'd do it, but instead, gave the man a hand up and shoved him toward the cart.

"Go now."

"Gimme that." The man reached for his whip.

"You're going to have to make that horse go without it. And don't come back this way until you've put some meat on its bones."

Amid cheers from several men who'd stopped to watch, the carter stumbled to the horse's head and gave its bridle a yank. Startled into motion, the horse kept on going, spurred on perhaps by cheers that were clearly for the horse and not the man who led it up the street.

Daniel snatched off his hat and slapped it against his leg with disgust.

"I'd like to have given him a beating, but it'd do no good," he said to no one in particular. "Sooner or later, he'll kill that horse, then begin on another."

Without a backward look, Daniel turned and strode through the shipyard to the dock. Andrew watched him go but his thoughts followed the horse. He wished he could have bought it from its cruel owner. At least that poor animal would keep another from a similar fate for a while more. Perhaps the man would get his just deserts and the new horse would have spirit enough to trample him if he used the whip. With that bit of hope, Andrew went back into the tavern to take his turn at working the tap.

He'd seen Pyke often enough in the Faals' tavern and on the street but never had reason to speak to him. Their regulars spoke of him often enough and his name came up when his father was looking for watermen to carry trade goods between Annapolis and other Bay ports. They told him Pyke kept his boat just off Wapping Wharf at the end of Prince George's Street.

That was where Andrew found Pyke the next day unloading barrels into his punt.

"Mr. Pyke?"

A curt nod was small encouragement, but he plunged on.

"My name's Faal, Andrew Faal. My father and I are keeping tavern in Thomas Pool's house. We do some trade on the Bay and might have business for you."

"So, you think we can do business?"

The man's frown wasn't encouraging.

"I *was* thinking we might. Your first drink's on me, if you've a mind to come in sometime."

"I know where you are. Tom Pool was my friend, my partner til he took up that place. Thought it was a good idea at the time, but he was a fool. And I was more fool than he."

Andrew stood in stunned silence to watch the waterman step down into his punt and shove off without a backward glance. He'd expected a better reception after the incident with the horse.

That evening, there were plenty in the taproom to tell him about Daniel Pyke. A hard, bitter man, they told him. In time, Andrew pieced together his story.

Daniel had, indeed, spent many a night drinking Tom Pool's gin. That was where he was when his little house at the edge of the marsh caught fire. His wife Peggy was there alone. The men figured that no one was close by to hear her screams.

Daniel was among the first to arrive with leather buckets but the house was already engulfed in flames. He wildly searched the ground around it and in the nearby marsh, but found no sign of Peggy. It took three men to knock him to the ground and keep him there so that he wouldn't run into the fire.

There was nothing for the firefighters to do but keep the blaze from spreading. They were lucky that night. There were no winds off the Bay to carry the flames to other houses or outbuildings. Daniel's house burned quickly. It wasn't much of a house, the men said.

In the end, when nothing was left but the blackened and crumbling brick chimney, a few men remained through the night to help Daniel stir the ashes and drown the last glowing embers. In the pale light of the waning moon, they could find nothing of Daniel Pyke's wife.

At dawn, Daniel sent the men away. Alone, he searched the still-warm ashes until he found Peggy's blackened bones and collected them, one by one, in his coat. Carrying the pitiful bundle to a charred stump in the door yard, he sat, her bones cradled in his lap, scrubbing at her soot-coated skull. Sooty smears streaked his cheeks where he'd wiped uselessly at his tears. Several friends who'd watched from afar tried to approach.

"Get away, God damn you! I'll see to this."

Exhausted, the men trudged away. A few who lingered close by, saw him tie up what was left of his wife in his coat and place it gently in his punt. He took the parcel out to his schooner, they supposed to cast her into the Bay. A fitting place to bury her, they thought. Next to his wife and his boat, he loved the Chesapeake.

The men were sad for him. She was a pretty little thing. Hair near the color of golden rod. Shouldn't have left her so much alone. He was gone, days, a week or more, running up and down the Bay. But a man had to make a living. The water was where Daniel made his, fishing the seasons, carrying freight when he could get it.

Ashore, he worked at the shipyard, trading his time for the use of tools and materials to keep the *Seagull* tight and able to do whatever he asked of her. During the Faals' first year in town, Daniel was never around long enough for Andrew to get to know him. Nor was Andrew at home that often.

IX

William Faal's Death

When Andrew returned to Annapolis at the end of the Faals' second summer in Maryland, the packs slapping at *Robin*'s flanks carried six fine beaver pelts that were offered in lieu of coin or notes for some of his leather work. He'd also traded the repair of a harness and other leather goods for a bolt of linen cloth, woven by a farm woman and her daughters when winter's snows kept them confined indoors.

His purse was pleasingly full and made trading goods for services a satisfying change. His parents were also satisfied. But, the pleasure of his homecoming was fleeting. The next time he saw the farm woman's linen, it was stitched into a shroud to bind his father for the grave.

Not two weeks after his return,

Andrew's father took to his bed with the summer ague as Doctor Hamilton called it. Like the Faals, Alexander Hamilton, a Scotsman, had recently arrived and suffered through the seasoning fever. Chinchona or Jesuits bark, as some called it, put the doctor on his way to recovery. He made sure he had a ready supply and counted on it to get most sufferers through Maryland's sickly season.

The doctor assured Mehitabel that William would soon be on the mend. When the fever didn't respond to the first dose, or to a second and third, the doctor cursed his own ill health, the weather, and the general deficiencies of the town in which they'd settled. The best he could do was suggest that the foul exhalations from the marshes flourishing along the town's myriad creeks and inlets were the cause. Neither bleeding nor blistering or anything in his apothecary seemed to combat whatever ailed William.

Hours stretched into days when William swung between tooth-rattling chills and fevers that drenched his clothes and bedding in sweat. Mehitabel and Andrew were constantly at his bedside with cool cloths for his brow when the fevers came on and extra blankets to combat the chills that followed. Nothing seemed to help. Nearing the end, he was mercifully unconscious. Dr. Hamilton left Mehitabel and Andrew to sit by turns at William's bedside awaiting the inevitable.

William's absence in the taproom was

quickly noted. Men who lived or worked nearby had made a habit of stopping in throughout the day for William Faal's cider and cheap, home-brewed small beer. Many of them had survived the ague and fully expected to see the amiable Scot at the bar again.

The regulars didn't complain about the simple meals that Belle had to prepare alone. By the fifth day of William's illness, however, the mood in the taproom grew somber. They knew to expect the worst and curbed their usual boisterous talk in deference to the man struggling for his life above stairs.

As Andrew watched his father pass into oblivion, he didn't know what to do, how to comfort his grieving mother, or deal with his own feelings. If the taproom didn't require his attention, he slipped away to the shadowy recesses of the barn to muck out the stalls or curry *Robin* and the cart horse *Cato*. But when he knew the end was near, Andrew couldn't face the stable's silence.

Instead, he found the wedge and maul and attacked a pile of logs the wood corder had left in the yard. He was encircled by a litter of badly split wood when Belle came running from the house. He felt as if he were waking from a deep dreamless sleep as he followed the black woman to his parent's chamber.

"He's gone."

His mother didn't look up.

He approached the bed, but had to look away from the pale, hollow-cheeked man who lay there. He didn't want to remember him that way.

"What can I do?"

"Empty the house. Then send Belle to me."

Andrew stood silent, willing her to look at him, but she didn't.

"Go, Andrew."

He left, almost bumping into Belle waiting just outside the chamber door.

"She wants you."

He dared not look at her before he headed down the stairs.

After Belle brought a kettle of hot water and cloths to wash her master's body, Mehitabel sent her away. When an hour later she called Belle to take away the dirty clothes and bed linens, her husband lay dressed in his best breeches, ruffled shirt, and waistcoat.

In the meantime, the coffin Andrew had ordered the day before arrived. He lifted William's frail body into it, laying him out as his mother directed, then had James and Harry carry it down to the store. Alone in the painfully empty bed chamber, Mehitabel remade the bed and paused staring at the fresh coverlet.

As she looked around the room, she realized it was the only place she'd felt was her own, in a house, a town, a land still foreign to her. Now it was only a sad reminder of William, of his illness, and the last agonizing days they spent together. Clenching her jaw, Mehitabel shut and locked the door and went below.

She was relieved to find herself alone with William's body. The smell of tansy and rosemary was heavy on the still air and, she assumed, already at work warding off dangerous humors. Still, they had to bury him quickly. She hoped Andrew was off seeing to that. She couldn't think what else needed to be done and was just too weary to care.

She sank into a nearby wing chair and would have fallen asleep if Andrew hadn't appeared. Silently he handed her a mug of cider refreshingly cool from the ice house. Mehitabel welcomed the cider with a nod but couldn't look at him as she took it. Her own flesh and blood, the only kin she had in the world now, and she didn't know how to turn to him for comfort. The one person who ever could comfort her lay cold as stone in the box at her side. She was relieved when Andrew left.

As the shadows spread, Nate arrived to light the candles. He left quickly, relieved when his mistress found no other chores to keep him in the room. Worn down by the past week's strain and lulled by the cider and flickering candlelight, Mehitabel's chin dropped to her chest. She passed most of the evening asleep and offered only a mild protest when Andrew took her arm and guided her upstairs to her bed chamber.

Without a word or any effort to prepare herself for sleep, she sank onto the bed and turned toward the wall. Andrew stood, for a moment at a loss, looking at his mother's back, then folded what he could of the coverlet over her. With nothing more to do, he returned to sit by his father's coffin in the chair his mother had left.

A steady stream of men came through to pay their brief respects then crossed into the taproom to drink toasts to their departed friend. Some ate the bread and cheese that Belle set out and sat smoking their pipes and talking in the flickering candle light. One by one, they took their leave and were all gone by midnight.

Daniel Pyke remained with Andrew. As the night lengthened, Andrew fell asleep in his chair and Daniel stretched out on a nearby table. When Andrew woke before dawn, Daniel was still asleep, unbothered by the hard surface beneath him. Andrew wished he could find such release.

Mehitabel was up at daybreak and determined not to delay the burial. She defied the prevailing custom and paid extra to have William buried that morning. When the time came to leave for the graveyard, she left Belle and Sukey tending four plump chickens turning on the spit and a pot of hominy and another of greens cooking over the coals. Four pans of cornbread and three apple and raisin pies were ready for baking. The midday dinner would be her thanks to the men who'd kept watch the night before, fashioned the coffin, and would accompany them to the graveyard.

On the hill above town, the church bell had begun to toll when Andrew brought the wagon to the front door of the tavern where other strong arms joined his to lift the long pine box into the wagon bed. Andrew helped his mother up onto the wagon seat and climbed up beside her. He flicked the reins on *Cato*'s rump to begin William Faal's last ride through town to the hilltop churchyard.

A crowd of some thirty men and a scattering of women and curious children followed the wagon. Sitting straight as a ramrod, Mehitabel neither acknowledged their presence nor shed a tear during the ride or at the grave-side as the minister said the necessary words. For his part, the reverend could offer nothing about William Faal. He didn't know him.

The Faals had paid the burial fee of 40 shillings and their poll tax, which went toward his salary, but the rector had never seen them as he looked out over his congregation. When he finished, he offered hasty condolences to Mehitabel and Andrew and excused himself to attend to business in the church.

Back at the house on Prince George's Street, rum and beer ran free that day and night. Mehitabel did little more than speak a word or two or nod and soon people left her to herself. She saw that food was available, admonished Belle to clear away the dishes when all had eaten their fill, then went up to her room. Andrew kept tankards and glasses filled until early morning when he drove everyone out into the street and turned the key in the front door lock.

Andrew was sure his mother was asleep when he slipped into his room across the hall from hers. He was glad, at last, to be alone, but once he'd shed his clothes and stretched out on his narrow bed, the darkness and silence left him no choice but to face the gathering storm of doubts and questions about what lay ahead for him. But too much strong beer had muddled his thoughts.

Exhaustion was nudging him toward sleep when a sound the likes of which he'd never heard wrenched him full awake. He tried burying his head in the bedclothes, but he couldn't shut out his mother's strangled sobs coming from her room across the hall from his. Nor could he stem his own tears when they came on without warning. Soon, his throat ached with his struggle not to let out any sound of his own grief. It was a long time before that grief released its grip on either mother or son.

X

Dealing With Mehitabel

Martha returned from cleaning the public rooms to find Belle chopping fresh vegetables for a pot beside her on the table. Outside the door to the kitchen yard, she saw Sukey husking corn and headed toward her.

"You, girl. Stop. Where do you think you're going?"

Martha turned to face Mistress Faal.

"I was just going to see what she's doing. I've never seen that."

"Don't play the fool with me. I suppose you think you're finished in the public room. Come with me. You can't have done a proper job in such a short time."

Martha had to bite her tongue as she managed a quick curtsy.

It's more than has been done in a while, I'd wager.

"Yes,'m."

Is there any reasonable way of dealing with this woman?

A quick glance at Belle gave her an answer. The slave woman's face and eyes showed nothing of what she might be thinking or feeling before she looked back at the carrot in her hand. Martha quickly set the broom and pail aside and followed Mistress Faal back toward the house.

In the public room, Mehitabel made much of looking under tables, rubbing at imagined spots, and carefully inspecting the freshly swept hearth, then suddenly stopped to look at the mantel. There, beside the candle box, were the two candle stubs that Martha had replaced.

"You removed these?"

She held them up to Martha.

"Yes 'm, I thought it would save someone the task of changing them before long."

"That is not for you to decide. We don't have candles to waste."

"Perhaps I might have them to light my room..."

"It *is not* your room. Don't think it's settled that we'll keep you."

Mehitabel slipped the two candle stubs into her pocket and looked around again.

"I suppose until that's decided, you'll do well enough as a scullery maid. You'll clean these public rooms and the kitchen..."

Just then, three men stamped through

403

the door, removing their hats to wipe sweaty brows. Each in turn gave Mehitabel a slight bow, but the eyes of all three were on Martha.

"Ye have a new servant, have ye, Mistress Faal? Not from around here, I think."

"No. She's not."

Mehitabel cut off further inquiries by shoving Martha toward the door to the kitchen. The men's voices trailed after them.

"She come in on the *Sea Nymph*, I'd wager."

"Aye, one of them transports. You don't see many as looks like that one."

Martha and Mehitabel didn't hear what else they said, but loud laughter followed them to the kitchen.

****

Later, in the taproom, Martha lit the candles as the sun dropped behind the prison across the street leaving its face dark and ominous. That was where Mehitabel found her for one last task that sent her with Sukey to the pig sty at the end of the yard. She suspected the black girl was happy not to have to carry the heavy pail full to the brim with the leavings of the day's meals. That would be her job from then on. The waiting creatures greeted the girls' arrival with a chorus of eager grunts and squeals.

"You jes pours it over. Like so."

Sukey took the heavy pail from Martha,

lifted and steadied it briefly on the top rail, then tipped it into the trough on the other side. Though she was nearly a head shorter than Martha and the fence rail was almost as high as her chest, the girl completed the task with ease. The pigs dove into the trough in a frenzied rush and soon were snout deep in the slops.

"I've never seen the likes of that."

Martha was pleased at last to think of something to say to the girl, but Sukey's puzzled look told her she needed to say more.

"Where I come from, the only live pigs we ever saw were in a cart going to market. Never saw where they came from. Most were in the butcher shop, cut up and ready for roasting."

"There's a man over town has a shop like that, but we'll be slaughterin' these shoats out yonder by the smokehouse by summer's end. Got some sheeps and cattle out to pasture we'll do come cooler days."

Martha looked again at the lively scramble and hoped she would have other chores by slaughtering time. But there wasn't time to think of that. The black girl had turned with the empty pail to walk back up the yard to the well.

"They be needing water, too. Harry or James, they gets it for them in the mornin'. You just be doin' it at night."

She quickly hauled a bucket of water from the well, filled her pail and returned to the pig stye to slosh its contents into a second trough.

After two more trips, they headed back toward the kitchen. Halfway there Sukey stopped.

"You see that little house over there?"

She pointed to a neat little building.

"That be the necessary. I s'pose you'll be using that. But I put a chamber pot up there in that garret for you, 'case you needs it."

"I'm much obliged. For the time being, I'll be asking the Mistress any time I want to go out."

Martha said it with a grin, but Sukey's serious look told her the girl accepted what she said and saw nothing to make light of in the mistress's doings. Sukey dropped her eyes and continued up the yard to where a dozen chickens and as many chicks scrabbled in the dirt at one end of the stable.

"These be my chickens."

"They're yours, then?"

"No, Miss. They be Mistress Faal's, but she leaves it to me to raise 'em up."

Martha thought she caught a hint of pride in the girl's voice.

"See them babies? She's hoping 'fore too long to have enough hens to be sellin' they eggs at the market."

She collected a broom leaning against the wall and began to shoo the protesting flock into a roughly made house attached to one end of the stable. She looked around to be sure all were inside and then latched the door.

"Mr. fox, he be around here somewheres. Was catching one or two every night till Mr. Andrew built this."

She pointed to the hen coop.

"Some don't like layin' in there, though. I still has to go lookin' for they eggs. But they's four more hens sitting on eggs in there now. I'll be havin' me some more fine chicks soon. If that devil fox don't get 'em."

She tested the door latch once more then turned.

"We'd best be gettin' back."

With one last look around, she hurried on toward the kitchen where Mehitabel was waiting in the kitchen door, arms crossed on her chest. Sukey quickly scuttled past her mistress and disappeared indoors.

"We don't need you any more tonight. You'll take the back stair from now on."

With a peremptory wave of her hand in Martha's direction, Mehitabel shooed her toward the kitchen door to the breezeway and into the taproom. Just like Sukey herding her chickens, Martha thought. From what she could see of the taproom, it looked like a busy night. But Mistress Faal and the smokey haze allowed her no more than a quick glimpse toward the front of the crowded room as she hastened up the stair. In the upper hall, Mehitabel nodded toward a second narrower flight to the garret.

"Go up, now. I'll call you when you're to come down in the morning."

"Yes 'm."

The light from the hall's single lantern extended only as far as the second step in the stairwell. As she moved into the darkening shadows, Martha paused. Blast! She'd forgotten to ask Mistress Faal for a candle. But to face the woman again was more than she could countenance. She suspected Mistress Faal hadn't forgotten to give her a candle.

Cautiously, she continued on her way, running her hand along the wall's rough planking. At the top, she stepped up into a shaft of moonlight that came through the garret's rear window. She stopped there for a moment to let its pale light and her memory recreate the room in which she'd spent so little time. Gradually, the moon's faint glow molded some of the shadows into recognizable shapes. She could just make out the cot, the table, the chair.

Suddenly anxious, she walked as quickly as she dared to check on her bundle on the cot. It was just as she'd left it. Tears of relief and fatigue blurred her sight, but she didn't have to see to untie the knotted fabric and find the familiar folds and stitches of her quilt. She took it and her blanket out and laid them on the bed, then put her bundle on the floor. She was about to collapse on the bed when she was struck by a sudden, surprising feeling of freedom.

For the first time in months, she wouldn't be afraid to close her eyes before her final surrender to exhaustion as she had on the prison's stone-cold floor or the ship's cramped berth. Though she wasn't welcomed here, for that night at least, she faced no real danger. The night would be her own. Martha quelled an urge to laugh out loud.

Slowly, luxuriating in a breeze that came through the rear window, she unlaced her bodice. Growing tighter with every passing day, it was an unwelcome reminder of the life she'd carried with her to the new world. But she was too tired to think any more about that or anything else.

She slipped off the offending garment, untied her apron, and shed the petticoat. Laying each over the chair, she opened her arms and twirled as her sweat-dampened shift fell away from her body. Bit by bit, she slowed and came to a stop.

This won't do, she thought, and spread out the blanket on the bed. *Best get a good night's sleep.*

Martha knew all too well there was no certainty she'd be in that room on the morrow. She kicked off her shoes, folded her quilt to pillow her head, and sank onto the cot, luxuriating in the night's prospects that were better than any she'd had in months. She gently rubbed her belly where sweat had gathered beneath the waist of her petticoat.

I suppose you'll be needing some more room. Poor little mite. We'll get through this together.

Unless Mistress Faal had her way. Martha was certain that if the woman won the strange contest of wills with her son, she wouldn't spend another day in their house. Then, there'd be no knowing where her child would come into the world. But as low moans and muffled curses rode the night air through the window from the prison across the street, she was reminded how much better her life was for the time being at least.

She was tempted to close the window to shut out the mournful sounds, but wasn't about to lose the occasional cooling breeze. Instead, she looked toward the rear window and concentrated on the moon, a lopsided silver disk that cast a bright patch of light onto the floor. She couldn't remember ever seeing the moon so bright and clear. At home, even when it occasionally snuck out from behind clouds to shine feebly through the soot-filled air and cast its poor light on the rooftops, it was no match for the darkness of Wapping's streets. But that night, not even the wonder of the near-full moon could keep sleep at bay.

XI

A New Day

Martha awoke with the first light of day and lay still, not sure where she was. The memory came soon enough, prodding her to swing her legs out of bed. But there she stopped to clutch her belly as her innards gave a lurch. Till then, she'd attributed most of her discomfort to whatever poor excuse for food she'd had that day. But this was different.

Would the child move like that?

As if in answer, she felt another distinct movement she couldn't blame on bad food. Nor could she mistake the urgent need to relieve herself. Quickly, she squatted over the chamber pot and blessed Sukey's forethought.

Careful not to make a sound, she pulled on her petticoat and apron and stuffed her feet back into her ill-fitting shoes. As she stepped away from her bed, the small force within her moved again and brought her to a stop.

411

Mr. Faal won't be pleased to find out about this. But Mistress Faal will be. She'll now have good reason to urge him to be rid of me. She's certainly not the motherly sort and certainly not toward a servant's child.

Despite the morning's warmth, Martha felt a chill.

Can they make me get rid of it? Can they take it away from me? These colonials think nothing of keeping slaves and treating them as they will. They'll not put a fine point on the rights of a convict servant. If it takes every bit of my strength and wits, they'll not take this child.

With a resolute shake of her head, Martha crept to the room's front door to listen. Not a sound came from the bed chambers below. A glance out the window offered only an empty street, dark and silent, but a cock's crow drew her to the rear window. She saw no sign of the fowl but just below the black man, Nate, stood in the kitchen door looking off toward a pale, pink glow spreading above the far shore of the Bay.

Martha ran her fingers through her hair to work out the worst tangles as she watched the man walk down the path toward the bottom of the yard. Shortly, one of the young slaves arrived with water for the kitchen and came out eating a chunk of cornbread. He carried a second piece. For the other slave, Martha guessed, and was suddenly aware of her own hunger.

Her mouth watered at the memory of

412

the bread she'd had the day before. God and Mistress Faal willing, she might soon have the pleasure again. She sent a prayer into the rough beams overhead that the woman had slept well and would wake in a better frame of mind.

"You there, girl. Come down!"

Ah well, at least I can hope for breakfast.

Dreading what might lie ahead, Martha took a deep breath and hurried down the stair. At the bottom, Mehitabel waited with a scowl and an angry set to her mouth. Silently she scanned Martha up and down, ending with a disapproving shake of her head.

"That won't do. Go out to the kitchen. Belle will feed you, then, wait for me there."

With a dismissive wave of her hand, she was off across the public room.

In the kitchen, Belle nodded toward a small table where a mug of cider waited beside a plate. As Martha sat, the woman appeared with a frying pan in which the last of the butter still sizzled around two thick slices of wheaten bread. She forked the bread onto Martha's plate along with what looked like the roasted hindquarter of a small animal. A hare perhaps?

Without a word, Belle returned to the table where she was working on two large fish. Mouths agape, their silvery skin glistened in the sun shining through the east-facing window and open door.

Martha picked up a piece of the hot bread and immediately dropped it, sucking her singed fingers. More carefully, she tore off a piece, remembering Belle's warning the day before. The black woman had made sure she ate slowly. Out of the corner of her eye, Martha could see the woman watching her. Probably didn't trust her any more than Mistress Faal did.

Truth to tell, she wouldn't rush to trust anyone fresh out of prison. But there was nothing she could do about that. At least she'd be facing the trials of the coming day on a full stomach. She took a swallow of cider and turned to the meat, sinking her teeth into the warm, well-browned flesh. It didn't taste like hare, but it had been a long time since she'd had any sort of recognizable meat.

"This is good."

Belle quickly fixed her attention on the fish.

"Hare is it?"

"Muskrat. James caught it in his trap yesterday. That weren't what he was trappin' for. Trying to get one of them rabbits that's getting into the garden. And Mistress Faal, she likes a couple o'good fat hares ever so often. She don't be likin' muskrat, but she let me cook him up for us to eat."

She pointed toward the food on Martha's plate and turned away.

"You better eat fore the Mistress gets back."

Put me in my place, thought Martha cleaning the bone. If it was slave food she'd be eating, she had no complaint. It was as good as some of the common fare they'd served at the Black Horse. Belle didn't have to prod her to eat. She quickly finished the bread, grateful that the woman was intent upon stuffing onions into the fish splayed open before her.

"Thank you."

Martha licked the meat's juices and the butter from her fingers and drained the last of the cider.

"That was a fine breakfast. Best I've had since I can't remember when."

Belle feigned not to hear her.

Maybe blacks and whites don't talk. More likely, Mistress Faal doesn't allow it. Probably better that way, if you're a slave. The mistress most certainly wasn't about to do more than give orders. Certainly no thanks.

With a shrug, she carried her dishes to the sink, but remembering the day before, left them unwashed. As if she'd sensed Martha had finished eating, Mistress Faal appeared with a basket on her arm.

"Come with me."

She beckoned for Martha to follow. In the passageway between the kitchen and the house, she stopped and shoved the basket into Martha's arms.

"I'll not have you going about in those filthy rags."

The curl of her upper lip spoke eloquently of her distaste.

"We'll be doing a wash within the

415

fortnight. If they come out well, we'll see. Till then, you'll make do with these. They're the only ready-made we have in the shop. I hope you know how to use the needle you have with you. You'll find thread and scissors in the basket. Go upstairs and do what you can."

She plucked at Martha's skirt.

"I don't want to see you in those things again. Now, go."

With a nod toward the house, she stood aside watching until Martha disappeared inside. Once in the garret, Martha emptied the basket, laying out each overlarge and shapeless garment on the bed. The bleached linen shift and pale green bodice were both much too large. So was the brick-colored petticoat. She'd have to remake them to fit.

With a sigh, she shook out the black and white checked apron and plain linen neck cloth. At least, they needed nothing done to them. With thread and scissors in the bottom of the basket, Martha found a wooden comb and a rough linen cap.

She had to wonder how long it took the woman to find such a particularly unattractive cap. For the first time, in more than a year, Martha thought almost kindly of Mary Rawley and her unwanted lessons in stitchery. Thanks to Mary, she knew what she could do to make the cap more to her liking. And the bodice. The last and most satisfying things Martha pulled from the basket was a pair of shoes and grey worsted stockings. The shoes almost fit and were of softer leather than the ones she'd come with.

Martha quickly slipped out of her bodice, apron, and petticoat, but unlike the night before, it brought no relief from the morning's heat. Not a breath of air stirred in the room when she pulled the damp shift away from her body. As she set about snipping thread and ripping out the seams of the bodice, she kept her apron close by to wipe the sweat from her eyes and palms.

Though the room's swelter was a distraction and the clothing wasn't of the sort she once worked on, the job at hand brought a contentment she hadn't felt in a long while. Using her old bodice as a guide, she went to work and soon thought no more of where she was or the passing of the morning.

Not until the sun climbed beyond the midway point did Martha realize how long she'd been at work. She rose and stretched, walking to the rear window where the smell of meat and fresh bread drifted up from the kitchen. Dinner preparations were underway, but no one called her. Tortured by smells that made her mouth water, she returned to her cutting and stitching, trying to shut out the voices of men beginning to gather for midday dinner in the taproom below.

This time she was sure the disturbance and grumbling in her stomach were not caused by the baby. Her hunger spawned images of tables at the Black Horse laden with platters of meat, bowls of stew, plates of vegetables and warm bread. Ah, for a meat pie. But, no, she couldn't give in.

If no one would bring her dinner or call her down, to the devil with them. She'd as soon starve as appear without her new clothes to ask Mistress Faal for something to eat. Like as not, she'd be denied. She had several hours yet before she lost the sunlight streaming though the front window. She could do it, with fast, loose stitches if need be, just enough to hold together till later when she could finish the seams properly.

Just as the sun began to slip beyond the roof of the prison across the street, Martha tied off the last row of loose stitches in the shift where they were least likely to be seen. She quickly discarded her old shift, now damp with sweat, to don the new one. With no looking glass, she had to guess how well the new bodice and skirt fit. From the feel of them, she decided she'd done as well as anyone could have. She was grateful that she'd lost the flesh that once shaped her hips and stretched her old skirt and bodice. Though she could still feel her ribs and hip bones, her expanding belly made the new clothes fit.

She hastily combed out the worst tangles, rebraided her hair, and tied it with a ribbon of cloth cut from the green bodice. Finally, she donned the cap, reduced in size and edged with tucks that made it more attractive. Satisfied with the result of her afternoon's

418

work, she headed for the stairs and a much longed-for supper.

In the kitchen she was rewarded by Mehitabel Faal's look of surprise as she clamped her mouth shut on whatever she'd been about to say.

"It's about time."

"Beg pardon, Ma'am. I worked as fast as I could. If you please, Ma'am, might I go down to the necessary?"

"Aye. Go."

Mehitabel waved her hand in the direction of the door.

"Don't tarry."

Before returning, Martha stopped at the well to hoist a bucket of water. She splashed some on her face and took a long drink from the tin cup that hung on a chain nearby. That afternoon she'd noticed when she wiped the sweat from her brow and cheeks, her apron came away streaked with dirt. She was glad to see that her new apron was unmarked.

She arrived in the kitchen just as Andrew Faal emerged from the storeroom with a keg of rum on one shoulder. He came to an abrupt halt when he saw her.

"That's better."

He nodded in Martha's direction, then toward his mother whose sour expression only deepened.

"Much better."

"Thank you, Sir."

"Get yourself something to eat and come

to the taproom."

Without another look he headed through the door to the house.

"Andrew, I must speak to you."

Relieved to see the woman hurry off after him, Martha turned to find that Belle had set out a plate of food and a mug of cider for her. Hungry as she was, Martha forced herself to eat the bread, cheese, and stew of meat and vegetables slowly. After the long day's confinement and a second filling meal, she felt ready to face whatever the Faals would demand of her.

XII

Meeting Daniel

"Andrew!"

Daniel Pyke burst through the taproom's front door carrying a dripping basket.

Ain't here," said one of the afternoon's half-dozen customers. He didn't even bother to look up from his backgammon game.

"Ask the girl, there."

He pointed to the bar. Martha had almost finished emptying a tray of clean tankards and glassware. She'd welcomed the work that got her out of the kitchen and away from Mistress Faal. As Daniel approached, Martha hastily stretched out her hand when he hoisted the basket up to the bar.

"Don't you dare!"

Ignoring her, he let it drop, sending a spray of dirty water over the bar and the tray's remaining glasses.

"Look what you've done!"

"Blast! Move the damn things. They'll come clean."

"And I suppose you'll be pleased to clean them. It's you should move that mess. This is no place for it."

He shrugged.

"As good a place as any. Look at these oysters."

He lifted out a seaweed-covered shell as big as his hand.

"Mr. Faal will be right pleased. Go fetch him."

"I'll do no such thing. Take that away."

Martha shoved the basket toward him.

"You're an insolent piece."

He pushed back against the basket to keep it on the bar.

"You cleaned up right well. I'd hardly know you for a fresh-bought transport. And looking like you belong here, too. Does Mistress Faal know you treat her customers like this?"

"If she was here, you wouldn't dare to put that foul thing on the bar. But I beg your pardon, Sir. You're right. I shouldn't speak so to a customer."

Martha had to bite her lip and look away to hide angry, unexpected tears. She wasn't angry at him but at herself. Her retort had sprung to her lips as it might have at the Black Horse. And he had a way about him that reminded her of Charley at his most irritating.

And endearing. That memory and the feeling of loss caught her unawares. But she wasn't at the Black Horse, wasn't free to speak as she once might have, and thoughts of Charley only increased the pain.

"You needn't worry about me. I deserved that. Most of the wenches hereabouts wouldn't care what you put on the bar or anywhere else. There's not a lot of pride in that lot."

Daniel moved the basket from the bar to the floor and pulled his kerchief from his neck to sop up the water.

"Leave it be."

Martha bent to search for rags beneath the bar and recover from the rush of painful memories. With her feelings under control, she rose.

"I'll finish this. You'll find Mr. Faal in the back somewhere." She nodded toward the basket of oysters.

"You can take those to the kitchen… The Mistress is there too, I think."

"I thank you for the warning."

She pretended not to see his wink.

"Yes, Sir."

"That's better. But don't call me *Sir*. The name's Daniel."

Making a deep bow, Daniel swept his hat from his head and with another wink and a grin was off through the rear door with his basket.

Martha was relieved to see him go. Not

only was it too easy to speak and act with him as she had with Charley, he was also too like the men of Wapping who believed they could win favors from a girl with their roguish ways. She vowed this rogue would be as sorely mistaken as the men of Wapping had been. She wasn't about to trust him. Or any man, come to that.

Driven by that thought, Martha vigorously sopped up the water and scrubbed the bar, then cleaned the spattered glasses and tray. Once everything was clean and dry, she scanned the room, hoping everything was ready for the evening. Mistress Faal most certainly would be looking for something she'd left undone. And just so she wouldn't be accused of it, Martha picked up the full bucket of ashes the girl Fanny had left on the hearth and headed for the rear door.

"You there, girl. Where are you off to? We need a bartender in here."

Martha put the bucket down by the door and turned back as several men came into the taproom.

"I was just going to fetch Mr. Faal."

"I'd wager you can draw a pint as well as he can. And I've got a terrible thirst."

He pulled a coin from his pocket.

"And there'll be a little something for you."

"There will not!"

Mehitabel's look was fierce.

"I knew you'd be up to something like

this."

Mehitabel pulled her away from the bar.

"Mr. Faal will be here shortly. You gentlemen can wait. And if you can't, there are other places on the street."

Suddenly angered by the woman's fingers digging into her arm, Martha had to force herself not to resist as Mehitabel dragged her toward the door.

"Go find Mr. Faal. And quickly. I'll wait here."

At the door, however, she came to an abrupt halt.

"What is this bucket doing here? Don't you know better than to leave ashes in the house. You'll set us afire. Get rid of those after you fetch Mr. Faal."

Martha snatched up the offending bucket and carried it out through the breezeway and into the yard.

A pox on that girl.

She found Andrew in the yard, intent on whatever Daniel Pyke was saying. Neither noticed her approach.

"They say it was a Spanish privateer that took John Stone's *Molly* off the Carolinas. John put up a good fight, but there were too many. The bastards killed two of his men and put him and one other adrift in the dinghy. Sailed off with the *Molly* and her hold full of wheat. None of us are safe, Andrew, but if I keep my wits about me, the *Seagull* will give me a better chance than most have."

Martha paused to let him finish. Andrew turned on her with a frown.

"What is it?"

"Beg pardon, Sir. Mistress Faal sent me to ask if you'd come in and tend the bar."

Daniel grinned at his friend.

"I'd wager she wasn't asking. Go on, Andrew. We can talk more later."

Rolling his eyes skyward, Andrew headed inside.

"Here."

Daniel reached for the bucket.

"I'll carry that for you."

"No thank you, Si...Mr. Pyke. There's no need."

The bucket's weight caused her to make a lopsided curtsy, but she recovered quickly. Aware he was watching, she continued down the yard with a sure stride.

On her return to the house, she was relieved to see that Daniel Pyke wasn't among the men clamoring for ale and rum punch. At the bar, Andrew was filling tankards as fast as he could.

"It's about time you got back. We're going to be busy tonight. Let's see what you can do."

"She's needed in the kitchen, Andrew."

Martha hadn't noticed Mistress Faal behind her.

"She's needed here, Mother, not in the kitchen."

He nodded toward the room nearly full

of men.

"Unless you care to serve them."

Martha pretended she didn't hear the last or see Mistress Faal's black look. She quickly turned away to answer a call from one of the far tables. When she returned to the bar, she paused to study the board on the wall behind the bar as if she needed to check the price of a pint of ale.

Mehitabel was still there, perched on a stool like some predatory bird. Martha easily took to the work, reveling in the familiar routine and trying to ignore the woman as she traveled between tables and bar, delivering drinks and occasionally returning with coins to count out on the bar and push toward Andrew.

"Have I got it right, Sir?"

With a quick glance, he scooped them up and dropped them in the purse he wore at his waist.

"That's a good accounting. Wait here, I'll have their drinks for you to take back."

Back straight as a ramrod, Mehitabel could barely contain her anger, as Andrew hooked four pewter mugs by their handles and began filling them with ale. One by one, he put them on the bar in front of Martha. She easily took two in each hand and headed off to deliver them. She returned quickly to take four more drinks for another table and, from then on, worked steadily taking orders and delivering drinks. If she didn't collect money, she took names to go on the chalkboard where Andrew kept track of certain customers' running tabs. She was surprised how easily it all came back to her.

She was also acutely aware that Mistress Faal was enthroned at the end of the bar, supposedly working on her embroidery, but mainly watching hawk-like, ready to pounce if she thought she'd found Martha at fault. She could keep from meddling just so long and waved Martha over.

"Come close, I must speak to you."

Eyes on the room beyond them, Mehitabel lowered her voice.

"Mind you, we don't serve everyone who comes through that door. You can't trust half of them and the other's are just up to no good. Tell Mr. Faal and he will get them out. Some respectable men live and work nearby. You'll get to know them. But not all are trustworthy. We don't want common seamen stopping here. And never serve a black, even if they claim to be free. Not ever.

"No Ma'am."

Martha nodded.

"Mind you. I'll be watching."

"Yes 'm."

"We allow games of dice or cards and backgammon, but if they get too rowdy, have Mr. Faal deal with them. Some will come looking for cockfighting. I do not allow that. Send them down to Judd Pyke. And I don't want to hear of you going near that place. It's bad enough Andrew has dealing's with young Pyke.

428

But never mind that. Just have a care who you serve. Now go. And see that they pay."

"Yes 'm," she said and put the money she'd just collected on the bar in front of her.

"Some are asking for supper, Ma'am. Might I fetch it out for them?"

"Yes, go. Belle will give you what you need."

Mehitabel watched her leave then leaned close to Andrew.

"You keep a close eye on her, Andrew. We can't afford any thievery. I don't trust her. Nor must you."

"I doubt we have anything to worry about, but I'll watch her, Mother."

"We don't need her idling about either. There's work to be done in the kitchen."

"And you have Belle and Sukey to do it. Are we in need of yet another servant?"

Mehitabel ignored his question. She wasn't about to have her attention diverted from the girl weaving through the room full of men.

"Watch her with them, too. I'll not have her getting up to no good."

"Aren't you needed in the kitchen?"

He caught the angry flush that rose in his mother's face as he turned back to the rum punch he was mixing.

"I'm warning you, Andrew. Mark my words. She'll be trouble."

Angrily she gathered her sewing back into her basket and stalked out.

Martha had dawdled at the far side of the room until Mehitabel left before returning to deposit an empty tankard on the bar. She nodded toward the drink he was preparing.

"I'll be back for that punch. But I must tend to something else first."

Andrew looked up puzzled.

"Those two, there by the door. I've been watching them. They figure I'm new and they can slip out without paying."

"Never mind. I know them. They're already on the chalk board. I keep tab and will catch them another day."

"No, Sir. It's not good for them to get off like that, even if you have them pay later. Others see it and, just you wait, they'll be taking advantage."

Andrew raised a questioning eyebrow, then nodded.

"Go to it then."

You've got a good head on you, Martha Pratt.

He stopped to watch as she waylaid the men at the door.

"I think you're forgetting something, gentlemen."

She stepped in front of them.

"It's six pence apiece you owe."

"And who are you to be saying so?"

The man snarled at her, fully expecting her to back down. She raised her voice just enough to be heard at nearby tables.

"I'm the one served you each two pints

of ale. Six pence, if you please."

Hardening her look to match theirs, Martha held out her hand.

"Mr. Faal knows we're good for it."

"Maybe so, but I don't. And I'm the one must account for it to him. Six pence, gentlemen."

By then, silence had fallen at the closest table. One by one, the men nudged others to pay attention. Most thought of themselves as honest men. One leaned forward about to step in and help the girl, but a companion stopped him.

"She don't need help. Let her handle 'em."

Martha heard his words, but wasn't so sure.

Should I ask again? No. Too much like begging.

As she argued with herself, Martha prayed Mistress Faal wouldn't come back into the public room just when she was creating a scene. The two men realized the same thing and began digging in their pockets.

The second one to hand Martha his six pence, leaned close, his raspy voice low, ominous. But it was his foul breath, not fear caused her to jerk back.

"This ain't over, slut. One way or another, there'll be a reckoning."

At the bar, Daniel had come in from the back and joined Andrew to watch the little drama across the room.

431

"I don't like the turn that's taking."

"Let them go, Daniel. She's handled it right well I'd say. It's clear she's no stranger to this business."

"That may be true, but I know those two. They'll not let it drop."

Before Andrew could stop him, he was gone, close on the heels of the men who were already out the door. Andrew was relieved.

At least he'll deal with them outside.

He'd watched Daniel start fights often enough, usually just for the sport of it. He hoped it didn't come to that.

"What's going on here, Andrew?"

Andrew was surprised by his mother's return, prompted, he guessed, when she saw Daniel pass through the kitchen yard on his way in.

"A pair of skin-flints tried to make off without paying their tab. Martha saw that they settled it. Daniel's gone to make sure they're well away and won't cause any trouble."

"Humpf. Brawling in the street, no doubt."

Before Andrew could respond, Daniel reappeared, crossing the room with a bit of a swagger.

"That's taken care of. They'll not be coming back any time soon."

Andrew was eager to hear how he'd achieved that, but not with his mother standing there.

"Ahh, Mistress Faal, good day Ma'am."

432

Daniel removed his hat with a quick bow.

"Andrew and I've just been talking about taking the *Seagull* after that privateer's been preying on our traders off the coast. It's about time he saw a good fight. She's a fine…"

"Andrew will do no such thing. He's needed here."

Mehitabel clamped her mouth shut on the last words as if she were sinking her teeth into the offending Mr. Pyke.

"I was about to tell him just that."

Indeed, Andrew would have if Daniel had actually said anything about the schooner or privateers. He would have liked to join in such an adventure, but the thought of leaving his mother to manage the pub with just a girl and a handful of slaves was beyond imagining, much less actually considering.

"You needn't worry, Ma'am. I'll not be takin' your son away."

Mehitabel ignored him.

"I'll have a glass of cider, Andrew."

Resuming her seat at the end of the bar, she waved Daniel off.

"Good day, Mr. Pyke."

"Good day, Ma'am."

Unruffled by her peremptory dismissal, he bowed ever so slightly in her direction as he left.

XIII

Sally's Story

Late one September morning, Mehitabel arrived in the kitchen and beckoned to Martha.

"Leave that and come with me. I've marketing to do."

Martha quickly took a swallow of ale to wash down her last bite of buttered bread and hastened to catch up with Mehitabel, who was already on her way toward the public room. There she grabbed handed her shopping to Martha and led the way to out to the street.

They'd gone just a short way when they were forced up against the prison wall by a half-dozen head-strong geese barely controlled by two small girls.

"A penny, Mistress? A scrap of bread?"

A filthy hand stretched through the bars of the prison's gate. The face behind it was gaunt, dead-eyed.

"I've had naught to eat for two days. Please have mercy, Mistress."

Mehitabel snatched Martha away and quickened her pace.

"Don't even look at him. Those horrid men are forever begging. The colonial officials expect townspeople to feed them if their families don't. It's a disgrace they let them accost us like that."

"The officials don't feed them?"

Mehitabel simply shook her head and hurried on.

"Might I take them something when we return, Ma'am?"

"Certainly not. Whatever kindred feeling you have for those wretches, I'll not have you consorting with anyone from that horrid place. Or anywhere else. I won't tolerate such behavior."

With an angry shake of her head, Mehitabel clutched Martha's arm as she caught her toe in a rut.

"These streets! Impossible to walk on. They're a disgrace. Nothing but dust or mud. Now they've strewn oyster shells that make it even worse. And this a capital city. They should be able to do better."

Mehitabel was going at a good clip when suddenly she stopped short, her hand pressed to her breast, her face flushed.

"Are you all right, Ma'am?"

Martha held out a hand as if to support her, but Mehitabel angrily waved it away."

"Of course I am. This heat is enough to overcome anyone."

With her breath coming in short, rapid puffs between words, she didn't look well.

Martha edged closer, just in case she went down.

Should stick to walking or talking. Not both.

She looked around to see if anyone was nearby to help, but the only people on the street were two unkempt carters and several blacks, their eyes stolidly averted.

They weren't about to help, wouldn't dare touch a white woman.

Martha kept her silence.

"Here, girl. Give me your arm. I'll go back, rest a bit."

She grabbed Martha's extended arm to lean on. At first their progress was slow, but Mehitabel became increasingly sure-footed as they neared home. Once inside, she dropped Martha's arm and headed up the front stairs to her room, pulling herself along, hand over hand on the rail. As she reached the stair's turn, she stopped and looked back.

"Send Belle to me with cool water and cloths. I don't want to see anyone. Belle knows what to do for dinner. You could help her this time, I would think."

"Yes, Ma'am, I will."

Mehitabel gave the slightest of nods and turned away, but stopped.

"We still must have bread. The rest can wait. You've been often enough to know what we need, haven't you?"

Martha nodded.

"Four wheaten loaves this time?"

"Aye, go now. Tell Mr. Faal I said he's to go with you."

Without another look in Martha's direction, she disappeared around the stair's curve. Once she'd delivered Mistress Faal's orders to the slave woman, she sought Andrew. He was at his workbench and was clearly irritated by the interruption.

"What is it?"

"Beg pardon, Sir. Your mother was feeling poorly and can't do the marketing this morning. She's gone up to rest. All we need is bread and she would have you go with me to the baker's."

With a grimace of disgust, he looked from her then back to the saddle bag he'd been stitching.

"Wait in the other room. I'll call you when I've finished this."

Martha busied herself at the bar, checking the supply of limes and counting the bottles of cider, bitters, and rum. She'd gone through everything twice before he appeared.

"I assume you know what she wants."

"Yes Sir. Four loaves of wheaten bread."

"That's all? I suppose it's needed. Let's go."

Striding past her and out the door, he walked ahead without a backward look.

Putting me in my place. Or, more likely, just wanting to get back to his work.

In either case, she had no desire to talk to him and didn't hurry to keep up.

"Good day, Mr. Faal."

Now there's something interesting.

Martha slowed her pace again to watch the approach of a girl tossing her profusion of blond curls as she greeted Andrew. Drawing closer, the girl gathered her skirts in a curtsy to reveal more than a bit of stocking and smiled at Andrew as if expecting a show of appreciation.

For his part, Andrew simply touched the brim of his hat and with a curt "Good day, Sally," went on his way. He failed to see the girl's pretty face twist in anger, but Martha caught the full force of it. She was sure the girl would have attacked with words at least, if Mr. Faal hadn't been just a few steps ahead. Martha quickly looked away and hastened to catch up.

Better not meddle with that one, whoever she is. Interesting that Mr. Faal gave her no more than a nod.

At the baker's shop, Martha quickly chose the necessary loaves of bread and they hastened on their silent way back to the house. He left her in the front hall to go upstairs.

"I'll see to my mother."

"She said she wouldn't be down for dinner and now, I must help Belle, if that's all right Sir."

"Yes. Yes. Of course. Do that."

Martha spent the rest of the morning in the kitchen until at midday she heard the first of the men from the waterfront calling for

Andrew. They both arrived in the taproom at the same time.

"Is Mistress Faal better?"

"She seems to be doing well enough now. It was the heat, I suppose. It's a good thing you were with her."

Martha nodded, a bit surprised at the acknowledgment. As the afternoon progressed into evening, she found herself fending off more groping hands and lewd offers than usual. No doubt the Mistress's absence at the bar had a freeing effect. Her playful rebuffs kept most at bay.

When a group of sailors fresh off a ship in the harbor joined the regulars, Andrew kept a closer eye on the room. He seldom worried about Martha, but several of the sailors were emptying their mugs more rapidly than usual. They'd made a game of trying to pull Martha onto their laps. Worried, Andrew was halfway around the bar when Martha appeared, an empty tankard in her hand.

"I fear, Sir, I've spilled this. The gentleman will require another."

Across the room, Andrew could see one of the sailors mopping at his crotch with his neckerchief amidst laughter and jests from his companions.

"So I see. I take it, you're all right."

She nodded with a smile.

"I'll speak to him."

"Thank you, Sir, but there's no need. He did me no harm and I believe I've seen to it."

She handed him the tankard.

"He'll need this filled, though. I'm afraid I left him no more to drink."

"Perhaps you'll teach these colonials some manners."

Andrew turned quickly to hide his grin as he refilled the tankard.

Clearly she spoke the truth about coming from a public house. And he had to admit that Martha was a great improvement over the wenches they'd had so far. He had to admit that his mother wasn't entirely wrong about them. Sally in particular. And good riddance.

****

Sally wasn't about to be dismissed so easily. The sight of Martha walking behind Andrew with pride and self-assurance further salted that wound. A week later, she waylaid Martha on Prince George's Street and blocked her way.

"I've seen how you walk the streets lookin' so high and mighty. But folks hereabouts won't forget you're Newgate trash. There's plenty don't want the likes of you around."

She nodded toward the gaol.

"We'll be seein' you in there before long."

With a toss of her head, she flounced off up the street.

"Pay her no mind."

Daniel Pyke stepped out of the tavern's doorway. He'd stopped there when he saw Sally bearing down on Martha.

"Sally's her name. Used to work the taproom here til she ran amuck with the Mistress. Offering more than food and drink, if you take my meaning. Would have been better for her if she'd worked on pleasing Mistress Faal instead of the customers. But then, most likely you wouldn't be here now."

He jerked his thumb over his shoulder toward the tavern.

"The Mistress is the one to watch out for. I'm careful to furl my sails when she's about in there. But don't let her put you off. If you ask me, you're the best thing to come to that house in a great while. So good day to you lass."

With that, he was off toward the wharf and his house at the street's end. He was a strange one, Martha thought, wishing he'd tarried to talk more. He was the first person to talk to her as one might a friend. She shook her head, chiding herself that she'd even thought such a thing. There was danger in that.

What was it that Sally did to send Mr. Faal out looking for another servant.

Martha wasn't about to ask Daniel Pyke. Or Mr. Faal. But they weren't the only ones to know. From what little she'd learned about the Faals' slaves, they knew a great deal more about whites than their owners supposed.

441

Sukey had warned her enough times about things that might get her into trouble with the Faals.

From what she'd observed, neither the Faals nor the men who filled their taproom gave a thought to a slave girl who might overhear a white man talking of private matters. The men she served were deaf to Sukey's "yes sir" or "no sir", as she went about her work, wiping up spills, sweeping the floors, tending the fires.

She missed nothing as she delivered drinks and food or cleaned away a customer's leavings. She knew the regulars' likes and dislikes, who cheated at cards and dice, and who seemed most likely to get into a fight or drink himself under the table. She also knew who was short of money, who carried tales to government officials, and who was having trouble with his wife or mistress. Or both.

Although Martha'd been brought to the new world in chains just as Sukey's people had been, that didn't mean the black girl trusted her. She was white after all. An insurmountable barrier. Sally, however, was another matter. Sukey had few qualms about sharing what she knew.

"She's got a mean streak. 'Specially towards people like me and some poor folks around town, but that's not what got her in trouble with the Mistress. She was always comin' in late when she was workin' in the taproom. Didn't take much to figure it was 'cause she was goin' off at night with some man took a fancy to her. Mr. Faal never seemed to pay that any mind, but when the Mistress caught on, she got mighty angry. She went stormin' round to Miss Sally's place to tell her not to come back. That was just afore you come here."

And reason enough to be wary of Sally, thought Martha.

"When she come back, I hear'd the Mistress tell Mr. Andrew she'd come up against Miss Sally's Ma. That's one mean-spirited woman. She chased the Mistress out'n her house with a broom."

Martha laughed at the thought, but stopped at Sukey's look of dismay.

"Don't worry. I won't let on that you've told me anything."

With a fearful survey of the room, Sukey ducked her head and hurried out.

Blast. I hope she won't get into trouble talking to me. My lot may be bad but the lot of these Negroes is far worse.

She couldn't help wondering if the girl bore scars like those on the backs of newly arrived slaves she'd seen being driven through town in chains. Fresh from the wilds of Guinea, she'd been told. She had to turn away from the sight of the horrible wounds inflicted by their white captors.

Few of the men and women in the crowd that had gathered to gawk at the captives seemed to be bothered.

"Don't usually get to see new ones brought in here," one of the men in the crowd told her. "Norfolk's usually where the slavers come in. Like wild animals, they are."

She hoped never again to see the vicious iron-toothed collars a few of the Africans wore. Earned when they'd fought their captors, she guessed, but they showed no sign of resistance now. Poor souls had no idea what lay ahead of them that day on the auction block. She hoped Sukey hadn't come naked to the port like the black women and girls she saw herded off the ship. But Martha had little doubt that her mother or grandmother had come that way. As for the men, all each wore was a poor excuse for a loin cloth.

The white women in the crowd didn't seem bothered when their male companions examined the slaves, poking and prodding them as they would livestock. They had few qualms about joining the men in examining the black women and girls. Sickened by the sight, Martha turned away. What she'd endured was nothing like the scene before her. Never again could she count herself unlucky or ill used.

XIV

An Unwelcome Encounter

"Well what have we here?"

Martha froze and willed herself not to look away from the tankards she was arranging behind the bar. She'd never expected to hear that voice again. Her fingers gripped a tankard's handle as she turned to face Hal.

"Thought you'd seen the last of me, didn't you?"

Grinning, he approached the bar with a cocksure swagger.

"I heard you was bought in town. A fine place we was brought to, ain't it? I've took employment right across the street til I learn the way of things here."

By the late morning light coming through a front window, two men idly tossed dice. Welcoming the diversion, they paused to watch the man and girl by the bar. They were regulars and the Faals' new wench had been proving herself good for a show.

"You can fill that with ale."

Hal nodded toward the tankard she held and went off to a table in a shadowy back corner of the room and well away from the other men.

Martha's knuckles were white around the handle of the mug she'd been holding. Slowly she put it on the bar and took a deep breath to still the pounding of her heart.

He can't do anything to me here. He wouldn't dare. He's as much a stranger in this place as I am.

"I'll fetch Mr. Faal."

"I'm here."

Andrew had heard the exchange through his shop's open door. He normally would have let her draw the ale, but didn't like the stranger's tone. He liked the look of the man even less.

"Ah, Mr. Faal, is it? An ale, Sir."

Andrew offered the slightest of nods as he passed the table and went silently to the bar. He couldn't help but notice that Martha's hand shook as she handed him the tankard. Ignoring his questioning look, she turned abruptly and hurried off to where the two men by the window had quickly downed the last of their cider.

"Got a thirst this morning."

One of them said as he handed Martha his empty mug. Actually, he and his companion were eager to see the drama to its end.

"Aye," said the other shoving his mug

across the table to her as he picked up the dice and gave them a careless toss. They resumed their game with divided attention.

Martha dared not look at Andrew when she returned to the bar. Would he think she'd been consorting with Hal aboard the ship?

A pox on the man. Could it really be chance that he found work so easily? And so close?

She'd hoped for a fresh start in Annapolis and a chance to prove herself. He was just the sort of trouble Mistress Faal expected her to bring into their house. Martha quickly delivered the men's cider but stopped on her way back to the bar to scrub a table with unnecessary vigor.

Something was amiss, Andrew thought as he watched her. She was biting her lip and, more puzzling, avoided Andrew's eyes when he put the man's ale on the bar.

She knew that man, Andrew realized as he watched her carry the mug across the room. And, for some reason, she was afraid of him. The man *was* intimidating. Andrew was glad there were others in the room. Normally, he'd have returned to his shop. In truth, he wanted to, but he couldn't in good conscience abandon her to deal with him alone.

He took a deep breath in hopes of relieving the tension building in his chest and poured himself a mug of ale. Aside from giving him something to do, a long swallow helped not at all.

"Looks like you ain't done so bad for yourself."

Hal grinned up at Martha as she put his drink in front of him.

"Better than some. Most of them got sold off to the country. They work 'em hard out there, I hear tell."

Hal took a long swallow of ale and wiped the back of his hand across his mouth. Martha stopped, as he undoubtedly knew she would.

"That woman, the plain-faced one was with you. That's where she went. I guess she was too old for field work. She was bought for a washerwoman or some such. Didn't go for much."

He took another drink and leaned back in his chair. He was enjoying himself.

"You was lucky. Captain wasn't happy with what he got for the rest of those women. Course, if they'd been black, he'd ha' done better. I hear tell, the white ones go for a lot less than the blacks they got all over this place. Bet they got a black wench or two working in the back worth more than you. So don't get no high-minded ideas."

His expression changed suddenly as Andrew appeared just behind Martha.

"I'll be working just across the street, Sir. So if you have any trouble with this one or any others, just let me know."

Andrew ignored him and spoke to Martha.

"We're low on lemons. Get some from the storeroom."

Puzzled, she hesitated. She'd filled the basket with lemons just that morning. Andrew gave her a light shove.

"Go. *Now*."

"Yes, Sir."

She hurried off, but stopped just outside the door.

"I'll not have our servants ill used. Finish your drink and get out. You're not welcome here."

Hal's answer was a low snarl.

"That ain't no way to run a place. Lettin' prison scum serve decent, law-abiding citizens. But I guess the people you get comin' in here don't mind drinking this piss you serve."

He slammed the tankard down, splashing most of its contents on the table and floor, then shoved the table just short of hitting Andrew.

"Don't think we're done with this. I'll be keeping an eye on this place. Any wrong-doing I hear of, the sheriff'll know."

Hal crammed his hat on his head and stomped out.

When she heard the door slam behind him, Martha returned.

"I'm sorry about that, Sir. I didn't know he would come here. His name's Hal Lowcross. He's off the *Sea Nymph* and carries a grudge against me. I fear he'll cause you trouble because of it."

449

Andrew shook his head as if it was of no concern.

"He's not the first to try to cause trouble, nor the first we've thrown out."

Well that may be a stretch of the truth...

"We can see he doesn't return. Now get up that mess."

"Yes, Sir. Right away."

As Andrew turned to leave, he stopped.

"He won't bother you here, but what will you do if you meet him outside?"

"I've come this far, Sir. I'll just have to keep my wits about me."

"Brave words. I hope you can."

"What's going on? Who slammed the door?"

Mehitabel Faal looked from Andrew to Martha and back to Martha.

"Just a troublemaker I had to throw out, Mother. No harm done."

"No harm? Look at that mess."

Mehitabel nodded toward the table.

"I'm just about to clean it up, Ma'am."

As Martha grabbed the tankard and hurried to the bar for a cloth to mop up the spilled ale, Mehitabel crooked a finger for Andrew to follow her. In the breezeway, she stopped abruptly and nodded toward the half-open door to the taproom.

"Close that. It was that girl, wasn't it? I knew she'd be trouble and that won't be the end of it."

"That man would cause trouble

wherever he went, Mother. He won't be coming back here."

"Humpf. You think that'll end it? You see no more than you want to see, but never mind that now. Go back and see she cleans the mess off the table. And the floor."

Shaking her head in disgust, Mehitabel headed back to the kitchen. Andrew sighed with relief and sank back against the wall. Who was he to be talking to the girl about brave words. He suddenly felt weak. What would he have done if the man had refused to leave? And what *would* the girl do? He couldn't see her standing by and wringing her hands. She'd already proven she could handle most of the men who came into the taproom.

But this one was different. Why would he have a grudge against her? And how did he get to be a prison guard? From all he'd heard, the sheriff was a gentleman of some standing in town. But probably he had no hand in the hiring. That man didn't look like the sort a gentleman would choose for a guard. The sheriff certainly wouldn't knowingly approve of one who'd mistreat his charges or cause trouble.

Andrew's concern was still festering several days later when he saw the sheriff out in town and hastened to catch up with him. They'd never met and the man barely hid his annoyance. It seemed to increase when Andrew introduced himself and asked if he knew a prison guard named Hal Lowcross.

"Only from afar."

The sheriff brushed angrily at something on his waistcoat's sleeve. The subject was clearly distasteful and he was eager to be away.

"You have the house across from the gaol haven't you? Did he cause you trouble?"

Andrew paused, surprised that the sheriff would know him.

"He tried. Accosted a wench who serves in our taproom, but no harm done. He left easily enough."

"Easily, you say? That's surprising. You're not the only one to complain. The man's a scoundrel. He's no longer in our employ and was advised to leave town. I didn't know he was still around. In the meantime, vigilance is the answer. That's my suggestion to you. Vigilance! Let us know if you see him."

"I will, Sir. And thank you for the warning."

With a quick nod and touch of his hat brim, the sheriff strode off without another word.

XV

An Accounting

As leaves on the trees behind the stable turned to shades of red, orange, and gold, Martha let out the first of the tapes that fastened her petticoats. She'd already remade her bodice to hide her expanding middle and spent as much time behind the bar as she dared.

She worked on building Fanny's confidence so that she wouldn't have to deliver drinks or take orders. As it was, the girl had trouble getting the proper drinks to waiting customers without mishap. Martha knew she could only stay behind the bar for a short while more. Mr. Faal wasn't likely to notice her growing middle, but the Mistress surely would. She'd have to tell them soon. But how?

Martha was certain Mistress Faal would be enraged and not without justification, but that wouldn't make her any easier to face. She was less sure of Mr. Faal. Most certainly he'd be angry when he found out about her deception,

453

but she guessed that it would bother him more that it might keep her from tending the bar. She could tell how reluctant he was to leave his workbench during midday dinner and in the evening. At other times, he let Martha draw pints of ale, cider, or rum, collect whatever was due, and keep a running tab.

The only thing that ruined her pleasure in the work was the presence of Mistress Faal watching from her throne-like chair at the end of the bar. She made sure that Mehitabel saw her count the money and make her entries in the account book for Mr. Faal to total the next morning. She also made sure that he knew when potables were running low.

Midway through the morning of her third day at the bar, Andrew called her to his shop.

Now, what have I done? Or more likely, what does the Mistress think I've done? Or not done.

She paused halfway across the public room.

Have they guessed?

She wished she'd given more thought to what she'd say if that was the case, but there was no time for that. She was almost relieved to see through the open shop door that he was waiting with the ledger in his hand.

"You've done well with your accounting. When I questioned you on the ship, you said that you'd kept accounts. Is that true?"

"Yes, Sir. That was a very simple

accounting though."

"Do you think you could settle a day's bar account?"

Stunned, Martha struggled to grasp what he was asking.

"It's been a while, Sir, but I suppose I could."

"Good. I'd like to give that a try. Look here."

Andrew beckoned her to come closer and opened the ledger on his work bench. He ran a finger down the columns as he explained what he needed and how he wanted her to keep track of the money and, eventually, the supplies. In effect, their bar business. They were so absorbed in the bookkeeping that they didn't notice Mehitabel standing in the door behind them.

"Andrew! What are you doing?"

He and Martha spun to face his mother. She was livid with ill suppressed rage. Martha quickly stepped away from his side and turned to face the woman advancing on them. She wasn't about to wait for the coming onslaught and cautiously edged around Mehitabel to escape into the taproom pulling the door closed behind her.

So, the obedient son has defied his mother?

If she weren't so sure that she was at the center of the impending storm, Martha would have been pleased. As it was, her dread increased as she returned to bar.

"What are you thinking, letting that girl keep our accounts? Have you lost all reason, Andrew? We know nothing about her but what she tells us. I've no doubt that she's an accomplished prevaricator. She could ruin us."

"Ruin us? Mother, be reasonable. What damage do you think she can do? I intend to check her accounting and you're welcome to do the same."

"I'm no accountant and if you're busy, you won't have time to properly check what she's done. Who knows what she'll try to get away with? And does the business of the public room interfere so much with your work?"

"Yes, it does. I'm not Father. I have more than enough to keep me in my shop all day. And when daylight's gone, I'll still tend the bar. The point is that my time is more profitably spent at my bench. And your time during the day would be better spent above stairs than sitting there at the bar.

"I saw Mistress Jennings' servant girl deliver that bolt of linen. You were half a day at her house taking measurements. She won't be pleased if she doesn't receive the clothing she's ordered in good time. You can't deny that you wouldn't rather be at your needlework or even in the kitchen than overseeing the taproom."

Mehitabel said nothing. She wasn't about to admit that he was right. But it was hard for her to give up her taproom vigil. Sooner or later, she'd find the girl at fault. And she tried. For three more days. As usual, nothing untoward happened, and she found reasons to be in the kitchen. Usually, from there, she retired to her room and her sewing. But for the next few days, she made a show of going over the account book. Her understanding of sums had never been good, and it was galling when she realized that the business was showing a profit.

At his mother's behest, Andrew checked the book and came up with the same result. He also realized more than that. In addition to the profit, in the short time Martha had been there, she'd brought order to serving the food and drink and seen that Sukey and Fanny kept the public rooms clean and orderly. She'd even found other chores to keep poor Fanny out of his mother's way. But of greatest importance, her presence meant that Andrew seldom had to leave the saddlery during the day. His business had never been better.

As for Martha herself, she took no pleasure or satisfaction from her industry. No matter how hard or long she worked, she couldn't overcome her fear of what lay ahead, assuming she survived. And if she did, how would it change her life and the lives of the Faals. She couldn't imagine how Mr. Faal would react, but the Mistress was another matter. She was sure the revelation would send her into a towering rage.

She knew she could bear the Mistress's ranting but what would Mr. Faal do? She'd deceived him and he had every right to sell her and her child, but from what she'd come to know of him, she didn't think he'd do such a thing. That didn't change the fact, though, that she'd be all but useless for a time, especially with a baby to care for. Could she make that up to him? And how much longer could she maintain her deception?

XV

A Secret No More

Martha was crouched in front of the taproom fireplace, stirring the embers in advance of the oncoming evening's chill. She didn't hear Mehitabel's approach.

"How long did you think you could deceive us?"

Lurching to her feet, Martha turned to face Mehitabel. The woman stood, fists on hips, her mouth twisted in anger.

"Leave that and come with me."

Without waiting for an answer, she marched across the room and into Andrew's shop. Close behind, Martha paused at the door.

"Don't just stand there. Come in."

Mehitabel yanked her through as Andrew turned from his work, a mallet and awl forgotten in his hands.

"What is this?"

"Look at her, Andrew. Just look."

She waved toward Martha's waist.

He looked but had no idea what he was meant to see.

"For heaven's sake, Andrew. Did you know she was with child?"

Her look told him he better not have known. She turned on Martha.

"How far gone are you?"

"Going on six months, Ma'am."

Although Martha had dreaded the day that the Faals discovered her secret, she realized she was relieved to end the uncertainty.

"You really didn't know, Andrew?"

"No. How would I?"

He was shocked and clearly embarrassed to look at Martha. He seldom looked closely at her and even now that his mother pointed out her thickening waist, he wasn't sure he could tell.

"Well, now that you know, what are you going to do about it?"

"I suppose we must deal with it when the time comes."

"We? I didn't bring this upon us. It's you who must deal with it."

"Ma'am."

Martha stepped forward.

"I didn't mean to…"

"You thought we wouldn't guess? That *I* wouldn't guess? What sort of fool do you take me for?"

"I'd never judge you so, Ma'am. I've wanted to tell you, but I was afraid…. I didn't know how."

"Afraid. I'd think it was shame kept you silent. Did you really think you'd be able to hide that?"

She waved a hand again toward Martha's protruding middle. For a long, uncomfortable moment, Andrew and his mother waited for Martha to reply.

"I'm sorry, I didn't tell you. I didn't know how, but it's not for shame. I've done nothing to be ashamed of."

As Martha placed her hands protectively over her belly, she was sure she felt a stirring in response.

"I got this child by no wilful act on my part. There was a man... he... he called himself a gentleman."

Martha couldn't look at them, didn't want to go on, but their silence was unrelenting.

"But he wasn't a gentleman. He was a wicked man. My mistress sent me on an errand to his room. He wasn't supposed to be there. But he was. When I tried to leave, he caught me and wouldn't let me leave. He...he... When I wouldn't do what he wanted, he beat me near senseless."

Martha's voice shook as the words tumbled out amidst tears now streaming down her cheeks.

"I couldn't stop him. When he'd... When he'd finished, he saw he'd bloodied my lip. He didn't want anyone to know what he'd done, but there was no hiding the blood all over my kerchief. I begged him and told him I wouldn't say anything. If it weren't for the blood, I think he'd have let me go."

"I said I'd tell people I'd fallen, but he still wouldn't let me go. He said I should have been willing to give him what he wanted. I think he was pleased at the result. He wiped at the blood with some pound notes that lay nearby and dragged me below, yelling for the constable. He said he caught me stuffing the notes in my bodice. That he had to hit me to get them back. That bloodied my lip and the notes, he said, and waved them for all to see."

Martha dared not look at the Faals as she wiped uselessly at her tears. She forced herself to continue.

"He'd say nothing to keep me from prison. I'm sure it suited him that I was transported. Because of him I've lost everything, and this child will be a bound servant until it's near grown. I...I won't cause you trouble and I will do what I can to repay you to allow this child to have a decent life."

Mehitabel couldn't remain silent any longer.

"That's a fine story. You can't tell me you didn't know you were carrying a child."

"I didn't know until I was in prison. And by then, I knew that it wouldn't keep me from being transported. It would just keep me in prison until the child was born. I said nothing because I knew, if my mistress found out, she'd

462

want to take the child."

"And why wouldn't you want that?"

Martha had to look away from Mehitabel at the thought of Hannah Chinn.

"That was how she got me. My mother was a servant in Mistress Chinn's house. She died birthing me. The Mistress could have sent me to a foundling home, but she didn't. She raised me as if I were her own. I knew she'd raise my child the same way and I couldn't do that to her.

"It's been seventeen years since she took me to raise. She might not have that long to care for another and there was no one else I'd trust to take it. I decided to take a chance, to keep and raise it. If the child and I survived."

Glancing quickly from one listener to the other, Martha stopped. Mehitabel's face hadn't softened. Andrew's bewildered look was puzzling.

"I don't know what more I can say, but I won't let the birthing interfere with my work for you any more than is necessary. I hope that it will only be a day or two before I'm able to get back to work. I'll honor the terms of my indenture and will do my best not to let the child interfere."

Andrew stood silent, struggling to take in what Martha was telling them. He knew very little about what was involved in the birth of a child. And til that morning, he hadn't thought about the girl's life before her arrival in Annapolis."

"Arrested for theft, Adam Muir said. He would most certainly have told him if he'd known more. But that made no difference now. The impending birth offered any number of uncertainties and he wasn't at all sure what he thought or felt about any of it. But first, he'd have to settle things with his mother. He wasn't going to have it out with her in front of the girl. He turned toward Martha.

"Leave us, now… and close the door."

Only when Martha shut the door behind her did Andrew toss the tools he'd been gripping back on his bench. He stretched his cramped fingers as he braced himself to hear what his mother had to say.

"So, you'll accept what she said? Just like that? She admits her deceit. Or what she wants us to believe. We have no idea what more she's keeping from us. And, whatever she says, you'll see. We'll be getting less and less work out of her as her time nears. And even less after the child is born."

"We can take her at her word or not, Mother. I don't think it makes much difference."

Andrew was measuring his words, trying to be reasonable.

"She won't be the first wench to work that way. Whether she speaks true or not doesn't change anything. That's always been the case with her. Or any other indenture. Nothing need change. Unless and until she gives us reason, she'll continue as she has."

"I don't understand you, Andrew. It's not just how she'll go about tending the bar. It's about when her time comes."

Mehitabel threw up her hands in exasperation.

"We don't know what trouble she might have. We must think about such things. You must get a midwife. And don't wait until the time is upon us."

The last she flung over her shoulder as she yanked open the door and headed for the stairs and her room.

Andrew closed the door with more force than necessary in the grip of an unexpected surge of anger.

Damn the girl. Everything was going so well. Work aplenty and time to do it. Not since Papa was alive could I count on that.

He stood looking at his bench and the work he'd just left.

I'll just have to wait and hope the birthing won't take her away from her duties for long. Or after. Lord knows, there are women enough in this house to help tend the child.

He picked up the supple piece of leather he'd just left, rubbing it appreciatively. His latest work had already brought in new customers and he expected soon to have more of his finely-tooled leatherwork to display. Just the day before, he'd placed an order with the tanner for the rarer hides such work called for.

Has she put all of that in jeopardy? Am I foolish to believe she was raped? That she was nothing more than a common whore? No one forced me to buy a convict servant. Can't even blame Daniel for that. If only a better man than Wilson had stepped forward to take her. And, if I hadn't, where would I be today?

Andrew looked at the unfinished leatherwork on his bench.

Still looking for a servant. Or dealing with another servant and a new set of problems. The girl's proved herself and we've certainly had none better. Nor half so good. God willing, if she comes through this, she'll soon be back to work.

A new thought brought him to a halt. His mother was right. They had to prepare before the girl's time came. He'd heard talk of a midwife near the town gate. Sukey could help. And Belle. The black woman had most certainly birthed her share of babies and helped with more. He could only pray that nothing went wrong.

Things were going so well. If only Mother could see that. At least we'll have time to prepare ... whatever the outcome.

XVI

Consequences

Andrew returned to his bench, but his work couldn't hold his attention. Near sundown, he was relieved to lay his tools and leather aside when he heard Daniel's voice in the taproom. Andrew went out and drew himself a pint of ale and one for Daniel, then beckoned him into the saddlery.

"What's this?" Daniel raised an eyebrow. "Some nefarious business?"

Andrew shook his head. He was in no mood for banter.

"The girl's with child."

"Girl? What girl? Ahh. So, you got two for the price of one. Not a bad bargain."

"You can make light of it, Daniel, but *you* won't have to deal with the consequences."

"Can't be much to it. There's a good midwife out by the town gate."

"I'm not worried about that."

"Ahh. The formidable Mistress Faal, is it? As I said. Get the midwife. Edna Jasper's her name. She'll take things in hand. Believe me, she can deal with your mother."

467

"But what's to become of the child?"

"I assume she can raise it here as well as anywhere else. And you've got women in the house to help. Far better, when all's said, if you think where she could have gone. You're a good man, Andrew. Chance has dealt her a better hand than she might have had. And from what I've seen of her, she can make the most of it. She's not the first woman to birth a bastard and she's not likely to be charged as a result."

"Charged?"

"Ah, Andrew."

Daniel shook his head in disbelief.

"Where have you been? Bastardy's a crime here. There's more than a few poor souls have been whipped or gone to gaol or both. But there's none likely to raise that issue. Aside from that, I'm guessing you'll be able to see she's taken care of. And her bairn. She's a fine lass, Andrew. Under better circumstances, she'd make a man a fine wife."

"What are you saying?"

"Don't tell me you haven't thought of bedding her. Clearly someone's had the pleasure."

"I'd never. And don't you be thinking of it."

At Daniel's sudden look of anger, Andrew hurried on.

"Whoa, Daniel. I spoke in jest. She says she was violated. Some scoundrel took her against her will. A lodger in the house where she lived, she says. He concocted a tale to cover what he'd done and got her charged with stealing. She went to trial and prison and the rest you know."

"For reasons I can't fathom, the foolish girl told no one what happened. She says she was in Newgate by the time she knew she was carrying his child. I suppose the consequences of keeping silent were worse than she'd expected. And once she came here, she says she didn't know how to tell us. Mother guessed."

"And you believe her?"

"If you'd heard her tell it, you would too. Whatever the truth, I choose to take her at her word."

Daniel nodded.

A sorry state of affairs, but she's proved worth believing it seems.

"That puts things in a different light. I'll follow your lead. But I warn you. You'd best be prepared to defend her. And the child if it lives."

"I've thought of that. But there's nothing I can do about it now."

"Aye. I'll stand by you, if it comes to that. But now, I've trade goods to carry to the head of the Bay. The word is that the Susquehannocks' have had good hunting. With favorable winds, I should be back in a fortnight with some decent hides. First choice is yours before they go to the tanyard."

Martha's thoughts were in a muddle after the Faals' grueling. At the taproom hearth, she placed a fresh log on the fire and absentmindedly stirred the coals beneath.

"Martha. Come to my shop."

Startled, she dropped the poker on the hearth with a clatter.

"Leave that."

Andrew was already walking away by the time she'd shoved herself to her feet. Worried by the sharpness of his command, she hurried after him.

"We... I understand that your situation is unfortunate. There's nothing you or we can do about it. Thus far, you've served us well and so long as you're able, you'll be secure in your place here. And after... I fear I don't know what we might expect of you... but I assume you'll be able to work as you have for a while longer."

"Oh, yes Sir. I should think so."

Nearly overcome with relief, she gestured toward her middle and felt a flush rise in her cheeks.

"I don't expect this to hinder me for quite some time yet, but I fear I know very little of that myself."

"Then it's settled."

He breathed a sigh of relief, his immediate duty done.

"I needn't tell you, Mother isn't pleased, but she's resigned to see it through. I'll leave it to you to let me know when you are no longer able to work."

"Yes, Sir."

She nodded and stood silent as if she expected him to say more.

Unsure what that should be, he rushed on.

"We don't want you to be doing anything that will bring it on. I've heard it's no good for a mare to throw a foal too soon. I suppose it's no different for a woman."

Damnation! What am I doing spouting such foolishness?

Flustered, Andrew turned toward his workbench.

"I suppose not, Sir."

She was no more comfortable than he and quickly turned away.

"And I'd best get back to the fire."

He nodded, but didn't look around.

"Yes, do that. Perhaps you could let Belle know. I suspect, she'll be of help when the time comes. And there's a midwife we can call to attend you."

"Thank you, Sir."

Martha paused, in case he had more to say.

He didn't.

"Close the door when you leave."

There was only the faintest click as the door closed behind her.

XVII

Preparations

By November, Andrew noticed that Martha was taking the spiral stair to the garret more slowly than she once had and for the first time since she'd come to live there, he wondered how she fared. It had been a long while since he'd ventured into the upper room and remembered it only as a cramped, low-ceilinged space. Prodded by the thought, he found a time when Martha was busy in the kitchen and went up.

Beneath the roof's peak, he stood upright and looked around. The room was cold, taking very little warmth from the chimney. There, along one side, Martha had put her cot with a pallet, a feather bed, and a heap of blankets piled atop. A table and chair were on the back side of the chimney opposite the window. Beside a candle on the table, he recognized the small leather-bound Bible he'd seen when she'd opened her bundle on the kitchen floor. Around, on the other side of the chimney, was a clutter of trunks, boxes, and broken furniture Martha'd moved out of her way.

The room, if it could be called that, was worse than what he remembered of the slaves' quarters over the kitchen. At least they were warmed by the fire and ovens below. As he looked around, he was ashamed of himself. He'd worried more about the stabling of his horse, than how the girl fared. And he couldn't blame his mother. He doubted she remembered the space, if she'd seen it at all when they first moved in. And he'd given it not a thought.

He guessed that Sukey and Belle had gathered the bedding to make it just barely a fit place to sleep when the weather turned cold. Neither they nor Martha would have dared say anything to him or his mother about what a poor place the garret was for sleeping. And it certainly wasn't a fit place for birthing a baby. As little as he knew, he could see it was no place for that. But where?

Back in his shop, Andrew sat fingering the piece of leather he'd been working, but his thoughts were elsewhere. Tossing the leather aside, he rose to wander aimlessly from one end of the shop to the other as he thought. After several turns around the room, he arrived at the foot of the ladder to the loft and realized he had the answer.

A quick inspection told him there was room above for a cot and even a table and chair. He'd often had worse accommodations when he was peddling his leatherwork and collecting pleasant memories his first year in America. Once he had James and Harry clean out the loft, it would be comfortable enough for him to sleep in, and the girl could birth her baby in his bedroom.

Pleased with his solution, he sank onto his stool to think about what next to do. It wouldn't be easy convincing his mother. She'd want none of it.

He found her in her bed chamber.

"A servant sleeping in your bed chamber? Have you lost all your good sense? A thieving criminal just across the hall from my room? And you nowhere nearby? I won't be able to sleep a wink."

He ran his fingers through his hair. Whether his mother liked it or not, that was where Martha'd have to be.

"She's given us reason enough to trust her. And you've a perfectly good lock on your door. We can add another, if that will ease your mind, but you have nothing to fear from her. Be reasonable, Mother. There's nowhere else for her to have her baby. Now, let that be the end of it."

"That won't be the end of it. You don't think, Andrew. Where will you put them once the child is born?"

"I have thought about it. We'll have time between now and then to make the garret into a proper bed chamber. Martha and her infant can sleep there. Once it's born, the child can be kept in the kitchen during the day. There'll always be someone to look after it while she goes about her work. But we don't even know how the birth will go. There's no need to think beyond that yet, Mother. And now I have work waiting below."

Allowing her no time to reply, he turned abruptly, leaving his mother speechless, staring at the closed door. She'd never admit it, but what he said made sense. She had seen the garret but thought it no more that a storeroom, certainly no place she'd want to sleep, but when the time came it had suited her to have Martha sleep there. It would keep the girl in her place, she'd thought. But such a cramped, dismal space certainly wasn't a suitable place for a birth, any birth.

Despite herself, the upcoming event had taken over Mehitabel's idle thoughts. It invariably brought on sad memories of the two dear children she'd lost. Remembering Emily's death was almost more than she could bear.

As Martha's time drew near, Mehitabel's feelings were in turmoil. Though she worried little how Martha would come through, she couldn't shake the fear that the child wouldn't survive the trials of its birth. In a more hopeful frame of mind, she dearly hoped that the baby would be a girl.

By mid November, after Martha moved into Andrew's bed chamber she could seldom escape encounters with Mistress Faal. Things were bad enough with the woman ever present during the day, but sleeping just a few steps away with no more than a door between them meant uneasy nights as well.

To avoid that as much as possible, Martha made sure she was up and out of the room before Mehitabel rose in the morning and returned after her mistress had gone to bed. She fought the temptation to risk meeting her mistress and spend a bit more time abed. Though her cot in the garret had been more comfortable than anything she'd slept on in a year's time, Andrew's soft, warm bed brought back memories of hers in the chimney corner of the Black Horse. As time passed, however, it wasn't fear of the Mistress that drove her out of bed but the increasingly active infant.

Though Andrew was busy in his shop from dawn to dusk, the leatherwork seldom taxed his mind enough to keep him from worrying about the impending birth. To ease his uncertainty, he sent James off with a note to Edna Jasper. The midwife arrived in the taproom one morning soon after. With the exception of three men lingering over the last of their breakfast, Mehitabel was the only one in the room. She looked up from the ledger page, her finger poised above the row of figures she was checking.

"I've come to see Martha Pratt."

Mehitabel studied her with suspicion. Women rarely came into the taproom. To her mind, none should be asking for a servant.

"What's your business with her?"

"Mr. Faal told me she's in need of a midwife. Edna Jasper's my name and that's what I've come for, if you'd tell me where I might find her."

She crossed her hands on the basket she carried, waiting for Mehitabel's answer.

"It's not her time yet and she has work to do in the kitchen."

Mistress Jasper wasn't a woman to be intimidated.

"It's necessary that I see her before she's brought to bed and where that will be."

"You'll be above stairs."

"That may be so, but I must see it so that I will know how to prepare. Do you have someone who will fetch her for me? Ah, here she is. Martha Pratt is it not?"

Martha hadn't expected to find anyone when she arrived in the taproom. Wary after a quick glance at Mistress Faal's angry frown, Martha nodded.

"Aye."

"I'm Edna Jasper. Mr. Faal asked me to call. And I can see you'll soon be in need of my services."

Edna stepped forward and took Martha's arm.

"Let's go somewhere to talk. I must see where you'll be birthing this baby."

Mehitabel sprang up and marched past them toward the front hall.

"I'll show you the way."

"Your pardon, Mistress, but I'll speak

with her alone. You need not bother yourself."

Taken aback, Mehitabel stopped short, her anger evident in the rush of color to her cheeks and glint in her eyes. For what seemed an eternity to Martha, the two women faced each other in silence. But Mehitabel was no match for the midwife's quiet calm and determination.

"Go then. But don't disturb anything."

"Not at all. Not at all. Let's go dearie. It's this way is it?"

Without another look at Mehitabel, Edna Jasper patted Martha on the back urging her toward the door and the stairs to the room above.

In Andrew's bed chamber, Martha turned to face the older woman, unsure what was expected. It had been less than a week since she moved into the room and was still uncomfortable about being there.

"Ah, this will suit us well."

Edna went directly to the bed, a sturdy, well-made one covered with Martha's quilt.

"This is good. But have you a cover and bed tick that are not quite so fine as this bedding?"

"Aye, above in the garret where I used to sleep. This is Mr. Faal's chamber."

"Have someone bring them down. This room will be easy to move about in and the fireplace is close by. We'll need linens, diaper, other things, but we'll see to those when the time comes. If you will allow me, lie on the bed.

I must see where we are."

Edna helped Martha to lie down, then began to poke and prod, pulling up the long shirt Martha had taken to wearing over her skirt to press an ear against her belly.

"Breath slow, dearie. Slow. I can't hear it with you panting so. I fear your Mistress has got you upset."

"That's often the case. This time I think it was the stairs."

"Just lie still for a bit."

Edna stepped back and pulled a chair up to the bed.

"So that is Mistress Faal. I had not the pleasure til now."

Martha nodded.

"This is her house, but I am Mr. Faal's servant. I'm a...."

Edna patted her arm.

"I know, dearie. There's little that people in this town don't know about each other. I know how you come to be here, and, truth be told, there's many an upstanding citizen of this fair city who came the same way. So think no more of it. Now let's have a listen."

Edna pulled a small brass horn from her bag and used it to listen intently, then lifted her head with a satisfied nod.

"There's a strong heartbeat and it's moving about, but I'm sure I needn't tell you that. All's well. Now, we'll just wait. I'd say a month more. As soon as you feel the pains coming on or anything worries you, send word.

I'll come to you straight away."

"There will be someone to help. The girl Sukey has only ever watched, but the cook has birthed her own and attended the birth of many others. The Mistress might want her to be in the kitchen, though. I fear she'll want to have a hand in this herself."

"That she will not! Don't you worry about her."

Martha nodded with a sigh of relief, but appeared no less worried.

Edna paused and looked hard at her.

"There's something else bothers you, I think."

"My mother died birthing me. She wasn't strong, they said. I *am* strong, but I know things can go wrong. What about the baby if I should…if anything happens? Will you help Mr. Faal to find someone? The baby will be bound to him, just as I am, but I'm sure he'd have no interest in keeping it. I worry what Mistress Faal would press him to do and dare not think what will happen if I'm not here."

"Don't you worry. I've taken the measure of your Mistress Faal. But nothing will happen. We'll see this through together. Don't give it another thought. You'll be the one to care for your little one. And on that score, I'll speak plain.

You'll still be a servant and required to work as you have been, but don't let them put your child out to be suckled by a Negress. That's often the custom here. And the child

480

doesn't know that's not its mother. You must keep it near so you can feed and care for it. That's as much for you as for the child. And it needn't keep you from your work. I'll come 'round to see that the mistress doesn't interfere with that."

Edna patted Martha's hand and left her close to tears at the thought she'd have someone who cared about *her* welfare and could stand up to Mistress Faal. Martha wasn't alone in her relief. Behind the half-open door to his shop, Andrew had overheard his mother's encounter with Edna Jasper, and what the midwife told Martha.

He breathed a little easier at the thought of the impending birth. Still, he worried about its outcome. It would be sad it they lost the infant, but if Martha were to die... he couldn't let himself dwell on the possibility, couldn't explain why it disturbed him so. For the first time he could remember, the leather's demands couldn't shut out his troubled thoughts.

Edna Jasper had left Mehitabel in the grip of bitter feelings that carried her into the kitchen. One look at their mistress drove Belle and Sukey to attend to the midday's meal preparations with extra diligence. But it was Mehitabel who most wanted to be busy. She waved Belle away from the chickens bound for the stew pot and gutted them with a vengeance.

She has no right to come into my house,

giving orders, telling me what to do. No right! I know what to expect about birthing. I...

As she looked down at the entrails in her hands, Mehitabel felt bile rising in her throat. Wiping her bloody hands on her apron, she fled out into the kitchen yard where the bitter winter air almost took her breath away. But it didn't stop her retching or the brown liquid she spewed over the winter-hardened earth. She couldn't remember the last time she had to examine anything she said and almost welcomed the searing pain in her throat.

No! I deserved that. She had every right to put me in my place. I can hear Mama now. "Mitty, curb your tongue." That's what she'd say.... Much as I'd like to be rid of that girl, I don't want her to die. Or her baby. God forbid that the child should die. I've had enough of unhappy memories. My own dear children gone. William gone. And me left alone to bear the trials of this life he thrust me into.

Ignoring the cold, she paced the yard in the grip of warring thoughts.

And now Andrew has brought this girl and her troubles into our lives. What if that awful man who came looking for her returns? What if there are others? She tells a fine tale, but can we believe what she's told us. Ill used? Falsely charged? Was it really no fault of hers?

Mehitabel came to an abrupt halt staring into the icy blue sky.

But what if she's telling the truth? What if she really has arrived here through no fault of

482

her own? She's paid dearly. And worse, the poor little mite she bears will suffer too. The girl knows nothing of birthing a baby. Or caring for one, I'd wager. But I can do something about that! She'll soon get her comeuppance. Humph! We'll get her back to work. At least she can do that.

XVIII

Acceptance

Not long after the midwife's visit, Martha found a high stool behind the bar. Not sure of its purpose, she shoved it back into the corner.

"You'll be needing to get off your feet, I suspect."

Mehitabel nodded toward the stool.

"Thank you, Ma'am."

Martha had to admit she was grateful, but couldn't help being wary of the Mistress's concern for her comfort. Something had changed though. She hardly ever complained any more. Was it Mistress Jasper's doing?

Mehitabel hoisted a basket onto the bar and took out a long infant dress, yellow with age. She laid it out tenderly.

"You might as well do something useful. The child must have clothing. A dress something like this, but I won't leave it with you. My children wore it and it's very dear to me. But here..."

She reached back into the basket and pulled out several bundles of cloth.

"Here are the makings for two dresses, some finer cloth for nightcaps, and plenty of diaper for napkins and tapes to secure them."

Without looking at Martha, she rushed ahead.

"I've cut out two dresses and finished a third and a cap so you'll have something to use as a guide. I presume you can stitch the others together. While you're at those, I'll make a warm winter gown."

Unable to speak, Martha took more time than necessary looking at what would be the bib of the little dress.

"Thank you ma'am. I... I hadn't thought what to do about clothes."

"I thought as much."

Mehitabel nodded with knowing satisfaction.

"And I'll see that Mr. Faal's chamber is made ready with what else you'll need. We'll not wait til the last moment. Until then, it will be better if you're not idle. You can continue your work here in the public room for some time yet."

"Yes Ma'am. I've no liking for sitting about with nothing to do."

"Good. You can get started then."

With a nod, Mehitabel shoved the basket along the bar toward Martha and, without a backward look, left for the kitchen. Martha sat for a long while fingering the pieces of cloth. They suddenly made the impending event very real. In a short time she'd be dressing a baby, her baby, in these little clothes. The reality of that thought had never struck her with such force.

But where were the feelings of joy and happy expectation? Instead she felt nothing but resentment and loss. The child would be a constant reminder of its despicable father and all that he'd caused to be taken from her. Mistress Chinn, Charley, a home…

No that's no way to think. This baby had nothing to do with what happened. Come what may, it mustn't suffer for that. I have a new life now and I must do what I can to make it a good one for this child.

****

"Bet you done in the man what did that, di'n't ya?

John Hutton leaned back in his chair as Martha tilted her pitcher of ale into his mug and shoved it toward him.

"And got yerself shipped off to America 'cause of it."

His companion grinned at Martha.

"Naa. She'd 'a got her neck stretched if she'd done that. Just havin' a bit of fun, she was."

Martha froze, fighting the urge to strike out, to fling the contents of her pitcher in his face. But that would only bring more attention to herself and gain nothing. The rest of the men in the room needed no more of a show.

"How I've come to be here is no business of yours."

She raised the pitcher and was pleased to see him flinch.

"I'd as soon douse you with this, but it's too good to waste on the likes of you."

Pleased with her forbearance, she hurried to the rear door, struggling to contain her anger. Behind her, she could hear the men teasing John Hutton, then taking bets on when the baby would be born and whether it would be a boy or a girl. Martha stumbled through the breezeway to the kitchen yard and took a deep breath of wintry air.

As Mistress Jasper said, a small town kept few secrets. Martha was sure hers would be common fare around town. When she returned to the public room, she was relieved to find that her tormenters had left and been replaced by men more intent on their midday meal and fresh tankards of ale.

Balancing on the stool, she pulled out her basket from beneath the bar and lifted out the infant dress she'd finished basting the day before. Though she welcomed the chance to get off her feet, she couldn't help wishing it was with a book instead of sewing, especially the painstakingly fine stitchery the little dress now required. At least her diligence seemed to put Mistress Faal in a better frame of mind. She actually nodded her approval when she stopped to look at Martha's handiwork. Indeed, Mehitabel left Martha wondering what had come over the woman.

****

Mistress Jasper's visit had spurred Andrew to ask Daniel to search for a cradle on one of his trading runs down the bay. He was puzzled when a sudden hardness darkened his friend's face. But it passed quickly causing Andrew to suppose he'd imagined it.

Two weeks later, Daniel struggled to contain the aching sadness that nearly overwhelmed him as he stood at his tiller guiding the *Seagull* up the Bay to Annapolis. Stowed below was a cradle that he told Andrew he'd found in a Norfolk joiner's shop, but would take no money for it. His gift to the girl, he said, but made Andrew swear she wouldn't know. Something in the look in Daniel's eyes kept Andrew from arguing. They clasped hands and Daniel agreed to keep the cradle hidden on the *Seagull* until it was needed. He quickly put it out of sight, back where it had been for nearly ten years.

Daniel hadn't looked at the little bed since he'd come so close to throwing it overboard with the remains of his dead wife. But it was the only thing that remained of his life with Peggy. He couldn't bring himself to do it. Wrapping the cradle lovingly in sailcloth, he'd shoved it into a dark corner of his cabin. And his mind until Andrew made his request.

Slowly, reluctantly, he unwrapped the cradle and the memory of his pent-up excitement the day Peggy told him she was carrying their child. He'd begun work on the cradle the very next day, finding scrap wood and time in the shipyard for the happy task. Now, as he drove the *Seagull* south to Norfolk, he forced himself to haul the little bed out into the light of a new day.

Using the times he could secure the boom and let the boat sail without his full attention, he cleaned and oiled the neglected wood. Driven by anger at himself for leaving Peggy so much alone and a perverse satisfaction in his purpose that day, he scrubbed away the years of grime. By the time he'd reached Annapolis, he'd brought out the wood's ruddy sheen. That pleased him and helped dull some of memory's pain.

The girl should have it. She'd been ill served by fate and the life she'd been cast into. Especially in that house. She'd get little sympathy there. Damn Andrew. Bends too much to the will of that harridan of a mother. I'd like to knock some sense into his head. Leastways, I can see the girl has a proper bed for her little one.

Daniel couldn't call Martha by name. Couldn't allow himself the familiarity it implied. Nor could he admit the warring feelings that the sight of her stirred in him and the thoughts of her that plagued him during his solitary nights and days on the water.

XIX

The Black Horse

Hannah sat savoring dawn's quiet before the gaggle of girls hired by Rebecca came straggling in from the courtyard. The new cook would follow in her own time. At the sight of her, the two odd-job boys broke off their noisy banter and hastened to stir the fires for the ovens and great hearth at the other end of the newly expanded kitchen.

Hannah much preferred the old hearth and was already warming her toes by its fire. Along with the growing flame came thoughts of days past, of the old cook Agnes Quinn, and of her own arrival at the Black Horse as Arthur Chinn's new bride.

How far she'd come from those happy days. But with Annie's help, she was still making the meat pies and hearty stews that brought men in from the wharves. She took a mean satisfaction from how much it rankled her daughter to see the old taproom fill up daily. Hardly a day passed that Rebecca didn't complain as she'd done the day before.

"Why must we continue to feed those men. There are other places they can go. We don't need the trade of wherry men and such. We serve gentlemen now, Mother. They want finer fare...pastries, not meat pies."

"I hadn't noticed. The men who've been coming here for years have been well pleased. And not a few are gentlemen. All have been welcome and they've been faithful to us. It's you and your high-minded airs that will drive them away."

"Good riddance!"

With a toss of her head, Rebecca was off and didn't see her mother's smile of bitter satisfaction.

And I'll be saying the same ere long.

Hannah had to bite her lip to keep from telling her daughter that in a matter of weeks, she'd be gone. And Charley with her, bound for the Chesapeake Bay and the colony of Virginia.

****

Though she and Charley made their preparations carefully and behind closed doors, Hannah doubted that they needed the secrecy. Rebecca's attention seldom strayed from meeting her *gentlemen*'s demands and keeping her new kitchen staff in line. She rarely paid Charley any mind unless he neglected

492

some chore or appeared late in the upper taproom where Joseph Rawley was happy to see his son whenever he arrived. Neither of his parents knew that helping his father at the bar was the only thing that kept Charley at home at all. It worried and saddened him to see his father's natural good humor wearing thin.

Unlike his wife, Joseph Rawley wasn't gladdened by the fact that more and more of the men he served seldom, if ever, got their hands dirty. Or sought to empty their woes into the ears of a non-judgmental listener. Gone was the easy comradery of the old taproom, full of men Joseph once called friends. One night after a row between his parents, Charley sought Hannah out.

"No matter what I do, I can't make it better for Papa. Like as not, I'll only do something to get Mama's dander up. But that's not all, Nana. I don't want to spend my life tending bar. Not any more. I spoke with Uncle William to see if he'd help me to sign on to one of the company ships. He said no. Mama wouldn't like that. But he did think she'd agree to let me join him and learn the business. If I applied myself, he said, I could be running it one day. But I don't want to do that, Nana. I don't want to be getting up every morning to spend all day in the shipping office."

He took a deep breath, then let out a long sigh.

"I want to go to sea, Nana. To see more of the world. And I'm going to. Please don't tell

493

Mama. I'll tell Papa, but you're the only other person I'm telling. When Uncle Jamie gets back, he's promised to take me on. We're going to the Chesapeake ...to make our home there."

"To make your home there?"

Charley's sudden guilty look told her that he'd let on more than he was supposed to.

"I aughtn't tell you more. Uncle Jamie'll have my hide. He wants to tell you himself. And I don't know the whole of it."

And that was all that Hannah knew until Jamie's return when she learned the rest and made the decision that changed her life.

****

On Jamie's last visit, he'd promised his mother he'd inquire about the ship that took Martha away. It was bound for the Chesapeake Bay and he knew those waters well. Not many ships carrying transported convicts traded there, so he thought he could find some trace of hers. As it turned out, that assurance brought little cheer for Jamie'd also told her that he'd decided to remain in the Chesapeake.

"Three times now I've been to the Chesapeake. I wish you could see the bay. They call it an inland sea, Mama, but you're never far from its shores. They're lined with forests and meadows, ashen cliffs, and rivers and bays that offer some fine harbors. But it'll test the most seasoned mariner with fickle winds and tides that can run you aground on its shoals.

Mariners there have even devised their own breed of sailing craft. It's fast as a bird in flight, they say and can outrun any pirate. They're not burdensome enough to carry cargo, though, or I'd have one by now."

"It sounds as if you're about to forsake us for your new mistress."

Hannah had to laugh at her son's look of shock and dismay. It wasn't entirely feigned. Mothers weren't supposed to speak of mistresses.

"Why must you trade so far away? If you put into port here more often, perhaps you could take a wife and start a family."

He'd laughed and hugged her with such unabashed joy she had to step back to get a full look at his face.

"That's just what I have to tell you. I have found the woman I will take for a wife. She lives in Virginia, in a fine port called Norfolk. I can prosper there, trading in American waters and south in the Caribbean."

At Hannah's continued stunned silence, he rushed on.

"She's a widow, Mama, but young. Twenty-eight. Her name's Polly Adams. I wish you could meet her, but let me show you."

He fumbled in his waistcoat pocket for a small leather sack.

"On this last visit, a traveling artist was in Norfolk and I got him to paint her portrait."

All thumbs, he fumbled to untie the sack and finally could let the small image slip out into his hand. He held it out for Hannah to see.

"It doesn't do her justice, Mama, but at least you'll have some idea..."

A pretty little thing, Hannah thought as she studied the young woman's delicate features framed by honey blond curls escaping from her bonnet.

"She's sensible and has a good head on her shoulders. Her husband Tom has been my friend ever since I began trading in the Bay. If he hadn't been there first to ask her, I expect I'd already have married Polly. But that caused me no ill feeling toward him.

I mourned Tom as much as she when he was lost at sea last year. He left her with a small son and daughter but she has no other family in the colonies. I was there for little Tom's baptizing and I suppose I'm closer than anyone else. For the past year, she's been working for a milliner to support herself and little Tom and Meg."

As if to prove her worth, Jamie proffered his coat sleeve to show Hannah the tear Polly had skillfully mended.

"She gets by, working at home with a slave woman to help care for the children."

A slave woman? What a strange world that Virginia is. And once he returns this time, I'll never see him again.

"A slave woman? Is she so wealthy she can purchase a slave?"

"No. Tom worried about her and the children when he was away. He got the woman so Polly wouldn't be alone. We've agreed to free Aggie, but she has no other home or means to live, so I suppose she'll stay on with us."

We'll free Aggie? So he's already thinking in terms of we?

Hannah listened with an increasing sense of dread.

"The bans are already posted and we'll marry when I return to Norfolk."

Blind to his mother's look of distress, Jamie rushed on.

"We'll have a proper home. Polly's house is small, but it's a welcoming place and it'll suit us well. When I visit, it feels just like home."

****

"I imagine Jamie will be arriving before long, now," Hannah said when she was able to get Charley alone.

"You must think seriously about what you're doing and all it will mean. Your mother will be angry, but that's nothing new. Your father's the one I worry about. It will be a hard thing for him. He loves you dearly."

"I know. Saying farewell to Papa and to you is the worst part of leaving. But if anyone understands why, I think you do, Nana."

"I do, son, and I'll miss you terribly. But if you're sure that's what you want, I'll help in any way I can and wish you Godspeed."

Brave words, she told herself that night

as she struggled with the thought of losing Charley before she fell into a troubled sleep. Though she prayed for Jamie's safe and speedy return, she dreaded the thought of watching the pair of them sail off soon after.

Little more than a week later, in the early dusk of a gray winter's day, sadness outweighed her joy when Jamie's voice brought her out of her chair by the kitchen fire.

Once past their greeting and settled at the kitchen table, Jamie announced that he had good news for her. While in Norfolk, he'd met Adam Muir, captain of the *Sea Nymph* just returned from delivering transports to the town of Annapolis in Maryland.

"He wished he'd never taken on such cargo and wants no more to do with trafficking in humans."

Jamie shook his head.

"Lost a young girl and several others, but your Martha fared well. He thinks the innkeeper who purchased her bond would be a kind master. Andrew Faal, Adam said his name was. Given some who came looking for servants, she couldn't have done better. But beyond that, he could say no more about her."

At least,it gives us some hope he'll use her well. But it does no good to dwell on that.

"That gives me hope at least. Now, tell me about Polly's children? How will they take to you? I'd think they miss their father"

"They were so young and Tom was so much away at sea, the children hardly knew

498

him. I suppose I seem as much a father as he did."

"So now you'll take on a father's duties as well as a husband's?"

Her hopes and prayers dashed, Hannah couldn't curb the hurt she felt.

"I'm sorry, Mama. I didn't plan for this to happen."

"I know that. I wish I could be happier about it. And Charley? Is it true that he's going with you?"

"Aye, I told him what John Muir told me about Martha and he's determined to go to look for her. Beyond that, I don't know what he'll do. He'll have no money to buy her freedom. Nor can he be sure that Mr. Faal will release her."

Jamie paused, then shrugged and plunged ahead.

"There's more to it than that, Mama. From what Charley tells me, Rebecca makes his life miserable. And his father's, but there's little he can do to make that better. I doubt Rebecca sees or cares what she's doing to either of them. But I'm sure, Mama, even if Charley can't find or free Martha, he won't come back. He'll have no trouble making his way in Norfolk or working the water … with me if that suits him."

"So, I'll never see either of you again?"

Jamie shook his head. He could think of nothing to reassure her or lessen the hurt he was causing. But Hannah's thoughts had suddenly veered on a different course.

Why must that be so? I'm of no use here.

499

Rebecca's made that clear. But I'm not useless and certainly not helpless or without means. There's nothing here for me anymore? Haven't I wished I could see the places Arthur and Jamie spoke of? And if I could find Martha …. What do I care about the expense or hardship?

"I won't stay here and watch you and Charley leave. I'm going with you."

"To Virginia? And leave home? How can you give up the Black Horse? Think what you're saying, Mama."

"I know what I'm saying. There's nothing left here I care about. The Black Horse is no longer the place I've known. Most everyone I've loved has gone or will be gone. That'll be intolerable. The truth is, in many ways, life here is already intolerable. For all intents and purposes, your sister directs what happens in the Black Horse. She and Joseph might as well have it. Rebecca doesn't need me. I've little doubt, she'll be pleased to see me leave."

Jamie knew that much was true, but was troubled by the thought of taking his mother on a sea voyage to a new world, to meet a soon to be daughter-in-law and two grandchildren.

And Polly. What'll she think when I arrive with my mother in tow? She's not one to give way easily. And she's already in a stew about preparing to wed.

Jamie offered the only other arguments he could think of against his mother's plan.

"You don't know how bad the sea can be

at this time of year, Mother. You've never been to sea. You don't know what it's like. There's no place on the *Speedwell* for a passenger, especially a woman. And some of my men may desert me. They think a woman aboard is bad luck."

"I'm sure I've stayed in worse places in my lifetime. I'll just have to get used to rough weather. As for your men. If they're worth their salt, they won't object to a paying passenger. I can make it worth their while. And yours too."

"Ahhhh!" Exasperated Jamie threw up his hands.

Whatever happened to the sweet and loving mother who used to welcome me home and send me off again with a kiss and a wave?

"I'd best go and prepare them," he said over his shoulder. "We leave in a fortnight, if you can manage that."

"Aye, aye Sir. I'm sure I can."

When he looked back, he couldn't help but grin as he acknowledged his mother's salute.

****

"You're going to do what?"

Rebecca confronted her mother, fists on her hips, cheeks an angry red.

"Have you looked at yourself in a glass recently. How can you be so adle-pated. You're too old, too worn out for such a voyage. And if you should survive, how will you live if you get

501

there? This Polly that Jamie plans to take for a wife, does she know she's getting his mother too?

Hannah had no intention of answering. She knew from experience that she could say nothing that would make a difference.

"You and Jamie have no right to lure my son away. None. His place is here, helping his father. How can he do that to Joseph? How can he give up the Black Horse? It'll be his one day. What will he have in that place? Nothing."

Hannah raised her hand to stop the tirade.

"Enough! I'm leaving the Black Horse in your hands and I'm sure you'll keep it for your son's return. He'll be better able to manage it when he's learned more of the world."

XX

Mitty

In the early dark of a February morning, Mehitabel's call to Belle brought Andrew out of bed with a start. Pulling on his britches and shoes and carelessly tucking in his shirt, he quickly climbed down to his shop and hurried out to the taproom. There he found his mother behind the bar shoving bottles and jugs around.

"Ah, there you are. The girl's time has come. As soon as there are people about, you must go to see if Mr. Middleton has white wine. We have none and we'll be needing a posset before this day's out. It will soothe the nerves."

"I suppose I'd best go straight away for Mistress Jasper."

"There's no need. Belle's rousing Nate to go for her. But look at you. You can't go out like that. Go back and make yourself presentable."

Andrew made a quick sortie into his shop and returned with his shirt tucked in and his hair freshly tied back.

"That's better."

His mother gave him little more than an absent-minded glance.

"The girl said she didn't need me, but I couldn't lie abed listening to her moaning and carrying on. Sukey's up there now. She's got the fire going and a kettle on. There'll be hot water at hand when needed."

"Now, go up, Andrew. Tell them I've sent for the midwife. Then, off to Mr. Middleton's."

Andrew hurried upstairs, but near the top, he hesitated. Cries, not unlike the sounds of a laboring animal, brought him to a halt. He'd seen the births of cattle and pigs, but had only the vaguest idea of a human birthing. From what he'd seen of their cow laboring to deliver a calf, he was glad he didn't have to witness what was going on. He hastily gave Sukey his message and hurried below trailed by cursing he'd heard only from hardened watermen.

Edna Jasper arrived with surprising speed, creating an authoritative bustle of activity. She was clearly pleased with the arrangements and, perhaps as a peace offering, thanked Mehitabel for having prepared everything as she would have done herself. As the morning progressed, she welcomed Mehitabel's posset. In the meantime, Mehitabel kept busy in the kitchen getting breakfast out to the few morning regulars and starting the midday dinner. Andrew could only marvel at the change in his mother and hoped that it would last for the benefit of all concerned. Especially the girl.

Girl?

He chided himself.

Martha's seen more of life's darker side than any girl should have. More than I have, come to that. And soon, she'll be a mother if all goes well. But what if it doesn't? What if she...? No, that can't happen. She's strong. She'll bear it well. With luck, she won't be abed too long. Then, Mother can help with the child and Martha will be back at work.

****

Gripped by pains that grew in intensity, Martha ceased to care who heard her curse the loathsome piece of offal who'd ruined her life. When Edna Jasper stopped in during the day to check Martha's progress, she paid the cursing no mind. She didn't doubt the girl had good reason to curse the despicable man who'd raped her. What worried the midwife was how she'd accept his child. By evening, Edna had settled in, prepared to stay the night.

As the sun sank below the prison across the street and supper was out of the way below, Sukey joined her. In her pain, Martha angrily pushed them away when they forced her to her feet to walk or to lie still so that Edna could check the baby's progress. At the end, her screams made some of the men below so uneasy that they hastily finished their pints and left. A few remained hoping to know before the night was out if the child was a boy or a girl and which of them had won their wagers.

At the bar, Andrew kept his mind occupied trying to recreate his father's recipe for flip. He offered the results free to any who wanted to try the hot, frothy drink. Aside from assembling the right combination of ingredients, he couldn't accomplish the task with his father's enthusiasm as he plunged the red-hot iron into a tankard. He offered the last one to Daniel who had been keeping him company and returned the iron to the fire.

Daniel shook his head and shoved the mug back toward Andrew.

"I have to be out on the Bay by sunup. You're the one could use that."

He nodded toward the half-dozen men still in the taproom.

"I were you, I'd drink this, send them home, and get yourself to bed. I'm sure if Mistress Jasper needs you, she'll let you know."

He grinned and rolled his eyes toward the ceiling.

"I'd say things are moving along. Don't take me wrong, Andrew, but you have the look of a worried husband. If I didn't know it was another's bastard, I'd think that's your bantling about to come into the world. From the sound of it, that girl is in fine mettle. You've no cause to worry. I've heard there are none better at a birthing than Mistress Jasper. You can be sure she has it well in hand."

With the touch of a knuckle to his forehead, Daniel nodded his goodby and grabbed his hat from its peg by the door. Outside, he welcomed the gusty northeast wind that hit his face and ruffled his hair. He liked the wild feel of it and folded his soft cap, tucking it beneath the broad belt at his waist.

In such a wind, the *Seagull* would be twisting and swooping like her namesake and would leave him no time to wonder how the girl was faring. She was young and strong, he reassured himself. And none better to be in charge than Mistress Jasper. By the time he returned in a fortnight, she'd be up and about and suckling a fine, strong bairn. He kept repeating that thought as he lay awake on his bunk until past midnight as thoughts of Peggy came unbidden.

They had been so happy anticipating the upcoming birth of their child. He'd taken to smoking a pipe in the early evening. When he wasn't on the water, he'd join Peggy by the hearth, smoking as she did her needlework. They'd talk of the son she insisted she wanted as much as he did. And he'd promised to build her a proper house for more children who'd help and keep her company when he was away.

But that memory wasn't as sharp as it once was, unlike his new quickening of feelings for Martha so like those Peggy had stirred the first time he laid eyes on her. Ordinarily he never gave serious thought to his feelings of desire for a woman and regularly satisfied his need in a brothel. He couldn't deny, he desired Martha as he would any fetching woman, but this was a deeper longing that couldn't be satisfied by an hour or even a night of coupling. He wanted more, much more. He wanted the home and family he'd given up thinking he'd ever have. But he couldn't see how Martha Pratt might fit into that picture. He was a damn fool to even imagine such things.

****

Across the hall from where Martha labored, Mehitabel couldn't shut out the sounds from Andrew's room. She felt a tightness in her gut and loosened her bodice as she stretched out on her bed, remembering her own labor, the pains, the fear. Early in the day, Mehitabel told Mistress Jasper she'd be available if needed, but she had no desire to help with the birthing.

She managed to stay busy in the kitchen and the men in the taproom enjoyed a midday meal of puddings and meat pies far from the usual. With the coming of evening, however, Mehitabel concluded that she was doing no good hovering about in the kitchen. She left preparations for the next day to Belle and joined Andrew in the public room. That proved as distasteful as ever and was made more so by the sounds from above.

Her son was clearly in no mood for her company and she lingered only a short time before retreating to her bed chamber. The best she could do there was to put plugs of cotton in her ears to shut out Martha's cries.

She lay awake thinking of the infant dresses Martha had finished for the baby and quickly drifted off to sleep imagining herself dressing the new arrival. A baby's cry woke her in the early morning darkness and she lay until daylight, drifting in and out of sleep thinking it was a dream.

****

"You've got a fine, strong girl."

Edna stood by the bed, the bundled baby in her arms.

"A moment, please."

Exhausted and fearful, Martha wasn't Ready to see the baby.

What if she's fair-haired, blue-eyed? What if she looks like her father? No! Even if she does, she's not to blame for how she came into this world.

"Let me see her."

Holding her breath, Martha moved aside a corner of blanket that partly covered the baby's face and took in a gulp of air. She could see nothing of John Randolph in the tiny red-faced creature. She let out her breath in a sigh of relief. The child's still damp hair was auburn like her own. In the flickering candlelight, her dark eyes were open wide with a look of studied, if unseeing, seriousness. A narrow ring of grey encircled the pupils. Martha looked up at Edna.

"I suppose her eyes will be blue?"

"Could be. But it's too early to say. Takes a year sometimes for the color to set. One thing for sure, she's hungry."

The baby's lips were already working hungrily and Edna helped Martha guide the infant's searching mouth to her breast. When the baby latched on, Martha gasped with surprise, then drew the tiny head close so she wouldn't lose her grip. Curious, she opened one of the baby's clinched fists and smiled as it curled around her finger.

While the baby nursed, Edna and Sukey gathered the soiled bedding and when the baby fell asleep, Sukey took her and helped Martha put on a fresh shift. Martha could easily have joined the infant in sleep, until she remembered there were others she was sure wanted to see the child.

"Has the Mistress risen yet?"

The midwife was a moment answering.

Now what would she want with that woman? I'd think Mistress Faal's the last person she wants to see.

"I believe so. In the kitchen, no doubt."

"I'd like her to see the baby."

"You would?"

"Aye, I can't leave her out of this. It will go better for this little one if she's not another bone for the Mistress and me to fight over."

"Humpf! I hope Mistress Faal shares your feeling."

When she left to find her mistress, Sukey's look told Edna that she was just as doubtful.

"Is it too soon to put a proper dress on her?"

"A day or two will be better. She's well swaddled and warm. That's enough for now."

Edna Jasper went to the nearby bureau where the baby clothes were neatly folded.

"There's some fine work in one of these."

"Aye, that's Mistress Faal's doing. Not mine."

"My, my. She's provided for your little one quite well. Who would have thought..."

The girl's right. For better or worse, Mistress Faal will have a hand in raising this child.

Martha's thoughts were following a similar course. She didn't know what to think about Mistress Faal anymore and couldn't imagine how she'd react to the child of a servant and a rapist... assuming she'd accepted what Martha had told her.

Oh bother! That's too much to think about. I'm so tired and this bed feels so good. I'll just close my eyes for a few minutes.

Martha had slept for more than a few minutes when she woke with a start. The baby was gone from her side.

Did I dream it? Was it real? Yes. A girl. Could they take her away from me?

Alarmed Martha flung off the bed covers

and tried to rise.

"There, there, dear. Don't get up. You're not strong enough yet."

Edna Jasper gently pushed her back on the bed.

"My baby. Where's my baby?"

"She's right here."

Mehitabel stepped from behind the midwife with the child in her arms.
"You needed sleep and your little one didn't."

Mehitabel held the swaddled infant out to her.

"You woke just in time. She's hungry again."

Martha didn't know what to say but forced a smile as she took the baby.

"You need to eat, too. I'll go fetch you some supper."

With a quick nod, Mehitabel turned and hastened out of the room.

Were those tears in Mistress Faal's eyes?

Martha and Edna looked at each other in puzzled silence.

"Was she weeping?"

"Aye." Edna nodded.

"I suspect there's been some sadness in her life where a baby's concerned. But let that lie."

Just outside the room, Mehitabel stopped with the closed door at her back and used her apron to mop uselessly at her tears. Instead of going below, she crossed the hall to her own bed chamber and sank onto the edge of the bed as she gave way to the rush of feelings unleashed as she'd cradled Martha's baby in her arms. After Emily, she'd never expected to hold another. Not even as she'd stitched the clothes for Martha's baby did she think she'd want more to do with it.

A servant's child? God only knows who the father really was. It's no more to me than the child of a slave would be. Just one more creature to provide for. But why do I feel this…this longing?

Mihitabel rose and shook herself as if it would be that easy to shed the unwanted feelings. Wiping away the last of her tears, she poured the last bit of that morning's tepid water into her wash basin and felt a little better after washing her face. A check in her mirror showed little sign of anything amiss. Donning a fresh apron, she went below to supervise breakfast preparations.

****

"What you gonna call her?"

Sukey took the sleeping baby and laid her carefully in the cradle beside the bed. When Martha pulled herself up in bed to sit, Sukey handed her a bowl of porridge sweetened with dried berries and honey. Martha frowned, the spoon halfway to her mouth.

"Call her? Oh dear, I don't know. I've no family to take a name from. Not that I'd want to anyway."

"There's no doubting she's yours. Got your hair. When she grows up, you'll think you're looking in a glass."

If you only knew how glad I am of that.

"You got a fine name, Miss Martha. It'd be fittin' to share it with this little one. Don't have to call her the same way. I was full grown 'fore I knew my true name. It were too big for a bitty little black baby, my mama said. Her mistress named me Susanna, but 'fore long everybody was callin' me Sukey. That's what was writ on the paper Mr. Andrew's papa got when he bought me."

"I can't think how anybody could make anything out of Martha. But more than that, I'm afraid that people won't soon forget how Martha Pratt came to be here. I must think more about it."

I can't let her carry my name around with her. That could be a heavy burden. Once I was proud of it, but none here know that Martha. Not yet anyway.

Her moment of defiance quickly vanished in a flood of memories of better times in her life, of how much she missed Mistress Chinn and the Black Horse. Though the details of Hannah Chinn's face were an ill-defined memory, her steadfast love and kindness were still very real.

Hannah? Hannah Pratt?

Martha had no one dearer to her than Hannah Chinn. And beyond her freedom, she'd

514

suffered no greater loss. The name Hannah would be a constant reminder of better times.

When Sukey left with the empty porridge bowl, Martha eased herself down onto her side so that she could reach into the cradle beside the bed and touch her sleeping daughter's soft cap of dark hair.

Who are you little one?

As she drifted off to sleep, Martha remembered Mehitabel Faal's tears as she relinquished the baby. She as much as anyone else would be a large part of the baby's life, her early life, at least.

Maybe the Mistress can suggest a name. Maybe... Martha sank back onto the bed and was quickly asleep.

****

"I think it's high time you gave this child a name."

Martha struggled to come fully awake. Mehitabel was looking down into the cradle.

"I was thinking that, too, but nothing comes to me."

"It requires some thought. My parents chose mine too quickly. I'm sure it wasn't my mother's choice. The name Mehitabel comes from my father's family. He was the only one who ever called me that. My mother wouldn't call me Mehitabel, despite his wish. She and most everyone else called me Mitty."

Martha turned to look down into the

cradle.

"Mitty? I like that."

Mehitabel shook her head.

"That's not a proper name. Think of something else."

What am I doing, talking with her like that? She's a servant. I can't have anyone thinking she's kin to me. But I can see that she makes a sensible choice.

"My mother's name was Sarah Pratt. She died because of me. I never knew her or anyone from her family. But the name Sarah makes me sad. I don't want to be reminded."

"That may be so, but it's a fine name."

"Mistress Chinn named me and was as much of a mother as I ever had. Her name is Hannah."

No sooner were the words out of Martha's mouth than she knew what she was going to name her daughter.

"I will call her Hannah. Hannah Pratt. But I still like the name Mitty. And you will be much in her life. If you'll permit it, Ma'am, I'd like to call her Mitty. None need know where the name comes from. But if you'd be ashamed that she has your name, I'll not do it."

She paused, waiting for Mehitabel to say something, but the woman didn't even seem to have heard her. And, indeed, Mehitabel hadn't. She stood gripped by a rush of confused emotions.

She's such a dear baby. But named after me? That won't do.

516

Mehitabel took a long shuddering breath and busied herself unnecessarily with a pile of linens on the nearby bureau.

What's wrong with me? The girl's a convict servant. She's nothing to me, nor is her child. What do I care about her and her bastard? She still owes us seven years. If she thinks I care a wit about that child, she'll use it to shirk her chores. The last thing I need is a child to worry about.

And soon enough, she'll be underfoot. Breaking and spilling things. Running about in the taproom. No! Not there. That's no place for a little girl. Not even a servant's child. I must... The devil take it! She isn't my concern. Mine is to remind that girl that she has no more privilege here than she did before. Mother or not, she'll tend to whatever's required of her.

Mehitabel turned back to look down at the baby.

"Hannah is a fitting name and I've nothing against calling her Mitty. That will be a pet name you've chosen for her."

Mehitabel hastily turned back to the linens. Angry at herself, she used the edge of one to wipe away tears that she couldn't control. Then waving it over her shoulder, she swallowed a sob as she hurried to the door. In the hall outside, she chided herself for letting her feelings take hold of her like that twice in one day.

XXI

Questions

After a restless night, Andrew woke in the loft's early-morning darkness to a confusion of thoughts and feelings.

It's done. And she didn't die of the birthing. Should I be relieved? She's a mother now. What must I do about the child? Nothing. Unless it keeps her from her work, it's nothing to me.

Andrew sat up in bed, staring unseeing at one of the loft's small windows where daylight was still only a pale suggestion.

Martha's a servant, nothing more. Nothing more. And mother or not, she has a duty in this house as a servant.

Andrew forced his thoughts to the day ahead.

There's work to be done. And first, I must get back to a room where I'm not bumping my head on the damned roof beams.

That thought drove him from the bed to search for his shoes in the room's half-light. Finally they came to hand as he groped under the bed. Once shod, he climbed down the ladder to his shop and luxuriated in the ability to stretch. Feeling better, he had to admit that he hadn't really begrudged Martha the use of his room. It was, after all, merely the place where he slept.

****

In Andrew's bed, Martha dozed with Mitty asleep in the crook of her arm. As the baby began to stir, she put her to nurse before she could cry and bring the Mistress from across the hall. She fell back to sleep until awakened by the door's soft click as Belle shut it behind her. The black woman nodded approvingly.

"Took her to bed did you? I come to see if you be needin' help."

"I'd like to go below, but first I must relieve myself."

"'Fore you do any of that, let's see how steady you is. You can't be doing nothin' when you goes down. An' don't you try carryin' that baby. I'll have James come get the cradle. Sukey can carry her down. I 'spect the both of you best stay down there durin' the day. If I remember rightly, there's an empty drawer in Mr. Andrew's bureau there. That'll do just fine as a bed for her at night."

Mitty squirmed but didn't wake as Belle put her back in the cradle and helped Martha sit up and tend to her own needs. Once Martha was clothed in a fresh shift, kerchief, and petticoat, Belle gathered up her dirty linens.

"The Mistress be down in the kitchen soon, so I'd better be there too. I'm sending Sukey up to get you and that little one down. Don't you try to do it alone."

Martha nodded. She had no intention of trying anything. She sank back on the bed to wait and was again asleep until Sukey appeared with James and Harry in tow. Silently, they hoisted the cradle and were gone. Martha wasn't surprised by their silence and haste. She was sure the last thing they wanted was to run into Mistress Faal.

Mitty had awakened by that time and Martha allowed her to suckle as Sukey fished Martha's shoes from under the bed and gathered a blanket and extra napkins for her and the baby. Once Mitty seemed content, Sukey helped Martha put on her shoes and stand. She then disappeared with the baby down the stairs leaving Martha to follow at her own pace.

Martha caught up with Sukey just outside the kitchen where she could hear Mehitabel fussing over where the slaves should put the cradle. They found her waiting expectantly with eyes only for the baby Sukey held. The slave turned quickly and shoved

Mitty into Martha's arms.

"You best take her now. You gonna be all right?"

"I'll be fine."

Martha nodded with a smile and took the sleeping baby. Walking slowly to the cradle, she was conscious of each unsteady step.

"Should you be up and about?"

Clearly Martha wasn't her concern. Mehitabel's eyes never left the infant she carried.

"I'd rather be here than above stairs with nothing to do. If that's all right, Ma'am."

"Of course."

Martha took heart. Mistress Faal had never agreed so readily to anything she said. She ventured a thought prompted by the sight of the cradle.

"I was told I spent my earliest days in a kitchen cradle."

For all Martha could tell, the Mistress hadn't noticed she'd spoken. Mehitabel pointed toward it.

"I've chosen a nice quiet corner. With a chair to rock her. We can keep an eye on her there."

We? Mitty is mine.

Rankled by Mehitabel's possessiveness, Martha managed to keep silent as she sank into the rocker. She looked up at the woman hovering over her.

"She'd be better in the cradle."

Mehitabel nodded toward the little bed.

Must we start contending for her so soon?

Martha hugged the baby to her and Mitty squirmed in protest.

Ah, sorry, little one.

"She's hungry. I'll feed her, now, but after that, she mightn't sleep. Would you take her?"

Not trusting her voice, Mehitabel nodded and, after a moment's hesitation, went to the table to check on the meat pies that Belle was preparing for the oven. Unable to think of another chore to keep her in the kitchen, she left for her bed chamber.

"Send word if I'm needed," she said to no one in particular.

Fanny and Sukey waited until their Mistress was out of sight, then left for the taproom with a pot of hot porridge, a basket of warm cornbread, and a pitcher of cider. In the breezeway, they met Andrew who helped himself to a piece of cornbread. He didn't expect to find Martha in the kitchen and hastily swallowed his mouthful of bread and wiped the crumbs from his chin. Gaining more time to prepare himself, he poured a mug of cider and took a swallow before approaching.

Andrew couldn't clearly remember his sister Emily as a baby except that she had their father's hair. Would this child forever be a reminder of its father? He braced himself, his jaw clenched, then let out the breath he'd been holding as he looked down at the tiny replica of her mother.

Puzzled by his apparent discomfort, Martha assumed it was the sight of the baby sleepily tugging at her partially bared breast and gently pulled Mitty away to cover herself.

"Ahh… She's healthy?"

"Aye, as near as I can tell."

"Do you have a name for her yet?"

"Hannah, but I'll be calling her Mitty."

His frown and a raised eyebrow demanded an explanation.

"The …your mother… that's what she was called as a child."

He shook his head.

I'll never understand the workings of women's minds.

"She was?"

How did she come to discover that?

Martha nodded.

Still puzzled, he decided to let the matter rest.

"You're well, now?"

"Aye. As well as can be expected, I suppose. I should be back to work soon. And my thanks for the use of your bed chamber. I'll see to moving back to the garret now."

That could be none too soon. She'd been living in constant fear of running into his mother leaving her room across the hall every time she opened his bed chamber door . Or worse, that her mistress would burst in on her if she heard the baby cry.

"There's no haste. When you're …

523

stronger, you can move back to … the garret.

Til that moment, he'd never really given much thought to where she'd been sleeping or how it would be with an infant to attend to.

"I'll have James and Harry go with you to make it more suitable."

Andrew paused. He didn't know how to go on. Now she was a mother, he wasn't sure what that would mean. She probably had little idea herself. But his mother most certainly would and somehow he'd have to keep her in check.

Martha's questioning frown brought him back to the present and why he'd come into the kitchen. He turned abruptly to Belle.

"I'll take breakfast now. Have you meat and more bread?"

Without waiting for an answer, he headed for the door.

"Send a plate to me in the saddlery."

Leaving Martha and Belle to exchange puzzled looks, he was gone.

In the uncomplicated familiarity of his shop, Andrew nursed his mug of cider and turned to his bench to let the demands of the leather capture his attention.

Turning back to the cradle, Martha stood with Belle looking down at the sleeping baby.

Belle straightened, nodding her approval.

"She's good and strong."

"You have children?"

Belle busied herself with tucking the edges of the blanket more tightly around the baby. She looked at Martha, then seemed to reach a decision. When she finally spoke, her voice was flat, her feelings contained.

"I birthed six. But I wished I didn't. Soon's they was walkin' good, they was took away. Ever' one sold off. I never knew what happened to them."

Martha stood silent unable to think what to say. The slave woman had never shared anything personal before. And she guessed this time had to be the hardest. She could only imagine what it must be like not to know her children's fate. Or, in Belle's or any slave's case, to know too well the fear, pain, and degradation their children would live in.

But she did know what it was to lose someone that way. She had to fight hopeless tears at the thought of Hannah Chinn and how much she missed her.

"I never knew my mother, but I've always wished I did. I suspect, your children wish the same."

Belle's only acknowledgment was to look away.

Martha hastened to fill the silence.

"My mother birthed me in a public house and died doing it. There was no family to take me, but I was lucky. The Mistress could have sent me to the poor house. But she kept me and raised me like I was her own child. She was just like a mother."

Martha looked again at Mitty.

"I wish she could see this little one. She never knew I was pregnant. She doesn't even know what's become of me. Come to that, I don't know what's to become of me. Or this child. Mr. Faal didn't expect to get a child. He'd have every right to sell us away."

"You don't hafta worry. The master's got a good heart. He won't be doin' nothin' like that."

"How do you know that?"

"I just knows."

Martha decided not to press her for an answer. The Negroes knew a lot more than whites gave them credit for. She suspected Belle would tell her if there was anything she needed to know to get through the next six years that she and Mitty were bound to Andrew Faal. Remembering the cruel-eyed man who'd tried to buy her, she knew their fate could have been far, far worse.

****

By early afternoon, Martha could spend no more time dozing in her rocker or tending to Mitty. She'd guessed that Fanny and Sukey had been managing well enough, but couldn't mistake the white girl's harried look. Martha had no doubt that was due to Mistress Faal's return to her vigil at the bar.

"I think I'll see if I can be useful in the taproom," she told Belle. "I'll send Sukey back to help you with the baby."

"Sukey be right glad of that. But you sure you be all right?"

"I'll be fine. I feel the need to be up and about. It doesn't sound as if there are many in the taproom."

As Martha thought, the few men in the taproom were regulars. They cheered when she appeared, causing Mehitabel to cast a disapproving look their way. Nonetheless, she lost no time in leaving for the more pleasurable demands of the kitchen. Andrew was equally pleased by Martha's return, but limited her to refilling mugs and glasses for Fanny to deliver. Each time the girl left with an order, Martha sank onto her stool with a sigh and realized that she couldn't continue long into the evening. Not only was she tired, she'd soon have to nurse Mitty.

"I think I'd best get out to the kitchen," she said. "It's past time for Mitty's supper."

He nodded.

"I'll not be needing you."

Once she'd returned the baby to her cradle, Martha sank back into the rocking chair and quickly dozed off. The lamps were lit when Mitty's cries woke her. After nursing the baby and an early supper of cider and a meat pie, she rejoined Andrew at the bar. He allowed her to do no more than she had earlier and after an hour or so, ordered her to take Mitty and herself to bed. She was surprised how welcome that was.

XXII

A Return to Work

The following noonday, when Martha appeared at the bar, Andrew waved her away.

"Sir, I'm no good at lying about with nothing to do. Or stitching the baby's napkins. I must be up and at work."

"What does Mistress Jasper say?"

"I'm sure she would agree. I'll take care."

Still skeptical, he nodded and handed her the pint of ale he'd just poured.

"For Tim McAlister."

A carpenter from the shipyard, McAlister was one of their regulars. He greeted Martha with a broad grin.

"Glad to have you back, girl. It ain't the same without you."

"I'm glad to be back. I heard Mistress McAlister is abed and waiting for your ... what is it, seventh?"

"Aye. We're praying for another boy."

"I'll keep her in my prayers too. Please tell her I wish her well."

She hurried back to the bar.

"Sir. I've had an idea."

She surveyed the room and could see there'd be no calls for more ale as the men waited for Fanny and Sukey to arrive with their midday dinner. In addition to the usual breads and stewed fruit, bacon, chicken, and fish, there'd be lamb, beef, and venison or some other game brought in by local hunters and fishermen.

"Fanny can fetch us if need be. Let me show you."

Without looking back, she led the way across the room and out through the front hall to the store. The room's musty smell spoke eloquently of its abandonment, as did the layer of dust on the sheets covering several tables, benches, chairs, and what remained of unsold goods. Andrew hung back, remembering the scent of tansy that had tinged the air long after his father's body had been carried off to the grave.

"Is something wrong?"

"Foolish memories. My father had thought a shop would be more to Mother's liking than keeping a public house. As you can see, he was wrong. And then, when he died, he was laid out here."

"I'm sorry. But perhaps you can replace those sad memories."

She pointed to the door at the back.

"This room might serve you better as a saddlery than the one you use now. With the kitchen yard and cartway to the street just behind, people could bring a horse or a cart up to your door if need be. And most important, you wouldn't constantly be at beck and call from the taproom. During the day, I can tend to that and Fanny's there to help."

He stood silent. His imagination had already leapt to the workroom she'd described. He could picture where his bench would be and where and how he'd store the increasing variety of leathers he needed. The shipyard uptown, vessels in the harbor, and businesses around the waterfront could keep him busy dawn to dusk. Then too, the room had a good fireplace to chase away the fall and winter chill. With a quick nod, he turned back to Martha.

"I think it will work ... yes, it'll work very well."

"With a good clean-out, your shop room would do very well for serving coffee. I've heard in some public houses, coffee's getting to be a favored drink, especially with gentlemen."

Still lost in possibilities for his new workshop, Andrew had to force himself to concentrate on what she'd just said. It made sense.

"You're right. I've heard that too."

Martha stepped past him to bend and lift the corner of a sheet that covered a jumble of chairs, tables, boxes, and barrels. As she stood, pulling the sheet away, she staggered and falling backward, was seized by a sudden panic. It wasn't Andrew Faal but John Randolph trapping her, pinning her helpless to his chest. Her fear suddenly turned to anger and she twisted, shoved herself away, and raised her fists.

Startled, Andrew was able to catch her wrists and hold them until he felt her relax. As she realized where she was and whose arms had caught her, Martha returned to the present. Slowly, he let her go and stepped back.

"Oh, Sir, I'm sorry. It was as if I wasn't here, but back in that room again, and that horrid man...

"You don't have to be sorry. And don't worry. You're safe now. And always will be, if I have aught to do with it."

Begun as a thought, the words had come out of his mouth before he could stop them.

For a moment, they stood, silenced by the turmoil of unexpected feelings and looking everywhere but at each other. Something new had passed between them, but neither could be sure what it meant. Unable to linger in that feeling, Martha quickly turned away, snatched up a bolt of linen close at hand, then tossed it aside. Thus revealed was a basket full of laces, ribbons, and thread.

"Ah, look, the Mistress will certainly be able to make use of these."

Andrew could only nod.

"There's much here could be used in the new room and these ..."

She poked into a nearly empty barrel, pulling a cream-colored plate and several bowls out of their cushioning straw.

"I suppose they could be used in the taproom. Ahh, and here..."

She beckoned for him to look into a nearby box as she pulled out a brass candle snuffer, several razors, a pocket knife.

"I'm surprised you haven't sold these."

"We were even worse at shop-keeping than tavern-keeping."

He took up a packet of memorandum books.

"I can make use of these."

He joined her to rummage through the box, ashamed of all he'd neglected to attend to since his father died.

"Mother was no better at attending to these things than I was. No, that isn't fair. She lost more than I. Father was the one who chose this life in America. She wouldn't have chosen it for herself and, without him, she's had noone she really cared about. Not me certainly. But your little one is the only thing I can remember bringing her real pleasure since ..."

Emily, he was about to say, but thought better of it. That unpleasant memory was best forgotten.

"... in a very long time."

He joined Martha to concentrate on what else of use they might pull from the box's straw bedding. Neither heard the hall door open.

"What do you think you're doing?"

Mehitabel stood in the doorway, a flush rising in her cheeks and an angry glint in her eyes.

Andrew moved quickly to ward her off.

"I've thought of another use for this room, Mother. I think you'll...

"You thought? What's she up to?"

"It has nothing to do with her."

He took his mother's arm and turned her away.

"I've been neglecting my leather work for too long. This room does us no good. With that door to the yard... It will do far better as a saddlery than the one I'm in now."

He rushed ahead, hoping to divert her, and stem an angry tirade.

"We can use the other to serve food and drink, coffee perhaps. By then, Martha will be back at work and I can return to mine. But it's no small matter. Come, I'll tell you..."

Mehitabel shook his hand off her arm and spun on her heel.

"Not now, Andrew. I've work to do above stairs. But rest assured, we *will* talk about it."

****

Upstairs, Mehitabel paced angrily from one end of her bed chamber to the other. Finally she sank into her rocker to draw some comfort from its protesting creaks as her toe kept it going with angry pokes at the unyielding floor.

Move his saddlery? Posh! Is he so blind? That conniving girl is planning something. She's no good. Worse than that slut Sally. Too smart. And not above using tricks to get what she wants. She's taken Andrew in. He gives her entirely too much freedom. Why can't he see it? He's the master here. She's a servant. Nothing more. Definitely nothing more.

Martha had caught the warning in Mehitabel's scowl as the woman marched past her out of the room. A moment later, her door's slam above rattled the lower room's window, spurring Martha to hurry out with a wave to Andrew.

"Let me draw you a pint before you go back to work, Sir."

She hastened to the bar where he took the tankard she slid across to him and headed for his shop. There he sat a long while before his unfinished leatherwork. His thoughts were still with Martha and the sudden sense of loss he'd felt when she pulled away.

Would she always be so fearful? Could they start again ... not as master and servant? Could she, would she come to accept him as ... as what?

He didn't know how to think of her or what he felt, but couldn't escape the fact that thoughts of her took him off to sleep at night and, come morning, the anticipation of seeing her hastened his waking. But his feeling that day was more intense, an ache he had to relieve.

Been too long without a woman, Daniel would say.

Andrew wished he was in town. He often helped put things in perspective ... when he wasn't urging him to join in on his round of Bay ports or on a visit to the house by the town gates before he left on his run to Bermuda.

That's all well and good for him, but I'd as soon do without. It's more than that. Is it what's called love? I don't know what she thinks of me. I'm not even sure she trusts me. But it she could come to trust me, mightn't she begin to care? To love me? But there's no use thinking of that as long as she's bound to me. She must be free to do what she will.

Andrew shook his head, trying to clear it.

But what if she chooses to leave? She must know how hard it would be to make her way alone. But with a baby? Would she stay here just for the child's sake?

He raked his fingers through his hair and rose from his stool.

I'll just have to risk it. And first I must free her.

****

In his shop, Andrew opened his writing desk, shuffling through bills of exchange, deeds, and bonds, to pull out Martha's indenture. He didn't like to remember what it was like before she arrived. Too often he had to put aside his leatherwork to tend to the bar and other tavern business. She'd freed him from that and much else in the day-to-day running of the pub and more than fulfilled her debt to him. Not only that, she seemed to thrive on the work and had made a success of the tavern.

Even the child, as unfortunate as its conception was, had improved their lives. For the first time since they left England, his mother was content, almost pleased with her life. That tiny, squirming creature might well have come into the world unwanted, but it had greatly brightened his mother's outlook. And his. But there remained one thing yet to set right.

He hastened to call Martha into his shop and without a word unfolded the indenture and handed it to her. Though she could see it was an official document, she'd never seen the paper he'd signed aboard the ship.

"I don't understand."

"This is the indenture from Captain Muir. I'm taking it to a lawyer to declare that you've fulfilled your obligation to me. Once it's witnessed and signed, you'll be free. You owe me nothing more..."

He stopped, struck by the reality of what he'd just done and the momentary desire to take it back. With that paper, she was free to leave, to find other work, other lodging. Would she? She had every right. But he didn't want to lose her. What could he offer to entice her to stay?

Martha struggled to understand...to accept that it was her freedom she held in her hand.

Free? Really free to make my own way?

He cleared his throat. He'd have to say something more, something to let her know that he wanted her to stay.

"As I said, you're free to do as you will ...but I hope you'll want to stay."

Her continued silence forced him to rush on.

"We can settle on a proper wage that will provide you a living. And enough for a place to live if you don't want to stay here."

Andrew paused, unnerved by her silence and the frown that had settled above her dark eyes.

"There are places to let nearby," he rushed on, "and I'll see that you have the means to get settled. Despite what's written there, I've never thought of you as property, mine or anyone else's. And as soon as it can be done, you'll be free of that bond."

Looking down at the paper she held, Martha struggled to grasp what he was telling her.

I'm free? Really free? I can leave ... go wherever I want? ... But I don't want to go anywhere.

She handed the indenture back to him.

"You must keep it. I've no safe place. I

don't understand why you've decided to do this. But I've no desire to leave, and as best I can, I'll see that you don't regret it. I thank the Lord nightly that you were the one to purchase my bond. This has come to be the only home I know here. Thanks to you, it's a far better one than I could have expected. I don't know where I'd go, or that I'd want to leave, if I can remain here. But what does your mother say about it?"

"Ahhh" His sigh of relief was audible. "Yes, well, she's had nothing to say. She doesn't know."

"Oh my. Perhaps you'd best wait. Don't do anything now. At least not until you've told her. Whatever the law might say, and what you've chosen to do, it's every bit her right to know and to have a say in the decision."

Andrew's relief was tinged by concern. He could well imagine what his mother would say. Indeed there could be hard times ahead that even the infant she adored couldn't allay. Ultimately, though, losing the child would be his strongest argument when the time came to tell his mother.

****

Feeling more satisfied and more in command of his life and affairs than he could ever remember, Andrew went ahead with new energy to move his saddlery. He put James and Harry to work carrying tables and chairs into his abandoned workshop off the taproom.

Throughout, he studiously ignored his mother's long, morose silences, punctuated by angry snorts, grunts, and mournful sighs.

The furniture was soon cleaned, arranged, and rearranged several times until Mehitabel expressed a grudging satisfaction and was making plans for the extension to the taproom. After the slaves had cleaned the unwanted furniture and sale items, Andrew posted notices for an auction and hired a crier to carry word of it around town.

As the auction was underway, Martha helped Andrew tend the bar. During one stint, she noticed that Fanny appeared particularly beleaguered as she brought food from the kitchen and caught the girl's arm.

"You look troubled. Is something wrong?"

"No, not with me, but it's not going well with the cooks."

"The cooks?"

"Aye. It's the Mistress. She's got them in a real state."

"Oh my." Martha shook her head. "I'll see what I can do."

As she passed the bar, Andrew stopped her.

"I heard what Fanny said. I'll speak with my mother."

"Thank you, Sir. I think I can manage it. Let me see."

"Very well, then. But, if you have a problem, let me know."

"Yes, Sir. I will."

"Good. Also, before you go there's something I've been meaning to suggest. It's time you called me Andrew not 'Sir'."

She stopped and turned toward him with a puzzled frown.

Now where did that come from?

"And what will your Mother say to that?"

"It doesn't matter. It's between us. Well..." he went on with a rueful shrug. "... you'd best continue to call her 'Ma'am.'"

"Aye," she nodded with a smile. "I will. But I'd as soon not let it turn into a battle royal."

Though such a battle between two cocks was common in Wapping, she'd seen women go at it with equal ferocity, scratching, biting, pulling hair. And there were still times when Mehitabel looked at Martha as if she'd like to engage in such a battle.

Martha braced herself as she hurried on to the kitchen where dinner preparations were well underway. Apart from the usual busyness, nothing appeared amiss, except for Mehitabel who was needlessly ordering Belle and Sukey to fetch this, redo that, or start something else. Martha managed to step in and relieve the beleaguered cooks who quickly found reasons for trips to storeroom and garden.

Eventually, things settled down in the kitchen, heaping platters and steaming bowls were delivered, and at the other side of the house, the auction went well. Andrew and his mother were surprised and pleased with the results and both went to their bed chambers that night, absorbed with plans for new use of the two rooms.

XXIII

Hal's Revenge

Hal Lowcross caught the arm of the serving wench as he passed her near the entrance to the Horn and Crown. Dark with smoke from poorly tended fires and candles guttering in their sooty lanterns, the pub served less discriminating travelers entering Annapolis through the town gates.

"I'll be wantin' a pint."

"And I'll be wantin' to see your coin before I set it down."

After looking around, he leaned close, pressing a coin into her hand as he lowered his voice.

"More 'n that, I got a proposition will make it worth your while."

"And why'd I be interested?"

"It ain't that kind o' proposition."

Sally looked at him hard, then shrugged and headed for what passed as a bar in the shadows at the back of the room. Hal took a chair at a table nearby. At that time of the morning, the pub was nearly empty except for a man sprawled in a drunken stupor on a corner bench and two others playing a desultory game of cards at a table well away from the door.

They eyed Hal suspiciously, then returned to their game. Mean-looking solitary types like him were best left alone. Sally, however, earned a second look as she thumped a tankard down on the grimy table in front of Hal. They hoped she'd be able to keep him at a distance.

"So, what do you want of me? I got work to do."

"You was workin' at Mrs. Faal's house over on Prince George's Street wasn't you?"

"How do you come to know that? And what's it to you?"

"That's my business. Let's just say I got a score to settle there."

"What kind of score?"

"Do you want to earn a coin or two or not?"

"I can't be goin' in there. Was a time I was keepin' that taproom full and more. Those men wasn't comin' in just for a pint of rum at the end of a day. I don't know what Mrs. high and mighty Faal's got against a girl makin' a little extra money out of it. And now that transport he's brought in goes about in town like she's not some whore straight out of Newgate."

"You and me 're thinkin' a lot alike. Seems we both got scores to settle in that house. Let me tell you what I got on my mind. See to them others, then come back."

Sally lost no time in checking and refilling the other men's tankards and returned with a rag to scrub Hal's table.

"I come in on the *Sea Nymph*, same as that girl," Hal began. "And who's to say I didn't know more about what put her on that brig than the captain said and what she's been saying since she got here."

He stopped and looked around to be sure no one was listening. Sally nodded for him to continue.

"Let's say, the truth is, she'd been playin' fast and loose and got caught at it. Say she was taken right and proper for stealin' that money. Robbed an upstandin' gentleman, she did. And what she's been sayin' about gettin' that babe and being took against her will ain't true either. Suppose… just suppose, I heard talk when I was aboard the ship what brought her… that when she was in Newgate, she was earnin' a better lot for herself by givin' the guards special favors.

"There was a lot of women come through their time in the cells that way. And she was earnin' favors on the ship too. Ain't none here but me can say she was or wasn't. None can say I don't speak the truth. And if that Mistress Faal gets wind of it, the trollop will be in for a heap of trouble. It won't be lookin' good for her and that son of hers either."

Hal leaned back in his chair so he could look Sally full in the face.

"So why I'm tellin' you all that is 'cause I got reason to want to put that girl in her place and I'm goin' to need some help. I'm thinkin, you know a lot of those as takes a meal or a pint in the Faals' taproom. All you got to do is get out the word that you heard talk of her doings in Newgate. Just what I been tellin' you.

You could say that now she's done with the birthin', she's ready to go back to her old ways. That she's lookin' to entertain those as can pay for something extra. You don't have to make a lot of it, just say enough to get people thinkin'. And like I said, there'll be somethin' in it for you beyond the pleasure of puttin' that girl in her place. What do ya say?"

"I've got no likin' for those people. Turning me out like they did, near put my Ma in the grave. Took the fight right out of her. And I've been working for the both of us ever since."

"There, you see, I knew you'd be just the one to help. Go easy, though. We don't want it comin' back to you. Just a bit of gossip dropped here and there will do it. There'll be a shilling or two in it for you, and I'll be around to see none cause you trouble."

****

From a table on the far side of the taproom, Daniel waved to Andrew as he came in from his shop.

"Get yourself a pint and join me."

Andrew gave his friend a questioning look, then went to the bar where Martha already had a mug ready for him. Once settled at the table, he leaned toward Daniel.

"You're not here just to share a drink. What's on your mind?"

"Aye, you're right. There's talk around town." He looked toward the bar. "About her."

Andrew shook his head.

"What about her?"

"Someone's spreading word that she's lying to you, that she wasn't raped, just unlucky. He's saying that she was thieving and justly sent to Newgate. Whoever started it, claims he knew her from before she went to gaol. Says she was earning better treatment in the cells and on the ship by selling her favors."

"And you believe that?"

Slapping the table, Andrew thrust himself back in his chair.

"She's given us no cause to think she's that sort and I can't believe Adam Muir would lie about her."

Daniel shook his head.

"No, never. It was none of his doing. Something else is going on and I've a good idea what and who started it."

"Who was it?"

"Don't trouble yourself, Andrew."

"Don't trouble myself!" Anger brought Andrew out of his chair.

"Sit, friend." Daniel grabbed his arm to pull him down. "Now you've got her looking at us. Try not to look as if anything's wrong. Let me see if I'm right. Until then, don't say anything. I don't want my prey to go to ground."

Daniel took a long drink as he waited for Andrew to relax then asked.

"So, how's the coffee business going?"

"Coffee? What are you talking about?"

"You've got trouble written all over your face. Let's talk of something else. And I do want to know about the coffee. I hear there's a good supply due in Norfolk, if you want me to see if it's worth the price. Down that way, it's going high."

"Aye, you're right. Do that. The coffee's doing better than I expected. And what's more, Mother's taken to it. Of course, 'twould be better still if she'd get back to needlework. She's keeping everybody on tenterhooks. And here she comes."

"Which is good reason for me to leave. With luck, I'll be back with news before the day's out."

"News of what?"

"Ah, good day, Ma'am. I'm off, but I look forward to coming by this evening for one of your fine meat pies. Until then, Andrew."

With a wink, he clapped his wide brimmed hat on his head and left Andrew to find an answer for his mother.

"What was he talking about?"

547

"Coffee, Mother. He's bound for Norfolk in a few days and will try to find us a new source. At the rate we're going, we'll need one. If the price is right, he wants to know if we want any? I told him I'd have to talk it over with you."

"I don't know why you must do business with that man, Andrew. I'm sure he's not the only one going there."

"He's a good friend, Mother. And I know he'll deal honestly with me, which is more than I can say for many others I know."

"Never mind that. If you must use him, we're sorely in need of more coffee. And there are other things we need. I'll make a list."

Back in his shop, Andrew couldn't clear his head of what Daniel had told him. His friend was too much at loose ends when long ashore and liked nothing better than to go looking for trouble. Or, if he couldn't find any, to stir some up.

****

Later that day, Sally was puzzled to see Daniel come through the door of the Horn and Crown. He'd sworn off drink, she knew, so his appearance in the pub more than likely meant trouble. She was certain when he hailed former drinking companions but continued through the taproom's smokey haze. At the bar, he slapped a coin on the lead counter.

"You've taken to drink again?"

"If it will get me some companionship, I'll have a pint. You'd not begrudge a man just come ashore a little company, would you?"

"I've never known you to be wanting for that. And since you're spendin' all your time down on Prince George's Street, I'd have thought Mr. Faal's wench would be ready to oblige now she's birthed her bastard. Or doesn't Mr. Faal like to share?"

Damn.

Daniel turned his head, biting back what he wanted to say.

"He's got nothing to do with it."

Suddenly suspicious, Sally cocked her head and frowned up at Daniel.

"No? So why you comin' in here?"

Daniel shrugged and took a swallow of ale.

"I've been hearing talk about her, but I never get the whole story. Wouldn't be surprising, her coming straight out of Newgate."

Scanning the taproom, Sally leaned closer to Daniel and lowered her voice.

"I hear there's some who knew her. One come with her from London. He says, she's took everybody in with her sad tale."

Daniel shrugged. "How's anybody to know its not true? I'd wager no one's been asking."

"There's one come in on the boat with her. He knows what she was up to."

"Ahh, I think I know. It's that Hal... Hal

Lowcross isn't it?"

Suddenly realizing what she'd done, Sally grabbed his arm.

"Don't you dare let on you found out from me. And don't you come here lookin' for him. If he finds out I told you, he'll kill me for sure."

And he will. Daniel shook his head and covered her hand with his.

"Don't worry. He'll hear nothing from me. I won't be talking about it and best you don't go repeating what you just told me. If I were you, I wouldn't trust anything he says."

He gave her hand a squeeze.

"You chose a bad one to be in league with."

Sally snatched her hand away and looked wildly around the room.

"You get out of here. Get out now. And don't come back."

"Don't worry. But you've been foolish. If he gives you any trouble, send someone to find me. *Seagull*'s my boat's name. Or…" With a rueful grin, … "you can have them leave word at Mr. Faals' taproom. It would give me pleasure to set Lowcross right."

Daniel took a second swallow of ale with a grimace. Foul swill, he thought and put a second coin on the bar for the girl. He'd seen real fear in her eyes. As he pushed the coin toward her, he leant forward.

"I meant what I said. Send word if you need help."

With a wave, he was off acknowledging calls from a back table as he stepped out into the street.

That's a bad business she'd got herself mixed up in. Should have better sense than to get caught up in that scoundrel's scheming ... or me either, come to that.

Daniel had seen Hal Lowcross just once. He'd come upon a drunken street fight and Lowcross was getting the best of two men. They were too drunk to know better than to take him on and their blows hit each other as often as they did Hal. Daniel would have left them to it until Hal began kicking one of them when he was down, aiming for the fallen man's head with his hard-toed boots.

Daniel stepped in and, joined by several others, pulled Hal away. They held him until the two men escaped into the Horn and Crown. Clearly outnumbered and his advantage lost, Hal scooped up his hat and stalked off. Daniel had thought no more of the man until the rumors about Martha Pratt took him to the Horn and Crown in search of their source.

Martha had touched something in him that he couldn't put into words. Not since Peggy had he felt any strong emotion for a woman and no desire beyond the ones he could satisfy with a few coins. Anger, hate, fear, those were words he knew and used, but love? That was for others and for the books that put ideas in the heads of high-born young ladies.

No, that wasn't for him, but what he did

know was that he had to protect Martha from animals like Hal Lowcross. She needed no more trouble. She'd borne enough from the lies that had brought her to Annapolis. And by the same token, neither should Andrew or his mother suffer from such lies.

****

Daniel found Andrew in his shop.

"It's Hal Lowcross has been spreading the slanderous talk. Using that wench Sally you had here a while back. She hasn't got good sense. But I've set her straight. I just hope she doesn't suffer for it. He's a mean one and will turn on friend as soon as foe. I've told her, if he goes after her, she can send word to me here. But don't you do any fool-headed thing if she does. Or any other thing where he's concerned."

He grinned and put a hand on Andrew's shoulder. "Don't take this the wrong way, my friend, but you're no match for Lowcross. I'll take care of him."

"You know I'm no fighter, Daniel. I had a run in with him once and it was pure luck it didn't come to blows. I'm not sure I'd have come out in one piece."

Andrew didn't like to think of the encounter and wasn't about to start anything with the man. He was no match for Hal's brawn, but he hoped if he had to stand up to him, he could do it without getting killed. As for that, he hoped Daniel wouldn't be taking a chance if he took the man on. He was equal to Hal in stature and strength and was no stranger to a fight, but could he strike the blow that would kill if he had to? Andrew had no doubt that Lowcross could.

XXIV

Andrew's Stand

Sad chance brought Hal to the Widow Simpson's rough public house near the foot of Prince George's Street. There, Sally had found new employment and, she hoped, refuge, after her encounter with Hal. He had no trouble tracking her to the widow's house. Already drunk and looking for trouble, he slapped a coin on the bar demanding an hour with Sally in the Widow's back room. She cared little for what went on in that room and knew nothing of Hal. A bite told her his coin was good. Ignoring Sally's protest, the Widow pocketed the coin.

"It's not your place to pick and choose, my girl," she said and shoved Sally toward Hal.

Far more agile than Hal, she slipped past him to plead for help from four men rolling dice at one of the pub's three tables, but they knew Hall and weren't about to take him on. With an angry growl, he took two unsteady steps after Sally, then stopped, aware that the men were watching. Managing an uncaring shrug, he returned to the bar and the pint that the Widow shoved toward him. He downed it in two long, slow gulps, swiped a sleeve across his mouth, then leaned back against the bar to steady himself. Once he'd got his bearings, he walked carefully across the room and out into the street.

Running with skirts hoisted nearly to her knees, Sally burst into the Faals' public room, praying that Daniel Pyke was in town or, at least, that someone in that taproom would help her. Her cries for help caused heads to turn, but several knew the girl and remained seated waiting to see what might develop.

"I'll see to her."

Martha waved Sally back past the bar to the rear stair.

"Who's got you running like a scared rabbit?"

"Lowcross. That bloody-minded dog, Hal Lowcross."

Martha stopped frozen at the foot of the stair as if an icy hand had reached down into her gut and taken hold. That name was too real a reminder of the fear and pain she'd thought was behind her. But as much as she dreaded confronting Hal, her fear this time was for Andrew who'd headed for the door.

"Sit there," she told the girl, shoving her

onto a lower step, "and don't move."

Martha didn't wait to see if Sally obeyed as she hurried through the taproom. Ahead of her at the street door, Andrew had come face to face with Hal. Primed for a fight and certain he'd prevail, Hal grabbed a fistful of the slighter man's shirt.

Completely unprepared, Andrew surprised them both as he drove his fist into Hal's face. Staggered by the blow, Hal reeled backward into the street where he came to a stop. There he kept a precarious balance bending forward, hands on knees as he struggled to breathe through his painfully bloody nose.

In pain, Andrew nursed his hand. Though he was fearful that he'd broken several fingers, he was more afraid that Hal would revive and come back at him. Martha saw the danger too, but she'd also seen several faces in the taproom windows and shoved Andrew back inside. There she accosted the onlookers.

"Now that he's shown you how to handle a blowhard are you such cowards that you won't help us keep him away from that girl? She needs no more trouble from him. Nor do we."

"Let her call the sheriff. It's not our job to keep the peace."

With a snort of disgust, Martha turned on the man.

"You know as well as I that the sheriff's not needed."

She turned to wave at the prison across the street.

"And no need to send anyone to that place, not even him."

"And none would know that better than you, would they girlie?"

Stray bursts of laughter were cut short by angry nudges from the pub's regulars. They knew how she came to be in Annapolis and the change she'd brought to the Faal's taproom. They believed her, but to take on Hal? The scrape of a chair being shoved back brought silence as a burly seaman, fresh off a brig newly arrived in the harbor, walked past the cluster at the window.

"Come on, you scurvy dogs. Ye're not goin' to let a worthless bit of offal like that bring trouble in here are ye?"

He didn't bother to see if any followed him as he shoved past and out into the street. By then, Hal had managed to stand and pull himself together. He knew he was no match for that man, or most of the others if they were given half a chance at a fair fight.

"The sheriff will be hearing of this," he growled as he pulled off his kerchief to mop his bloody nose.

"From what I recollect, the sheriff's the last person you want to hear about it," said one of the onlookers. "Wasn't so long ago, he ordered you out of town. If you value your hide, you'd best go this time. And if you come back again, we'll see you get a fine coat of tar and feathers to wear as we ride you out on a rail."

Snarling behind his bloody kerchief, Hal staggered across the street to where none could see him and sagged back in the shadows of the prison wall. Finally, he took a deep breath, pulled himself upright and trudged across the dock and up town to the Horn and Crown. Martha felt like cheering. She signaled the stevedore to follow her and Andrew back into the bar.

As they passed, several of the regulars raised mugs and glasses, saluting Andrew with a new respect. At the bar, he quickly filled a tankard and handed it to the seaman, then offered a free round to those who followed. Once all were served and their attention was turned elsewhere, Martha drew Andrew aside.

"You're not using your right hand. Let me see it."

"No need to bother. It'll mend soon."

He shook his head and tried to hide it.

"No it won't. I can see it pains you. If you're to go back to your work, we must tend to it."

Slowly, he held out his hand for her to see his reddened knuckles.

"Come with me. A cold compress is what you need."

When he hesitated, she nodded toward the full taproom.

"They'll be content for a while yet. Fanny can come for me if need be."

Allowing him no time to protest, she

gently pushed Andrew ahead of her. At the back of the room, they passed Sally who hadn't moved from where Martha left her on the stair.

"Oh my, you too. Come with us to the kitchen."

She beckoned for the girl to follow Andrew and herded them out into the breezeway.

In the kitchen, she was relieved to see that Mistress Faal was nowhere in sight and quickly enlisted Sukey to fetch cold water from the well. Tsking and shaking her head at the sight of her master's hand, Belle soon had a piece of linen torn into strips for a bandage.

"You drink this, Sir," she said and put a mug of hot cider on the table where Andrew sat examining his injured hand.

"Ah, good," he said with a smile and a nod toward Sally.

"Give her one, too."

Though Andrew didn't notice, Sally caught the full force of Belle's look of disapproval. Slowly, painfully, he moved his fingers, one at a time, and sighed with relief. None appeared to be broken. There'd be swelling that would keep him from his workbench for a day or so, but he couldn't deny a sense of pride. He'd actually put that damned Lowcross in his place. Gritting his teeth, he plunged his hand into the cold water, once, twice, then, pulled it out with a grimace.

"Enough of that. Let's wrap it."

"Let me see."

Surprised, Andrew looked up from his hand and hesitantly held it out toward Martha.

"You needn't worry. I've dressed my share of wounds and broken bones."

She quickly pushed away the image of Charley that came to mind and took Andrew's hand in hers. Carefully, she ran her fingers over his. When she too was sure that none were broken, she crossed to the kitchen hearth to rummage through the kindling.

"We'll need a small bit of wood to keep it still."

Nate had come in from the kitchen yard and joined her to pull a bit of shingle from the box.

"This 'un will do jes fine. Le'me smooth it up," he said, heading for the door. "Don't be needin' splinters."

As they waited, Martha sent Sukey to the taproom for a glass of ale for Andrew and one for herself.

"A little something to fortify us."

She was heartened by his nod and rueful smile.

"Twas good to see him brought down."

The thought of Hal put in his place and, with luck, out of her life forever, lightened the weight of sad memories she'd carried with her from England. For the first time, she felt a real hope for whatever might lie ahead.

Though Andrew wanted badly to ask what she had against the man, the look on Martha's face suggested that it was not the time to ask. Instead, he fumbled in his waistcoat pocket with his good hand and handed her a coin.

"You'd best take Sally back to the Widow Simpson. I assume she'll still have a place there. Give her this and let's hope she'll keep out of trouble now."

"You're a kind man. I hope this is all you'll have to pay for it."

He nodded. "I'd say it's money well spent."

With a smile and a nod, Martha beckoned Sally to follow her into the kitchen yard and handed her the coin.

"Mr. Faal asked me to give you this."

"Give him my thanks. I heard what you said to him. He is a kind one. There's not many as would help someone like me. Specially after the trouble I brought him."

"You were lucky."

"Aye. But I didn't see it like that. And my Ma was madder than a scalded cat. 'Specially when Mr. Faal took you on. And there's the devil in that Hal. He told me things about you that I come to know wasn't true, but til then, I was spreading his tales around town. I was wrong to be doin' that and I'm sorry. You'll hear no more of that from me."

"You couldn't know what he said was a lie. He's a vile man. I won't be holding it against you."

Martha turned toward the kitchen, then stopped.

"Let's say no more about it. Wait here and I'll go along with you to see that you have no trouble from the Widow."

Standing just long enough to see Sally sink onto a stool by the garden gate, Martha hurried back toward the kitchen. As she neared the door, Mehitabel's raised voice caused her to slow her pace.

"Getting rid of a troublemaker? You?"

"Yes'm, he did."

Martha hastened inside before Andrew could say any more.

"Sent him off with a broken nose and there were others to see that he won't be coming back."

"You broke his nose? Why would you be brawling with someone like that here?"

"He'd come after Widow Simpson's girl. She ran in here to get away from him."

"Widow Simpson? It's that minx Sally. I thought I heard the Widow'd taken her. I told her that girl was nothing but trouble."

Andrew held up his bandaged hand.

"It was no fault of hers."

"So where is she now?"

"She's outside, Ma'am, and I'm about to take her back to the widow. I just wanted to be sure that Mr. Faal had been seen to."

Martha hurried out before she had to listen to any more from Mehitabel on Widow Simpson and her wayward wench. Or her own shortcomings.

Mehitabel stood in the doorway

watching the two girls.

"Two of a kind, I'd say."

"You're wrong, Mother. But it's over and done with."

He lifted his bandaged hand.

"This should get me through the rest of the day. And there's no one tending the bar. I'd best get back to the taproom til Martha returns."

Testing how far he could bend his fingers, Andrew hurried through to the taproom where a resounding cheer greeted him. Two of the regulars rose, one to guide him to a table and the other draw him an ale.

XXV

Hannah & Charley

Fifty-nine days out of London, the *Speedwell* sailed past the barren, windswept dunes that marked the entrance to Chesapeake Bay. From there, leafless trees and scattered evergreens along the waterway's eastern shore promised a vast forest of green come spring. Across the bay, however, the forests gave way to signs of civilization with open stretches waiting to be tilled and rough landings serving an occasional farm or homestead. Their westerly course finally brought them to the broad mouth of the James River where the *Speedwell* inched her way in among the assorted vessels that crowded Norfolk's harbor.

The sun was high and pleasingly warm on that cold winter's day. At the helm Jamie barked orders to his crew and guided the brig toward one of several busy wharves. Hannah was used to seeing great varieties of ships and smaller vessels but none like those Jamie identified. The single-masted sloops, as he called them, were fast and nimble craft and, as a result, often chosen by privateers. A few sleek, two-masted schooners, he pointed out, were more versatile and growing in number on the Chesapeake Bay.

Hannah tried to show an interest, but the scene ashore was what captured her attention. Ahead of them were none of the well-aged buildings so familiar along the Thames. Winter-shorn trees were scattered among buildings of brick, stone, and weathered clapboard. The streets, she learned when she went ashore, were paved with the crushed shells of clams harvested from the bay.

Rough as it looked, Hannah could see that Norfolk was a busy and prosperous port, but it was the small army of black stevedores laboring on the docks that captured her attention. She'd heard tales of dark-skinned people in distant lands and the trade that carried them as slaves to the American colonies. Still, that knowledge hadn't prepared her to see them in such great numbers. Except for a contingent of British sailors loading supplies into a longboat from the frigate that stood out in the harbor, she saw few other men engaged in such labors.

Hannah had little time to study the scene. As soon as Jamie could leave the *Speedwell*, he led her and Charley ashore and into the town. Pointing out this or that business in rapid-fire order, she suspected her son was more than a little nervous about how Polly would react when they appeared on her doorstep. For that matter, Hannah had to admit that she was just as uneasy about the prospect.

As they entered a narrow street of neat frame houses set back behind small dooryards, Jamie left them to follow on their own as he hurried ahead to tell Polly of their coming. Hannah put a restraining hand on Charley's arm and stopped. She'd seen Jamie rap on the cottage door and when it opened, step inside with arms open wide.

"We'd best give him time to break the news and for Polly to prepare herself. I suspect this won't be easy for her."

"I don't think it will be easy for us either, Nana. And what I want to know is where will we stay. From the look of her house, she's got no room."

"You're right and I've already noted an inn or two that will be suitable until we can make further plans. We'll stay just long enough to meet Polly and her children. I don't want her to think that I've come to meddle in their lives. And for today, I'll be more than content to get settled someplace with a bed that's not heaving beneath me at night."

"That will suit me too. But I don't want to tarry here, Nana. Uncle Jamie said that soon he'll be going up to Annapolis town, but he's made no plans."

"I'm sure it won't be long."

Exasperated, Charley rolled his eyes

skyward.

"I have to know what's become of her, Nana. Good or bad, I won't be able to settle on anything else until I know."

"I know. I feel the same. She's as dear to me as you are ... as if she were my own flesh and blood. I've told Jamie that I want to go up the Bay and he thinks we can set sail within a fortnight. In the meantime, we'll do well to take our time."

"Why must we do that."

Hannah had to turn away to hide her smile as he stamped his foot, then stalked away and back, just as he'd done when he was a little boy.

"We've just arrived. I'm sure things are very different here. Let's get a sense of this place before we start making plans. The first thing you must do is talk to Jamie about what's involved, and I must meet this young woman he plans to take as his wife. Ah, here they are."

With arms open wide she strode forward to set Polly's mind at ease and begin her own life in the new world.

XXVI

Annapolis

"Mistress. There's a man."

Fanny waved over her shoulder toward the front of the house.

"He's askin' for Martha."

As usual, the unfamiliar threw the girl into a panic, worsened by Mehitabel's sudden scowl.

"What did you tell him? Nothing, I hope."

"No, Ma'am, just I'd get you."

"I'll go see what it's about, Ma'am."

Martha hoped her voice didn't give way to the sudden fear that gripped her. Could it be Hal or some scoundrel he'd found to cause trouble? She prayed someone would be in the taproom. There had only been the usual half-dozen or so who came in for a bit of breakfast most mornings and they didn't linger.

568

Mehitabel held up a hand to stop her.

"You'll do nothing of the sort. Stay right there. Where is Andrew? Fanny, go fetch Mr. Faal."

Flapping her hands, she shoved the girl out the door and into the yard, waiting just long enough to be sure that Fanny was bound for the saddlery's open door. Satisfied, she turned to Martha.

"You have no idea what he might want?"

"No, Ma'am, how would I? But I'll go with you. There should be someone in the taproom to help us if need be."

Loath to admit that Martha was right, Mehitabel nodded and motioned for her to follow her to the taproom. A few steps behind, Martha came to a sudden stop and gripped the frame of the doorway to steady herself.

Could it be?

"Jamie?"

"You know this man?"

Martha could do no more than nod. She'd never expected to see anyone from that life again. Indeed, to ease the pain of remembering, she'd put them out of her mind.

Jamie snatched his hat from his head with a slight bow toward Mehitabel but his eyes and words were for Martha.

"Aye, she knows me, Ma'am. And it's my great good fortune to have found her at last. I think she's fared better than we could have hoped."

Jamie assumed a more deferential

569

stance to deal directly with the woman.

"I beg your pardon Ma'am. I'm James Chinn, captain of the brig *Speedwell* moored now in your harbor. She's my mother's ward and was taken from us by the machinations of a lying rogue. We sorely feared for her life until we learned that she'd been brought here."

Arriving from his shop, Andrew came to an abrupt halt behind his mother, who shoved Martha to one side with a restraining hand on her arm.

"We know nothing of what you say. This girl is indentured to us ... well, to my son here. She hasn't begun to work long enough to repay what is owed."

Damnation.

Andrew cursed himself. There'd been no time to tell her he was freeing Martha.

"You said *we*, Jamie?" Martha pulled out of Mehitabel's grasp as she spoke.

"Aye, Mother and Charley are waiting aboard the *Speedwell*.

He turned toward Mehitabel.

Best tread carefully here. There's trouble between this woman and Martha. And no simple way to deal with her, I'll wager.

"I didn't know if I'd find Martha and thought it best that we not all appear at your door, Ma'am. Also, I must find lodging. My mother is weary after being so long at sea."

He paused to look from Martha to Andrew, then his mother. "And I think there are things that must be dealt with before I bring them here."

Though Martha wanted badly to run to him and give way to threatening tears, she dared not lose control.

The Mistress is here? I'll see her soon? And Charley?

She wanted to laugh and cry and give in to a confusion of joy, disbelief, and sudden fear.

They don't know about Mitty. The Mistress will understand. But Charley? Or Jamie? He must know before he goes back to the ship.

"The Faals have treated me well."

She nodded toward Mehitabel and Andrew.

"But there's something you must know before you fetch Mistress Chinn and Charley. Wait here. I'll be right back," she said over her shoulder as she ran to the breezeway.

Ignoring Belle's and Sukey's startled looks, she scooped Mitty from her cradle and hurried back to the taproom.

Jamie and Andrew stood as she'd left them in awkward, guarded silence. At the sight of the bundle Martha carried, Mehitabel reached out to stop her then quickly drew back.

Approaching Jamie, Martha pulled aside a corner of the blanket.

"Jamie. This is... my daughter."

"Your daughter?"

Jamie looked up at her puzzled. Then at Andrew. No, she hadn't been in Annapolis long enough for him to be the father. Then, it struck him.

Randolph.

"That scoundrel," he said, his voice a low growl that only Martha could hear. Then with a smile.

"There's no doubt she's yours. What do you call her?"

"Hannah Mehitabel Pratt, but we call her Mitty."

"Good idea, I'd say."

"That's Mistress Faal's suggestion."

"If I remember correctly, she looks just like you did. Mother will see it, I'm sure."

"But she and Charley must know about Mitty before they come ashore. It'll be best that it doesn't come as a surprise. Charley won't take it well, I fear."

"Aye. You're right about that. The word is that damned Randolph returned to Virginia. And I hope well away from Norfolk. I'll be sailing out of that port and Charley with me. With luck, their paths won't ever cross. But we'll talk of such matters later."

Jamie stepped forward to enclose Martha and the baby in a quick embrace, then turned to Mehitabel and Andrew.

"I have business to attend to before I return to the ship with the good news, so I'll say good day for now. I plan to bring my mother and nephew ashore this evening."

He bowed toward Mehitabel with what he hoped was a winning smile.

"Might we take supper here, Ma'am?"

Mehitabel returned a tight-lipped smile

with a peremptory nod.

"Aye, please do," she said, her white-knuckled fingers clasped at her waist.

****

Jamie left and Mehitabel turned without a word to disappear up the stair to her bed chamber. Wrapped in a sense of unreality, Martha watched her leave.

Can this really be happening? I never imagined ... to see the Mistress again? I've missed her so. And Charley. But I'm not the same person I was at the Black Horse, certainly not the girl Charley knew.

Only as she turned to take Mitty back to the kitchen did she notice Andrew, and was struck by his look of dismay as he spun on his heel and left.

What can he be thinking? When he set me free, I had no place to go, no reason to leave. Is he thinking now that I might?

Even as she awaited the family she'd never expected to see again, Martha knew she wouldn't be leaving, knew she didn't want to.

I belong here now. Andrew didn't have to tell me he has feelings for me. I've seen it in his eyes. To leave this place, to leave him... No. I do care for him. I must let him know.

****

"Your people have come."

Mehitabel found Martha in the kitchen, rocking Mitty in her cradle.

"Oh, my. She's eaten, and I hoped she'd be ready to sleep. Would you mind seeing to her?"

Mehitabel's look of pleasure was a relief.

"Oh yes, yes. You go on now."

"Thank you. I'm not sure what to expect of this visit."

"Don't worry. Mitty will be fine til you're ready for her."

Martha paused, suddenly uncertain, as Mehitabel scooped the baby from her cradle.

"Go now. No wonder she won't settle. You're in a stew and she's in need of changing. Don't you worry. We'll see to that right away."

Martha took a deep breath to steady herself and hurried to the taproom. She was surprised to find it nearly empty. Andrew had managed to get most of the men to forego their favorite tables for those in the far room. Only a half-dozen remained by the front windows. They knew Martha's story and were waiting with avid, but discreet, interest as the grey-haired woman opened her arms.

"Oh my dear," Hannah said, clasping Martha to her, then leaning back to look at the girl through tear-filled eyes. "I never dreamt I'd see you again."

Hastily she fumbled for the handkerchief tucked in her bodice to wipe her eyes. Martha had only a corner of her apron to stem the threatening tears as Hannah stepped back to get a better look at her.

"I needn't ask if you are well and that gladdens my heart."

Martha could only nod, realizing as she did that she truly was well. And, over Hannah's shoulder, she saw Andrew. He'd been waiting none too patiently in his saddlery listening for the Chinn's arrival. He'd stopped just inside the taproom door, struck by the joyous meeting before him. Martha greeted him with a smile.

"I've been very lucky."

She beckoned Andrew to join them.

"This is Andrew Faal. It was my great good fortune that he purchased my bond."

Andrew acknowledged the introduction with an awkward bow.

"And our good fortune as well. I'm no innkeeper. My mother and I are indebted to Martha for what success we've had in the time she's been here."

"And we're grateful for this dear child she's brought us."

As one, Martha, Andrew, and Hannah turned toward Mehitabel, who, with a self-satisfied look, handed Mitty to Martha. A quick nod was all the thanks Martha could muster as she settled the baby in the crook of her arm.

You may have claimed this moment for yourself, but you won't claim my daughter.

"This is Hannah Mehitabel Pratt," she said, pulling the blanket aside. "It's a long name for such a little mite, so we call her Mitty."

"She's the very image of you!"

Hannah turned to Mehitabel.

"Martha is more a daughter to me than my own flesh and blood and I can't tell you how thankful I am to see that she's well. She was fortunate to find a home here with you. And for her daughter to be born in your house."

Mehitabel could only nod and quickly turn away, overcome by the sudden memory of her own little daughter and the faded charcoal rubbings Andrew had taken from the stones that marked Emily's and young Will's graves. After William's death, she'd taken the framed images from their bed chamber wall and packed them away with his favorite waistcoat in a small trunk she kept under her bed. At first, she'd regularly replaced the herbs that warded off insects and mold, but now couldn't remember the last time she'd done that.

"It's near suppertime," she said abruptly.

"I must get back to the kitchen to see it's well underway."

And with that, she left them speechless and hurried off, stumbling through the breezeway and out into the kitchen yard. There, she paused, welcoming the bite of the evening's chill as she fought to compose herself before going on to the kitchen.

****

Andrew pulled a large high-backed chair to the fireside and beckoned for Hannah to sit with Mitty, then drew up a chair for Martha to sit near her. They nodded their thanks, but soon were oblivious to anything going on around them. Mitty quickly fell asleep in Hannah's arms as she and Martha talked. Often smiling through tears, they tried to fill in all that had passed since last they were together but, in the end, it was enough that at last they were.

"I think you've found a life for yourself here. Am I right?"

Martha nodded.

"It hasn't always been easy...."

She paused, then decided there was no need to go into her troubles with Mehitabel.

"Mitty has been a Godsend. Until recently, the Mistress was so unhappy. Andrew's told me that her sadness began years ago when his older brother was run down by a cart and killed. Then his little sister died of fever. I think that was the hardest for Mistress Faal to bear. Indeed, I'm certain of it since I've seen how much she cares for Mitty. My guess is that Mr. Faal hoped to escape those sad memories by coming here, but that only brought the Mistress more sorrow. He died of fever after their first year in Annapolis.

"But since Mitty was born, she's been a different person. She adores Mitty and I have to admit that I'm relieved she's happy to take over much of her care. With that and her kitchen, I think she seems much more content. And I am, too."

"Andrew is a saddler, but he does other sorts of fine leather work. So he's quite content for me to run the public room during the day, then he joins me at night. It reminds me of the Black Horse, but I've never stopped missing it. And you. But how could you leave? It must have been a hard thing to do."

Hannah shook her head.

"It wasn't at all. You wouldn't recognize it, what with Rebecca and her grand ideas. She's doing well, but it's not the place her father and I created. And when Jamie said he was going to marry and move to Virginia, that was all I needed. He has a young wife, a widow with two dear children. We get on well and I'll be content there. She's a milliner and I'll live with them to help keep house and tend the children."

Hannah's recounting had come in such a rush that Martha could hardly take it all in, but could not have had better news than that Hannah would no longer be an ocean away.

"And Charley? What brought him?"

"Charley had no desire to spend his life behind a bar and Rebecca made it worse. He was forever in trouble with her. It broke Joseph's heart, but I think he understood Charley's need to get away and make a life for himself. He was as relieved as I that Jamie was willing to take him on as crew. I don't know how long that will suit him, but, for now, he's content with life at sea."

Hannah couldn't imagine her grandson

settling down. She'd watched him with young women in the taproom of the Black Horse. There'd been one or two, she feared, would lead him astray and his mother encouraged them, but, as much as anything else, that put an end to any desire he might have had. Martha, however, was a different matter. Hannah knew that she and Charley had cared for each other, but Martha's life had changed too much and Charley, most certainly, wasn't ready for fatherhood.

****

Martha and Charley concluded the same. When they saw that Hannah was content to rest with the sleeping baby and Mehitabel was busy overseeing supper preparations, they were left for an uneasy moment in the taproom.

"We're not needed here," said Martha. "Let's go walk a bit."

Not waiting for his reply, she grabbed her shawl from it's hook by the door and led the way out to the street. Charley hastened to catch up.

"Would you believe, they call this part of town Wapping?" she said.

"Ach!" she said, stubbing her toe on an ice-hardened rut.

"But beyond that, it's nothing like our old neighborhood. I still miss it."

She stopped suddenly and turned to

look at him.

"I've missed you, too. And Mistress Chinn. But I've been lucky."

"Lucky?"

Charley shook his head in disbelief.

"Aye. It could have been much worse. This place, this new world is much different. But not in a bad way. Maybe that's why I've come to like it."

Leading the way, she headed down Prince George's Street to the water and a small plank wharf.

"This place calls itself a city - a metropolis some call it. That's wishful thinking, I'd say, but it's the center of this colony's government and might amount to something more one day. The royal governor lives here and he and wealthy planters are building fine brick houses uptown."

At the wharf's edge, they paused looking out at the creek, then, down into the water where the bottom was littered with oyster shells. Charley squatted the better to see them.

"What sort of creatures lived in those?"

"Oysters. Slimy grey things, larger than clams. Watermen come in here with their catch and before they unload, they'll make a meal of the ugly creatures, scooping them out with a knife and swallowing them whole. The Mistress wanted nothing to do with that, but she makes a fine winter stew of them with butter and potatoes."

"I plan to see a lot more of these waters

now that I'll be living in Norfolk and sailing with Uncle Jamie."

Charley glanced sideways at Martha.

"I couldn't believe it when he told me he'd found you, that you'd fared well since you came to this town."

"And that I have a daughter?"

"Aye," he snapped. "That bastard Randoph!"

"Mitty is a dear little thing and I cherish her. She will hear nothing of that. As far as she'll know, her father's dead. I'll not let her suffer because of him. And since I've come here, I haven't either."

"The Faals don't hold the past against me. They've given me a chance for a new life. And Mistress Faal dearly loves Mitty. Indeed, she's been more mother to that child than I have."

Charley was struck by a confusion of emotions and could only nod. He hadn't stopped caring for Martha, but knew he could never accept another man's spawn. But better to say nothing about it, he decided.

"So this place suits you now?"

"Yes," She paused struck by the thought.

"I never would have believed it at first, but now this feels like home. It's nothing like it was for us at the Black Horse, but, then, I'm not at all like I was then. I'd wager you aren't either."

Charley cocked his head.

"No, I'm not. Once I had a chance to

leave, I couldn't wait. It was hard to leave Papa, but he urged me to go. He knew that I wasn't cut out to spend my life behind a bar. He wanted me to get away and see some of the world.

"And your mother?"

"She went into a towering rage. I just let her go on. I've never been able to please her, nor did I want to try anymore. And since I've been sailing with Uncle Jamie, I can't imagine settling down, not this soon. I've too much to do, a world to explore, and I plan to see as much of it as I can."

"I hope you'll return to tell us of your travels and that you won't forget you have family and those who care for you here."

"Don't worry about that. Uncle Jamie, plans to trade here in Maryland as well as in Virginia. There's a small town just north of here, up a river called Patapsco, one of those Indian names. I hope we'll see some of the savages ere long. Have you seen any?"

Martha shook her head.

"I've heard they're not really savages. They're quite peaceable and trade here sometimes, but I've yet to see one."

She shook her head. "And after all this time, why are we talking about Indians? I want to hear about the Black Horse, what's to become of it? And your father?"

"As well as can be expected. Mama has taken full charge and Pa's got help at the bar. He can spend time with old friends, sitting back with his pipe and a glass of ale and sharing tales."

"He's content, then. I'm glad. But I'm sure he misses you."

"Aye. And I miss him. That was the hardest thing about leaving. But Uncle Jamie plans to make one more trip back. So Papa will know all's well with us. And with you."

He grinned.

"Mama will be fit to be tied."

"I've no doubt."

"We were best friends once," he said, suddenly serious. "I hope that won't change."

"Never. I can think of nothing better than to have you back in my life. And Mistress Chinn."

****

When the Chinns' visit came to an end, Hannah and Martha said a teary goodby, but were comforted by Jamie's assurance that they'd be seeing each other again ere long. As the *Speedwell* passed down the Bay and out of sight, Martha dried her eyes and turned away.

I must get home. Home? When have I ever said that?

With that thought, she couldn't help but smile as she saw Andrew coming toward her.

"I see they got off well. Are you sorry that you didn't go with them?"

"Sorry? No, I'm sad to say goodby, but it won't be forever. And as I said the other day.

583

This is where I want to make my home if that suits you and your mother."

"I think it would break Mother's heart to lose Mitty, and though I doubt she'd admit it, she'd be unhappy to lose you too. And so would I. To know you want to stay here makes me exceedingly happy. And if I have aught to do with it, I hope you will...."

Suddenly at a loss for words, Andrew raked his fingers through his hair, cleared his throat, and stumbled on.

"Ahh, Martha, I've been afraid that something or someone would take you away ... that we..., no, I might lose you. Will you marry me? Let me be a proper husband? And a father to Mitty."

Her look of surprise caused him to stop, then rush on.

"I know this is sudden. I'll make no demands that you're not ready to accept, but I must know. Is there hope for me at least."

He paused, unable to read anything in her dark eyes.

Martha felt a sudden release, akin to the rush of steam upon lifting the cover of a boiling kettle. She had to look away.

"I thought I'd never trust a man again. But that's changed since I've come to know you. You have my trust. And my love. Yes, I will marry you, Andrew."

Made in the USA
Monee, IL
15 March 2021